Maybe Kevin

Brian Kiley

Cover Design by Dwayne Booth

Published 2019 by HumorOutcasts Press
Printed in the United States of America

ISBN: 0-9600085-2-7
EAN-13: 978-0-9600085-2-0

Chapter One

Curt was acting weird right away. When he came in he kissed her without making eye contact. He sort of missed, his lower lip just grazing her upper lip. Technically, it was a kiss but just barely. She'd have to look at the replay. *Fuck, he's breaking up with me.*

Normally, he'd take his coat off and sit and they'd talk and smooch a bit before they went out, but now he remained standing with his coat and even his gloves still on. In his left hand, he clutched his car keys. *What's the rush?* She didn't have her shoes on so they stood eye to eye, or would have if he had looked at her.

It was because of last week. It was because of "The Christmas Debacle." Julie liked to name the events in her life like "The Great Balloon Fiasco" or "The Day We Were All Almost Killed." She had dubbed last week "The Christmas Debacle." *That couldn't be it, we have laughed about it on the way home. That must be it.*

This was the first time they'd seen each other since Christmas and its debacle. He said he'd been really busy, some of his workers were away for the holidays. When they spoke on the phone, she chattered away while he barely said two words, so everything seemed normal, but kisses don't lie. Not lower lip to upper lip kisses any way. That had been her experience.

When you're supposedly "in love," six days apart is a long time. She knew he was shorthanded and busy and she could accept that but she also knew that two days earlier he had gone to visit his father and his terminally ill uncle without her. *Why didn't he bring me? I've still never met his Dad and I like visiting the terminally ill as much as the next guy.*

He seemed nervous, he never seemed nervous. After all he'd been through this year, the shooting, the funeral, the pre-trial hearing, the visit to the home for the criminally insane, he'd handled it all with aplomb. Yet, he was standing in her living room, fidgeting with his keys in his gloved hand and looking uncomfortable.

"Do you want a drink?" she asked.

He looked at her funny. Julie didn't really drink but it was New Year's Eve. 1989 couldn't come soon enough.

Julie didn't drink because her mother drank, drank enough for both of them. Julie didn't drink because she knew Kevin wouldn't like it and she wanted to be a good mother. She promised herself many times that she'd be a caring, empathetic, fun mother. The kind of mother that Kevin deserved. The kind she didn't have.

"I bought some gin today. Do you want a gin and tonic?"

"All right," said Curt, "One quick one."

Julie traipsed from the living room to the kitchen of her tiny apartment, trying to appear as though there was nothing wrong. Her bare feet were chilly on the kitchen tile. She poured a healthy shot of gin into two glasses, not really sure what she was doing.

Even before Curt when she was unattached and went out with "The Committee" on Thursday night, she didn't drink and often ended up giving the other committee members a ride home. "The Committee" wasn't really a committee. It was what she called her friends from work because they acted like a committee. They acted like every personal decision was a group decision to be proposed and discussed and decided on by consensus.

She handed him his glass and he took it without sitting down.

"I made reservations for eight," he said, "So we should probably go."

"Gimme a sec," she said, ducking into the bathroom and bringing her drink with her. She stared at the mirror looking at her thirty-six year old face wondering if it still looked good and for how much longer. She hadn't eaten all day so she could fit into her New Year's Eve dress. She had squeezed herself into it with grim determination just before he showed up, mind over matter. It was a little too tight and made her look a little more boobalicious than she actually was. "What the hell," she thought, propping them up like a woman trying to get out of a speeding ticket, "Maybe these will change his mind."

She couldn't believe he was breaking up with her. She was convinced he was "The One" almost from the moment they met, at least since the funeral.

He was perfect. Okay, he was shorter than she would have liked and quieter than necessary, sometimes maddeningly so, dispensing valuable information in tiny dribs and drabs and he had an odd habit of mumbling to himself when he thought no one was looking. Other than that, he was perfect.

It was only recently that things had gone bad. Her birthday and Christmas, even before they drove to New Jersey when he said, "I have something for you." For one micro-instant, she thought it might be a ring but the box was long and slender instead of short and square. It was a watch and not an elegant one for evening wear, a digital one she could wear to work.

"I noticed you didn't have one," he said.

Julie didn't wear a watch on purpose because she found when she did, she looked at it compulsively, sometimes two or three times in the same minute. "Miss, do you have some place to be?" one customer asked one day at the bank, the last time Julie had ever worn a watch.

"I love it," she said pretending she loved it, not wanting a watch. Isn't a watch what a company gives someone when they're retiring? "Here you go, here's a watch, now get the fuck out of here."

"We really should get going," he said from outside the bathroom door.

"Okay," she said cheerfully. She finished her drink.

If he was breaking up with her, she wanted him to do it and get it over with, not like with Michael, her most serious boyfriend before Curt. That relationship ended but wouldn't end, hanging on for years like the Ottoman Empire, a slow, painful death. She'd rather a quick death like Pompeii, buried in a sudden heap of lava and ash where nobody knew what hit them.

As he drove she stared at his handsome profile looking for clues but his dark, inscrutable eyes revealed nothing. She thought about asking about his terminally ill uncle and then decided against it. *That won't lighten the mood.* She made a joke about the tollbooth collector instead and he laughed. *That's more like it.*

Curt liked that she was funny. It was what Michael hated about her. When she got laughs at college parties or with friends, Michael sulked. The bigger her laughs the bigger his sulk. He wanted to be the funny one. He always had the latest joke at the ready but it was never his. It was always something he'd heard somewhere. Julie was actually witty which was what Michael wanted to be that more than anything else.

Their last night together was a year after graduation. They went to a dinner party where Julie told her classic anecdote about her days at an all-girls Catholic school. Sister Beatrice was a neat freak, always wiping her hands with one of the wet naps she kept stashed in her desk drawer. One day, while lecturing the class, Sister Beatrice discovered among her wet nap stash a condom and went ballistic. That's what really happened. In Julie's embellished, dinner party version, Sister Beatrice took out the condom without noticing. She kept her lecture going as she opened the condom and rubbed her hands with it. It wasn't until after she had dabbed her lips with it that she realized what she was holding. It was a story Julie had told many times, a carefully honed piece of comedy material that she had added to over the years until the laughs built to an explosive crescendo. It was a story everyone loved but Michael, who barely spoke the whole way home. "You jealous, insecure fuck," Julie called him when they broke up the next day.

Curt had laughed so hard the first time he heard that story. He laughed often at her, a jarring, explosive laugh so contrary to his quiet nature. A particularly hearty laugh would cause his eyes to squint and his nose to scrunch. He would then add a line or two and build on the reality she had created. God, how she loved that.

"Where are we going?" she asked.

"I made reservations at that French place downtown, Maison Richard."

"I know that place," said Julie, "It used to be called the Chateau Rich Douche." Curt laughed again. She was on a roll. *See, he's not breaking up with me. I'm too funny.*

He pulled off the Pike and exited under the Pru. Maison Richard was one of the fanciest places in Boston. It was a former residence turned into a restaurant amidst the banks and shops. It was set back against the street and guarded with an iron gate. Revelers in fancy dress heading for the First Night festivities strolled past them as they valet parked.

When they got to the table, he was nervous again and wouldn't look her in the eye and once or twice, she caught him mumbling to himself. *Shit, He is breaking up with me.* They ordered another gin and tonic and some escargot that took forever. "Those snails must be walking to the table," she cracked and then told herself to take it down a notch. No need to bludgeon him with jokes.

Her humor wasn't for everyone. It had an edge. When her boss Simon had suddenly dropped dead and Bob was promoted from assistant branch manager to branch manager, it was too much for him. He couldn't make a decision on approving a loan or even when to allow tellers their breaks. He was the perfect Number Two man but the type who panics when made Number One. When a story spread of a bank employee killed in a bank robbery out in California, she remarked how Bob had envied him. The tellers loved that one but her magnum opus came a week later when Bob had to call the district manager at home over a minor matter. "He's Bob-solete" Julie cracked and the name stuck. From then on, the tellers called him "Bob-solete" when he was just out of earshot and sometimes when he wasn't quite. He knew it had come from her. Who else would be so scathing? A few weeks later, Bob had a fainting spell and had to go home. The next day, Julie was called into the boss' office and made branch manager. Bob would go back to his old job as assistant manager when he returned in a week. She was his enemy for life.

The waiter was middle-aged, which made Julie sad. Whenever her family made the trek from New Jersey to a restaurant in New York, the waiters were always young guys who thought they were actors. The waiters in Boston had no such pretensions. Here was a middle-aged guy resigned to his lot in life. The special was something with rabbit.

"You're not having the bunny, are you?" Julie asked.

Curt looked confused.

"Bunny?" he asked.

What is with this guy?

They had the duck instead and another drink.

Julie talked about work and Curt yawned. Curt wasn't a night person, and neither was Julie. They'd both rather be up at five and get the day going. It was one of the many things they were simpatico about. They even fucked in the mornings.

She was getting hungry and didn't feel so great.

"I fuckin' hate New Year's Eve," she said.

"You're talking kind of loud," he said. "And you're swearing a lot."

"Oh, fuck, I am? Oh, sorry," she said. "I'm going to go to the bathroom."

"That's a good idea," he said.

Why did he say that?

"Going to the bathroom is always a good idea," she said. "I mean who wants to pee their pants?"

"Good point," he said.

She meandered into the ladies' room almost entering the men's room until she veered off at the last moment. *I'd better slow down a little bit on the gin.* She entered the middle stall, peed and wiped and then decided to stay seated for a minute and not get up just yet. She knew baby Kevin was inside her somewhere and thought he might die right there on the toilet without anyone ever knowing about him. She leaned back, her head resting on the wall behind her. She closed her eyes and fell asleep.

Chapter Two

Tom didn't want to visit Eddie but Eddie was finally back home after the Japanese blew his leg off and Tom knew he had to go see him. His mother had bumped into Eddie's mother at a prayer vigil at Immaculate Heart and said Eddie had been asking for him. She put her off by telling her that Tom had his final exams but his Latin final was his last one so now he had to go see Eddie.

Tom was the first in his family ever to go to college, enrolling in Boston College, just a mile or so from home, in the fall of '41. His brother Billy had done even better in high school and left for Holy Cross a year later. Tom's mother's father had to drop out of school and get a job and help support his family and she was determined her boys would go to college. She talked about it their whole lives and she wasn't about to let the war get in the way. Tom had done all right on all his finals, except calculus and knew Billy and his straight A's would be home tomorrow.

Tom waited for the trolley to pass before he crossed the street. There was no snow yet and ever since the war had started Christmas was subdued and half-hearted. The shops only had a sprinkling of decorations in the window. It was cold, and when the wind blew, it was damn cold. He didn't like to swear out loud, his mother didn't approve, but he'd swear in his mind especially when it was damn cold. It was two more blocks to Eddie's house.

He didn't really like Eddie. They'd been friends when they were kids more out of proximity than anything else. Eddie lived a block over but they went to separate high schools and hung around less and less.

Eddie was always working a deal and always had an angle. Tom didn't have a car, but if you had a car Eddie could fix it for you. He was a crackerjack mechanic. He fixed up Charlie Matthews' Packard, then drove it around for a week before giving it back to Charlie. That was the kind of angle Eddie worked.

Tom beat Eddie up once when they were twelve. They were playing football in the street and Billy kept dropping Eddie's passes and Eddie started riding Billy pretty good. Billy couldn't catch a ball if you put it in his lap and Eddie rode him pretty hard 'til Tom decided enough was enough. He sat on

Eddie's chest and made him cry. They patched things up after that but not really.

A couple years later, Eddie and his mother got some money when Eddie's father croaked, and his mother bought him a pool table for the basement. Eddie liked to bet and liked to take Tom's money. Tom felt guilty about having beaten Eddie up and about his Dad dying so he thought giving him the money he made shoveling snow made them square.

Tom rang the doorbell and stood waiting on the stoop. *The house could use a new coat of paint*. He looked over at the garage and wondered if Eddie's Studebaker was still inside. Eddie had gotten a deal on a broken down Studebaker and had fixed it up and drove it around town. Tom never had a girl but Eddie always seem to have one and he'd drive her around in his Studebaker and show them both off. Eddie liked to be a big shot.

He rang the bell again and Eddie's mother opened the door. She was in the middle of dyeing her hair and her head was wet and half of it was blonde. Tom's mother would never open the door while she was dyeing her hair.

"Tom, you finally came."

"Hi, Mrs. Curran."

"C'mon in. He'll be happy to see you. He hasn't been himself since he came home."

Tom took off his head and stepped inside the house. He noticed the legs of the coffee table were broken on one side so it leaned onto the floor in the shape of a triangle. *It must have just broke.*

"He hasn't been himself since he got home," she said again, leading him down a narrow hallway. "He'll be so happy to see you."

"Eddie," she said, knocking and then not waiting for an answer before opening the door, "Look who's here to see you."

Eddie sat up in bed with a white sheet pulled up to his chest reading a car magazine. The first thing Tom noticed was the bottle of Scotch on the nightstand. There was half a bottle of Scotch on the nightstand and he wasn't making any attempt to hide it from his mother.

"Tom, you came," said Eddie, quite loudly.

He's drunk. It's eleven o'clock in the morning and he's drunk.

"I'll leave you two alone," said Mrs. Curran, closing the door behind her.

"Move those shirts and sit in that chair, Tom."

Tom lifted some shirts off a chair and looked for somewhere to put them.

"Just dump at the foot of the bed."

Tom put the shirts on the bed and sat down, still with his coat on. He noticed a pair of crutches leaning against the wall. Eddie's face was rounder than it had been with the beginnings of a double chin. He'd been a bit of a ladies' man but now he was pale and plump and glassy-eyed.

"I've been back for two weeks."

"Sorry," mumbled Tom, "I had final exams."

"Yeah, college," said Eddie and he poured himself half a glass of Scotch.

"You want some?"

"No, thanks."

Tom didn't drink and didn't know anybody who drank at eleven in the morning.

"I was in a hospital in Hawaii before this for four months. You should've seen the nurses."

He put his drink down and made the "curvy" sign with his hands.

"I was at Coral Sea," he said, "when the Japs got me."

"Sorry," mumbled Tom.

He stared at Tom for a minute with his glassy eyes and Tom shifted in his seat uncomfortably. He still had his coat on.

"You want to see it?"

See what? The Studebaker? He had seen it. Eddie picked him up once when he was walking home from school doing him a favor but being a big shot nonetheless.

Before Tom could say, "I've seen it," Eddie pulled the sheet back revealing his stump. Tom gasped just loud enough to be heard.

"Here it is," he said, rubbing the hand around the rounded lump where his leg had been. It was reddish and blotchy at the base with some jagged scarring. Tom winced.

"Sorry," he said again.

"Me, too," said Eddie, mercifully covering it back up with the sheet.

Tom wanted to leave but he'd only been there for two minutes. They talked for a while about some of the fellas from the neighborhood and what they'd been up to. Eddie took another swig from his glass and then took in some short breaths of air.

"You don't like me much, do ya Tom?"

"What are you talking about Eddie? We're old friends."

"You just never took a shine to me."

"We've been pals since we were kids. We played baseball and had snowball fights."

"You didn't come and see me before I shipped out," said Eddie, pointing a shaky finger at him, "And you didn't write to me."

"I prayed for you, Eddie. I prayed for you and…"

He stopped himself before he said "the others." Each week at mass at Immaculate Heart, the whole congregation prayed for Eddie and the boys from the parish who'd been killed. Tom had prayed for Eddie and the others.

"Prayers," said Eddie, waving his hand dismissively, "look at what good that did me."

You shouldn't blaspheme.

Eddie closed his eyes and leaned his head back, resting upright against his pillow. Tom sat still with his coat on and his hat in his lap. When he started to stand up Eddie's eyes popped open.

"You never liked me," he murmured and he closed his eyes again.

Tom lifted himself out of the chair and tiptoed out the room, silently closing the door behind him.

"Good bye, Mrs. Curran," he said, reaching the living room.

Mrs. Curran emerged from the kitchen with her head still wet but all blonde now.

"Oh, you're going so soon, Tom. I was going to make you boys lunch."

"He's sleeping."

"He drinks now," she said, "Since he lost his leg. He makes me buy booze for him and I can't say 'no' on account of what he's been through."

Tom nodded.

"Merry Christmas," he said after a moment.

They didn't have a tree.

"Yeah, Merry Christmas. Say hi to your folks for me."

"Will do."

"Come back and see him, Tom. Won't cha?"

"Sure. Sure, Mrs. Curran."

The next morning, before Billy came home with his perfect report card, Tom went to the army recruiting office and joined up.

Chapter Three

Julie's body shuddered and she opened her eyes and nearly fell off the toilet. Her hands leapt from her lap ready to protect herself from danger. It took her a moment for her to get her bearings. *Where am I? Oh, okay, it's New Year's Eve, I'm at the Maison Richard and my boyfriend is about to break up with me.*

Between Michael, her first boyfriend and Curt, there had been a series of disasters. She and Michael dated her senior year of college and stayed together when their group of friends found jobs around Boston. Their college clique got together almost every weekend until Julie and Michael finally broke up and the whole thing fell apart.

Julie worked downtown in those days for one of the accounting firm monstrosities where she'd never amount to much. She abruptly quit one day telling her boss to fuck off in the middle of a meeting and storming out after he accidentally called her "Julia." She was really mad at Michael but didn't know it at the time.

After Michael, there was what she called "The Bozo Parade" or a series of relationships flawed from the start. Most notable of these was "Dutch" a nickname Julie hated but he insisted on. It was what his jock friends called him and he needed constant reassurance that he was still a jock at thirty-two even though it had been years since anyone gave a shit. Her parents nearly divorced at that time and she could have used a sympathetic ear instead of a narcissistic douche.

Earlier in the week, it had occurred to her that she'd been with Curt for eight months and that the eight month mark was when she and Dutch broke up. She found out he'd been cheating when she spotted another woman's panties in his pile of clothes one day when he was doing laundry at her apartment's basement. He probably wanted her to see them so he wouldn't have to break up with her. Men are such cowards.

She grew suspicious after that. Every guy seemed to have one or two women on the side or at least in the wings. She was suspicious of Curt at first. That was the real reason she went to the funeral, despite what she told herself at the time.

Yet, she had gone to the funeral, hadn't she? And the pre-trial hearing and was with him for the long drive to the Home for the Criminally Insane, the only time she'd ever seen him cry. Who else would have done that? *Every other woman would have run from a guy with a family so fucked up and now he was breaking up with me. That little shit.* She didn't have time to fuck around. She was thirty-six years old and Kevin needed a father. *Let's get this over with and go home.*

When she returned to the table, he stopped mumbling to himself and he looked at his watch in an exaggerated pantomime. It was a bit animated for him and he seemed exasperated.

"That took a while. Are you okay?"

"If you must know I peed twice."

He looked at her not knowing how to respond.

"Okay, thrice," she said.

She looked around at the other patrons quietly going about their dinners. It was not a rowdy New Year's Eve crowd. Over his shoulder, she saw a well-to-do black couple in their fifties. The man had a gray beard and looked distinguished. Julie liked seeing successful black couples. It made her feel good about America. Her Dad had a habit of seeing a well-dressed black man and assuming he must be somebody famous, an athlete or an entertainer.

"Who is that guy? He's somebody I bet," he'd say.

Julie would chide him good-naturedly, "Dad, black people can be doctors and lawyers and businessmen too, you know."

"I know," he'd say, "It's just that that guy looks like somebody important."

Living in Boston had made Julie more racially sensitive. She didn't like when she was back home in New Jersey and heard cracks about "racist Boston." Although she saw stories on the news of racial incidents and occasionally, heard racial epithets, the people she knew didn't speak like that and would shun those who did. She even fantasized from time to time of one day having a black friend.

"I like seeing successful black couples," she said.

Curt laughed, barely managing to swallow first.

"Really," he said, "I'm partial to wealthy Oriental families myself. I've always had a soft spot for Eskimo billionaires."

He seemed to be making fun of her and Julie didn't know why.

Neither spoke for a moment. *Let's get this shit over with.* She balled her hands into fists under the table.

"You got something you want to say?"

He more smirked than smiled.

"Um, okay, I was going to wait until midnight."

Midnight? Why wait 'til midnight?

"Well."

He reached into his pocket and pulled out a small velvet box. It was small and square. She froze as he lifted the lid revealing a ring with a diamond on top. He slid down on one knee next to her.

"Julie, will you marry me?"

Chapter Four

The night of Tom's party, the night before he left, his mother spent almost the entire evening in the kitchen. Every now and then, she would bring out a tray of food, set it down without saying a word and then turn and walk back out of the room. Tom would follow her into the kitchen and try and coax her into joining the others, but she wouldn't budge even when the radio in the living room played her favorite song, "Moonlight Serenade" by Glenn Miller.

"Are you still mad at me?" he asked.

She shook her head "no" but wouldn't look at him directly. Tom's Uncle Brendan, the priest, his father's brother finally convinced her to come into dining room when it was time to cut Tom's cake, the one she had baked for him that morning. It wasn't his birthday so nobody sang, but Uncle Brendan said a little prayer.

His father was there, of course, and his brother Billy had hitched a ride back home from Worcester with one of his college buddies. Billy sat next to him while they ate. They used to banter back and forth about their rival colleges but that came to an abrupt end the previous November. Tom's college was undefeated and on its way to the Sugar Bowl when Billy's school pulled off a stunning 55-12 upset. Neither of the boys played football and Billy wasn't even at the game, yet it somehow seemed to symbolize their relationship; the smaller, craftier one outshining the bigger older brother.

Billy never got to tease Tom about the game because that night, a fire broke out at the Cocoanut Grove nightclub. The exits had been locked to prevent patrons from skipping out on their tab and then the fire started, trapping 492 people inside. It would have been many more had Boston College won. "God played for Holy Cross that day," said Father Brendan.

There was an additional cousin or two and a handful of neighbors, but it was more of a gathering than a party. No one had invited Eddie Curran because a fella with a missing leg would have upset Tom's mother. Tom didn't have a girl and his rational side was glad. A girl was apt to cry and make a scene and be just as angry with him as his mother was and for two weeks now, his imagination grew annoyed with this fictitious girlfriend. *Didn't she understand he had to do his duty?*

"Didn't who understand?" he asked himself in a moment of clarity. Sometimes Tom let his daydreams carry him too far away and he wondered if that was the first step in losing your noodle.

His Uncle Brendan, the priest, had been the first to arrive. He happily accepted a "snort" of whiskey.

"It's my dipsosis. I was born with a powerful thirst, you know," he often said with a twinkle in his eye, and Tom smiled when he said it again tonight. Uncle Brendan or Father Brendan depending on who was addressing him had gotten by for many years with only a handful of jokes and a handful of stories in his repertoire.

Uncle Brendan had always delighted Tom with his vocabulary, choosing words he never heard elsewhere. "Honey-fuggled" and "Rat-baggery" and "caterwauling." When the boys were little, he would scold Tom's Mom for being too strict, "Don't be a harridan now, Kitty. Even the best boys sky-lark." Both boys adored him.

Tom was grateful his uncle was there. Tom's father had been too young for World War I but his Uncle Brendan had gone and so had his Uncle Donald. Brendan liked to call the Great War "The Great Kerfuffle" and though, he'd been a chaplain, he saw plenty of blood and innards. Tom felt his mother was comforted by his presence knowing he had gone to war and come back without being killed or maimed or losing his noodle.

The eldest brother Donald wasn't so lucky. Tom's father only drank on special occasions, for his mother never would have tolerated a tippler, but on those special occasions when he did imbibe, he would invariably talk of Donald.

"Donald lost his noodle in the war."

That was how his father put it. Whether it was shell shock or battle fatigue, Tom didn't know but Donald lost his noodle in the war. He had stripped naked and tried to climb out of the trench. "I'm invisible, I'm invisible" he yelled over and over and his brothers in arms pulled him down and beat him. He was sent to a hospital and then eventually, sent home, and upon returning, he told his family the whole story, withholding nothing. His candor disturbed them.

Tom's father told Tom and Billy the story of Donald's return two or three times a year every year their entire childhoods. He was like an African tribesman continuing the oral tradition, retelling the same story the exact same way each time. Tom could recite it verbatim.

"Are you proud of yourself?" his father, Tom's grandfather, had asked Donald.

"I'm telling you what I did."

"You were sent there to be a soldier. You're a disgrace to your family and to your country."

"You don't know what it was like, with the shelling and the mustard."

"No, but I know a coward when I see one. I won't have you in the house. Look at how you've distressed your mother."

Tom's father kicked Donald out of the house and then, a year or two later, Donald hanged himself in New York City.

"He died the way Judas Iscariot died," Tom's father said, each time he ended the story, "He died the death of a traitor."

Tom's father didn't drink the night of Tom's party and didn't wish to speak of his brother Donald but after the others left and Tom's mother and Billy had gone to bed, Brendan brought up Donald. It was only Tom and his father and his uncle, the priest, who by this time had more than a few "snorts."

"It wasn't the war that did it to Donald," Brendan said in not much more than a whisper. Most men got louder when they drank; the more Uncle Brendan drank the quieter he became. "Did what?" Tom asked.

Tom's father looked at Tom and shook his head "no." Tom's father could see where the conversation was going and tried to head it off, but Father Brendan's was undeterred.

"Your Uncle Donald" he said looking only at Tom, "He lost his marbles before the war."

Father Brendan emphasized the word "before" to make sure his point was made. Tom wanted to correct him.

"It wasn't his marbles, it was his noodle," he wanted to say but instead he kept quiet.

"No one wants to hear about him, Brendan," said Tom's father.

Tom's father always called him "Father Brendan" in front of the boys but his Irish was up, and he dropped the title.

"We're all thinking about him," said the priest.

"No one is thinking about him," said Tom's father.

"We're all thinking about him and we should be."

Uncle Brendan said all of this without taking his eyes off Tom.

Tom's father got up with a groan and went to the water closet and closed the door. It wasn't quite a slam, but he shut it more forcefully than necessary. Brendan looked at the closed door for a moment then looked back at Tom. His eyes were watery and big behind his spectacles.

"Your Uncle Donald didn't go crazy in the war," Uncle Brendan whispered tapping Tom on the knee with his glass, nearly but not quite spilling some of his drink.

"He went crazy before that. One time, he took off his clothes in Oak Square and the cops had to lock him in the pokey. He said there were bugs all over his clothes and he had to take them off and the cops thought he was drunk and locked him up. He wasn't drunk, Tom, he was as sober as I was."

The fact that Uncle Brendan was drunk now didn't seem to factor into the story. Tom nodded slightly not knowing how he was supposed to react to this new information.

"It's true," said Uncle/Father Brendan and Tom knew it was. "There were other episodes too. He caused public scenes. He was an embarrassment to the family. That's why they made him join the war. They didn't want him around anymore."

Uncle Brendan looked right at Tom with glassy, blood-shot eyes. Tom's father was back from the bathroom now.

"Why the hell are you telling him about Donald?"

Tom had never seen his father speak sharply to Uncle Brendan before because he was both a priest and his older brother.

"He doesn't need to know about that. Donald was a disgrace to the family."

"He should know. The boy's going off to war and he should know. He should know that the war didn't make Donald lose his marbles. You'll be all right, Tom," he said with a nod and a sip. "You'll make it through full chisel."

As he lay in bed that night Tom decided to be brave. His uncle had been a coward and had gone insane and disgraced his family. Tom would be brave. His family would be proud of him, his current family and his future family, if he ever had one. He would be brave at every opportunity he had to be brave. He made a promise to himself then said a slow and solemn Hail Mary sealing the deal.

Chapter Five

There was a momentary stillness as Julie took in what was happening. She covered her mouth and hiccupped. *Fuck, I wish I were sober for this.*

Her first thought was of Debbie. Debbie was just a teller and at work, Julie was her boss but outside of the bank, when the Committee met, Debbie was the chairwoman and though no one ever said it, everybody knew it.

Julie and Debbie were friends but the kind of friends who deep down couldn't stand each other. Debbie knew that Julie was prettier and made more money and had the potential of attracting a man and she resented her for it.

Debbie didn't appeal to men but it wasn't because she was fat or ugly. Cara was fat but had a pleasant face and big tits and a willing vibe and she got laid more than any of them. It wasn't so much Debbie's physical appearance that chased away men. She, as far as Julie could tell, had an anti-charisma. Part of getting laid involved laughing at men's jokes and putting up with their bullshit and Debbie wouldn't do that. She saw through men and scowled at them because she knew what they were up to and men didn't like that and took an instant dislike to her. Even drunk men in bars kept their distance from Debbie and ended up in the parking lot later on making out with Cara.

Debbie, in Julie's view, was a foul-weather friend. If you got dumped, Debbie was the one to take you for drinks or talk on the phone with to hear your tale of woe and tell you how you were too good for him. She'd be your best friend just as long as your life was as miserable as hers. Julie stared at the ring with one thought in mind, *Debbie is going to be pissed.*

Curt looked down at Julie awaiting her answer.

"Yes," she said, her eyes filling up with tears. "Yes," she said again.

He kissed her, standing and leaning over the table, while she sat, letting him be taller than her. The other patrons whooped and cheered and applauded. Curt was red-faced as he sat back down. Julie laughed.

"What?" said Curt.

She leaned towards him so no one could hear, "I thought you were breaking up with me."

He looked puzzled, "Why would you think that?"

What could she say in response? She couldn't say, "Because of what happened at my parents' house last week" or "Because of the shitty Christmas gift you got me" or "Because of the shitty birthday gift you got me" or "Because right around eight months was when Dutch and I broke up." Even drunk she knew couldn't say any of those things, so she merely shrugged.

The waiter brought them duck and champagne while they talked about their wedding. They agreed on September just as the leaves were changing. They discussed the pros and cons of their apartments and he agreed to move into hers since she had more room and a place where he could park. He'd move in as soon as possible to save on rent. The champagne caused her to hiccup again and he laughed. Her meal was tasty but tiny and she told her what her Dad always says about gourmet restaurants, "Five stars and four scallops." She told it to him twice more in the next five minutes.

"Where do you want to live after we get married?" she asked.

"We just decided on your apartment," he said.

"No, I mean after that."

He shrugged and took a bite of his duck. She glared at him.

"I think we should live in either Wellesley or Newton."

"Why Wellesley or Newton?"

"Weston is too expensive and Wellesley and Newton have good schools and are good places to bring up kids."

Curt wiped his mouth with his napkin and put his fork down.

"Julie, we've been over this and over this. I can't have kids."

Julie put her fork down.

"You can't have kids? I've been on birth control for six months."

Curt chuckled.

"You know what I mean. I don't mean I can't have kids," he said softly, "I mean I can't have kids. Not with my family history."

"I don't care about that."

"Three weeks ago, you and I went to the Home for the Criminally Insane. Remember?" he said, using his hands for emphasis. "You didn't see him, but I did. You have no idea what he did to my mother."

"Okay, but that has nothing to do with our children. You're normal" she said, ignoring the fact he mumbles to himself from time to time, "And I'm extra normal. I'm like 'Uber Normal.' My uber normal genes would cancel out your abnormal genes."

He didn't laugh. His dark eyes darkened.

"Mental illness runs in my family. Schizophrenia runs in my family. This goes back generations. My father's uncle was kicked out of World War One. How crazy do you have to be to get kicked out of a war?"

The waiter started to approach, thought better of it and quickly retreated. Someone placed two pointy hats and two noise-makers on their table so they stopped talking momentarily.

Curt leaned over and whispered, "I witnessed what my mother went through. I would never put you through that."

"I'll risk it," she said.

"I've been upfront about this since the beginning."

Had he been? He might have said he didn't want kids, but guys always say that. Michael had said that to her more than once and now he had three kids and another on the way, not that she was keeping track.

Dutch used to talk about what great athletes their kids would be since Julie was good at tennis and he was good at everything else. Kevin wouldn't have liked Dutch but Kevin would like Curt.

They went back and forth and Julie got a sick feeling in her stomach. She knew there had to be a catch. Someone couldn't just love her, she had to give up something. True happiness wasn't for her. She pleaded with him.

"I'm sorry," he said, "I promised myself a long time ago that I would never have children."

"So" she said, "I promised myself I'd be in Josie and the Pussycats and I got over it."

Curt started to say something but was drowned out by the people around them. They were counting down loudly from ten. For ten long seconds, Julie and Curt said nothing but stared or in her case, glared across the table. They were the only ones not wearing paper hats. "Happy New Year," people shouted. Noise-makers bleated. Curt came over and kissed her. She didn't put much into it. He sat back down in his seat. A different waiter came over and poured them each some champagne. Julie drained hers with one flick of the wrist. 1989 wasn't going very well.

"If you loved me, you'd have children with me."

"I do love you," he said, "I just asked you to spend the rest of our lives together."

They were at an impasse. *He's digging his heels. He is like his father. So stubborn. He's a stubborn little fuck.*

"Excuse me? Did you just call me a 'stubborn little fuck?'"

She hadn't meant to say it out loud. In fact, she hadn't said it very loudly at all, at least in her mind. He looked at her with an expression that was 60% shock and 40% hurt. Maybe 55/45. She didn't know how he even heard her with noise-makers still bleating and mixing with the car horns honking from outside.

"I have to go to the bathroom again."

It was unraveling. She felt a wave of nausea as she entered the bathroom. She had had too much gin and too much champagne and not enough snails and not enough duck. *Maybe I should have had the bunny.*

She sat on the toilet with the lid down catching her breath. The possibility that she might throw up had passed but she needed air. She knew she should be happy. The man she loved had just proposed to her. She should feel happy and hopeful and loved. Instead, she felt nauseous and dizzy and drunk. *How could he do this to baby Kevin?* Curt knew nothing about baby Kevin but these days baby Kevin was all Julie thought about. *Kevin would need a father and if this guy was unwilling it was time to move on.* She took off her engagement ring and held it in her hand making a fist. *Fuck him* she decided again, *I am going to be a mother.*

She got up and exited the bathroom stall. A middle-aged woman entered the ladies' room. It was the wealthy black woman Julie had taken delight in seeing just a few minutes earlier.

"Come here," Julie said to the woman before she could enter a stall.

"Pardon?"

"Come here," Julie opened the door a crack. Curt's back was to them. "See the guy sitting there? The little shit with the dark hair?"

"The guy who just proposed to you?"

Julie looked at the woman with surprise.

"Honey, we all just saw you get engaged. We were all cheering."

The woman had kind eyes and a serene face. Julie closed the bathroom door.

"Can you give him this?" Julie pressed the engagement ring into the stranger's hand.

The woman opened her mouth and looked at the ring in her hand.

"Sweetie, I can't do that. If you don't want to marry him, you have to tell him."

She tried to hand the ring back to Julie.

"I can't," said Julie, "And I can't marry him."

“You have to tell him that. You need to tell him why.”

Julie thought she might throw up again. There was too much to explain. There were members of his family who were criminally insane and therefore he didn’t want children. But she did want children and he was neither criminal or insane. It was as simple as that, but Julie didn’t want to get into it with a total stranger. She just wanted to go home.

“He’s a bad guy,” Julie said, “He uses the “n-word” all the time.”

The woman’s face dropped, and the serenity drained from her face.

“And he hits me sometimes,” said Julie, “when he gets drunk,” she added in an effort to make her story more plausible.

The woman gripped the ring in her fist.

“Pee first,” said Julie, “Then tell him.”

The woman nodded gravely. Julie slipped out of the bathroom. The coat check was not far but Curt might see her if she moved towards it. She couldn’t take that chance. She turned the other way, down the stairs and out the exit.

Chapter Seven

Julie slipped out of Maison Richard's and was immediately met with a bracing combination of noise and cold. It was New Year's Eve in downtown Boston, and she had intentionally forgotten her coat. Car horns honked and revelers surged down the street after making it through another year. Julie negotiated the cobblestone walk to the street carefully, mindful of her heels and aware she'd had too much to drink.

As she approached the gate and opened it, a sandy-haired twenty-something blocked her exit with his back to her.

"Excuse me," Julie said, causing no discernible reaction. "Excuse me," she yelled pushing him causing him to rock forward and back but not move out her way. Startled, he turned and stared at her face to face. He was younger than she thought, maybe nineteen and his face well acned and his eyes glazed. *He's drunker than me.* Julie knew Curt would be coming soon and felt a panicked need to be home.

"Get the fuck out of the way," she yelled, and nearby heads turned her way.

The boy moved and Julie turned and bumped into another drunken teen, this one with dark hair with a handsome, smooth skinned face. The dark haired one gestured to the sandy-haired one who gestured wildly back. *Fuck, they're deaf. I just thought they were drunk but they're deaf and drunk.*

Passing revelers stopped and stared.

"What the fuck is your problem, lady?"

Julie winced. She had a proposal and a break-up and now had bullied the handicapped and the term "lady" wasn't helping. Had the boys just been drunk teenagers the crowd may have been on her side, but they were drunk deaf teenagers and the moral high ground was no longer hers.

"I didn't know," she murmured and the revelers stopped walking and blocked her way.

"How could you not know? They're obviously deaf, you dumb bitch." *Dumb bitch? That's almost as bad as lady.*

"I swear I didn't know," Julie said again and gave up heading right and turned and moved back towards the deaf.

The deafs had multiplied now and seven or eight of them gathered near the gate of Maison Richard. A slightly older woman, older than the deafs but a little younger than Julie, emerged from the pack. She was chubby and mannish and bundled up.

"These young people are out here for a good time on New Year's Eve just like everyone else. They should be treated with respect."

Julie gleaned that the woman was some type of caretaker of theirs and she wondered why she had let them get drunk. "This is your fault," yelled Julie and the woman's mouth made the shape of an O.

"My fault? How'd you like it if I pushed you?"

She lunged at Julie as Julie turned. The woman's right-hand struck Julie's right breast. *Ow!* Julie spun around and would have fallen if not for the fence that sheathed Maison Richard's. "Fight, fight, fight" the revelers yelled.

Julie wasn't looking to rumble, she merely wanted to go home. As the woman came at her again, Julie pushed this time, hard and the surprised woman fell backwards and landed on her considerable behind. Julie seized the moment and scurried between the cars waiting at the red light, wobbly on her high heels and nearly falling but determined to make it to the safety of the other side of the street.

The light changed just as she reached the opposite sidewalk and the cars began moving forcing her enemy to remain where she was.

"I'll fuckin' kill you," she yelled at Julie over the din.

"Yes, I'm sure you will," thought Julie spotting a cab in the distance and waving frantically at it.

Julie had never been much of a fighter. She played tennis and was brotherless. The only physical fights she'd ever had were with her sisters and they involved hair-pulling and kicking and ended at around age ten. Her strength was the wise crack which was not the sort of protection she needed from the Deaf Defender.

My boob hurts.

Julie waved her hand desperately at the cab that was still a half a block away. The cabbie nodded in her direction and put his blinker on. Julie looked back across the street at her assailant.

"Bitch, I'm going to fuckin' kill you."

Her eyes were wild, and she shook her right fist at Julie. She was surrounded by drunken deaf teens and indignant revelers who began chanting "Bitch" in Julie's direction. The drunk deaf teens began gesturing what Julie assumed were similar sentiments. Car horns honked and noisemakers bleated as the cab stuck behind traffic crept slowly closer.

"Bitch, Bitch, Bitch!"

"This isn't over," her enemy yelled.

Oh, yes, it is.

The light changed and the cars stopped and the bully darted across the street. It was now a race between her and the cab to get to Julie first. Julie, frightened, ran down the street, tottering on her heels from side to side, towards the cab.

"I'll rip your face off, bitch."

Maybe, later.

Julie reached the cab ahead of her assailant and opened the door, jumped in and closed it with only seconds to spare.

"Go, go, go!" Julie yelled.

The woman smacked the cab's window with the palm of her hand.

"Do not do that," the cab driver yelled with a heavy accent as Julie slid to the other side of the backseat.

He pulled away from the curb and away from her assailant while Julie gave him her address. The light had changed again but the cars were slow to respond. Julie rolled down her window as she approached the revelers still looking on.

"Deaf people can be assholes, too, you know," she hollered out the window as the cab drove past. Someone yelled something indecipherable back and in the middle of the angry crowd and drunken deaf teenagers and outraged New Year's Eve revelers, Julie could see Curt's bewildered face.

Chapter Eight

After basic training ended, the men in Tom's unit were shipped to England and Tom caught a bug and spent the entire voyage below decks vomiting and sweating and shivering. He got healthy in time to join his buddies on a 48-hour pass to London knowing that any day after that they'd be sent to France to join the war.

By the time they got off the train in London it was dark and not the normal darkness of a major city in the 20th century but an eerie, fog-shrouded enveloping darkness. Tom had been envisioning the London of his school books. He had expected to see Big Ben and Buckingham Palace with a hint of Oliver Twist. It was as though everyone in the city had left leaving Tom's little group alone in the misty black.

"Haven't these people heard of street lights?" said Simms.

"You, dumb fuck," said Moretti, "It's blackout conditions."

Tom had gotten used to Moretti saying "fuck" all the time even though he'd never say it himself. Moretti was the one who told him about the trip to London and made sure he was included in their plans. He knew his parents wouldn't approve but he liked Moretti.

"I can't see a thing," said Simms.

"It appears these Londoners are involved in some sort of global conflict," added Leckie.

Tom laughed. Leckie had a way of saying things in just the right way to make them funny. When Tom tried to recreate what Leckie said in his letters home it didn't work, and he'd find himself ripping the page up and leaving it out. It was only funny in the moment coming from him.

"How the hell are we going to find a pub? None of them have their lights on," said Simms.

Tom had to admit Simms was right. *How are we going to find a pub?* He kept his thoughts to himself. Tom was always the quietest member of every group, even with his friends from high school, even with his family. He sometimes wondered why his friends wanted to hang out with him.

"There's plenty of fuckin' pubs. You can't take a piss in London without hitting a fuckin' pub," said Moretti, "We'll find one."

"Look out" yelled Tom and he grabbed Simms by the collar and pulled him back from the street as a car approached.

"That bastard almost hit me" said Simms. "That British bastard almost hit me" he said again in case someone missed it the first time.

"They drive on the left side of the fuckin' road here," said Moretti, "You gotta watch out."

"Pip, pip," said Leckie with a fake British accent, "Someone should inform that chap he's driving on the wrong side of the motorway."

Tom and Moretti laughed. Tom wished he could be funny like that.

"The bastard didn't even his headlights on," said Simms, not letting it go.

"The headlights have been painted," said Tom.

He had no patience for Simms either. Whereas Tom was big and quiet, Simms was small and wouldn't stop with the stupid questions.

"Here, look," said Tom.

They stopped at a parked car and Leckie lit a match and they gathered around the bumper and looked closely. The headlights had indeed been painted.

"It's part of the blackout conditions," said Tom.

"How the hell can they see anything driving around with black headlights?" said Simms.

"Black fuckin' headlights are better than no fuckin' headlights," said Moretti.

The street was quiet again. Leckie blew out his match and complete darkness returned. "You have to hand it to the British," thought Tom. His grandfather hated them, "Bunch of Protestants" but they were all in. Back home, it got dark but not like this and some people went about their business just the same as before the war but here everybody was all in. Black headlights and dark houses and dark streets and shortages of butter and sugar and their monthly allowance of two ounces of cheese.

"Look at that," said Simms.

"At what? I can't see a fuckin' thing," said Moretti.

"The Limeys didn't blackout the moon."

Simms, for once, was right as the moon peeked around a cloud and through the mist. They had just enough light to see the ruins of a building across the street. They got a closer look. Moretti nudged Tom, "It must have been hit in the fuckin' blitz."

"Could have been a fire," said Simms.

"It couldn't have been a fire, you dumb bastard. The fuckin' houses next to it weren't touched. It must have been a direct fuckin' hit."

"Holy shit."

A Luftwaffe plane had slipped past the RAF and dropped some sort of incendiary device on the house in front of them. Those were the facts. It was something out of a history book or the newsreel and it was right there in front of them.

"Filthy Germans," Tom muttered.

This was their first real evidence of the war. The war up until now was only a rumor but here it was right in front of them and they all knew that next week they'd be part of it. No one spoke for a little while, even Simms.

Tom glanced at the silhouetted faces of Simms and Leckie and Moretti. They were going to war soon and he knew it was unlikely that they would all return home safe and sound. He knew it was even more unlikely that they would all be brave. He wondered which of them will be killed and which of them will be maimed and which of them would lose his noodle.

Chapter Nine

For Julie, New Year's Eve had turned out even worse than Christmas, which had been the worst day of her life. The day before Christmas, she and Curt had drove from Boston to New Jersey so he could meet her family. She was so nervous she'd talked for almost the entire six-hour drive.

She had enough self-awareness to appreciate the absurdity of her situation. His family, thanks to violence, psychosis and hatred, had been virtually obliterated leaving him all alone. Yet, she couldn't help but worry about what he'd think about her family.

Prior to this trip, she had told him some of the bad stuff about her family thinking it would make him feel better knowing every family has its problems. It was a foolish endeavor, for as competitive as Julie was there was no competing with this guy when it came to whose family was the most fucked up.

She briefly recapped the story of her parents with one new wrinkle. He knew Julie's Mom was a recovering alcoholic and that her parents' marriage had nearly ended a few years earlier. What he didn't know was that their near break-up occurred not while she was drinking but after she stopped. She'd been a relatively pleasant drunk but without alcohol she'd become caustic and mean and hurtful, "a real bitch," said Julie knowing that wasn't a nice thing to say about your mother. Whether it was due to her father's love or patience or some vestige of Catholicism or perhaps, simply habit, the two stuck it out and have seemed to work out some sort of truce.

She, then told Curt of her two sisters. Cheryl, the older one, was the pretty one, the one her mother fussed and fretted over, the blonde one, the one with the nice singing voice to be trotted out as the show pony whenever company arrived.

"You might decide you picked the wrong Rossi girl," said Julie.

"Hmmm," said Curt, nodding, "Sounds like it."

Julie had been in competition with Cheryl her whole life, at least in her mind. Cheryl may have been prettier, but Julie was smarter and funnier.

Cheryl would get the solos in the school plays, so Julie fought to make the tennis team, giving up on her mother but hoping to win over her Dad.

Cheryl dropped out of college to marry a handsome cop named Nick and produce three postcard perfect children, twin girls and a boy. Year after year, Julie dreaded coming home for the holidays with no boyfriend, no husband, no Kevin and having to watch her mother fawn over Cheryl and her children and look upon her with pity.

Meg, the younger sister, was always the loser of the bunch, plump and dumb without a nice voice or a nice backhand, she became a hellion, always in trouble, always with the wrong sort of boy. She eventually calmed down and with few prospects married a New Jersey redneck named Ned. Ned was the kind of guy, who, if "funny" was synonymous with "racist" would have been a riot. They had a three-year-old boy Julie had already deemed "a moron" and an infant who was probably well on her way to becoming one.

"Nothing worse than a three-year-old moron," said Curt.

Julie always dreaded the holidays but this Thanksgiving, Nick wasn't there, and Cheryl hinted at the possibility of divorce. Meg overheard her saying something to her mother about "some young slut" and now, Cheryl, with no husband and three kids and a no job, had lost her advantage. Meg was never a threat, so now, Julie with a good job and a cute boyfriend and Kevin on the horizon, might win this race after all. Her mother had backed the wrong horse. It was all so sudden and overwhelming.

As they pulled off the highway, drawing closer to her house, Julie became more nervous, almost frightened and her breathing became irregular.

"Are you okay?" he asked.

"Yeah, yeah," she said, "Aren't you nervous?"

"No," said Curt and he didn't appear to be.

When she pulled in the driveway, she saw Meg's car but not her parents.

"Maybe they left the country," said Julie, "and you won't have to meet them after all."

Julie retrieved the presents she'd picked up for her nieces and nephews from the trunk of her car and entered the house. They found Meg and her three-year-old moron sitting on the kitchen floor, playing with Tupperware bowls and wooden spoons.

"Meg, Curt, Curt, Meg," said Julie.

"And who's this?" said Curt, extending a hand to the little boy who didn't know what to do with it. *See*, thought Julie, *a moron*.

"That's Jared," said Meg as Curt slid down onto the floor next to the boy.

It suddenly occurred to Julie she'd never seen Curt interact with children before and here he was sitting next to Jared playing the Tupperware drums along with him. The two of them seemed to be having fun. *Imagine how good he'll be with Kevin. This kid isn't even cute.*

"Where are Mom and Dad?" asked Julie.

"They went to get Aunt June," said Meg.

The possibility of Aunt June making an appearance hadn't dawned on Julie when she gave Curt the unauthorized biography of her family members. Aunt June lived in a retirement home just a bit too far away and usually spent the holidays being shuffled between other branches of the family. This Christmas was apparently their turn.

"Who's Aunt June?" asked Curt.

"She's my mother's aunt, said Julie, "I was named for her. Sort of."

"Yeah, sort of," said Meg. "Mom, called an hour ago to warn me. Aunt June is losing it."

"What do you mean?" asked Julie.

Aunt June had always been her favorite relative, a career woman before such things were in vogue.

"Mom says she has 'hardening of the arteries' and can't remember who anybody is and repeats the same stories over and over."

"I do that now," said Julie, looking down at Curt with a smile, "No one will be able to tell when I start losing it."

"Oh," said Meg, "And we're doing take out at Sal's."

With the big turkey dinner on Christmas, no one liked cooking the night before, so her family usually did take-out. Her family name was Rossi but they were only one-quarter Italian and eating occasionally at Sal's was about as close as her family got to their paternal roots.

Jared continued to rock out on the Tupperware until Julie's parents' car finally pulled into the driveway.

"I was afraid they'd come home," said Julie, "Let's get this over with."

"Thanks for playing for us, Jared," said Curt, pulling himself up off the floor.

Julie's Mom and Dad had just gotten out of the car when Julie and Curt came out of the house.

"Hi, Daddy," said Julie, knowing he preferred "Daddy" to "Dad" and wanting to be on his good side right now.

"Hi, Sweetheart," he said, kissing her head.

"Hi, Mom," said Julie, and she went around the other side of the car to hug her mother.

"Hi, Julie," said her Mom, while looking over at Curt.

"Mom and Dad, this is Curt."

"Hi," said Curt, right on cue.

"I'm Bill," said Julie's Dad, warmly.

Julie's Dad was a salesman and liked when people liked him. Julie's Mom didn't have a job and didn't care if people liked her or not.

"I'm Ellen," she said without warmth.

They were probably expecting someone a little taller. Well, too bad. He's better than that two-timing Nick and that awful Ned. Besides, they're not perfect. Dad's has a comb-over and Mom's arms jiggle when she moves them. Julie was having an imaginary argument in her head.

"Julie, help your aunt out of the car," said Julie's Mom, "And Bill, get the food out of the trunk."

Julie opened the door to the backseat and pried her aunt out. *Oooh, she does look bad.* She'd gotten shorter and become hunched, her hair was newly dyed and looked all right, although implausibly black, her make-up askew and her eyes glazed and far away.

"Hi, Auntie," said Julie.

"Hello, Ellen," said Aunt June.

"Aunt June, I'm Ellen," said Julie's Mom, "That's Julie. You remember Julie. She was always your favorite."

"Thanks a lot," said Meg, who had suddenly appeared with Jared in her arms.

"Aunt June, this is my boyfriend Curt," said Julie.

Aunt June turned her glazed, zombie-like eyes towards Curt and gave him the once over.

"Oh, my," she said.

"What did that mean?" thought Julie, escorting the old woman into the house. Julie got her aunt's coat off and plopped her down in a seat at the dining room table.

"Sit here," the old woman said to Curt, who did as he was told but looked uncomfortable for the first time.

Just before dinner, Ned came downstairs with the baby. "Peaches and I slept like two Mexicans in a field," he announced proudly.

"What an entrance," said Julie.

"You must be Ned," said Curt.

Julie laughed silently and took a seat next to Curt, sandwiching him between herself and her aunt.

"Edgar Trevin Burris, the second" said Ned, shaking Curt's hand across the table, "white people call me 'Ned' but everyone else calls me, 'sir.'"

Julie tried to gauge Curt's reaction but he didn't seem to have one. *I'm glad I warned him.*

Moments later, Julie's other sister Cheryl arrived with their seven-year-old girls and their little boy. Cheryl looked thin and pale and Julie took note. Auntie June called Cheryl "Ellen" and then called Meg "Ellen." As far as she knew, she was seated at a table with four "Ellens." She called Curt "Richard" and Julie watched as she patted his knee.

"Who's Richard?" asked Cheryl.

"Who knows?" said the real Ellen.

"So Curt," Julie's Dad said, "I understand you own your own cleaning business."

"Yes," Curt swallowing a mouthful of pasta, "For eight years now."

"Richard is a lawyer" said Aunt June, "He's leaving his wife for me."

No one said anything for a moment.

"Well," said Julie, "The plot thickens."

"Sounds like someone was getting his wick dipped," said Ned.

"Edgar Trevin Burris" said Julie's Mom crossly. She turned to Curt and asked, "So how did you two meet?"

"We met at the bank, Mom. I told you that," Julie cut in.

"I was taking out a loan," said Curt, "We were adding two more cleaning crews, so we needed two more vans and supplies."

"I was the collateral," Julie added, getting a laugh from Meg and no one else.

The twins stared at Curt and whispered to each other.

"What are you two whispering about?" said Julie.

The two of them giggled identical giggles and said nothing.

Ned started a story about a Chinese co-worker, using the term "Chinaman" when Aunt June interrupted.

"Richard takes me to the Ambassador Hotel on Tuesday afternoons. Don't you, Richard?" Aunt June said turning to Curt, who blushed.

"No wonder I never see you on Tuesday afternoons," muttered Julie.

"Ooooh, I bet it would get pretty hot in the middle of June," said Ned, laughing at his own "wit." Meg laughed too and her Mom glared at the two of them.

"Aunt June, that isn't proper conversation for the dinner table," said Julie's Mom with a raised eyebrow.

"It's more interesting than cleaning crews," said Julie getting both her sisters to laugh that time.

"We're going to mass first thing in the morning," said Julie's Dad, "We better get there early. It's always crowded on Christmas morning with the twice-a-year crowd."

"What about the kids opening presents?" asked Cheryl.

"They can open one present before we go," said her Dad, "You know the rules."

At bed time, Julie and Curt were relegated to separate rooms. Julie had warned Curt on the drive down. They met in the hallway before turning in.

"Thanks for putting up with my family," said Julie.

"They're all very nice," said Curt.

"Ned?"

Curt shrugged and gave a "What are you going to do?" look.

"I think my parents really like you," whispered Julie.

"Not as much as your aunt does," said Curt.

"The Ambassador Hotel? What the hell was that?" she asked before kissing him good night.

At five in the morning, Julie was wide awake. She lay there thinking about Curt. He'd been so kind and playful with Jared. She thought about the way Curt tolerated Ned while simultaneously fending off the lascivious advances of a daft, elderly woman. She couldn't fall back to sleep so she opened the door a crack and listened but couldn't hear a thing from the whole house. Slowly and carefully, she tiptoed down the hall and into the room where Curt was sleeping. She felt a thrill of excitement as she slid into bed with him. He stirred and opened one eye.

"What are you doing?"

She kissed him.

"What about your parents?"

"I'll be back in my room in no time."

Within a minute, they were both naked. As he kissed her neck, his fingers moved up her thighs, to her waist and began caressing her breasts. She began to moan softly. Curt was breathing heavily. So heavily, neither one of them heard the door open.

Chapter Ten

They put as many men as they could onto the ship. Tom was one of hundreds, all standing, packed in tight, shoulder to shoulder, all facing away from England and towards France. As small boys, every single one of them, Tom included, had played at war and daydreamed about war, and as grown men, they had all been trained at war. All of that playing and daydreaming and training had been in preparation for this day.

When the ship started moving, the talking and the joking stopped and the quiet began. It wasn't the "serene quiet" of a congregation after the homily or right after communion. It was the "fear quiet" when an entire crowd felt the same pervasive fear. Tom had only heard this kind of quiet once before. It was during a high school football game he was playing in his junior year. A player on the other team had been hit in the neck reaching for a pass and he lay on the field with limbs that could no longer function. That crowd which had been noisy and boisterous just moments earlier suddenly had nothing to say. Tom watched from the sidelines while the paralyzed boy was carted away.

Whether it was a clean hit, or a dirty hit was a matter of conjecture. The boy who hit him, a boy named Hank Phelps, took himself out of the game. In the locker room, afterwards, the coach and the other players tried to convince Phelps that these things happen. It was nobody's fault, but Phelps, racked with guilt, quit the team anyway.

The incident had affected Tom, too. After that, he never tackled anyone as hard as he could. He didn't want the guilt of paralyzing someone. He even said prayers for the other boy for several weeks until it gradually slipped from his mind.

Tom wasn't on the sidelines now, he was in the middle of the pack and was tall enough to stare over the heads in front of him at the gray mist in the distance. He was one of the hundreds of men all staring straight ahead not saying a word. He could hear the waves lapping up against the hull and the steady hum of the engine and the occasional squawk of a distant bird. He fingered his rosary in his pocket and silently said his "Hail Marys."

After a few minutes, a wisecrack or two broke out and then eventually some guarded and subdued conversation. Tom spotted Moretti a dozen or so feet away with a dozen or so men in between. He could see Moretti's lips moving but couldn't hear what he was saying. *He must be praying*. They made eye contact and Moretti nodded.

"Fuckin' Nazis!" yelled Moretti.

Tom chuckled.

I guess he's not praying.

Tom looked around and became aware of other troop ships crossing the channel. It was nothing like D-Day. He'd heard the stories and even met a man who'd been there. A paratrooper on leave back in England told them all about it.

"There was an armada that day. Everything that could float was thrown across the channel at them," he told Tom and a few others.

"We knocked the Gerrys off the coast."

This is nothing compared to that.

Tom had barely slept the night before. *What if I die tomorrow? If I die, I'll go to heaven.* He knew there was a heaven and a hell and hell was for fornicators and murderers and rapists and masturbators and he wasn't any of those things. He'd even gone to confession and confessed his venial sins to a disinterested chaplain used to hearing juicier stuff. *If I die, I'll go to heaven.*

But what if I kill someone? That was the big question. Hitler and the Nazis were evil. They had subjugated the Poles and the Czechs and the French and the Dutch and the Belgians and others and were still going. They had to be stopped. *I'm here to stop them. Killing them was the only way to make them stop. God knows that. I'd still go to heaven.*

What did it feel like to kill someone? Could I forgive myself for killing someone or would I be racked with guilt like Hank Phelps? Could I kill someone and not lose my noodle? He was more afraid of losing his noodle than he was of dying or having his leg blown off like Eddie Curran.

Tom could make out the silhouette of French coast in the distance now. The men grew quiet again as it came into view. The breeze felt good on his face and he knew there were only a few minutes to go.

He became anxious and the ship grew closer. He could make out figures now on the beach and could hear airplanes, but he didn't look up. He wanted off the ship. He gripped his M-1 tightly with his left hand and held his rosary in his pocket with his right. *Almost there.*

He knew his orders. The night before they'd been shown a map and a rendezvous point. Once they landed, they were to move at double-time to the rendezvous point and wait there.

"We'll be lucky if we see any fuckin' Germans," Moretti had said the night before.

"They won't be lucky if they see me," said Leckie.

Some of the men seemed anxious to kill. Was it just tough talk? Part of him was excited, he was part of something big, something important. "Be brave" he had told himself the night before and as they got close, he reminded himself once more.

They inched closer and closer and the signal was given. *This is it.* Tom and the other men leapt into the shallow water and he clutched his M-1 tightly. Bombs began dropping from the planes overhead. "Not ours" thought Tom. The water was knee high and he splashed his way onto the beach right behind the man in front of him. When he ran, Tom ran. There were orders and screams that were drowned out by the explosions from the bombs. Tom could hear gunfire and the sound of airplane engines. *I'm in combat. This is combat.*

Everything happened slowly and quickly at the same time. Tom wanted to look around and take everything in, but he knew better. He focused on the helmet of the man in front of him and ran to keep up. He heard someone nearby shrieking in pain but didn't turn to look. Bullets hit the sand nearby. *Someone is trying to kill me.*

He ran faster now, and the Luftwaffe planes disappeared into the distance, bringing an end to the bombing and the shooting. There was still yelling and shrieking and Tom continued to follow the man in front of him as his training had taught him to do. He held his M1 the way Harroway had shown him and he ran with his knees up. He was aware of the other men now, not just the man in front of him. He saw the rendezvous point just beyond on the beach and ran toward it. He had never been a fast runner and other men had gotten there first. He reached the spot where other men had gathered, and bent over at the waist catching his breath.

The disembarkation from the ship to the shore couldn't have taken more than a minute or two. They had been fired on by German planes and they still hadn't seen any enemy soldiers yet and it wasn't technically, "a battle" but they had officially seen "action" and Tom felt as happy as he could ever remember feeling.

His hands shook as he drank from his canteen. Moretti sidled up to him.

"Well, Tom, we made it this fucking far."

Tom smiled and drank. He still didn't know if he could kill someone. He would learn that the answer to that question was "yes."

Chapter Eleven

It was still early enough that the light that filtered through the window blinds into the guest room was a half-light with a diffused, ethereal quality. Julie straddled Curt, her body rocking forward and back on top of his. As he caressed her breasts, her head lurched backwards, and her hair cascaded over her face. Her eyes were closed and so were his.

"Richard, what are you doing?"

Julie and Curt froze, their eyes popped open and they turned at the exact same time like synchronized swimmers towards the doorway. Julie shook the hair from her face and stared into the unblinking reptilian eyes of her Aunt June. All was momentarily still then Julie vaulted off of Curt, suddenly and violently, nearly taking his penis with her. He groaned and bent at the waist.

"Auntie June," said Julie with exaggerated caution, "This isn't Richard. Richard is dead. This is my boyfriend Curt. You need to go back to bed."

She spoke with her hands reaching out in front of her body doing her best to placate the old woman. Curt nodded in agreement, a look of terror on his face. He tried to cover himself in the sheet, but Julie ripped the sheet from his hands and covered herself.

"Richard isn't dead," the old woman squawked loudly, "Richard is my boyfriend."

"Auntie June," Julie whispered with urgency in her voice, "You need to go back to bed. You need to go back to bed right now."

But it was too late, a door upstairs creaked open and banged into something. The sound of footsteps pattered on the ceiling directly above them.

"He is my boyfriend, you hussy," Auntie June bellowed, her voice louder than ever.

Julie, desperate now, stood on the bed using both hands to hold the sheet to her body and whispered urgently back at the old woman, "Auntie June get of here, please, Auntie June go back to bed," but Auntie June refused to budge.

The footsteps drew closer now and Julie was helpless to stop their arrival. She began to have trouble breathing and she turned to Curt who had scrambled, still naked, into the corner. She looked at him helplessly and he looked back even more helplessly. Still standing on the bed, Julie turned back and looked down at Auntie June and then past her at the open doorway.

Her father was the first to enter. He wore pajamas and his normally combed-over hair stood straight up on one side. He was in the process of putting on his bathrobe and tying it as his eyes moved from Aunt June, up towards Julie, still standing on the bed, over to Curt, who was crouched behind a chair in the corner of the room, trying to cover his nakedness. His mouth opened and his eyebrows lifted as he surveyed the trio, spending a second or two staring at each of them. There was just enough light to see everything.

"Goddammit, Julie! What the hell?"

"I'm so sorry, Daddy." Julie mumbled.

Julie stepped gingerly down off the bed, still clutching tight to the sheet around her body. She was close to her father now as she murmured with great sincerity, "I am so sorry." She said this with her eyes cast downward, noticing his slippers for the first time.

Julie's Mom entered an instant later, her bathrobe fully on. She took in the whole scene and then whispered, "Oh, God."

"This one is a real peach," said Auntie June, pointing a finger at Julie.

Julie's Dad let out a "pfft" which may have indicated agreement.

"Richard is my boyfriend."

The old woman pointed at Curt, who was tucked in the corner, curled up in a ball, both naked and chilly. They all stared at him for a moment and his face reddened and he looked away.

"Auntie June, let's go back to bed," said Julie's Mom, trying to take the old woman's arm but Auntie June resisted.

"I'm not going anywhere until she leaves."

Quick footsteps made their way down the hallway and Cheryl's twins poked their heads in the doorway, one above the other.

"Jesus, get the goddamn kids out of here," yelled Julie's Dad and the violence in his voice caused both children to start to cry. Julie's Mom glared at Julie's Dad.

"Goddam it, Bill," she said.

Cheryl entered and her head darted around quickly like a squirrel sensing danger. Her eyes went from Julie to Aunt June to Curt and back to Julie where they lingered for just a moment.

I guess you win again, thought Julie.

Cheryl grabbed her twins and disappeared down the hall. Her entire cameo lasting no more than five seconds.

"Look what you've done, Julie," her mother yelled. Julie adjusted the sheet to keep it from sliding off.

"I didn't mean to. We all make mistakes."

Her father stared into Julie's face wondering what she meant by that remark.

"I'm so sorry," she mumbled again.

Her mother scowled at Julie while her father smoothed his hair down with his hand and shook his head. Julie looked over towards Curt, a look of terror clung to his still reddened face.

"Julie, I think you should go back to your room," said her father and Julie nodded.

"Okay, I'm going Auntie June," but before she could leave Meg entered with the baby and Ned. Ned looked around the room and then laughed out loud when he saw Curt. Curt still naked and red-faced and still crouched behind a chair covering his private parts with both hands.

"You've ruined Christmas, Julie" yelled her father and Julie said softly, "I'm sorry, I'm sorry," over and over.

Julie then wedged herself between Ned and Meg and out the door wearing the sheet like a Roman senator.

"I hope you're proud of yourself," her mother barked as a parting shot.

"Auntie June, you can go now," said Julie's Mom and this time the old woman let her take her by the arm. Meg moved out of the way allowing them out into the hallway. Julie's Dad glowered at Curt on his way out the door and Curt let his expression apologize for him.

In the hallway, Julie clutched the sheet tightly and carefully as she maneuvered herself towards the stairs. Auntie June yelled at her backside one last time, "Richard is my boyfriend."

Chapter Twelve

For the next three or four months until the Bulge, they pushed the Germans further and further from the French coast, hedgerow by hedgerow, until they were almost out of France altogether. Paris was liberated and a generous Eisenhower let de Gaulle and his men enter before he did. The Germans seemed to lose a few miles each day.

Tom was pretty sure he had killed some of them, but he couldn't be certain. He'd been placed on mortar duty and lobbing shells from a distance of six hundred yards while under fire made the precise results difficult to determine. The mortar shells fell with an ear-piercing, terror-inducing whistle and more than once, he saw Germans run from the whistle into machine gun fire preferring to die by old-fashioned bullets. He knew he had a hand in killing even if he hadn't done the actual killing.

Once a week, after mass, Tom found a chaplain to confess to and each one told him the same thing.

"It's not a sin to kill Nazis."

One went as far as calling it "The Lord's work" which got a hearty laugh at chow from Moretti, Leckie and Simms.

Tom grew to hate the Germans, a natural consequence of someone trying to kill you. He saw men killed and men with their limbs torn away. He saw a man he'd been talking to just moments before blown to bits not ten feet from him. Once, he saw a man whose jaw had been shot off and he stood, dazed, with a top half of his face but no bottom half.

Some men lost their noodle. They would shake and tremble and no amount of beer or whiskey could calm them down and they would be shipped out. A corporal from Ohio named Plesac, a man from his company that Tom had been friendly with, shot himself in the foot so he'd be sent home.

One night, while bombs from a Luftwaffe plane rained down on them, a brand, new man, ran unarmed, across the field into the German lines and disappeared forever. No one ever found out if he'd been killed or captured.

Many of them cried, usually at night, sometimes after a battle out of fear of death or grief over a lost buddy. Some men cried over homesickness. Tom didn't lose his noodle and he never cried, for he reasoned that it would break his vow of being brave.

In October, he volunteered for a mission. As it turned out, it wasn't really a mission, it was more of an errand. Back home, it might even be called "a favor" but Tom, reflexively, had volunteered for it not knowing what it entailed. He was told to drive a captain from the town they occupied back to headquarters. The Germans were being pushed east and the Captain was actually heading west away from the line. Tom didn't know why the Captain was heading west but he knew better than to ask.

He was issued a jeep and Moretti and Leckie helped him lift three unmarked crates onto the back.

"I bet it's wine," said Moretti. "The fuckin' officers love French wine. The dumb bastards, it's the Italian wine that's the good shit," Moretti said, with a chuckle.

"Oh, yeah," said Leckie, "I don't even know why we're fighting the Guineas since their goddam wine is so good."

Tom sat in the jeep and waited until the captain finally arrived.

"Are you my driver, private?"

"Yes, sir."

One of the first things Tom learned about the army was a lot of guys didn't look like the soldiers in the war movies. Simms, for example, was covered in acne. It was like leprosy. *The poor fella, you never saw that in the movies.* The captain was another one who seemed miscast. He wore glasses and had small unmuscular frame with a skinny arms and legs and a slight belly. He had a gentle, cherubic face. Nothing about him said, "warrior."

"Let's go, private. I'd like to get there by 0400."

In peace time, they'd have looked like father and son on holiday; the son having graduated from college, his wealthy father rewarding his efforts by taking him to Paris, Amsterdam, London and the other great cities of Western Europe. Tom had never taken a trip alone with his father to Europe or anywhere else.

The autumn air was crisp but clear and neither unpleasant nor unfamiliar to a Bostonian like Tom. They passed army trucks and tanks and jeeps. They drove through French towns ravaged by bombs and soldiers yet there were stretches, a winding road here, a wooded glen there, that the war had randomly and mercifully left alone.

"Pull over up here at woods, Private. Nature calls." "Yes sir."

After a minute or so, Tom pulled his jeep off onto the side of the road in a thicket. There was the sound of some airplanes in the distance. He ducked behind a tree and urinated while the captain walked deep into the woods. He chuckled to himself when he realized the Captain was responding to a more robust call of nature. Tom finished, zipped his fly back up and stood near his jeep. As the time passed, Tom knew he had a story for Moretti and Leckie. Here he was, all alone in the French woods, on a beautiful autumn day, waiting for his commanding officer to finish his bowel movement. Such were the oddities of life. It was nearly twenty minutes before the captain emerged from seclusion.

"Private, bring me a canteen."

Tom grabbed his canteen from the jeep and hustled toward the captain.

"Pour it on my hands, will you, son?"

He unscrewed the cap and poured water over the Captain's hands. It was almost like a religious ceremony. The two men avoided eye contact.

"That's enough," the Captain said before wiping his hands on his pants and getting back in the jeep. It was tough to say which man was more embarrassed.

They drove on through a small town and then back through French countryside. There was a convoy of Americans trucks in the distance heading in the direction on a different road. The trucks looked small like toys and gradually grew bigger as their jeep drew closer.

"Morrissey, is that Irish?"

"Yes sir."

"100%?"

"Yes sir."

"I'm 75% myself. There's one quarter English we don't like to talk about."

He nudged Tom in the ribs playfully with his elbow and Tom smiled.

"Yes sir."

In the distance, three airplanes came into view. *"Were they theirs or ours?"* The captain lifted binoculars from his chest to his eyes.

"They're Krauts" he shouted, pull over here and get down."

Tom swung the jeep to the side of the road and came to an abrupt stop. The Captain scurried behind a clump of trees as the sound of bullets came from the airplanes. Tom remained in the jeep, his hands on the steering wheel, ever determined to keep his vow of being brave. The planes swooped, ignored the jeep and fired on trucks in nearby convoy. The convoy managed to fire a shot or two back. Tom gripped the steering wheel defiantly and the muscles in his face tensed as he watched the fire fight. After a few more exchanges the planes climbed back up and disappeared and the trucks drove on unfazed.

The Captain stepped out from behind the clump of trees. His face was red and his eyes fierce.

"Private, what the hell kind of stunt are you pulling? I told you to 'get down.' I gave you a direct order, private. Didn't I?"

"Yes sir," Tom stammered.

The Captain stood over him while Tom looked up at an angle.

"Do you think that shows courage sitting here like that, Private?" Tom said nothing.

"What it shows me is you're a damn fool. Are you trying to get yourself killed?"

"No sir."

"You sure fooled me. If I ever see you pull a stunt like that again I'll have your ass thrown in the stockade so fast…"

The Captain's face remained red and there was spittle on his chin.

I'm just trying to be brave.

"Do you understand me, Private?"

"Yes sir."

"You are a goddam fool. Even the village idiot knows to get down when someone is shooting at him."

Tom's eyes looked downward and he stared at his hands which had never left the steering wheel. Then the captain got back into the jeep and the two men drove on in silence.

Chapter Thirteen

Julie lay on her back in her old bed with her pillow pressed against her face for an hour thinking about what had just happened. Her entire family had just seen her and her boyfriend naked on Christmas morning. This was the opposite of a "Christmas Miracle." This was a "Christmas Debacle."

What Julie regretted most, more than the ill-advised sexual romp, more than the nudity, was the crack she had made at her mother. That one snide comment, "You're not perfect either" showed she resented her mother's alcoholism and wasn't afraid to throw it in her mother's face. In that one instant, it was clear she had discussed her mother's secret with her boyfriend, and it was then her father really became enraged. Nudity was something her parents could forgive but disloyalty was not.

She got up, finally, to get ready for mass and pretend nothing had happened. Over the years, she entered her parents' kitchen in her pajamas or bathing suit and various other stages of dress. Today, she wore a skirt, a blouse, a sweater, nylons, earrings, and a scarf. She put on as many articles of clothing as she could, hoping it would compensate for her lack of clothing earlier that morning.

Entering the kitchen, for an instant, she thought she was alone until she turned and saw her father, tucked in the corner, scooping marmalade onto an English muffin. Once upon a time, she and her Dad had been pals. He'd taught her how to play tennis and would sneak out of work early to watch her high school matches. She'd accompany him to a Phillies game or toss the football around with him in the backyard whenever he felt the void of a life with no sons. She thought of this as she popped an English muffin into the toaster. Maybe the English muffin would remind him of all the other things they once shared.

Curt entered the kitchen, looking innocent in a dark blue suit with a light blue shirt. He smiled weakly at Julie who flicked her eyes towards the corner of the room. Curt recoiled slightly as he turned and saw her father.

"Merry Christmas," Curt mumbled.

Her father grunted something back that almost sounded like “Merry Christmas.”

Julie’s Mom came in from the living room and looked at both Julie and Curt without saying “hello.”

“Merry Christmas,” said Curt.

“Merry Christmas, Mom,” said Julie.

“Merry Christmas” Julie’s Mom said, begrudgingly.

The four of them then exchanged glances but no more words.

There were footsteps on the stairs and Meg entered with Ned and the baby. Ned laughed as he looked around.

“Nice of you two to dress for breakfast.”

Julie wanted to brain him with the toaster but stood staring at it instead waiting for her English muffin to pop.

“Curt,” said Julie’s Mom, “Would you care for some eggs or some fruit?” She gestured to a plate of each on the counter.

“I’ll just have some cantaloupe,” he said, lifting some onto a plate.

“Sure,” said Ned, speaking louder than necessary, “Grab the melons.” Meg laughed and Curt blushed.

Curt took his cantaloupe and sat at the table across from Julie’s Dad. Julie buttered her muffin as Curt, a hater of small talk, did his best. “It’s supposed to get very cold this week. In Boston, it’s supposed to get down to the single digits.”

Julie’s father nodded and chewed. “We should leave at 8:30,” he announced to no one in particular, “We’ll bring two cars.”

“Sounds good,” said Julie, overly pleasantly as she sat down. She tried to think of something to say to both her father and her boyfriend but could think of nothing.

Meg sat down at the table and unbuttoned her blouse to breast-feed the baby. Her Dad winced and excused himself from the table. Curt blushed and said something about brushing his teeth as he exited just as quickly. The baby began slurping from Meg.

"I'm next," said Ned.

Meg feigned disgust while Julie didn't have to feign.

"Honeybuns, I could use some milk in my coffee."

God, he's the worst.

A few minutes later, the family assembled in the driveway to divide into two carloads. It was sunny and not that cold.

"It could have been a beautiful Christmas if I hadn't fucked it up," thought Julie.

"I'll take one car," said Julie's Dad, "And Cheryl, do you mind driving the other?"

"Not at all," said Cheryl, who was enjoying her rightful place as the number one daughter.

The backdoor opened and Auntie June emerged. Julie, inexplicably, had forgotten about her once again and yet, there she was, with make-up on one side of her face and not the other.

Aunt June cast a dirty look towards Curt, "I'm not talking to you."

"A lovers' quarrel," said Ned.

"Aunt June, why don't you ride in the front seat of my car?" said Julie's Dad.

While Julie's Dad escorted Auntie June to his car, Curt quickly hopped into the other car. Julie sat in the back of her father's car with Meg and Ned and the baby, desperate to avoid her mother's scowl and Cheryl's gloating face.

Julie sat pressed against the car door thanks to the collective bulk of Meg and Ned.

"So Dad, are the Eagles going to make it to the Super Bowl?" she asked.

"Your Aunt June doesn't want to talk football," he snapped.

So much for breaking the tension.

She caught a glimpse of her father in the mirror. His jaw was set, and his lips were welded together. It was his angry face. When they were kids, Julie and Meg used to call this "straight line mouth." Cheryl never caused "straight line mouth" and never used the term. Julie came up with it the day she was hitting tennis balls against the house and accidentally bashed one through a kitchen window. "Straight line mouth" always appeared the next morning if they'd been out too late the night before or anytime Meg's report card arrived.

I'm thirty-six years old and I still quake at the sight of straight-line mouth, Julie thought to herself. She tried to catch Meg's eye, but Ned's foolish head was in the way.

"Auntie June, look all the houses with the beautiful Christmas decorations," said Julie.

"Not all the houses," said Ned. "Jew," he said, pointing to a house without Christmas ornaments. "Jew," he said again a few moments later.

"Ned!" said Meg, disapprovingly but with a giggle all the same.

"We're celebrating the birth of a Jew," said Julie.

"The last good one," said Ned.

This fuckin' guy.

"Just ignore him," said Meg, giving him a gentle nudge in the ribs.

Julie looked at her Dad in the mirror again. His straight-lined mouth hadn't budged and his eyes looked away when they detected hers. Julie stared out the window. *I'm too old to cry.*

"Richard is very successful."

Oh, fuck, not this again.

"He drives a Packard. He takes me to the Ambassador Hotel."

"Auntie June," said Julie's father before she could continue, "This isn't appropriate talk for Christmas morning."

"Ha," said Auntie June with a scoffing laugh.

This is the longest ten-minute car ride of my life.

"Jew."

Chapter Fourteen

Did they think he was stupid? Tom knew where his buddies were going. They'd been before. They didn't tell him this time because they knew he didn't approve. So, they just slipped off without him, evacuated the area, their own little Dunkirk.

Tom didn't need them. He had a bottle and he had the graveyard. He'd get drunk on his own. At least he'd be able to hold his head up tomorrow and every day after. He'd go home when the war was over knowing he hadn't disgraced himself and his family by visiting a brothel.

The first time, they'd found the graveyard by accident. They were headed into town from the makeshift barracks when someone, (Simms, maybe?), stopped for a piss.

"Why don't we just stay here?" said Leckie.

Tom thought he was joking because Leckie was always joking.

"Why the fuck not?" said Moretti.

So, they sat in a graveyard, the irony not lost on any of them. They leaned against headstones and sat on grave markers smoking cigarettes and passing around two bottles and a flask. It was Tom and Moretti and Leckie and Simms and two other fellas who Tom didn't really know but mixed in well enough.

They got drunk and laughed at the things Leckie said. Moretti told stories about his neighborhood in New York and his "little fuckin' Italian father" and his "big fuckin' Hungarian mother." Tom laughed at Moretti's stories but would never tell stories about his own family. When the headstone Simms was leaning against toppled over and Simms went down with it, the whole group, even Simms, died laughing, drunkenly for many minutes without end. Tom couldn't remember a time when he had more fun or felt more a part of something. Now, just a week later, they'd gone off without him.

Moretti disappointed him the most. He had a girl back home, a girl he was always writing to and pining over, a girl who wrote back plenty whenever they got mail. Tom wished he had a girl writing him love letters, but he didn't and the other fellas knew he didn't. Yet, even with a girl back home, Moretti went with them. He even tried to invite Tom until Tom growled at him.

Leckie went. Leckie was engaged to his girl, put a ring on her finger the night before he shipped out. Yet, he went, and came back drunk and proud of himself.

"We're Veterans of Foreign Whores," said Leckie, getting laughs from everyone but Tom.

Leckie and Moretti were at mass the next day as if nothing happened. Hypocritical bastards. Tom let them know how he felt. When they tried to sit next to him at chow, he got up and moved his seat. Moretti's mouth hung open. For once, no words not even "fuck" came out of it.

The first time they went Simms got the clap. He'd had it before.

"If he gets the clap one more time it'll be a round of applause," said Leckie.

Tom wasn't surprised that Simms went. *Simms is a rat-faced, pimply little varmint who'll end up having to pay for a woman his whole life. No woman wants to face those beady eyes and pock-marked face and little rat body without kind of remuneration.* Women were as repulsed by Simms as Leckie was.

After Simms got the clap and Tom voiced his disapproval, he thought maybe they wouldn't go anymore but they had, all three of them leaving Tom to sit in the graveyard all alone. He took a drink. He looked from one headstone to another. It angered him that Moretti and Leckie had done this to him. He felt like a goody-two-shoes, a little Lord Fauntleroy. He felt his anger rise and he spat on the ground with feeling. He looked at the headstone that Simms had broken. They should be with him now drinking and telling stories like the night Simms had broken the headstone. Tom grew angrier. *They're degenerates. They're sinners. I'm not milquetoast. I was the second toughest guy in my unit, I could beat up Leckie and Moretti at the same time. Maybe I will.*

He drank some more and was starting to feel the effects. He ducked behind one of the gravestones and took a piss on the grave of someone named La Croix. *Monsieur La Croix won't mind if I pee here. He's been dead for eighty years.* There was no one around to see his privates yet even drunk, Tom wouldn't pee out in the open. There was just enough light to see the name "La Croix."

As his piss died down, he heard the sound of footsteps. He zipped his fly and turned to face the intruder. He didn't have his M-1, but his fists were clenched and ready as he looked through some tree branches toward the sound of boots scraping against gravel. A silhouette emerged from the blackness.

"I fuckin' knew you'd be here."

As Moretti came toward him, Tom dropped his hands to his side. He was glad to see Moretti but couldn't let on.

"I thought you went," said Tom.

"Changed my mind." Moretti smiled.

Tom didn't smile back.

"Can I have some of that?"

Tom shrugged and handed him the bottle at his feet, "It's a free country."

"Thanks to us," said Moretti, taking a robust swig and looking around at the headstones.

"What the fuck we standing for?"

They sat down and Moretti handed the bottle back to Tom. The grass was still wet from the rain that morning. They sat in silence for a moment, each taking a turn taking a drink.

"Why'd you change your mind? Why didn't you go with them again?" Tom's emphasis on the word "again" hung in the air between them.

Moretti chuckled though Tom didn't see anything funny.

"I didn't want to see you spend the whole fuckin' night alone. You might as well be on fuckin' guard duty or KP."

"Can't get drunk on guard duty," said Tom.

"You can if you want to get fuckin' court-martialed," he said laughing at himself. Moretti drank some more then stopped when Tom asked, "Why do you do it?"

Moretti swallowed and sighed.

"What? Fuck whores? It's natural, Tom."

"Not to me it isn't."

"Don't you have urges, Tom? You like girls. You must have urges."

"They're whores. I like girls, not whores."

"Besides" Tom said, going in for the kill, "You've got a girl."

Moretti stared at him for a moment, looking hurt.

"Yeah, I've got a girl," said Moretti, "but who knows what she's been up to while I'm gone."

That hadn't occurred to Tom. He'd envied the fellas with girls so much he didn't realize there was a downside. These fellas didn't just miss their girls, they were suspicious of them. *What if your girl was stepping out with some guy with flat feet or a bum ear drum while you're here? His brother Billy was back home but Tom couldn't picture Billy stepping out with somebody's girl.* Tom didn't know firsthand, but he'd heard enough stories about Dear John letters to know this kind of thing happened.

"Besides," said Moretti, "I might never see her again."

"Don't think like that."

"It's the fuckin' truth. Look where we are," Moretti said waving his hands dramatically. "We could all be killed by the fuckin' Nazis tomorrow, so eat, drink and be merry for tomorrow…"

"Knock it off," said Tom and they each took a drink.

"Finish it." said Tom.

Moretti drained the bottle and then threw it, high and far and listened and waited as it shattered in the distance.

Moretti stood up.

"Walk back with me, Tom?"

Part of Tom wanted to say "yes" but Moretti hadn't said he was sorry. He hadn't admitted he'd committed a sin. Tom shook his head.

"I'm going to stay here by myself for a while."

"Okay, suit yourself."

Moretti weaved between the gravestones, staggered a bit but continued. Tom felt the urge to catch up to him and forgive him and absolve him of his sins, but he couldn't. *It wouldn't be right.*

Chapter Fifteen

After mass on Christmas morning, the family gathered in the living room to watch the kids open their presents. Cheryl's kids didn't seem to like the board games Julie got them and Jared was too stupid to know what he liked. *This nightmare won't end.*

Julie stood up suddenly and announced, "We've got to be getting back."

"Okay," her Mom said instantly.

Her father said nothing. Julie just let her family know she was leaving on Christmas morning without having Christmas dinner and her family was okay with it. More than okay.

"See you later," said Meg.

"Good-bye," said Cheryl, "It was nice meeting you," she said to Curt. *Was that a smirk on her face?*

"Really, nice seeing you," said Ned to Curt with an exaggerated emphasis on the word "seeing." He smiled broadly, exposing yellowing teeth, proud of himself.

Aunt June was in the upstairs bathroom and Julie and Curt exited without saying good-bye.

"I'm glad that's over with," she said. He nodded in agreement.

"We'll have to stop at a Roy Rogers or a Howard Johnson's for lunch," she said, and he nodded again. It was several minutes later when they were on the parkway when he broke the silence.

"Your parents saw my dick."

"I'm sure they couldn't see it from across the room."

"Is that supposed to be reassuring?"

Julie hated the word "dick." She didn't mind "fuck" but she hated "dick." There were other words she hated more but "dick" was right up there.

"You were behind the chair, they probably only saw some of it."

She took her eyes off the road for a second to gauge his reaction. There wasn't one, he just stared straight ahead without smiling.

She turned onto the Garden State Parkway. Despite all the New Jersey jokes, there were huge chunks of New Jersey like this one that were actually quite wooded and quite lovely.

"How can I ever face them again?"

Is he breaking up with me?

She licked her lips and tried to appear casual.

"You've already have faced them."

She took her right hand off the steering wheel and placed it near his left hand. Sometimes when they drove on the highway, he'd hold the steering wheel with just one hand so they could hold hands with the other. He ignored her right hand and after a moment she put it back on the steering wheel.

"They must hate me. They'll hate me forever."

"No, they don't hate you."

Curt gave her another look.

"My Dad may be a little jealous…"

She patted his thigh with her hand, and he declined once again to take her hand in his. She had hoped to joke him out of it and when it wasn't working, she started getting a little nervous. *What if he really didn't want to see them again? Do couples really break up over extreme embarrassment? "I'm sorry but now that your parents have seen my penis, we can't be together. We should see other people and they should see other penises." Would he really break up with me over this?*

It was all her fault. If she had just stayed in bed in her old room, none of this would have happened. The idea of it was too exciting, tiptoeing into his room, slipping into bed with him, waking him up, she couldn't resist.

Why couldn't I have just held on until we got back? If I could have just held on for two days, we wouldn't be in this bind. Her horniness had put their entire relationship in jeopardy. They drove in silence for a while, Curt in his embarrassment, Julie in her shame.

The silence lasted for a good five minutes. She drove and he just looked out the window at New Jersey. *What is he thinking? When he said, "I can never face them again," was he saying, "I will never face them again"?* Five minutes of silence between two people who were supposed to be in love is a long time. They drove in silence for another five minutes while Julie thought about the ramifications of the previous five minutes.

Finally, she decided to jumpstart the conversation.

"You know, they didn't just see your penis, they got a pretty good look at your testicles, too."

She knew the prudent thing would be to change the subject, talk about something else, plans for New Year's Eve, New Year's resolutions, anything. Instead, as she'd done for most of her life, Julie went for the laugh.

He didn't laugh. He simply nodded and said, "Good point." She went further.

"They also got a pretty good glimpse of your ass."

Curt looked over at her and nodded again.

"You have a unique way of making me feel better."

Is he softening or am I making things worse?

Julie knew she had a tendency to sabotage herself but she couldn't help it. Years ago, during a job interview for one of the big eight accounting firms, the interviewer, a 50ish white male asked, "Any hobbies? Baking?..." Something about the way he said, "Baking?" rankled her. *She's a woman so she must enjoy baking. What century is this guy from?*

"Oh," she replied, "I have a couple of hobbies, tennis…embezzling."

He didn't laugh, of course, and she knew instantly she shouldn't have said it, accounting executives never laugh about economic malfeasance but the urge to amuse herself was too strong.

That night, Michael and her other friends weren't really amused either. They looked at Julie like she needed psychiatric care. *Who makes an embezzling joke when applying for a job as an accountant? Was she trying to fail? Did she have a fear of success?*

How many times in school had she known the right answer when called on and gone for the laugh instead? Her classmates expected it of her, and she felt she let them down when she answered correctly.

"You know," he said, "There is only one way to solve this. I'm going to have to see them naked to even the score."

"I like the cut of your jib," said Julie. "Of course, that includes Aunt June."

He looked shocked and then he erupted, finally giving Julie the laugh, she so desperately needed.

Chapter Sixteen

Tom didn't feel like volunteering. He was cold and his back and his shoulders and his legs ached from sleeping on the frozen Belgian turf. He'd been sharing his foxhole with a man named Dawes now that he and Moretti were no longer speaking. "A marital spat," Leckie had called it, the day before he died.

Tom was surprised at how much Leckie's death affected him. He had found him so witty, "the wittiest man I ever met," he would say whenever Leckie's name came up. Leckie was blown to bits on patrol one night and Tom was grateful he hadn't witnessed his friend's death.

Tom grieved inwardly for Leckie but didn't cry. He knew God punished Leckie for going with whores and for being a bully. Leckie would heap insults onto Simms even when enough was enough. Simms was killed two weeks before Leckie. Tom was certain God didn't punish Moretti because he had been nice to Simms.

Tom was tired and grieving, and when the Captain asked for three volunteers, he didn't raise his hand. *Let someone else volunteer this time. I've volunteered enough.* As the Captain's eyes searched from man to man a tiny almost imperceptible look of puzzlement came across his face as his eyes met Tom's. *If I don't, someone else will have to.* When the Captain's eyes came back around a second time, Tom's hand haltingly, begrudgingly, resignedly, lifted.

After Tom, a new man, a polite glasses-wearing gent named Reed, desperate for approval, raised his hand. The Captain now had two of the three men he needed and there was a momentary pause, a beat before Tom heard a low murmur coming from his right. "Oh, what the fuck," the murmur said, and he glanced over his shoulder to see the raised hand of Curtis Moretti.

"Will that satisfy you, Tom?" whispered Moretti.

"It's not about satisfying me," Tom whispered back.

Moretti's problem wasn't between the two of them; it was between Moretti and God.

Tom, Moretti and Reed had volunteered for a reconnaissance mission to be led by a Lieutenant named Faring. There were rumors of money attached to Faring. "His Pop is some kind of mucky-muck," was the way Tom had heard it, "with GM or Ford," the story varied slightly. Faring was so rich that the men wouldn't accept him. You could be an ex-con or a Jew and the men might come around eventually but you couldn't be rich, and you couldn't be a fag and Faring was rich.

Tom didn't know how rumors got started in the army; he only knew that the men clung to them, and once spread they were rarely dispelled. "He went to Brown" someone said of Faring when he first appeared, a month earlier. "No wonder he looks like shit" said Leckie as one of his final bon mots.

The Captain stood back, silent and impassive, as the men gathered around a map while Faring outlined the mission. The Germans had pulled back from the town nearby, a little Belgian town of no consequence. The Germans had pulled back just as the fog rolled in but had they really pulled back and how far? With the fog, the reconnaissance planes were useless.

Faring had only been around for a month and seen limited action yet; he spoke to the men as though they were new recruits. He spoke to them as though they hadn't been fired at and had fired back, as though they hadn't killed and hadn't had their friends killed.

"We're going to sneak into the town at sunrise, on foot, no jeeps."

He didn't need to say "no jeeps" since Tom and the others knew what "on foot" meant. Besides, you couldn't sneak into a town with jeeps since jeeps make noise. "We've done this before," thought Tom, "and you haven't." While Faring spoke, Moretti eyed Tom and Tom knew he was thinking the same thing.

The next morning, Tom was awakened at 0500. It had been a herky-jerky night's sleep disturbing Dawes with his restlessness. Tom had spent much of the night trying to pray away his fear. He had his rosary in his hands and meticulously counted out his Hail Marys 'til he dozed. He awoke with a start and panic surged in him as he fumbled for his rosary in the dark. It was his mother's and she had given it to him before he had left. She didn't say it was for good luck, for that would make a mockery of prayer, but there was a tacit implication of luck. He found it in his pocket after a second or two, and his body unclenched. It would have been a terrible omen to lose his rosary right before a mission.

The four men taking part in the mission assembled and Tom had a quick breakfast of the chopped ham and egg k-ration and two salt tablets. He said "hello" to Reed, whose glasses were fogged up, and Tom wondered how he could see through them. Tom looked at Moretti and nodded. Moretti smiled broadly counting Tom's acknowledgement as a victory. Then the four of them set out for the Belgian town.

They followed the road, hugging the tree line single file, with Faring leading the way. Tom was in the rear, peering over Reed and Moretti. He could see his breath and not much else as the night had not yet given way.

He could detect the smell of a wood-burning fire in the distance. He'd grown used to the smell of metal burning and of oil fires. He knew the smell of human flesh which made him queasy. The smell of wood burning reminded him of his childhood, of winter nights spent by the fireplace listening to radio programs with his brother Billy.

Despite the cold, beads of sweat dripped from Tom's helmet where his hairline met his helmet. There was a sudden rustling to their right and he turned with his M-1 cocked and his muscles taut. Something furry scurried away. Tom couldn't tell what it was. After a moment, the lieutenant said, "onward" and turned to return to the march. "Pompous fuck" whispered Moretti and Tom chuckled. He found it amusing when Moretti said "fuck" as a noun when he knew it to be a verb.

The men marched for what must have been an hour, with Faring finally stopping at a ridge overlooking the town just as dawn was breaking. It was either a large village or a small town with each home abutting against the other along narrow serpentine lanes leading to the town square. *The poor Belgians, they just want to go about their business in their picturesque little towns, but the Germans never let them.*

"Lieutenant?" Moretti asked and gestured towards the trees and Faring nodded.

Tom, Moretti and Reed each picked out a tree and urinated. Faring remained where he was.

"The Lieutenant is too good for this, I guess," whispered Tom and Moretti broke out in a grin.

They finished and stood by as the Lieutenant surveyed the scene with his binoculars. Outside of the village on the far hill, Tom could see a farmer crouching next to a cow. In the village, Tom could see a plump, white haired woman walking, carrying a basket.

The lieutenant spoke just above a whisper, "From here to the town, we need to move double time. There could be snipers. If a sniper opens fire keep moving. I didn't see any movement coming from the church steeple. That's most likely where the sniper would be. If there is one, keep moving."

While the Lieutenant spoke, Moretti scooped up some snow and put it on his tongue.

"Are you listening Private?"

Moretti nodded, "Yes, sir."

Tom could see the fear in Faring's eyes as he looked at each of them.

"Let's go."

Faring began to run with his knees up and his arms in sync like a track star. The three of them took off after him and Tom began to lag behind. The distance was maybe three quarters of a mile and he could not keep up this pace. *I am so damn slow.* Tom had always been tall and clumsy and lumbering. He remembered his high school football coach yelling "C'mon, Frankenstein" while the team ran sprints. His pace slowed to a jog and his breath grew heavy. *Reed and Moretti were too close together.*

"Snipers prefer clumps to individual figures," he knew from a lecture from someone somewhere.

Faring made it to the corner of a house at the village end and ducked behind a fence. *C'mon, c'mon.* After a few moments, Reed made the fence, and then Moretti, who glanced quickly back at Tom. He had a hundred yards to go. *Even a near-sighted sniper could get me now.* Moretti waved frantically. Tom wanted to quit but fear his propelled him forward. *Please God.* Almost there. He made it to the fence and collapsed. He was down on his knees willing himself not to throw up. Between labored breaths, Moretti mumbled, "Maybe the fuckin' sniper's sleeping in."

"Wait here. Lucky for you, I know French," Faring said before ducking around the corner.

"Of course, he does" said Moretti.

Tom had taken Latin for eight years and could decipher French words with Latin roots on paper but not while spoken. Tom was able to stand now, and Moretti passed out cigarettes.

"You a fuckin' runner?" Moretti asked Reed.

"Baseball," said Reed, "I played centerfield in high school."

"You must have stolen a fuckload of bases."

Reed blushed behind his still foggy glasses. Tom's urge to throw up had subsided, and after ten minutes, Faring was back.

"Put those out," Faring snapped when he saw the cigarettes.

"Jesus Christ, this isn't a picnic," Faring blasphemed and spat on the ground. It was an act of bravado and neither Tom nor Moretti nor even Reed were fooled.

"I made contact with a Belgian citizen," said Faring.

"Citizen?" thought Tom and Moretti smiled at him with his eyes.

"The Krauts pulled out yesterday afternoon and last night," said Faring. "They pulled back across the river."

"So, we head back?" asked Reed.

The sun was up now but low and each of the men cast a long shadow.

"No, no, we have to make sure. The old man said the mayor and town officials are here. Reed and I will go here."

Faring made a mark in the dirt.

"You two check out the church steeple and meet us here."

He made another mark on the ground and the men nodded. Faring and Reed left first, then, Tom and Moretti, ran towards the steeple. The two men leapfrogged each other, ducking in doorways and looking from side to side.

Tom leaned on a door that suddenly popped open. He jerked his M-1 up and saw a figure move. He swiveled, his gun cocked. A white-haired Belgian woman stood trembling in front of him clutching a black kettle. He pointed his gun downwards.

"Americans?" she said, patting the sleeve of Tom's coat while Moretti stood behind him chuckling.

There was a fire in the fireplace and the sparse room was illuminated by kerosene lamps. Her husband sat at a table eating something from a bowl. Seeing Tom and Moretti, the man stood up and smiled.

"No German," he said, "No German."

Tom entered the house and Moretti followed. A Belgian man and woman kissed them on both cheeks.

"What the fuck?" said Moretti.

The woman spoke in French, gesturing with her hands, offering them food and tea from the hearth.

"No, no, thank you," said Tom to the woman.

"Let's go," he said to Moretti.

"They fuckin' love us," said Moretti.

"Yeah," said Tom, "We're liberators."

Now that the danger was gone, Tom was desperate for sleep. They could hear the buzz of the townspeople gathering in the square after waking to find the Nazis gone. Tom and Moretti jogged to the church and the foot of the steeple.

“Are Belgians Catholic or fuckin’ Protestants?” asked Moretti.

“I don’t know,” said Tom.

Moretti shrugged and started up the serpentine steeple stairs. After a few minutes they were close to the top. *I’m hungry. And I need to sleep.*

“These fuckin’ steps,” murmured Moretti as he rounded the bend, Tom heard a loud crack. Tom turned the corner quickly. Moretti and a German were nose to nose. The gun cracked once more. Tom lunged for the German knocking him down with the butt end of his M1. Moretti slumped backwards and cried out.

“Jesus, Jesus, Jesus,” he yelled.

Again, Tom bashed the German in the face with the butt of his M1, this time bouncing his head off the stone floor. The German’s gun tumbled down some steps. Tom dropped his rifle and got on top of the German grabbing him by the throat with his bare hands. Moretti yelled, “Jesus” over and over. He could hear the panic in Moretti’s voice. The German’s fingers scratched at Tom’s face. Tom squeezed his throat harder as Moretti yelled and Tom became aware of how young the German was. He was a boy of sixteen with the neck of a sixteen-year-old. His face turned purple as Tom leaned forward with all of his weight. The boy’s neck snapped. The boy’s fingers fell away from Tom’s face. His eyes bulged.

Tom fell off the German boy and looked back at Moretti. Moretti’s eyes were just as open as the German boy’s and his chest was covered in blood. Tom recoiled seeing Moretti’s corpse. Tom slid backwards on the seat of his pants along the floor and leaned against the stone wall of the steeple. He had promised himself to be brave and he had kept that promise but here now, he couldn’t bear to look at his dead friend. He shielded his eyes and wept.

Chapter Seventeen

The Thursday night before the Christmas Debacle was the bank's company Christmas party. Curt worked late so he and Julie got there late. Nobody got drunk and nobody made out with anybody, even Cara and everybody kept their jobs.

The Thursday night before that, Julie went out for drinks with the Committee. She hadn't gone in a while after four years of almost never missing. It was a relief having a boyfriend and not having to sit and bitch about men and then drive everyone home.

"I have a fun weekend planned," she announced, "He's invited me to visit the Home for the Criminally Insane."

She liked to say things like that to the Committee. She knew they resented her for having a boyfriend and having graduated from the group. She knew they felt better knowing her life and her boyfriend weren't perfect.

Julie was caught off-guard when Curt invited her.

"I've been avoiding going," he told her, "I really don't want to see him but it's Christmas time and all that."

She felt the same way about going for drinks with the Committee. With Curt working late she'd be happier sitting alone in front of the TV but "it was Christmas time and all that..."

When Curt came to her apartment Saturday morning, he surprised her by asking, "Do you mind driving?"

"No, not at all," she said.

She knew this was a weird day for him and probably wanted one less thing on his mind.

"I have the directions," he said, brandishing a piece of paper.

He was extra quiet in the car. She didn't even catch him mumbling to himself. He just sat stone-faced looking glum and handsome until a sudden thought occurred to him.

"Do you think he'll be in a strait jacket?"

"I don't know," Julie said, gripping the steering wheel a little tighter and staring straight ahead.

"Hope not," said Curt softly and neither of them spoke for a few minutes.

Before she had met Curt, Julie had often described her family as "crazy" or at least "nutty." She liked to tell how her father couldn't bear the tense moments of Philadelphia Phillies' games. When the Phillies made the play-offs or the World Series and it was a make or break moment, her Dad would turn the TV up and leave the room trying to distance himself from a possible negative outcome. Once, as a teenager, Julie had entered the den, found no one nearby and changed the channel. "I'm watching that" her father had yelled from three rooms away.

Once she and Curt had become intimate, she confided to him about her Mom's alcoholism. It was the family secret. Her mother had been a quiet drunk, doing chores in the morning and then rewarding herself with a drink then one or two more during lunch. By the time the girls came from school, she'd be passed out on the couch or at the kitchen table. Julie's Dad was finally able to get her help, with just the family and their doctor and one or two friends ever finding out.

Meg's problem was not a secret. Meg was mentally unbalanced when it came to boys. She went through a prolonged promiscuous phase (much longer than Julie's) that began in high school and lasted through her mid-twenties, always falling for boys who were trouble. They were either too old or too violent; one ended up in the county jail for three months. Eventually, Meg settled down and married that loser Ned.

Being with Curt had made Julie realize her family wasn't actually "crazy," but "flawed" and a little "quirky," and while there is no such thing as "normal," they were at least pretty close. Everyone in Julie's family could at least function in society. Everyone could hold a job, sustain a relationship and not commit felonies. Curt wasn't so lucky.

A few drops of rain hit the windshield and Julie flicked on the wipers for a minute. It was one of those days that thought about raining but couldn't make up its mind.

"Did you ever see 'Titicut Follies'"?

"Is that from like the twenties or something?"

Curt chuckled. "No, you're thinking of 'Ziegfeld's Follies. 'Titicut Follies' is a documentary from the '60's."

"Oh."

"It's about the Bridgewater State Hospital for the Criminally Insane."

"You mean, the same place where we're going?"

"One and the same."

Julie nodded and bit her lower lip. *Oh, fuck, this is going to be some crazy shit.* Rain began to fall again, a little harder this time, and she flipped the wipers on and kept them on. *When he starts talking softly like this it's always something fucked up.*

"Why? What about it?"

"I saw it in college in my psychology class. It's all this footage of these guys in this hospital and they're all fuckin' crazy, most of them anyway. Some seem normal enough but not many. The director of "One Flew Over the Cuckoo's Nest" made the whole cast see it before they started filming."

"I love that movie."

"Never saw it."

"You never saw 'One Flew Over the Cuckoo's Nest'?

"I don't think I'd like it."

Julie nodded. *I guess a movie about mental illness wouldn't appeal to him. I don't like movies about alcoholism.*

"Any way, I wouldn't have watched 'Titicut Follies' if the professor hadn't shown it in class."

"Were the patients wearing strait jackets?"

"I don't remember seeing any strait jackets but there were a lot of nude guys."

She snuck a peek at him to see if he was joking but he didn't appear to be. The corners of his mouth always crept upward whenever he was trying to tease her and maintain a straight face.

"Why were they nude?"

"No idea, but they were always nude, and they were always being poked and prodded by doctors and the guards would gas them sometimes."

"What do you mean 'gas them?'"

"It was some type of tear gas, I guess. I'm not really sure. They used it to keep them in line."

Julie scrunched her face up.

"That was twenty years ago and I bet that documentary made them cut that stuff out."

Curt shrugged and got quiet. He stayed quiet for several minutes and Julie, with little choice, stayed quiet with him.

I hate when he does this. He just shuts down and withdraws from the conversation like I'm not even here. Earlier in their relationship, Julie would think she had said the wrong thing, had offended him in some way. They'd talk, he'd withdraw and suddenly he'd be back as if no time had elapsed. She understood now that was just part of his personality but a part of his personality that she hated. *Maybe he's a little crazy, too.*

"Why did they call it 'Titicut Follies?'" she asked, trying to pull him back in.

"It was some kind of talent show that the patients had. One guy really could sing but he was nuts and he just went around singing all day. I don't know if he could hold a conversation but he had this deep baritone voice and would going around singing all day. He was pretty good but he always fucked up the lyrics so they made no sense. It was kind of funny."

Julie was always surprised at what offended Curt and what didn't.

"So everybody in my class was cracking jokes. I mean, you can't blame them, we're in college and we're looking at a bunch of nude lunatics singing songs they don't even know the words to. I was probably the only one who wasn't laughing. I just kept thinking, 'I hope he doesn't end up in this place', and what do you know? This is exactly where he ends up."

They passed a sign that read, "Entering Bridgewater," and she knew they were getting close. It was her turn to withdraw. In some ways, after seven months of dating she was no closer to knowing him then when they'd first met. *Maybe the Committee is right. Maybe I should run away. Maybe his family is too fucked up. Maybe Kevin would be better off with someone else as his father.*

She looked over him staring straight ahead into the light November rain. She reached over and clasped his left hand with her right. She drove for a minute with one hand on the wheel.

"It should be coming up here any minute," said Curt looking at the directions. "There it is. It looks just like in the movie except the movie was black and white."

Julie looked at the barbed wire and high chain link fence and got a chill. She squeezed his hand tight and then put both hands on the wheel and put her blinker on.

"Sorry, you can't see him," he said.

"That's okay," she said, "I brought a book."

"They're pretty strict about just family."

Julie didn't want to meet him. Truth be told, she was afraid to meet him but she didn't want to tell Curt that. She nodded and kept her mouth shut. She was happy to drive him there and to be supportive but she could only handle so much psychodrama. In fact, she preferred to not deal with any at all.

"Be sure to say hi to the nude baritone for me."

Fuck, should I have said that? He chuckled. *Phew.*

She turned and pulled up to the guard shack while Curt leaned over from the passenger seat towards the open window. "We're here for visiting day. Or visiting hours," said Curt correcting himself.

"Inmate's name?" the guard asked.

Julie winced. "Inmate" was so much harsher than "patient."

"Thomas, ah, Thomas Morrissey," Curt said.

Chapter Eighteen

Tom came back a hero. He even came back with medals that were awarded to the men in his company. He had been part of a fighting force that had defeated Hitler and the most heinous regime in history's endless parade of evil regimes. More importantly to Tom, he had done all this without losing his noodle.

His family had another party for him, and Eddie Curran wasn't invited to this one either. Eddie had gotten in some trouble with the law and his mother moved them to Maine with her mother so the two of them could keep an eye on him. He didn't write Tom during the war either, so they were even.

The party he returned to was much like the party the night before he left with one notable exception, his Uncle Brendan had passed away. They didn't tell Tom until the war was over not wanting to upset him, apparently, thought Tom even though he had dealt with death in one form or another every day. Whether it was cancer or cirrhosis or something else Tom would never find out how his Uncle died.

Tom missed him the most at his party for the two had shared a rite of passage. It was his uncle, not his father, who had assured him he'd be all right, and the memory of his uncle saying those things had comforted him overseas.

This was a summer party, unlike the last one, and the windows were open, and a warm breeze sifted in and out. The music from the radio spilled down the street 'til late at night, but none of the neighbors complained for they all knew Tom was home, safe and sound.

His mother hugged him and kissed him at the train station and this time, at his party, she stayed out of the kitchen and joined in during the singing and the laughing. She kept close to him throughout the evening, petting his arm like a cat.

It was different with his father. Outwardly, he did the right things, he shook Tom's hand and took his bag at the train station and told him how proud he was. He told him again in the car, but Tom sensed a hint of resentment.

At the party, in front of the others, he teased Tom about wearing a wristwatch.

"Ladies wear wristwatches," he said, "men wear a watch fob."

It was all in good fun but it wasn't. Tom knew there was something below the surface. His father never said anything that didn't hint at something else.

He's envious. It's one of the seven deadly sins. He's envious because I've surpassed him. I've been to war and he hasn't. I've done something that would be remembered by our descendants for a thousand years and he hasn't and never would.

His brother Billy was home for good now, a college graduate, having sat out the war with a bum ear. He didn't meet Tom at the station with his father and mother. He was working at the lumberyard but when he came home, he smiled warmly and shook Tom's hand and told him how proud he was of him with more sincerity than his father had, yet, their closeness was gone forever. There was no more banter between them and there were long stretches when neither knew what to say to each other and Tom wished their Uncle Brendan had been there to fill in the gaps.

The closeness he had once felt for his brother had been transferred to Moretti and Leckie and even Simms. Although they were all dead, they were Tom's brothers now and Tom shared with them a deeper and eternal bond.

Billy made him show everyone the medals he won, and everyone remarked on them but his father. He even passed around the Luger he picked up as a souvenir, trading for it after V-E day with a German soldier who assured him, "No use, no use" in broken English.

Everyone commented on how Tom had changed, his voice deeper, his shoulders broader and his face fuller. *They had changed too.* His mother's face was lined and her hair gray and his father slightly stooped and no longer imposing. Tom caught his parents exchanging a look when he lit a cigarette but neither dared say a word. Later, he even drank a bottle of beer right in front of his mother even though she considered all forms of alcohol the "devil's juice" invented to "keep down the Irish."

While it was awkward at home, it wasn't until Tom returned to the lumberyard that he learned just how much had changed. His brother Billy was in charge now. His father was still the owner, but Billy handled the day to day operations, set the hours, placed the orders, hired and fired, while his father took an advisory role.

His first morning back, his father called him into his office for the three of them to discuss the new arrangement. Billy had graduated from college and was now full-time. Tom still had two more years of college and would continue part-time.

"After you graduate, Tom, you'll come and work for your brother."

He thought he had misheard. *"Come and work for your brother?" Meaning, I'm to work under my younger brother?* He stared at his father and felt his face become flush.

"Pardon?"

"There's no other way, Tom. You've got two more years of college."

"You want me to work for him?"

Tom said "him" with disdain, and he turned and looked at Billy who wouldn't look back at him. Tom had always been in line to take over, primogeniture and all that. He was being passed over. He was being penalized for going off to war, fighting Hitler, winning medals, risking his life, watching his real brothers die, making his family proud, all while not losing his noodle. He was being punished and it wasn't right. His eyes narrowed as he glowered at his father.

"There's no other way" his father stammered, "You've got to finish college. You promised your mother."

He was right, Tom had made a promise to his mother and now his father was trapping in that promise.

"Your brother has more of a head for this stuff. He's the best manager I've ever had."

"I'm not trying to take anything from you Tom," said Billy. "I'm not trying to push you out. When you graduate you can start full-time. I'd love to have my brother as my right hand man."

He turned from his father to Billy. *I should hit him. I should punch him square in the face. Right hand man.*

There was a tense silence as Tom considered who he should hit first, his brother or his father.

"So what is it you want from me exactly?"

"We're family here, Tom. This isn't 'take it or leave it'. We just want you to understand the situation and agree with the logic."

"We won't do it if you don't agree, Tom," Billy cut in.

"So you want me to agree to this? Working for my kid brother?" asked Tom.

"That's right," his father said.

He looked at his father and then his brother and back again. No one said a word while they waited several moments for Tom's reply.

"All right," said Tom, "on one condition."

Then Tom whirled sharply and took a step towards his brother. Billy's hands jerked upward to protect his face.

"I'll agree to this," said Tom slowly and carefully, "As long as you never shake my hand again."

"What?" said Billy, slowly dropping his hands.

"You heard me."

"Tom, what are you talking about, not shaking your brother's hand?" said his father.

"I don't think that's too much to ask. I'm giving up quite a bit. All I ask in return is that you never again shake my hand."

Billy looked helplessly back at his brother. There was emotion in his voice now as he said, “All right, Tom, if that’s how you want it.”

“I do. Then, we have a deal,” said Tom, and he looked at his stunned father and stuck his hand out. His father shook it, not knowing what else to do. Then, Tom turned and walked out of his brother’s office.

Chapter Nineteen

Julie sat at her desk staring across the way at Bob sitting at his desk talking to a hundred-year-old lady while his pinky finger rooted around inside his ear. She cringed and looked at the clock. It was ten past nine and Sasha was late. Later than usual. *She better have a pretty good excuse.*

It was November 1st. In exactly nineteen days it would be her birthday. Her birthday always made her feel reflective and vulnerable and insecure and this year's birthday was a big one. She was turning thirty-six.

Thirty-five had been swatted away with barely a ripple, one little crying jag in the bathroom at work and that was all. At thirty-five, she had no boyfriend and no prospects and had to settle for drinks with similarly situated Committee members. Yet, her recent promotion had made her feel like she was getting somewhere and being in her mid-thirties she was still young enough to get where she wanted to go.

At thirty-six, she would be on the other side. Thirty-five was mid-thirties but thirty-six hinted at late thirties. The fact that this year she had a man and a good one should have factored in, but somehow it didn't. She was still husband-less, and Kevin was still fatherless and although she wasn't depressed yet, but she would be in nineteen days. She was pre-depressed.

Her problem, as far as she could tell, was that she had never really had goals, she had feuds. She had gone to college only because she wanted to beat her sisters. Cheryl may be prettier, but she was smarter. If she could go to a better college and get a better job than Cheryl, she would win. Her parents would know that they were wrong all along, Cheryl was not better than her. Meg, of course, was hopeless.

In college, she majored in accounting. She never dreamed of being an accountant, but she'd always been good at math and one day, she heard her professor remark off-handedly to the whole class, "You can never go wrong with an accounting degree." That one comment, not even directed at her, by a man who no doubt wouldn't recognize her if they passed on the street, had changed her life. She declared herself an accounting major, got her degree and got a job right out of school with one of the big eight firms. *Take that, Cheryl. I win.*

Somehow, no one had ever acknowledged her victory. Her parents were dealing with their own problems and barely said a word. Michael told her they would "have to go out and celebrate" but her job paid better than his and envy got the better of him, so they never did mark the occasion.

Once inside the colossus, she discovered she was merely one in a billion, all tucked away in a tiny cubicle. She was funny and smart and a good friend but no one in the firm gave a shit. They were too busy focused on accounting and she didn't give a shit about that.

When she quit and joined the bank, she was happy to be around women her own age instead of married men with beer bellies who talked endlessly about Pop Warner football and Little League. Julie, with her college degree and work experience, was their boss during the day, while Debbie emerged as the boss after work. Julie didn't mind, she was glad to have friends and was preoccupied with her new enemy, Bob.

Bob had been to college and was pushing fifty and wore a suit and tie and had gray hair. Bob looked the part of the boss and anyone looking in the window would assume he knew what he was doing, and as assistant manager he was Julie's direct boss. There was only one problem. Bob was an idiot, and a lazy idiot, to boot.

More than once, Julie caught him at his desk preoccupied with his rotisserie baseball team in the middle of the day. Customers always seemed to leave his desk no better off than they were before they arrived, and his work somehow always ended up being foisted onto Julie.

When Julie complained to Simon, the branch manager, Simon never disagreed. He would nod his head and murmur, "I know, I know." Julie knew that Simon knew that Bob was a fuckin' idiot and a lazy fuck.

"I'm not going to fire him," Simon said in a rare moment of honesty, "He has a family."

Bob was divorced with three kids. His wife had left him for another man after having caught on that he was a fuckin' idiot.

Julie became obsessed about the unjustness of it all. She was better than he was. He had been there longer and he was a man and he was older but she was better than he was. After work, drinks with "The Committee" invariably turned into a bitch session about Bob initiated by Julie. The rest of "The Committee" grew tired of hearing about him despite how funny Julie could be. None of them were going anywhere so what did they care. Having a lazy boss allowed them to fuck off as well. They sympathized but didn't see the broad social implications the way Julie did.

Simon's death shocked everyone. It was so sudden and undeserved, and it caused the unthinkable. Bob, the newly dubbed "Bob-solete," ascended to the throne. Julie's tears for Simon were an uneasy mix of grief and indignation.

"The Committee" didn't want to hear it, so Julie would scream at Bob while all alone in her car. She would careen down the Mass Pike with the music blasting while she yelled all the things at Bob that she wished she could say. During the day, to his face, Julie struggled to even speak civilly to him and then only in front of customers.

Finally, when Bob imploded and Julie got his job, she had been triumphant. "The Committee" hailed her victory mostly because they could now speak of something else. Julie had conquered Cheryl and now conquered Bob. She took delight at the customers' surprise when Bob deferred to her. *"But he has gray hair" they must be thinking.*

Julie was the obsessive type and after two and a half years of obsessing about Bob she needed to find someone else or something else to obsess over. She was like a parasite looking for a new host. Her new obsession became Kevin. She thought about Kevin the way the Ancient Egyptians thought about death; all the time. Who should his father be? Will Kevin like this guy? When do I tell him about Kevin?

When she found Curt, she decided she had found Kevin's father, but there was a problem. He didn't want to be Kevin's father or anyone else's. Julie would sure she'd change his mind but now she wasn't so sure. She'd beaten Cheryl and beaten Bob, but would she defeat Curt?

Sasha rushed in late with a zit on her chin the size of a toddler that she had tried to cover up with a pound of make-up. *Good luck. You can spot that thing from the Space Shuttle.* Normally, when a teller was late Julie felt compelled to say something even if it was just a wise crack. Today, she let it go. A zit that big was a legitimate excuse.

She watched as Bob directed the old woman who'd been sitting at his desk over to her desk. *Typical.* As the old woman shuffled over, two thoughts crossed Julie's mind: One, *that will be me pretty soon* and two, *When the hell is Curt's birthday?*

How do I not know his birthday? Didn't I ask him once? She had, it was right after she lied to him about her age, shaving off a couple of years, but the waitress had come by or something happened and she never got an answer. She remembered when he signed the loan application that he was born two years after her but what was the date? It would still be on the loan application.

Before she could check Curt's file, she had to help the ancient woman put some money into a CD that she wouldn't be able to touch for a year. What optimism. She was helpful and cheerful and professional and all the while chastising herself in her head. Curt was her boyfriend. It was November 1st and they'd been sleeping together since May and yet, she didn't know when his birthday was. *I am a terrible person.*

After the old woman had been helped and sent on her way, Julie raced to the file cabinet and scanned the M's until she found the file labeled "Morrissey" and plucked it out. Before she could peek, Debbie sidled up to her on her way back from the bathroom.

"Did you see that zit on Sasha's chin?" whispered Debbie.

"Did I? It showed up five minutes before she did. She could star in a female version of "The Two-Headed Man."

The "Two Headed Man" joke was a gem she had used on Cheryl years ago and Debbie laughed a hearty, contemptuous laugh. The way to get close to Debbie was through a technique Julie liked to call "negative bonding."

With Debbie safely back at her post, she opened the file.

"Curtis Joseph Morrissey," date of birth, 8-6-1955--August 6th? *We were together August 6th.* By, August 6th, they'd been dating for five months and sleeping together for three. They must have seen each other that day or at least spoke on the phone and yet, he mentioned nothing.

Why does he do that? Why does he keep things from me? He didn't tell me how his mother died or about his brother's mental illness or the charges brought against him? He didn't tell me about his rich uncle and how he was the beneficiary. And now he doesn't tell me about his birthday. This guy is infuriating.

At ten-thirty, he made his daily call not expecting trouble.

"Hey," he said.

"Oh, hi, August 6th," she said nonchalantly.

"Pardon?" he said.

"Your birthday is August 6th, is it not?"

"Yeah, so."

"Why didn't you tell me?"

She was mad. He laughed.

"What did we even do on your birthday?"

"That was the night we went to that Mexican place in Harvard Square. It was good."

"But why didn't you say something?" she asked.

"Because I didn't want you to have the waiter bring out a cake in front of the whole restaurant and have total strangers sing that stupid song. I hate that kind of thing."

"You could have told me later on" she said, "I would have done something special."

"We did do something special," he said.

She blushed.

"Besides I don't care about my birthday," he said.

"Well, I do," she said.

She stood up and began to pace.

“Here’s what we’re going to do. Friday night, I’m making dinner for you and we’re going to pretend it’s August 6th and we’re going to celebrate your birthday. You got that?”

He laughed.

“Yeah, yeah, I got it.”

Chapter Twenty

The skinny girl was with her sister when she approached Tom at the trolley stop. He had started a new job at a department store downtown after keeping his promise to his mother and graduating from college. He still lived with his parents and still shared a room with his brother, and things had been tense ever since he quit his job at the lumberyard.

While his brother Billy remained chatty and pretended nothing had changed, the rift between Tom and his father was irreversible and out in the open. The two spoke only in short declarative sentences exchanging information but no warmth. His father looked at him as though he had betrayed the family, whereas Tom knew he was the one who had been betrayed.

The skinny girl was small and pretty and the other one was taller and plainer but with an obvious resemblance. He was minding his own business, waiting for the trolley and wishing he'd remembered his gloves, when the two sisters sidled up to him.

"I want to thank you for the pie your mother made," said the skinny, pretty one.

What was she talking about? Who is this skinny girl?

The plain one looked slightly familiar, being closer to Tom's age. He recalled maybe having seen her at church although this wasn't saying much. The whole neighborhood, except for the Rothmans went to Immaculate Heart.

"Pie?"

"Your mother made us a pie three years ago when my…our mother died," said the skinny, pretty one.

"Oh, sorry to hear that," said Tom. "I mean about your mother, not about the pie."

"Thank you."

The plain one still hadn't said a word so Tom spoke mostly to the smaller, prettier one. She seemed nervous and her lip quivered slightly when she wasn't speaking. *Am I making her nervous? Is her lip quivering because of me?*

"What kind of pie was it?"

The sisters exchanged looks and shrugs. The smaller one laughed, "I don't remember."

"So you're thanking me for a three-year-old pie that you don't remember what it was?"

She laughed again, "That's about the size of it."

Her lip quivered. Tom chuckled.

"How did our mothers know each other?"

"They were on the Helping Hand Committee during the War…for the troops," said the plain one, proving she had the power of speech.

This was the first he'd heard of the Helping Hand Committee. His mother must have joined after he left and she never mentioned it.

"I'm Tom Morrissey."

"Lydia Spellman," said the pretty one, "And this is my sister Kate. We live on the corner of Hobson Street, the brick house on the corner."

Hobson Street was only about two and a half blocks from Tom's house, but he'd never met these girls before. Of course, when he left for the war they were just kids, he thought.

The trolley finally came. He could tell Lydia was getting cold. Skinny people weren't built for the winter. They rode the trolley into town. He found out Lydia was nineteen and Kate was twenty-three. They were secretaries in an office downtown. Lydia did most of the talking. It seemed funny to him that the younger one was the spokesman for the two of them, but she was probably cuter their whole lives and people probably responded to that.

They got off a couple of stops before his and he didn't see them the next day. He went early for the train the day after that and let one go by and still didn't see them, see Lydia, more importantly, he didn't really care about seeing Kate.

That evening, Tom walked the long two and a half blocks over to the Spellman house, the brick one on the corner of Hobson Street. Her father answered. He wasn't tall and bald like Tom's Dad, he was short with a shock of white hair. His face looked like half the Irish mugs at mass at Immaculate Heart and Tom couldn't say for certain if he'd seen him before.

"Can I help you?"

"I'm looking for Lydia."

"Lydia?"

Tom knew what he was thinking. Tom was closer in age to Kate, but he didn't want Kate.

"You sure it's Lydia, you want to see?"

He was like a car salesman trying to pawn off one of his older models. *Oh, no, you don't.*

"That's right" said Tom pleasantly, "I was wondering if Lydia happened to be home."

The white-haired man eyed him suspiciously and called to Lydia over his shoulder. He held the door open and Tom removed his hat and stepped in the house. It was smaller than Tom's house, made smaller by an oversized piano. Pictures hung on the wall, including the same painting of the Last Supper that hung in his parent's bedroom.

Tom stood looking down at the older man. For an instant, he almost asked, "How's Mrs. Spellman?" but he caught himself in time. *Good lord, she's dead. I almost asked how his dead wife is.* The two men continued to just stand there, wordlessly, the older man making no attempt at small talk with the younger. Tom couldn't ask him about his work since he was now retired. *What can I say to him?* He could think of nothing. *I am such a numbskull.* The two men just stood there for close to forty seconds with Tom fumbling with his hat unable to think of anything to say.

They turned simultaneously when they heard footsteps on the stairs. Lydia wore a sweater and a skirt and no shoes and her hair was wet. *She must have just gotten out of the shower.* She smiled broadly when she saw who it was, “Well, well, well,” she said, “If it isn’t Tom Morrissey.”

Chapter Twenty-One

While having drinks with the Committee on Thursday night, Julie let it slip that she was having Curt over the next night to "celebrate" his birthday. She used careful, precise language not to say that it was his birthday, merely they were celebrating it. They didn't need to know his actual birthday had been three months earlier.

It was a passive aggressive move on her part and she knew it. They were both her employees and her friends and the dual roles created friction from time to time. When they would stretch a ten-minute break into fifteen or a half hour lunch into forty minutes, they were challenging her authority. When she reminded them that she had a boyfriend and they didn't, it was a way for her to assert her authority. *I'm better than you and don't you forget it.*

She spent most of the week preparing for his fake birthday. On Tuesday morning while he showered at her place, she read the labels on his shirt and pants and wrote down his sizes. She used that intel that night to pick him up some hipper clothes than he normally wore, finding dark colors that matched his hair and eyes.

She wanted everything to be perfect but there was one problem, she was a shitty cook. Her feminist side was proud of being a shitty cook. She had a career, she had gone to college, she had a good job with people who worked under her. Her mother had none of those things but could cook. Not knowing how was one more way for Julie to say, at least subconsciously, "I am nothing like you."

There are drawbacks to being a shitty cook. For one thing, you can't make yourself a nice meal when you want to and for another, you can't make one for your boyfriend either. Not even on his fake birthday.

"Why don't you learn to cook?" Michael used to ask her from time to time.

"I don't have to. I've got you," she'd say.

And he was good at it. He'd prepare chicken or fish or lamb all with an elaborate sauce taught to him by his Greek parents. One of the things she missed most when they broke up were his delicious meals.

Dutch never complained about her cooking. To him, chicken wings in a sports bar were fine dining. As long as there was a game on in front of him, he didn't notice or care what he was eating.

For Curt's birthday, Julie only really had one option.

"Any asshole can make spaghetti," Michael once said in a rare moment of insight.

She'd make spaghetti and meatballs, they'd drink Marguerites (something she could make) they'd have cake and then fuck. The perfect evening. Then Friday came and she forgot the meatballs and had to race back to the store and get them. *I'm such an idiot.* She was behind schedule now and was just boiling the water when the doorbell rang.

"Happy Birthday," she said, greeting him with a big kiss.

"Thanks," he said, "It's funny, I don't feel any older."

He was under strict instructions to pretend it really was his birthday and she appreciated his playing along.

"Did everybody at work make a big deal about your birthday?"

"Not really," he said, "It was weird."

"That is weird," she said, "Let me get you a Margarita."

She tried mixing the Margarita in the blender while zapping the meatballs in the mike and the lights went out.

"It's all going according to plan," she said after a beat.

She fished a flashlight out of the drawer and negotiated her way carefully to the front door and opened it. The lights were on next door and across the street.

"It's just us," she said, "Must have blown a fuse."

Julie called her landlords, the Perettis. They lived on the floor below and had the Perettis been home, Mr. Peretti would have taken care of it. This happened from time to time but the Perettis had gone to their house in New Hampshire and left Julie their number in case of emergency. This was an emergency.

She dialed while Curt sat at the table.

"We could just have a candlelight dinner," he said.

"We could," said Julie, "But the sauce and the meatballs would be cold. Mr. Peretti…" she said turning away from Curt. "It's Julie…no, it's not an emergency but the lights went out and we're the only house on the block without power…all right…yep…uh huh…on the right…got it, thanks. Enjoy your vacation." She hung up. "He's said there's a box of fuses on top of the fuse box. In the basement just past the stairway to the right. If you switch out the fuse, I'll zap the meatballs and get some candles then we can have a candlelight dinner."

She handed him the flash light and he shook his head "no." "Can't do it," he mumbled.

She chuckled.

"Seriously," he said, "I can't."

"What do you mean?"

"I can't do basements."

"What does that mean, 'you can't do basements'?"

"I mean, I can't go in basements," he said, and his tone was direct and nearly angry.

"Since when?"

"Since I was a kid."

Julie couldn't see his face clearly. There was a little light coming in from the street so she could make out the outline of his head but that was about it. She couldn't tell from his expression if he was playing with her and if he was, it wasn't making her laugh.

"So you haven't gone into a basement since you were a kid?"

"Correct."

"You clean houses for a living. Don't you have to clean a basement from time to time?"

"I prefer to think of myself as a small business owner but I'm glad you think of me as a guy who cleans houses for a living."

Oops, she had accidentally insulted him, and on his birthday no less.

"I know you have your own business I just thought that sometimes people would want you to clean their basement."

"They do."

"So, what do you do then?"

He was clearly getting annoyed.

"I have someone who works for me do the basement."

"Every time?"

Curt nodded his blacked-out head.

"Yep."

"So not once since you started this business have you gone into someone's basement?"

"Correct. The first thing I ask when I'm booked on a job is 'Do you have a basement that needs cleaning?' It's mostly two-person jobs anyway so I make sure the other person does it for me."

"Do the people you work with know you can't go in basements?" "Of course."

"So, you're telling me something traumatic happened to you when you were a kid in a basement, and you haven't been in one ever since?"

"Uh huh."

"Will you tell me what happened?"

"I will but not tonight."

Why is this guy so fucking secretive? Now she was getting annoyed.

"Why not tonight?"

"It'll kill the mood."

"You're pretty confident you're getting laid tonight, aren't you?" Curt laughed.

"So something caused you to develop this fear of basements and you know what it is but you're not going to tell me tonight?" "Right."

"What if I went down to the basement right now and while I was down there, I started choking and needed the Heimlich? What would happen then?"

He took a moment to consider that scenario.

"I guess you'd die."

Julie laughed.

"Really?"

Curt's silhouette said nothing.

"All right, I'll go down and try and switch out the fuse, but do you promise me you'll tell sometime what this is all about?"

"I promise."

He handed her back the flashlight and she started down the stairs.

"Don't choke while you're down there," he said.

Chapter Twenty-Two

On the way to Lydia's house, Tom was more nervous than he could remember ever having been. The evening was clear and cold and blustery, and he stuck his gloved hands in his pockets and smiled to himself. He'd been shot at, ducked Luftwaffe bombs and had fought at Massen and yet, he was just as nervous going out with a girl.

I promised myself to be brave. That was just during the war. That contract has expired. No, a promise is a promise. He enjoyed debating the great questions in his head.

Her father answered the door once again.

"She'll be down in a minute."

Tom nodded but didn't move.

"I suppose you can come in."

He stepped into the house after removing his hat and stood clutching it in both hands.

Kate entered.

"Hello, Tom, remember me? I'm the sister closer to your own age who you didn't find to be pretty or interesting."

In reality, she only said, "Hello, Tom." but he knew what she was thinking. He stood for a few minutes making small talk with the suspicious father and the jilted sister. *I miss the Nazis.*

Finally, he heard the sound of an upstairs door close and Lydia's footsteps coming down the stairs.

"Sorry to keep you waiting, Tom Morrissey," she said, halfway down, I had to fix my hair. I'm a blonde during the day."

Tom chuckled.

She plucked the same faded red coat and flowered hat off the coat rack that she had worn at the trolley stop. She slipped them both on and kissed her father good-bye. She pulled gloves from her pockets.

"Leave the light on," she said, "In case we don't elope."

Kate laughed but her father didn't. She's quite the wise guy, thought Tom, who knew better than to sass his own father.

When Tom had asked her to the movies a few nights earlier he neglected to mention he didn't have a car. As they walked down her front walk, he blurted out, "I hope you don't mind walking to the theater."

She gave him a puzzled look.

"I don't have a car" he said, adding, "at the moment."

"Of course you don't, Tom. If you had, we never would have met at the trolley stop. I don't yell things about pies at passing motorists."

He chuckled. *She's got me there.*

As they walked down streets he'd known his whole life he felt himself gradually relax. She chatted away and he noticed her lip quiver from time to time. *Could she be nervous about me? Will she let me kiss her good night?* She talked about her work and asked him about his and then there was a brief lull.

"Oh" said Tom, "I asked my mother and she said she made a cherry pie."

"Is that right?" said Lydia, "I remember it being delicious. Mostly people brought apple pies."

Tom realized his blunder. He'd inadvertently brought up the subject of her mother's death. The conversation had been pleasant and fun and now, he had spoiled everything. He began berating himself in his head, yet, she didn't seem sore. She even told him the whole story.

It wasn't much of a story. One day, when Lydia was in high school, her mother was cleaning the house and dropped dead. Vacuuming one minute, not vacuuming the next.

"I came home and found her that way."

She paused before she said, "that way." Tom thought of all the men he'd seen "that way" but kept his mouth shut and let her talk. He wondered if she'd been the nervous type before this or if this was a consequence of finding her mother "that way."

She spoke of the months following her mother's death and how she cried several times a day at first then eventually, once a day. "It's down to about once a week now" she said with a hint of a smile. She told him it was hardest on her father. He had been a machinist but an accident in the shop had forced his retirement.

"Kate and I hate leaving him in the morning when we go to work. He sits all alone in that big house all day with nothing to do." "It's a really a small house," thought Tom.

They had a few minutes to kill before the movie, so they stopped into Blake's Diner to get out of the cold. Tom had known Mr. Blake his whole life. When Tom was little his family would sometimes stop at Blake's after Sunday mass to buy doughnuts and Mr. Blake would give Billy and Tom free doughnut holes. Mr. Blake gave Tom a wink on the sly seeing him with a pretty girl for the first time.

She ordered a hot chocolate and he ordered a coffee and she talked about her mother some more.

"She was only forty-four when she died," she said.

All conversations led back to her mother. She was obsessed thought Tom, but he couldn't blame her. It had only been two and a half years and it had been so sudden.

"Sometimes I think about all the things she never got to do," she said.

Tom thought about Moretti and Leckie and Simms and all the things they never got to do.

"At least she got to be married and have children."

"That's true. She always wanted to go to Rome and never got there."

"I'm surprised she didn't want to go to Ireland."

Blake brought them their hot drinks.

"She was born in Ireland and lived there 'til she was fourteen. She didn't care for it. I asked her what it was like one time and she said, "It's Vermont, with more pubs."

Lydia laughed. She liked to laugh at things she said. Tom was surprised. Ireland was spoken of reverently in his house.

"She would have liked seeing St. Peter's Basilica and the Sistine Chapel and all that. I'd like to go to Rome someday."

"I've been to London" said Tom.

"Really? What was it like?"

"Dark," he said. "and noisy" he said, "with all those German bombs."

She laughed. He liked when she laughed at things that he said and not just things she said.

He talked about the war and he was surprised at the things she didn't know. She seemed unfamiliar with Antwerp and the Battle of the Bulge. She knew Ike and Patton but not Omar Bradley who he had fought directly under. She was just a kid, he thought.

He told her about Moretti and Leckie and Simms and that they were killed but they would always be his brothers. He left out the part about the German boy that he strangled to death. He would go to his grave without ever revealing that to anyone.

"Should we skip the movie?" she asked.

"Sure," he said.

The two of them seemed to be in the middle of something that a movie could only spoil so they each got a piece of cherry pie instead. It seemed fitting.

I think she likes me. When he spoke, she listened intently and didn't interrupt and locked her eyes onto his. She told him some more about her mother and how her parents were still madly in love after twenty-six years of marriage.

"I never heard them exchange a cross word."

He smiled and kept quiet. He'd heard his parents exchange cross words, and "madly in love" was not how he'd describe their relationship. They were more like East and West Germany; two former compatriots with a long history who lived contentiously side by side.

Tom had a special feeling about this little nervous girl from the time she approached him at the trolley stop. He had stayed away from the girls in France and when he returned home, he went to a handful of church dances and had been on a couple of dates, although, technically, they were double-dates. He had helped out a high school pal who had a girl who had a friend that she didn't want to leave home alone. Not much had happened on either occasion. At twenty-six, Tom had never had a steady girl.

When she finished talking about her mother and father, he found himself telling her about his Uncle Donald. He played with his tie and told her about his uncle and how he had lost his noodle. He had never intended to. He'd never spoken of his Uncle Donald to anyone outside of his family, not even Moretti. Yet, she had opened up to him and he felt an obligation to repay her. There was a softness to her face that made him want to tell her things. She looked at him without judgment and with an expression that said, "and what else?" and he found himself confessing most of his secrets.

"She'd make a good priest," Tom thought while acknowledging to himself that was a funny thing to say about a pretty girl. They were the last ones left in the diner and Tom could tell the owner Mr. Blake was itching to close. Lydia didn't seem to notice. *She must like me because she keeps talking.*

She finished her last piece of pie. He'd already finished his and Mr. Blake took their dishes into the kitchen.

"I suppose I should be getting home," she said.

It was even chillier now as they walked back, and Tom began to think how the date would end. He wanted to kiss her good night and he hoped she wouldn't mind. They had spent so much of the evening talking about her mother and her death and his friends' deaths that he didn't know if she would be in the mood for that sort of thing.

As they got closer to her house, he thought about how much shorter she was than him and how far he'd have to lean down to kiss her. He wondered if his face was too cold. His nervousness was back, and he felt his stomach tighten.

She chattered along until they reached the gate of her house and Tom struggled to get it open. He felt clumsy and it took him a minute. He wondered if her father were peering at them from upstairs. He walked her to the door and stayed a step from the top so as not to be too tall.

"Well, Tom Morrissey" she said, "I had a lovely time."

"Be brave," he thought as he leaned down and kissed her.

Chapter Twenty-Three

Curt didn't know Julie hated clowns or he wouldn't have sent one, so afterwards, she couldn't entirely blame him for what happened. *He didn't know.* On November 21st, he called to order balloons and the balloon guy told him a clown came with the deluxe package, so he figured, "What the hell?"

She wasn't keeping her hatred of clowns from him. It just never came up. *Why would it?* She assumed that clowns, like snakes, were universally hated. They were so creepy with that painted on smile and those sad sardonic faces. When that psycho in Chicago killed a bunch of boys dressed as a clown, Julie was not surprised. Clowns should have been their first suspect. As far as she was concerned any murder spree in any city should start out with an investigation into the local clown community.

She never had found clowns funny either. Even take away the "creep" factor, they never made her laugh. When her Aunt June would take her and her sisters to the circus when they were little Julie had never laughed at the clowns and had tensed up until they were gone. She couldn't tell Auntie she didn't like them. They were under strict orders to be grateful and tell Auntie how much they loved the circus. The circus wasn't cheap and Auntie didn't have to take them. Julie loved the acrobats and trapeze artists. She even liked the lion tamer although not the sound of the whip. She liked it all except the clowns and she couldn't tell Auntie. So, she'd sat with her stomach in knots and her face grimacing until they were gone.

"Are you feeling all right, Sweetie?" Her aunt would ask and Julie would nod and cringe and hold on until they were gone and she could enjoy the show once again.

It was a bad time for a clown to show up. There was never a good time as far as Julie was concerned, but she was particularly vulnerable on her birthday. Especially now that she was in her late thirties.

Marjorie, Julie's best friend and former college roommate, called to wish her a happy birthday and ask about Kevin. Debbie and the other Committee members were threatened by Marjorie and her closeness with Julie. They would have been even more threatened if they knew Marjorie had known about Kevin and they didn't. She was on the phone with Marjorie when the clown showed up in his Toyota Tercel. The bank robbery had been a mere three months ago so when Melvin saw a man with a hidden face, he assumed the worst.

"We got a problem here," he said in a loud voice.

Julie turned and saw the clown in the distance and gasped.

"Lock the doors," she yelled.

"I'm on it," said Melvin, and while the clown carefully and unsuspectingly pulled his bouquet of balloons from the backseat, Melvin had time to lock both the inner and outer doors.

"What should we do?" asked Bob.

"Push the alarm," said Julie.

"I did," said Debbie.

It was "The Day We Were All Almost Killed" all over again.

Everyone inside the bank watched the clown as he naively loped towards the entrance with his multi-colored balloons. No one made a sound as he reached the locked door and gave it a tug and then two more. *That should wipe the stupid smile off his face.*

"What if it's just a clown?" said Bob.

All the more reason.

"What if it's isn't?" said Julie.

The clown stopped tugging at the door and knocked instead.

"Hello" he said, his voice sounded far away, "I'm with the Balloon Platoon."

I thought clowns weren't supposed to talk.

"I think it's just a clown," said Bob.

There is no such thing as just a clown.

Julie ignored him.

"I think he's right," said Debbie, "It's just a clown."

"The police will be here any second to sort this out."

Sure enough, a siren blared and a few seconds later, three cop cars pulled in the parking lot and came to an abrupt stop.

"Freeze, get down," one of the cops yelled, loud enough to be heard through two glass doors.

The clown didn't want to.

"I'm just delivering balloons. I'm with the Balloon Platoon."

They told him to get down once more. They were quite insistent. Two of them had their guns drawn.

"I hope they don't shoot him," said Sasha.

Julie was, of course, torn.

The clown got on the ground and while they cuffed him, the balloons slipped from his grasp and began to drift upward. One cop, a younger one, made an honest effort to jump up and catch the string but he couldn't quite reach it and the balloons floated sideways at first then upward, skirting the telephone wire in between two oak trees and then into the troposphere, into the stratosphere then to the mesosphere and beyond.

"Those cost thirty-two dollars" the clown said, and his voice conveyed that real tears now mixed with his painted on ones. Julie, Melvin, Bob and the two customers watched from the front door while the cashiers huddled together behind the glass partition.

"I'm just here delivering balloons for Julie Rossi," he said.

Everyone turned and looked at Julie who was now suddenly implicated in the fiasco.

"Oh, I didn't know it was your birthday" Melvin said, "Happy Birthday."

"Thank you" Julie said, not taking her eyes off the proceedings outside.

"Happy Birthday," said Bob.

"Yeah, Happy Birthday," said Debbie.

"Happy Birthday" said Sasha.

"Happy Birthday," said one of the customers.

No chance of that now. Seeing a clown on your birthday was like a snowstorm on your wedding day.

The cops took the clown over to his Tercel. They searched the back seat and the trunk. Checking for other clowns, one would presume thought Julie. It was empty.

"I don't think this guy is a bank robber," said Bob.

Duh.

"Maybe I should tell them" suggested Julie. "Melvin, can you open the door?"

Melvin agreed it was safe and he unlocked the doors and Julie stuck her head outside.

"Officers, I think he's just delivering some balloons for my birthday," said Julie.

"Stay inside please," the older officer said.

Julie went back into the bank and Melvin relocked the door.

"Can someone take care of me here?"

One of the customers had gotten back in line and was standing in front of the ropes.

"I was here before you," the other customer said.

"But you got out of line to watch the clown."

"So did you."

"But I got back in line first."

Julie jumped in at this point.

"Debbie and Sasha, can you take these two customers please?"

Sasha was happy to oblige but Debbie always seemed put-off whenever Julie reminded her, she was her boss and not the other way around. Julie turned back to the customers.

"Neither of you will have to wait."

"We've been waiting."

It's the clown, they make everybody edgy.

Julie went back to the glass window. One of the cops was on the radio. The clown was angry now. He seemed to be berating the younger cop but was too far away now for the gang at the bank to hear. His hands were still hand-cuffed behind his back, but he seemed confident the police were about to realize their error. He began stomping his feet and his head moved up and down indignantly as he spoke. It the first time Julie had ever found a clown funny and she laughed out loud, drawing a few curious looks.

A customer tapped on the glass trying to get in and startled her.

"I think you can let them in Melvin."

Melvin unlocked the door letting in a young mom with a little boy.

"What's going on?"

"A clown showed up and looked suspicious, so we called the cops," said Julie.

"He's not really a bank robber" Melvin said, "He's just a clown."

"I hate clowns" said the little boy.

Who doesn't?

The phone on Julie's desk rang and she hustled over to answer it.

"Allston Bank."

It was Curt.

"Happy Birthday."

"Oh, thanks."

"I made reservations at the place on the Harbor you like."

"Sounds good."

"Did the balloons arrive?"

Julie cringed.

"Oh, they arrived."

She could have just lied, the way she been forced to with Auntie June as a child, but it wasn't her nature.

"You know how you feel about basements? That's how I feel about clowns."

Chapter Twenty-Four

By the time Tom got home from work, his father and mother and his brother Billy had finished eating their supper. He didn't mind eating alone, in fact, he preferred it. Ever since the "Handshake Meeting" he couldn't look his father or brother in the eye without feeling some resentment if not outright disdain. Even the closeness he had shared with his mother was gone. He'd never forgive her for standing by and letting his birthright be taken from him. *What sin had he committed?*

Tonight, as he entered his home, the three conspirators sat at the table with empty plates save for a few potato skins. Upon Tom's entrance all three exchanged glances and Billy's face wore a sneaky smile. Tom stopped and looked from one to the other. Something was up.

"I guess the mail's a little slow these days," said Billy.

His mother snickered.

Tom didn't smile along with them. He was in no mood to be made sport of. In the old days, it had always been two against two, now it was always three against one.

"What's this about?" said Tom.

"The mail," said Billy, getting up and going to the mail table near where Tom stood, "It's a little slow."

Billy retrieved a letter from the table and handed it to Tom. It was addressed to "Private Thomas Morrissey, First Class."

It was 1949. No one had called Tom "Private Morrissey" for four years. For an instant, he thought an old army buddy was reaching out but who was left? Moretti and Leckie and Sims were all dead. There was no return address. It wasn't typed. Someone had written Private Thomas Morrissey and so on in neat cursive handwriting.

He slid the letter opener off the table and turned to see his three family members staring at him with a curious look on each face. *The hell with them.*

"Who's it from?" his father asked.

"I'll have to read it and see."

He excused himself and ducked into the bedroom he shared with Billy and closed the door. He sat on the bed. His fingers trembled slightly as he slit the envelope open.

"Dear Tom,

I know you are far away in France and must be quite homesick.

Tom stopped reading and looked to the bottom of the page. *This is a letter from Lydia. Why is Lydia writing me? Is she breaking up with me? Why did she address it to Private Morrissey?* He continued reading.

"The newsreels say Eisenhower and Patton and Nimitz are giving the Germans heck and with any luck our boys will be home for Christmas."

Tom shook his head, not sure why she was pretending it was it was 1944. Not to mention that Nimitz didn't give the Germans heck, he was in the Pacific theater.

"It's so queer here with all the young fellas away. We're all worried sick about you and trying to do our part. I'm still in school but when I graduate, I'm gonna join the WACs or maybe I'll be your very own Rosie the Riveter. Can you picture me with a soldering gun? What a sight!"

He became aware that he was smiling as he read. *She's not breaking up with me.*

"I don't have much more to say. If you were here in person, I'd hug you and kiss you and kiss you some more. I hope you can whip those Nazis quick so I can show you what I mean. We want all you boys home soon especially you because you're my sweetheart. Take care and write back when you can."

Love,
  Lydia

P.S.

Tom when you told me you never got a letter from a girl the whole time you were a soldier I got so sad and indignant I thought I'd write you and pretend it was four or five years ago and you and I had already met and were going together then. Now you can't say you never got a letter from a sweetheart while you were a soldier. How's that?

Lyd

Tom, still smiling, sat clutching the letter between his thumbs and forefingers before looking up to see Billy standing over him in the doorway.

"Who's it from?"

He stopped smiling and stood up.

"None of your goddamn business" he snapped, placing the letter carefully in his top drawer.

Chapter Twenty-Five

In mid-September, Julie had to attend the regional managers meeting with Bob. It was two months before "The Great Balloon Fiasco" and three weeks after "The Day We Were All Almost Killed." Every third Tuesday, the branch managers would meet with the Big Boss. Bob was no longer a branch manager but they never uninvited him and he was too dumb to realize he didn't have to go anymore. The worst part was the two of them would drive together, fifteen minutes there and fifteen minutes back with nothing to talk about.

Now that Bob's kids lived in Maine with their mother and her replacement husband and he never saw them, he liked to talk about his cat Smudge. Julie didn't care much for cats but felt sorry for Smudge. *Imagine spending nine lives with Bob?*

On this Tuesday in September, Bob revealed that he had made the difficult decision to have Smudge neutered.

"That's nice," said Julie.

He parked and on the way into the building he said, "Oh, I forgot to give you this" and handed her a yellow post-it note. The message said, "Bill Morrissey called."

Bill Morrissey? Curt's Uncle Billy? Bill Morrissey called and you're just telling me now. I'd like to build a time machine and have your parents neutered.

"I'll be right there," she said, then circled the building looking for a pay phone. She spotted one at the gas station across the street that was being used by an unkempt, old hag but Julie scampered over, dodging puddles anyway. The hag using the phone spoke in Russian or some Eastern European language and she kept talking even when Julie coughed and fidgeted to let her know she was waiting. Julie looked at her watch. It was five past now, the meeting had already begun. She scampered back. *Fucking commie.*

Julie apologized for being late then sat in the meeting not paying attention. *Why was Uncle Billy calling me? I must have been in the bathroom when he called. Why couldn't that imbecile give me the message sooner?*

The meeting was Julie and eight men, eight, mostly married, mostly middle-aged men.

"I wouldn't fuck any of them if we were stranded on a deserted island for twenty years," she once told the Committee.

The Big Boss, short, fat and bald, a triple threat, was the type who knew everything and assumed everyone else knew nothing. He did all the talking and the subtext to everything he said was, "I'm great." A total asshole, and while he blathered on, Julie had plenty of time to imagine horrible things. *What if Curt had been in an accident? She had spoken to him around ten-thirty and he was fine but what if something happened since then? What if he had been killed or maimed and Uncle Billy found out and was letting her know. The note didn't say "urgent" but Bob could have left out that part. Maybe Bob doesn't know what urgent means.*

The meeting finally ended, and Julie peeked around the building again. The old woman was still on phone. *It's been over an hour. How much change does she carry with her?* She got back in the car with Bob and when he dropped her off at a T station, she finally found a pay phone.

"Uncle Billy, this is Julie Rossi, is everything okay?"

"Oh, yes, Julie, everything is fine, fine, just wondering if you wanted to play tennis with me."

Tennis? He's calling me about tennis? He does have his own court and he did say we should play some time. I guess it makes more sense that he called about tennis than Curt being killed while cleaning someone's house.

"Sure, that sounds like fun."

They made plans for Saturday. Twice after work, she practiced hitting balls against a brick wall, knowing she was rusty and not wanting to embarrass herself. On Saturday morning, Julie showed up exactly on time in a sweatshirt with white shorts and her old wooden racket. It was Indian Summer and pleasant, the last nice weekend before the endless Boston winter. Uncle Billy greeted her at the door in a maroon tracksuit holding a brand, new aluminum racket.

It was the second time she'd been to his house. It was actually a mansion with pillars out front, a tennis court in the backyard and a kitchen with an island in the middle.

"I could live on the island in his kitchen," she had told the Committee.

"I thought we'd play first and then have lunch," he said with a wink. She was used to his winks by now.

They loosened up by hitting easy ones to each other. He was dexterous and nimble, and his form was graceful and fluid. This guy has had lessons. After a few minutes, they got a pretty good rally going which she ended by slapping a hard backhand just inside the line.

"Whoa," he said, straightening up and looking at her in surprise.

She had fucked up. This was supposed to be a friendly game. It wasn't even a game, they were just hitting balls back and forth, but she couldn't help herself as her old instincts kicked in. She was competitive and she played to win. *I'm a terrible person. I just blasted the ball past a sixty-year-old man who is HIV positive. What is wrong with me?*

She lightened up after that, hitting them right to him and none too hard, maintaining long, boring volleys. After forty-five minutes or so, he was worn out.

"I had no idea you were Billie Jean King," he said with a laugh and a wink.

Hey, buddy, I took it easy on you.

"I thought we'd have some tuna melts," he said on their way inside.

She sat on a stool in the kitchen and rested her elbows on that island she loved so much. He removed a Tupperware container of tuna from the fridge and took out three different kinds of cheese from the crisper.

"I want to ask you a favor," he said.

What's this about?

"I want you to convince Curt to be my beneficiary."

I see, that's why I'm here.

She scrunched up her face.

"It's tough convincing him of anything."

"Ain't that the truth," he said before pointing at the cheese.

"Munster, Pepper Jack or Cheddar?"

"Munster."

"He's just like his father but if anyone can convince him, you can. He's obviously crazy about you."

She could feel her ears turning red.

"You think so?"

"I do" he said, putting a tuna melt into the microwave. "With his last girlfriend there was no chemistry, none at all."

Last girlfriend? The one he never talks about? The one who broke up with him because she wanted to get married and have children and he didn't want to? That one?

"What was her name?"

"Tracy?" he said, before taking a bite and correcting himself, "Stacy!"

I always hated the name "Stacy."

The microwave beeped and he took one tuna melt out and put another one in.

"What was she like?"

"Nice. Cute," he said, then quickly backtracking as he pulled out the other tuna melt from the mike, "Not as cute as you, of course. And they had no chemistry. You two have chemistry."

Julie promised him she would do what she could. *It's hard to say "no" to this guy.* They sat on the porch and ate and talked and laughed and he winked and then it was time to go.

On the way home, she popped in her mix tape and thought about Stacy who had wanted to marry Curt and have his children and she didn't get her way. Julie wanted those exact same things. She had outdueled Cheryl and bested Bob and bashed a backhand past Uncle Billy because she was someone who always had to win. Yet, Curt was stubborn and once he dug his heels in, he wouldn't budge. It was all leading to an epic showdown between the boy who wouldn't budge and the girl who has to win.

Chapter Twenty-Six

Tom had never bought a ring before. On the trolley ride home, every minute or so, he would reach up and feel the bulge in his top pocket. He'd outline the square box with his finger and then remove his arm from the inside of his coat. He did it compulsively over and over the whole way home as he thought about the young, cocky clerk at the jewelry counter.

The young man had smiled a smug half-smile when Tom asked, "What if it doesn't fit her finger?" The man paused and half-smiled and drawled out, "It can be adjusted so it fits, sir." Tom didn't like being half-smiled at. He nearly told the man to go to hell and turned and walked out. Let him half-smile about that.

How was I to know? I never bought a ring before. I never even had a girl before. How was I supposed to know a thing like that? The man was younger than Tom, twenty-one or twenty-two with slicked back hair and rubbery cheeks. Tom had gotten good at being able to tell who'd gone and who hadn't. The clerk hadn't gone. *He's too young*. Tom hadn't dropped out of college, enlisted in the army, been shot at by Nazis, watched his best friend die, lose the family business all so he could be half-smiled at by this smug sonofabitch. He reached into his coat and outlined the box again with his finger.

Was this a mistake? Was it too soon? It was only their fourth date. They had necked a lot their last two dates. *Were they falling in love? Were they already in love? What was the difference between "falling" and "being"?*

Maybe the fourth date was too soon to give her a ring, but she had sent him that letter. *Was it just a gag? Lydia liked to kid. Was it just a joke between the two of them because he didn't have a sweetheart during the war? It was more of a gesture than a gag. She had made a gesture and it was his turn to reciprocate. Was a ring too much? Would it scare her off? It was just a gesture like her gesture.* He reached under his coat and felt the box again.

Only his mother was home when he got home. He worked a half-day on Saturdays.

"You're home late."

"Had to work late."

He didn't like lying to his mother. It was a venial sin he'd have to confess, but he didn't want her to know about the ring and that he and Lydia were getting serious.

"Do you know where my ice skates are?"

He knew where they were but asked anyway.

"You're going to Rogers Park?"

"Lydia wants to."

He wanted his mother to know about Lydia, just not that they were getting serious.

He changed out of his suit and got the ice skates from the closet. He sat on his bed with the bedroom door closed and pulled out the box and looked at the ring. He polished it with his handkerchief even though it didn't need polishing. It was gold-plated and simple and there was no inscription. It had cost Tom twenty-five dollars, nearly a week's pay. Tom knew he was going all in. This was his D-Day, success would lead ultimately to victory, but failure would mean disaster. There was no middle ground.

He looked at his watch. He remembered how his father had mocked him when he came home from the war for wearing a watch on his wrist. "Ladies wear wristwatches" he said. "Men wear a watch fob." *Who the hell cares what he thinks? Someday, I'll be married, and I'll have nothing more to do with him.*

He would know four or five hours from now if she loved him the way he loved her. *What if she didn't? What if to her this was all a lark?* He felt a wave of nausea. He stood up and went to the bathroom. He splashed water on his face. *I felt the same way going into battle. Love and war. No difference.*

When Tom picked up Lydia, for the first time in their dating history, she was actually ready, bundled up with her skates flung over her shoulder.

She kissed her Dad good-bye and once they were a safe distance from her home, they held hands.

They skated holding hands, careful to avoid small children and old people in their forties and fifties. She chattered and he listened and the lights in the park turned on as the sun went down and the afternoon became night.

Tom's fear rose as the day faded and his gift bestowing grew near. He became preoccupied and withdrawn and stopped laughing at her jokes.

"Did I say something wrong?" she asked.

"What? Why would you think that?" he said.

"You've stopped talking. I've met walls that were more fun."

"You've met walls?"

"I have and they've enjoyed my company more than you."

She stopped skating.

"Are you mad at me, Tom Morrissey? Are you mad that I sent that letter?"

Tom realized he had made a tactical error. He hadn't mentioned or acknowledged her letter. The ring was his response and she didn't know about the ring yet.

"I wasn't mocking you but after I sent it, I worried you'd think I was mocking you for not having a girl. I didn't mean it that way." He could see she was on the verge of tears.

"No, no," he said with a trace of trepidation in his voice. "I loved the letter, Lydia. Let's sit, I have something for you."

They skated to a bench and sat. Tom unwound his scarf and reached into his coat. There was no bulge. He checked again and sat up and checked each pocket now in a state of full-blown panic.

"It's gone."

"What's gone?"

"I had it and now it's gone."

He skated away, scanning the ice for the ring while Lydia chased him.

"Tom, what's gone?"

"I had a box, a little white box about yeah big."

He skated away again, bent over searching the ice. Lydia caught up, she was crying now.

"What's happened, Tom?"

He stopped short nearly crashing into two children. He straightened up and faced her.

"I got you a ring and now it's gone."

"A ring?"

"A promise ring and now it's gone."

He started to skate away again, and she yelled his name. "Tom, we're not going to find it, it's too dark. We can come back the first thing in the morning and look for it."

He looked around, cold breath poured from his nostrils like a dragon.

"God damn it."

"Tom."

"I'm sorry," he muttered, knowing better than to take the Lord's name in vain.

"I don't need a ring," she said, "We can promise without one."

She smiled at him with cold tears still on her cheeks. He reached down and kissed her even though people could see. They had never kissed with other people watching before. Tom and Lydia were now promised to each other without a promise ring and it wasn't until he got home that he found it on his bed.

Chapter Twenty-Seven

No one could have seen the disaster coming. It was an early August morning, three weeks before "The Day We Were All Almost Killed," and the sky was already a clear and cloudless blue. It was exactly like the morning of Space Shuttle and Julie would always remember exactly where she was when it happened.

They had just had sex. Her favorite kind of sex. Superfluous sex. Maybe that doesn't sound sexy, but they had just had sex the night before and the plan was to just wake up, shower and dress and go to work but one thing led to another and before they knew it they were having superfluous sex.

It was during the afterglow when it happened. They should have been showering and shaving and putting on make-up and going to work but the two of them were just lying there, entangled, with Curt still partially on top of her. Right then, she blurted out "I love you."

It was the second worst mistake she could have made. Only telling him about Kevin would have been worse. That would have been a mortal wound and the patient would have died instantly. This was serious and possibly fatal. She'd know more in a day or two.

She knew right away it was a mistake. Not right after but a second after that when he didn't say it back. She knew better. She was supposed to wait until he said it first. More than once, she had had that conversation with herself. She would say it only after he did.

Over their first few weeks of dating, Julie had played her hand masterfully. Anyone who says "love isn't a game" is a fool or worse, a spinster. She had dated lots of guys and made lots of mistakes but she had learned from them and she was now a wily veteran, a crafty lefthander who knew what it takes to win.

Going to the funeral and the pretrial hearing were strokes of genius. It showed him that she'd be with him in the tough times. *I have character. He can't deny that.*

Holding off on sex was another brilliant move. *It kept him coming back and showed I'm not some slut. Not anymore anyway.* Other than that, she was funny and could feign being carefree better than anyone. When they got together, they would have long talks and long sex and they would have fun. She was the perfect girlfriend until this.

After her blunder, he kissed her a couple of times and then pulled back.

"I've gotta jump in the shower."

True to his word, he got out of bed, closed the bathroom door and turned on the water. Her stomach filled with air. She lay on her back staring at the ceiling. *I said, "I love you" and he said, "I gotta jump in the shower." Not even, "I've got to" or "I've gotta." If you're going to snub me, at least use real English.*

There was only one thing to do. Act like it hadn't happened. There was no other way. She jumped out of bed and put on a robe. She gathered up her clothes for the day and waited outside the bathroom door leaning against it, listening for the sound of the shower. When it stopped, she counted to three and then entered.

"Excuse me," she said, placing her clothes atop the covered toilet seat. In an instant, she had slipped off her robe and stepped in the tub and pulled back the curtain. She was a blur. She turned the water back on and began showering. He shaved and dressed, and she wasn't coming out until he was gone. He took forever. *I'm gonna run out of hot water.*

"I better get going," he said, finally through the shower curtain.

"Okay."

Her tone was cheerful. *There's nothing wrong. Everything's good.*

"I'll call you later."

"Great."

She couldn't have been more pleasant. She waited until she heard her front door close before shutting the water off and getting out. *I'm late. What the fuck took him so long?*

Julie relived her faux pas all the way to work. *Maybe he didn't hear me. I was two inches from his face. Even a deaf person could have read my lips. Maybe he thought I was joking. What woman jokes about that? I'd joke about cancer before I'd joke about that?*

When she was with Michael, he said it first. It was during the first time they had sex and even though he said, "I love you" she always wondered if he meant, "I love this." She and Michael said it all the time to each other although she now doubted that she was ever in love with him. They were so young, and it made them feel more mature to say it.

Dutch said it to her from time to time but only when he was drunk and then, he wouldn't stop saying it. It never felt that good to hear him say it because he was such a sloppy drunk, who would cry at a sappy commercial or when the Celtics were knocked out of the play-offs.

On the train to work, she sat chastising herself and growing angry at him. *Why the fuck didn't he say it back to her? What the fuck is his problem?* She arrived work looking haggard and was snippy almost immediately.

"You're in a mood," said Debbie.

"Bite me," she said.

She was in no mood for someone to tell her she was in a mood. She even barked at Bob to his face in front of a customer for something he didn't deserve. *He deserved it plenty other times.*

Finally, around ten-thirty, true to his word, Curt did call. She answered on the first ring, something she never did, and she knew she was still off her game. *Get your shit together,* she reminded herself. They chatted about nothing, she forced a few jokes and then, they made plans for the movies the next night. Everything seemed fine and maybe it was but with Curt you never knew. He was so inscrutable and after four months together, she still never knew what he was thinking.

She felt better after they hung up. It hadn't been a fatal error after all, just a blip and every relationship has those. Still, she knew her situation was too precarious and for her sake and for Kevin's sake she couldn't fuck up like that again. From here on in, she would have to be perfect.

Chapter Twenty-Eight

"Pretty swanky digs," said Lydia as the two of them entered the hotel lobby.

Billy was the best man and he paid for the hotel room for their wedding night as well as the car from the church to the hotel. Tom hated Billy but was bound by convention. When a man married, he chose his brother as his best man. His father, of course, had chosen Brendan over Donald but Tom only had one brother.

Though the two of them still shared a room, they hadn't spoken much in the past two years ever since the day they agreed to stop shaking hands and Tom convinced himself he always hated Billy. That wasn't true. When they were kids there were many hours laughing and playing and wrestling and swimming and a million shared experiences. When they fought, as brothers do, Tom always won handily, and Billy quickly learned to use his wits.

"Do you need help with your bags, sir?"

Tom turned to the bellhop, an older colored gentleman with flecks of gray in his beard.

"I can take mine" said Tom, "if you take my wife's."

He had never said the word "wife" before. Of course, he'd said the word "wife" before but always about somebody else's wife. Now married a little over three hours, he said if for the first time about his own wife.

Can I call her 'my wife'? We haven't consummated our marriage yet. She won't be my wife in the eyes of the Lord until we consummate our marriage. He was a curious mix of joy and terror.

The three of them, Tom, Lydia and the colored bellhop said nothing on the elevator ride up. Elevators do that to people. He was happy just looking at his pretty wife. She wore a simple light green outfit having changed from her puffy white dress, her hair and make-up still perfect. He rocked back and forth on his feet nervously. He was anxious to consummate his marriage and be "man and wife" in the eyes of the Lord.

He'd have to get used to saying "wife." While they were engaged, he never said "fiancée," finding it too pretentious and too French. He'd just say, "my girl." She was still his "girl," "his girl" and now, "his wife."

"What are you looking at?" said Lydia, looking back up at him.

As the colored fellow carried her bags ahead of them, Lydia nudged Tom and made a money gesture. "Oh, right" thought Tom, fishing a couple of quarters from his pants. "You folks have a wonderful evening" he said after opening the door and leaving Lydia's bags.

Tom surveyed the hotel room. There was a domed radio on the dresser and a bottle of champagne jutting out of a bucket of ice next to two empty glasses. There was a four-poster bed against the wall. "It's going to happen right there," thought Tom. He turned and saw Lydia still standing in the hallway.

"What are you doing?" he asked.

"Waiting for a bus," she said.

She motioned with her head for Tom to come out of the room.

"Oh" said Tom, it finally dawning on him. *The threshold.*

He leaned over and scooped up his petite bride.

"I'm not much of a challenge, am I?" she said.

"That's why I picked you," he said, "I didn't want to strain my back."

He carried her across the threshold and kissed her once or twice before putting her down. *Is she as nervous as I am?*

"What do you say we have a little champagne, Tom Morrissey?" He liked it when she called him "Tom Morrissey."

He opened the little card in the bucket. He had assumed the champagne was from the hotel, a thoughtful gesture for the newlyweds but he was wrong. It read, "All the best, Billy." Seeing his brother's name angered him. *Always the big shot. Was he flaunting his success? Rubbing my nose in it, that bastide* crumpled the card up in a ball and hurled into the wastebasket.

"What's wrong?" she asked.

"Nothing," he said, and he began opening the champagne. He took off the wrapper and the wire but couldn't get the cork out. He tried pulling at it and twisting it this way and that, but it wouldn't budge.

"Do you want me to help?" she asked.

"I got it," he said, continuing to tug, "It's just that I've never done this before."

Finally, it popped, catching him off guard and bubbling over with half of it spilling on the rug.

"Oh, hell," he said, who didn't usually swear in front of Lydia. "It's all right" she said, "We don't live here."

He poured them each a glass and they gazed out the window at Copley Square.

"Even the pigeons look pretty from up here," she said.

Was she stalling? Doesn't she want to do this? Maybe not. It's always the fella who wants to. It's pleasurable for the fella and the girl just goes along.

She sipped her champagne and stared out the window. *It's just Boston. She's seen it a thousand times.* He stroked the back of her neck and leaned down and kissed her more passionately than before.

"You trying to make me spill my champagne?" she asked when they finally stopped.

"I love you," he said.

"Yes," she said, "I think you mentioned that earlier."

He kissed her again and she seemed to get the message. "Oh, my, somebody's impatient," she said, setting down her glass. "I'll be back in a jiffy," she said taking a small bag with her into the bathroom.

He finished his champagne. He wanted scotch. Scotch was a manly drink. Champagne was too feminine and too French. He came home from the war "anti-French," not as anti-French as he was anti-German but anti-French just the same.

He took his tie off and then his jacket and hung it in the closet. He took off his shoes and socks. He hesitated for a moment and then took off his pants and hung them on a hanger. He took off his shirt leaving his undershirt on and then tossed the shirt behind his suitcase. He slid into bed and sighed loudly. He strummed the bed with his fingers nervously.

On their dates, they would neck and nothing more and then he would come home and invariably dream of her. Once he dreamt of her naked, a dream so vivid he woke feeling both guilty and aroused. He would never press her for sex before they were married. Lydia wasn't that kind of girl nor was he that kind of man. There was no place to go any way even if they were.

He'd been dreaming of this moment since they met a year ago. Now he wanted it to be done with. He knew it was supposed to be pleasurable, but he wanted it over and done with all the same. *How long does it take?* He didn't know. *Maybe an hour or two.* It should be all done within an hour or two.

He began saying his prayers and then stopped himself. He always said his prayers when he went to bed ever since he could remember. Was it sacrilegious to pray before sex? No, he decided. *I married a Catholic girl. I'm Catholic, she's Catholic. We're supposed to have sex. We're not sinners. They want us making more Catholics.* He finished his prayers.

He clutched and unclutched the under sheet waiting for her. *What could be taking so long? What if I fall asleep?* He was too filled with anticipation and adrenaline for that, but the idea made him smile. A bride climbing into bed for their wedding night only to find her groom sound asleep. He chuckled to himself.

Finally, he heard the bathroom door open and she stood before him in a light blue nightie. *She's beautiful.*

"I hope you didn't mind waiting," she said.

Tom jumped out of bed and closed the curtains. He didn't want anyone looking in. It was irrational, perhaps, since they were 14 stories up but he didn't want anyone looking in and seeing what they were about to do. She watched him curiously. He looked back at her and got aroused and then blushed at his arousal. He shut off the light and they each got into opposite sides of the bed.

"Well, here we are" she said as they began kissing. He climbed on top of her. He knew enough to know that the man always got on top. They kissed for a long time.

"Hold it," he said.

"Is everything all right?"

"Yeah, swell," he said, "I…I have to go to the bathroom."

A month earlier, a horrible thought had entered Tom's mind. *What if I urinate instead of ejaculate into her?* He had dismissed the thought then but now it was back. *I'd better piss now.* He stood in front of the toilet. His heart rate was up and he was sweating. It took several minutes for his erection to recede and the urine to come. Afterwards, he looked at himself in the mirror and whispered, "Be brave."

"Oh, you're back," she said as he climbed into bed and resumed his position. They began kissing again. They kissed for a long time and he arched his back which began to hurt bending over his petite wife.

"Are you ready?" she whispered.

"Yes" he said, his breath irregular and whispered back, "Are you?"

"Yes," she said meekly.

He pulled his underwear down but when he went to place his penis inside her, the fear came back. *What if I pee?* He felt his penis grow flaccid and his body tensed as he tried to will his erection to return. His penis stayed limp and he groaned softly.

"Everything all right," she whispered.

He climbed off of her and got out of bed. He was breathing heavily now, and he sat on the chair by the bed and panted. He was sweating and she sat up and turned on the lamp on the nightstand.

"Shut that light off," he snapped, "I'll be fine."

She stared at him curiously for a moment and then obeyed.

"I'll be fine," he said again.

What if I can't do this? What if I can't consummate our marriage? Will we be a childless couple? Would she divorce me? Would people find out why? The image of the German boy he strangled to death flashed in his head. *What if God is punishing me?*

"Tom, come back to bed," she said. "It'll be all right, come back to bed."

He got off the chair and got back in bed. She kissed him and kissed him again and he became aroused and climbed back on top of her.

His penis began poking around her upper thighs, near but not in its intended target. He grew frustrated. *Why won't it go where it's supposed to?*

"Let me help you" she said, taking her hands from his face and shifting them down to his penis. Tom couldn't believe she had touched it.

As she coaxed his penis inside her, she suddenly gasped and he pulled back.

"Are you okay?"

"I'll be okay, it just hurt a little."

"Do you want to stop? We can stop."

"No" she said, "It'll be all right."

They kissed some more and slowly she finagled his penis into her vagina. Within seconds, he felt an explosion of desire. He fell off of her, full of relief. He hadn't peed. Tom and his pretty wife were no longer virgins.

Chapter Twenty-Nine

Julie was on the phone with Curt when the men in the ski masks pulled into the parking lot. She was sitting behind her desk, holding the phone with her right hand and twirling the cord with her left and didn't look up when the faded, burgundy Impala stopped out front. Melvin, the security guard hadn't noticed them yet either.

Julie and Curt usually spoke for few minutes or so at this time of the morning five days a week. He always called her, and she let him know when her customers were getting impatient and it was time to get off. It was late August and much of Boston had emptied out for one last bit of sun on the Cape, or perhaps, Hampton Beach or Block Island. In a week or so, the students would be back, and the city would teem with U-Hauls and ski racks laden with luggage, and the bank would be crammed with twenty-year-olds opening up accounts, some with as much as a thousand dollars. *Where do kids that age get that kind of money? I never had anything close to that when I was in college.*

It was the slowest time of the year and Julie kept him on the line much longer than usual. She was regaling him with one of her favorite stories from high school. He had heard most of her stories by now but this one somehow had slipped through the cracks.

The story was of a red headed girl in her tenth-grade biology class named Celeste Sebastiano. The characters in Julie's real-life stories always had wonderful names like "Celeste Sebastiano." Celeste was round like a circle and just as simple. She had red hair from her Irish mother who worked at the DMV, and Celeste wore it short and sassy.

Mrs. Kelly, not one of the great names, was one of the few lay teachers and her subject was biology.

"The nuns would rather not discuss sexual reproduction."

The student body was too slight for an honors or AP classes. Once in a while, a girl was so bright she was moved up to a higher grade but generally, the smart and the dumb were thrown in the mix together.

"Celeste was one of the dumb."

Julie wasn't trying to be mean, she just wanted Curt to follow along.

"Any way, one day, Mrs. Kelly was teaching us about cell mitosis, you know mitosis? The way cells divide?"

"Sure, mitosis" said Curt with a straight face, "One of my favorite things to talk about."

The same could not be said about poor Celeste Sebastiano, who wasn't paying attention to Mrs. Kelly's lecture and was whispering and giggling with another girl.

"Knock it off, ladies" barked Mrs. Kelly. "Celeste, do you even know what I'm talking about?"

The funny part came when Celeste said, "Sure, you're talking about your tosis." It was a story that had delighted Julie for years but never had quite the impact with anyone else. After years of lying dormant in her brain, it popped in her head the night before last when her groceries were rung up by a girl with bright red hair much like Celeste Sebastiano.

Julie never got to the funny part. She saw a man with a black ski mask and camouflage pants and a shotgun heading towards the door followed by two other men with black ski masks also carrying shotguns.

She stood up and screamed, "Lock the door, lock the door. We're being robbed."

"I have to go," she said into the phone and hung up on Curt.

Melvin moved quickly for a man his age. The men entered the outer door, but Melvin got to the inner door first and locked it a second or two before the man with the camouflage pants could reach it.

"Now lock the outer door, quick, hurry Melvin," yelled Julie.

Melvin flipped the switch locking the outer door and the three men were trapped in the bank's foyer, not quite in but not quite out of the bank.

The man in the camouflage pants pulled again and again at the inner door but it wouldn't budge. The other two just stood by not sure what to do.

Then the man camouflage pants darted to the outer door and pushed and pulled hoping to get out. *They're trapped. They're trapped inside.*

"Let us out," screamed the man in the camouflage pants, his voice slightly muffled by his ski mask. "Let us the fuck out."

"Let us out" they screamed, "Let us the fuck out."

"Should we let them out?" asked Bob the idiot.

"No, no, we should not let them out" said Julie emphatically, "Push the alarm, push the alarm."

"I've been pushing the alarm" said Debbie. "I've pushed it ten times."

The alarm, of course, was silent.

Camouflage pants seemed to be the leader of his crew and had by now discerned that Julie was the leader of hers. He turned and looked at Julie through the holes in his ski-masked face.

"Let us out," he said, pointing the gun directly at her face.

"It's bullet proof glass," she said, trembling just the same.

"Let us out and no one gets hurt," he said.

Julie looked at the gun and trembled a bit more but said nothing and didn't move.

"Let us out, you fuckin' cunt."

"Maybe we should let them out?" said Bob-so-lete once more. "No" said Julie, "The police will be here any minute."

"Let us out of here, you fuckin' cunt."

"There's no need for that kind of language," said Bob, apparently, hoping for more polite bank robbers.

"We've got you boys now," said Melvin which made them curse again and hit the glass door some more.

An elderly man with wispy hair and light blue windbreaker approached the outer door. It was eighty-two degrees and Julie wondered why the windbreaker was necessary.

"Go back, go back to your car!" Julie called to him through to glass door waving her arms in an exaggerated fashion. "We're being robbed, go back to your car!"

Oblivious, the old man tried the door and found it locked. He tried it two or three more times. *Go away, you old fool, go away.* He cupped his hands around his eyes and peered into the bank. His head jerked back when he noticed the three men with ski masks and shotguns just a few feet away. He spun around and shuffled back to his car, his arms swinging like a man in a silent movie. *Thank God.*

One of the armed men, not the one in camouflage, bashed his gun against the ATM machine in the foyer. He smashed the machine three times. Julie cringed.

"That's bank property," Bob cautioned the man. *No shit.*

It was at this point that Julie became aware of the other customers. There were only two, both women, one about fifty and one about sixty.

"This will all be over in just a minute. Would you like to sit while you're waiting?" Julie asked.

The two of them stayed put, too stunned to move. In the distance, they could hear a police siren. *Finally.*

"The police are coming," said Bob.

Thanks for the tip.

The three men again pulled hard at the outer door until four police cruisers screeched into the parking lot. Several cops sprang from the cars with their guns drawn.

"Put your weapons down!" they yelled, "Put your weapons down!" Melvin reached for the button for the outer door. "Not yet," said Julie, "Not until they say it's okay."

The bad guys put their guns down.

"Kick them away from you," one cop said and "Get down on your knees with your hands behind your head."

Sheepishly, the men did as they were told.

"Now Melvin!" said Julie, and Melvin unlocked the outer door and the cops swooped in with handcuffs and placed a knee in the back of each bad guy and put the handcuffs on.

After the men were cuffed, the police lifted them to their feet and removed their ski masks. The camouflage man had shaggy, sandy hair and a boyish face.

"He's gorgeous," said Debbie.

Gimme a break.

"Melvin, you can open the inner door now," said Julie as the cops put each man in the back of one squad car.

"Sorry about that folks," Julie said to the customers.

"Well, wasn't that exciting," said the older one.

Curt's yellow van pulled into the parking lot. Curt jumped out wearing the yellow overalls he wore while he cleaned people's houses. He saw the police and the bad guys in the police cars and turned towards the bank. Julie waved to him from inside. In a moment, he was inside.

"Are you okay?"

She nodded but began to cry. She began to breathe rapidly and felt her heart race. She cried harder now like a little girl who'd fallen off her bike.

"It's okay, it's okay, it's okay," he said softly.

He hugged her tightly and her body shuddered against his. "I love you," he whispered.

Chapter Thirty

It was three years and ten months before Lydia gave birth. She had had two miscarriages and they prayed and prayed and Tom feared he was being punished for things he'd done in the war. Finally, God forgave Tom and Lydia had a baby boy.

Tom waited in the waiting room for nineteen hours, dozing here and there, but mostly sitting tapping his feet or pacing, too nervous to eat or read a book. He remembered hearing a story of an expectant father so overcome with worry he actually went into the delivery room to check on his wife. Imagine.

Tommy grew tall like his father, with the same pale blue eyes, yet his features were fragile and feminine like his mother's. His two parents marveled at his progress, speaking at nine months, walking at eleven months. Before he was two, Tommy could identify each letter, pulling the alphabet magnets off the refrigerator one by one to prove it. Their babysitter, an older woman, who had once taught kindergarten, said he was the "most verbal child" she had ever encountered, and Tom and Lydia felt the rush of parental pride.

After another miscarriage, it was another four years before their next child was born. It was a difficult birth for Lydia, and Tom, sitting alone in the waiting room, was unaware how close she came to death, her heart rate plummeting twice to dangerous levels. She was allowed to return home only after a full week in the hospital. She was over thirty now and the doctor, concerned that her heart might be frail like her mother's, warned against having another child and Tom and Lydia used the rhythm method from then on.

For their second son, Tom chose the name this time, naming him "Curtis" after his fallen friend Curtis Moretti. "Curtie" as he was called in those days, was small and dark with a fat face and a button nose. Tommy resembled Lydia while Curtie was all Morrissey.

Both boys were often asleep by the time Tom got home. He'd been promoted to floor manager and the store now stayed open 'til eight, trying to compete with Filene's and Jordan Marsh, a dying redwood fighting for sunlight in a crowded canopy.

The war came back to him from time to time. It would wake him up in the dead of night with images of Moretti or the German boy or of Leckie's headless body. He'd tramp to the kitchen when prayers didn't work and sip some Scotch and smoke a cigarette and try and push those thoughts away.

"Come back to bed, Tom Morrissey," she would drawl from the top of the stairs and he'd put his cigarette out and his bottle away and do as he was told.

He had grown heavier around the middle, still with long birdlike legs and his forehead had expanded. His wife was still pretty and slim and girlish despite the creases around her eyes.

One night he came home and found Lydia beaming at him from across the kitchen table. She wore a sly mischievous grin.

"We have a poet in the family."

He removed his coat and loosened his tie.

"Is that a good thing or a bad thing?"

Lydia grinned.

"It's a good thing. Robert Frost got to recite one of his poems at the inauguration."

"Did he get paid for it?"

"Oh, Tom, you know you're supposed to ask not what your country can do for you."

Tom smiled. His wife was witty, wittier than even Leckie.

"What's all this about?"

"Have your supper and I'll tell you all about it."

He sat at the little table in the kitchen while she lifted a TV dinner from the oven. She put it on a plate and pulled back the tin foil.

"Let it cool for a minute," she said, "I know how impatient you are."

He poured himself a glass of scotch and sat down across from his wife, whose finger caressed a mysterious envelope.

"I got this note today from Tommy's teacher."

Tom grimaced.

"You might like her better once you hear this," she said, placing her reading glasses on her nose.

"Dear Mr. and Mrs. Morrissey, Each year there is a poetry contest for students in the ____ school district. Each student in the primary grades is required to submit an entry, and Tommy's poem has been selected as the best poem in the third grade for the entire school district. His poem will be on display in the Town Hall and his name will be announced in Saturday's edition of the Town Crier. Tommy's poem displays a facility of language and clever imagery. It is quite remarkable for a boy his age."

Lydia removed her glasses, which hung on a chain around her neck.

Tom beamed, "Did you hear that? Remarkable for a boy his age."

"Hear that? I said it."

"I knew there was something special about that kid."

"Oh, Tom."

"I mean it. I've felt that since day one. That kid is going places. He's going to be something special."

Lydia chuckled.

"Far be it for me to argue with you."

Tom dipped a tater tot in gravy and took a bite.

"What's the poem?"

"Oh, I almost forgot."

She slid her glasses back on and took the poem from the envelope.

"It's called, 'There's a Tigress in the Egress.'"

"Egress? What the hell is an egress?"

"It's an exit, an exit to a building."

"How the hell does he know what an egress is and I don't?"

"Oh, Tom, kids today know everything."

He took a bite from his TV dinner.

"Read it," he said, his mouth full of Salisbury steak.

She cleared her throat and began.

"There's a tigress at the egress and she's full of meanness. There's a tigress at the egress and she has no niceness. Bite, bite, bite, chomp, chomp, chomp."

Lydia looked over his glasses at him.

"Go on."

Lydia cocked her head.

"That's it."

"That's it?"

She displayed the page both front and back.

"That's it" she said again.

"That's remarkable?"

"Apparently. The experts seem to think so. I don't think he's quite ready for the inauguration."

"But still" Tom said just before swallowing. "She called him 'remarkable' and 'creative' and she said he was more remarkable than all the other third graders."

"Oh, Tom Morrissey, she didn't exactly say that."

The end of World War II was the high-water mark for the U.S. Germany, Italy and Japan were devastated. The Soviet Union was reeling from the loss of twenty million men, China on the brink of Civil War, France and Britain and the rest of Europe were years away from recovery. America's prestige was never higher thanks to men like Tom Morrissey.

The night of the "Tigress in the Egress" was his high-water mark. While his brother Billy remained a bachelor, he had a pretty wife and two sons. There was an Irish Catholic in the White House and anything was possible. One of his sons was so remarkable his name was to appear in that Saturday's newspaper for the very first time. It would not be his last.

Chapter Thirty-one

Now that they had had sex, Julie and Curt began having sex all the time. They'd go to dinner or a movie and come back to her place and have sex. Sometimes they'd plan on going to dinner or a movie and have sex instead and then grab leftovers from her fridge. They'd rent a movie and have sex on the couch and miss almost the whole thing. Some nights Curt would decide to stay home and catch up on some sleep, but they'd talk on the phone and he'd end up coming over and they'd have sex. If they woke up early enough, they'd have sex in the morning before work. They fucked all the time.

"This is what it will be like when we're married," Julie told Marjorie one day on the phone.

Marjorie laughed.

"I don't think you understand married life," she said.

Why couldn't it be like that? In a couple of years, when we're married, we'll both look pretty much the same. When Kevin's born, we'll be even more in love. Babies go to bed early, so we'll have plenty of time for sex. We'll feed him and burp him and bathe him and we'll put him to bed and then put ourselves to bed, why not?

"Every couple goes through this phase," said Marjorie.

Every couple? Julie doubted this was true. She couldn't picture her parents ever going through this phase. Why would she want to?

She had never felt like this before. The nuns had warned her about the dangers of sex, and she had held off until her sophomore year of college. Michael was her first and they would have sex in her dorm room when her roommate Stephanie was at the library or doing a lab. Michael stayed over, once or twice, smushed alongside her in her little twin bed until Stephanie complained and then Julie would make him slink back to his dorm no matter what the weather or time of night.

After college, she still had roommates and she worried about the sounds she and Michael made during sex wafting about the apartment. Aside from the snickers, they had to take turns using the bathroom and it was not the life of a married couple.

With Dutch, sex was always secondary to whichever sports team he was currently on it, be it softball or basketball or flag football. When his softball team made the play-offs, he abstained from sex until after the big game.

"I need to conserve my energy," he said.

"You realize you're not on the Red Sox, right? Your shortstop sells pot for a living," she told him.

Julie stayed with Dutch hoping he'd grow up but he never did. When she caught him cheating, it hurt, but deep down, she knew part of her was relieved. It saved her from being the bad guy. Kevin would never have liked him anyway.

Curt was different. He opened up more post-coital then he did at other times. He'd even talk about his mother sometimes. One story that stuck with Julie happened during a thunderstorm when Curt was a little boy and he was terribly frightened. His mother climbed into his little bunk bed and held him 'til he fell asleep. *That's the kind of mother I want to be with Kevin*, she decided.

After sex, Julie would open up to Curt, too. She wouldn't tell him about Kevin, of course, but she'd talk about work and the Committee and Bob-solete. She told him stories about Cheryl and Meg and about the time her Dad grew a beard but kept finding food in it so he finally gave up and shaved it off.

"I'd say to him, 'What have you got your own private pantry there, Dad?'"

They laughed a lot lying in bed together. Aside from Kevin, the only thing Julie didn't talk about was her mother's alcoholism. She had never discussed it with anyone. Was she afraid of being disloyal? Was she worried about what he'd think about her family? Look at his family, Good Lord, but, still, she didn't say a word.

Julie's dating career began at sixteen and despite all the mistakes she had made after nearly twenty years, her decision to have sex with Curt was a stroke of genius. It wasn't made hastily or drunkenly or as an act of desperation; it was made rationally as the next step in their courtship and this time, it didn't lead to shame or abandonment, it led to intimacy. It drew them closer and confirmed the love she had felt all along. The nuns had never told her that.

Sundays were the best. Saturdays he'd leave early and work a long day but Sunday, they fuck, lounge around, read the paper, have breakfast then fuck again. Eventually, they'd get up and go for a bike ride or a hike or maybe even do something exotic like go to a play. She couldn't remember a happier time in her life than those Sunday mornings and Sunday afternoons.

She began to dread Sunday evenings. Curt would return to his apartment to do his laundry and get some sleep and get ready for the week ahead. She longed for the day when they'd live together and he wouldn't leave. Her daydreams about Kevin became three-person dreams with the three of them playing at the park or the beach or Disneyworld.

One Sunday morning, as she lay with her head on his chest, he surprised her by asking, "My Uncle Billy invited us over for brunch next Sunday at his place. Would that be okay?"

"Sure, sure," she said casually, as though, spending time with a member of his family was commonplace.

"I haven't seen him since the pre-trial hearing," he said, "I think he might have AIDS."

Chapter Thirty-Two

"I wish I knew why the hell she asked us to come down here. I gotta go to work, you know."

"Shh, Tom, don't say 'hell' we're in an elementary school. We don't want her to think we're those kind of people."

"There aren't any kids around."

"There might be."

"I just wish we knew why she asked us to come," he said.

He walked over to the water fountain built for small children and had to lean a long way down to get a drink. His back stiffened and he felt himself starting to get old. His mother had passed a month earlier just a year after his father. Billy was at each funeral, of course, but wisely kept his distance. Tom noticed his brother was still woman-less and overheard someone remark, "he'd have made a good priest."

Lydia walked over to where he was standing.

"She just said the three of us should talk about Tommy, that's all."

"You know she's going to want to double promote him," he said, trying to suppress a sly grin.

She took a drink at the water fountain, not having to lean over nearly as far and with her mouth full, shook her head "no."

"Why are you so opposed to that? He's the smartest kid in the fourth grade."

"Tom, you don't know that."

"Sure, he is and he's tall enough. He'd fit right in."

"The year is halfway done."

"So, he'll spend half a year in fourth grade and half a year in fifth."

"Kids should be with kids their own age. It's not about intelligence. It's about maturity."

"He's plenty mature."

Lydia didn't say anything, but she pursed her lips the way she always did when she disapproved of someone or something. "Let's see what his teacher has to say about it. She's the expert."

The door opened and Miss. Simon poked her head out.

"Mr. and Mrs. Morrisey?" she said.

She looked like she was right out of college with acne on her cheeks not quite hidden with make-up.

"I'm Miss Simon," said Miss Simon.

They shook hands and the three of them sat in tiny chairs with the little desks attached. Lydia held her coat folded over in her lap.

There was a manila folder on the little desk in front of Miss Simon. Tom was forced to sit at an angle with his knees near his chin.

"Sorry about the little desks," she said.

"That's all right," said Lydia, "I'm not much bigger than a fourth-grader."

Miss Simon smiled. Everyone smiled tight-lipped smiles. The small talk was over. There was a moment of two of silence before Miss Simon began what seemed to be a rehearsed spiel. "As you know Tommy is an extremely bright boy."

Tom sniggered and eyed his wife obliquely.

"Were you going to say something?" Miss Simon asked.

Tom folded his arms, "She doesn't think it's a good idea for him to skip a grade but I'm okay with it if that's what you recommend. He can go right into the fifth grade tomorrow as far as I'm concerned."

"I think children should be with children their own age" Lydia said, defending herself for the sake of her child.

"I agree," said Miss Simon. "That's not why I asked you to come in."

He looked over at his wife as if to say, "Do you know anything about this?" but she seemed just as puzzled as he was. "It isn't?" he asked.

"No, I'm afraid not."

Miss Simon looked down and measured her words carefully. "Tommy is a very bright boy but he's also very disruptive in class."

"How so?" asked Lydia.

"He's often yelling out in class and…"

Tom didn't let her finish.

"He's just yelling out the right answer. He was reading at three and a half. Actual words at three and a half, tell her, Lydia."

Lydia didn't tell her anything.

"Mr. Morrissey, I don't doubt that's true, but he's not just yelling out the right answer. He yells out things that frighten the other children."

"What do you mean?"

Mis Simon's voice got softer now the more of an edge crept into to Tom's voice.

"After lunch, the kids have recess, and last Friday, Tommy wouldn't go. He said there were werewolves outside and that if we went outside everybody would die. He frightened the other children, and no one would go outside for recess."

He smirked and Lydia looked him the face and shook her head.

"What? Maybe he knew it was cold out. He's got an imagination what can I tell you."

"He talks a lot about death for a boy his age."

"He's got an imagination, that's all. If you want, I'll tell him to go out for recess. I'll even spank if that's what you want."

"No!" said Miss Simon, "That's not what I'm recommending at all."

It was at this point that Miss Simon reached into her manila folder and pulled out a cream-colored piece of paper with a drawing on it.

"Here's some of Tommy's artwork."

She held up the piece of paper. It was a crude drawing done in black crayon of a man with a gun shooting bullets into a group of people. The bullets were long straight lines almost as big as the gun. Some of the people lay on the ground. There was red blood dripping from them.

"Oh, my," said Lydia.

"You can see the imagery is very disturbing."

Tom shrugged. "He's a boy. Boys like guns."

Miss Simon frowned. "I understand little boys like to play with guns, but all of Tom's artwork is very violent."

She pulled out another cream-colored piece of paper.

"This is Tommy's drawing of the first Thanksgiving."

It was a drawing of a pilgrim with a buckle on his hat holding the head of an Indian. Blood dripped from the Indian's head.

"Look, every TV show is about cowboys and Indians. He knows the Indians are the bad guys, that's all."

"Mr. Morrissey, please don't get defensive."

"I'm not getting defensive, I'm just telling you how it is."

"Tom," Lydia said gently.

"What?"

Is she saying he's the only kid that plays with guns? We played army all the time when we were kids and we didn't turn out so bad. Every kid that isn't a sissy, plays with guns.

Miss Simon pulled out three more drawings from her folder, two on the same cream-colored paper and one on white paper. Each featured guns and bullets and dead people, but these drawings also featured swastikas. Some of the dead people had swastikas on their bodies. One drawing was only partially finished. Lydia and Tom stared at the drawings and tried not to react.

"I had to take these drawings away from Tommy," said Miss Simon, "swastikas are inappropriate for a fourth-grade classroom."

Lydia looked askance at Tom who sighed heavily.

"Look, I was in the war…not Korea," he said. "The Big One. Tommy knows I was in the war and he knows that the Nazis are the bad guys. He's very smart. If you notice the Nazis are the dead ones. The good guys are killing the Nazis."

Miss Simon looked at Lydia and then at Tom.

"That may be Mr. Morrissey, but I can't have drawings of Nazis and swastikas in my classroom. Some of our students are Jewish."

He could feel himself getting angry. His ears felt warm and he knew his face was red. *Was she accusing them of being anti-Semites? Is she Jewish? 'Simon' could be. It was hard to tell. She wasn't one of the obvious ones. I risked my life to kill Nazis. My best friends were killed by Nazis. We did it to save her people and now she's accusing me of being an anti-Semite?* He glowered at her.

"I haven't shown you the worst one," Miss Simon said, only looking at Lydia now.

"How many more do you have in there?" he asked.

"Tom," said Lydia, putting a hand on his forearm.

"This is the last one," she said, and she unveiled it slowly from her manila folder and placed it gently in front of them. It was the same cream-colored paper and this one featured a snowman, a snowman with an unmistakable Hitler moustache and Hitler hair and a large swastika on its big, round base. Two figures, a small one and a large one, were attacking the snowman with axes. In Tom's mind it was a touching scene, a small boy and his Dad fighting evil together, maybe it was the two of them, but Miss Simon didn't see it that way. Lydia gasped and turned away from Tom.

He stood up with his hands out in front of his chest.

"All right, look," he said, "This is all my fault. He always wants a story at bed-time and I tell him a story about the war. It's my frame of reference. I tell him stories based on my experiences in the war. I won't do that anymore."

"Mr. Morrissey, I'm not tell you what you can and can't tell your son, it's just that I can't have pictures of Nazis and Hitler in my classroom. Tommy's was the only winter drawing I couldn't hang."

She gestured to the other drawings on the wall.

"Hey, point made. I'll tell him to knock it off. I'll make sure he doesn't do it again. Believe me, I'll make sure of it."

"Mr. Morrissey, please sit down."

"Tom, sit down."

He slunk back into his little chair. No one spoke for a moment, then Miss Simon began slowly with a slight tremor in her voice, "There is a psychiatrist who works for the school district who I'd like to examine Tommy."

Lydia opened her mouth in surprise. Tom jumped to his feet, "No, sir," he yelled, "No, siree!"

Lydia stood up and put a hand on his arm trying to calm him.

Miss Simon was standing now too, "Mr. Morrissey, the psychiatrist would just spend a few minutes talking to Tommy."

"No, no, no," he yelled, jabbing his index finger at her before he turned and walked out the door, "There is nothing wrong with my son."

Chapter Thirty-Three

When I told him my name, the male nurse kind of bristled. I'm used to funny looks, but this was very nearly a "bristle." What's his problem?

"Come with me," he said, "He's been asking for you."

"Asking for me?"

"Calling out your name, murmuring it over and over, that sort of thing."

I never would have pegged this guy as a male nurse. He looked disinterested for one thing and even a little mean. There was something about the energy he gave off, a kind of underlying aggressiveness. He seemed more like a cop than a nurse. Of course, my name doesn't match my appearance so maybe we're even somehow.

I hate hospitals, nothing unique about that I know, but I can't even visit a friend who's just given birth without feeling my stomach tense up and my legs wobble and today, I wasn't here for a birth.

The cop nurse brought me into his room. He gestured with his head towards the bed as if to say, "There he is. Tough shit."

"Oh God," I thought. It was much worse than I thought it would be. I don't know what I was expecting but I didn't think it would be this bad. He was skeletal. I don't know what other word to use. This big, strong formidable guy who in his eighties still evoked fear in his son was at ninety, a shrunken, gray carcass. Nearly completely hairless save for a few wisps, with pools of moisture around his closed eyes, he probably weighed half of what he weighed as a young man. I've seen the pictures. I don't know what I was expecting but one look at him and I knew one thing for certain. I was not getting married tomorrow.

"He's dying, isn't he?"

"Uh-huh," the male nurse said without hesitation.

He was the worst nurse I'd ever seen. I wondered if there had been some sort of mix-up and his high school guidance counselor was looking at the wrong file when he was doling out career advice. Maybe across town was there an overly sensitive, compassionate cop interrogating a hardened criminal and getting nowhere.

I hadn't been to see him since he went from the nursing home to the hospital. I was studying my ass off for the bar exam and then I had to focus on my wedding. There are plans you have to make and weight you have to lose and friends you have to see and bachelorette parties you have to go to and wear a penis hat one last time. It had been six maybe seven weeks since I had last seen him, and in that time, he had gone from "old" to "dying."

I sat down and covered my face with my hands and tried to figure out what to do next. I thought about crying and then decided against it. Instead, I decided to postpone my wedding. There was no other way.

I opened my eyes and took out my cell phone and texted David telling him to call me. That was protocol; I always had to text first in case he was with a client. I noticed the nurse was gone, back walking his beat presumably.

David called a minute later, and I answered right away.

"Hey…listen, I have some bad news…he's dying…thanks, so, we can't get married tomorrow…I know, I know but he's dying…I realize that, but I can't go to my wedding and then go to Paris for ten days like nothing's happening…"

He was pushing back. He wanted to marry me as soon as possible. Who can blame him? I wanted to marry him, too, but I had a tragedy on my hands and tragedies take precedence.

"David, look, I'm the only person in the world he loves and I'm the only person in the world who loves him…I can't let him die all alone…my Dad hates him and my mother dislikes him…he has no one…I couldn't enjoy my wedding or enjoy my honeymoon knowing he's like this…we'll just postpone it two weeks…our friends can come back, our good friends anyway…It's November, what else have they got to do?…I bet the hall will still be available…"

He was softening, I knew he would. The last thing he was expecting was a call from me postponing the wedding and I didn't blame him for being upset but he loves me after all, and I knew I could wear him down and get him to see things my way.

"If you tell Barry you'll work the next two weeks and then take the two weeks after that…Barry loves you, he'll let you do that…I bet he'd rather have you work these two weeks anyway and now you'll be gone over Thanksgiving when work is slow…then we can have Thanksgiving in Paris…I know that's not a thing but it could be…"

When he laughed, I knew the worst was over. He knew he didn't want me going on our honeymoon filled with regret, and if you're married for fifty or sixty years what's two weeks?

"I know it's a pain in the ass but he's dying, what can I tell you?...it's literally a matter of life and death…all right, I'll call the caterer…how 'bout this?, I'll call my friends and you call your friends, it's just easier that way…I've got all my friends' numbers and you've got yours…"

Luckily, it was a small wedding, thirty-five, maybe forty people. I don't like being the center of attention. My mother does, but I don't.

"We'll say two weeks from tomorrow…oh, right, all right, I'll call the airlines, too…thanks for being so understanding…we'll have a great story to tell our grandchildren…maybe they'll postpone their weddings when we're on our deathbeds…just a joke…okay, love you, bye."

I hung up the phone and noticed my grandfather's drippy eyes were now open and staring at me.

"I'm dying?" he said.

Chapter Thirty-Four

Julie met Uncle Billy at the pre-trial hearing, and she could tell from the way he dressed that he was rich, but she didn't realize how rich. As Curt drove from her apartment to Uncle Billy's, the houses kept getting nicer and the yards more expansive until finally they got to the top of a hill to a gargantuan white colonial resting on a sprawling manicured lawn. It was as though a mini-replica of the White House had been plunked down in suburban Boston.

"You're kidding, right?" she said, as he pulled up out front.

Curt chuckled.

It has pillars. His house has fuckin' pillars.

"It's pretty nice," said Curt.

"Nice? This is the kind of house that people give names to like "Pemberly" or "Wetherfield," she said, pronouncing the names with an affected British accent.

It began to drizzle as they trekked up the brick walkway to where Uncle Billy stood waiting in the open doorway.

"Come in, come in," he said thrusting a bony hand at each of them.

His turquoise shirt was oversized and the top three buttons left undone. He wore Jordache jeans, normally ridiculous on a man his age, but somehow appropriate on him. His feet were clad in velvet slippers.

"Do you mind taking your shoes off?" he asked then winked for no apparent reason.

"You have a lovely home," said Julie, unzipping her slippers.

"Thank you, would you like a tour?"

He led them up the front staircase. *Is this Italian marble? Is it rude to ask?* The first room, a guest bedroom, was larger than her living room/kitchen combo with a high ceiling unlike the one in her apartment that she could touch if she stood on her tiptoes. A queen-sized bed rested underneath some kind of avant-garde painting. *Were those supposed to be clouds or two naked bodies?* She couldn't tell. She hated abstract art, preferring definitive answers.

"I love your artwork," she said.

Next, they stood at the doorway of his office, two more guest rooms and then an exercise room with a stationary bike and one of those Nordic track machines they advertise at two in the morning. Julie alternated compliments back and forth between "beautiful" and "gorgeous." Curt had apparently been here before because he said nothing.

"Here's the master bedroom," said Billy and this time, all three entered the room.

There was a king-sized four poster in the center. *My whole family could sleep in this thing. Comfortably.* There was a blank space on the wall where a painting had been. On either side were two large walk-in closets, one stuffed with clothes, the other, suspiciously empty with unused wooden hangers clinging to a bar. *Someone left in a hurry.*

Uncle Billy gestured to two French doors leading to a balcony and a view of the Blue Hills. *It must be something during foliage season.* She peered out the windows to a tennis court below. *He has his own tennis court.*

"You have your own tennis court?"

Curt chuckled.

"Oh, do you play?"

"A little," she said. *It must be nice to play in your own backyard and not have to wait in line to play on a city court with a metal net.*

"She's quite good," said Curt, taking her word for it.

"We'll have to play some time," he said giving her another wink. He was a winker.

The master bath had a Jacuzzi tub and his and her sinks. *His and his sinks.*

"This bathroom is the size of my bedroom," said Julie.

Uncle Billy laughed. Sometimes Julie got laughs when she wasn't trying to. They followed him down a back staircase to the kitchen. *His refrigerator could fit four dead bodies standing up if you removed the shelves.* He had a microwave and a rotisserie and an espresso maker on the counter. He had set up the regular coffee maker and a waffle maker on the island in the center of the room. *He had pillars and a tennis court and a kitchen with an island.*

"Holy mackerel," said Julie as she looked around. "Holy Fuck" would have been rude.

"Do you cook?" he asked.

"No, but I would if I had a kitchen like this."

Uncle Billy laughed again. She was doing quite well without meaning to.

"I thought we'd have waffles," he said.

"Great," said Julie and Curt nearly in unison.

"Your home is truly spectacular," she said.

"Thank you," he said, pouring waffle goop into the waffle maker, "It's a bit much for one person, I suppose."

He poured them each a coffee and a juice.

"I miss your mother," he said, and Curt nodded. "She and I were quite close once upon a time until your father put the kibosh on that."

He fished a waffle out of the maker onto a plate and then poured in more goop.

"Curt's Dad stopped speaking to me years ago. One of those silly family things."

What am I supposed to say to that?

"Where does your family live, Julie?"

"New Jersey."

"Nice, just far enough away," he winked and sipped coffee from his tea cup.

The rain began to fall in sheets now and they chatted about the weather 'til the waffles were ready. They moved to the dining room and sat at the corner of a table that could accommodate twelve. He had a glass bowl filled with an assortment of fruit and there was another blank space on the wall missing its painting.

"How's your health Uncle Billy?"

"I'm all right at the moment. Phillip left, soon after I got sick. Some people just can't handle it."

They nodded sympathetically.

"This all goes to you, you know," he said, looking directly at Curt.

Julie stopped chewing her waffle. *This? What does he mean by "this"? This house? Curt is going to live in this fuckin' house? So if we get married, I'll live in this fuckin' house? Kevin will live in this fuckin' house? Holy fuck.*

Curt shook his head.

"I don't want it, Uncle Billy."

What? I think what he means is, "I'd would love it. Thank you, Uncle Billy. Thank you very much." This is the most beautiful house I've ever seen. Who wouldn't want to live here? If we lived here, we wouldn't have to be one of those couples who lived in an apartment for years and scrimped and saved and eventually bought a tiny house in a lousy neighborhood. We wouldn't have to be one of those couples she saw every week who dreamed of a nice home in a nice neighborhood and came in asking for a loan they would never get.

"Curt, your mother and I used to talk about this. Everything was supposed to go to you and your brother. Now it's just you."

Curt shook his head and Julie realized she shouldn't be here for this.

"Excuse me," she said, and she popped into the bathroom off the kitchen and closed the door but not all the way. If they lived here, Kevin could go to a good school in a safe neighborhood. They could put a swing set in the backyard and they wouldn't have to go to the park in her neighborhood where bums slept on benches. If they lived here, she could teach him tennis in their own backyard.

"I like to make my own way in life. That's why I went to Northeastern instead of Holy Cross or BC. So I could pay for it myself."

He was ruining everything, the stubborn little prick.

Uncle Billy said something she couldn't quite hear and then the pangs of guilt began. *I'm a horrible person. I'm rooting for Uncle Billy's death. He's the sweetest man in the world and I'm rooting for him to die so I can live in his house.* She knew that as much as she tried to make it about Kevin and how she was thinking of him she knew the truth. *I want this beautiful house. I am an awful, awful person.*

She flushed the unused toilet. She had to pretend she had been peeing and couldn't take too much time otherwise, they'd think she'd been up to something more elaborate. She washed her hands without looking at herself in the mirror.

On her way back to the table she heard Uncle Billy say with great gravity, "Don't be stubborn like your father, Curt. You'll end up like him, alone and bitter and full of hate."

Chapter Thirty-Five

Tom was having a few Christmas cookies when the boys began fighting. Lydia was out so it was safe for him to sneak a few cookies with his coffee and morning paper. He heard the ruckus from the living room and with great reluctance put his paper and his half-eaten snowman down.

"Stop it, stop it" he yelled as his two boys fought over a Tonka truck. Though Tom hadn't witnessed the scene it was obvious that Curt was playing with the truck and Tommy wrestled it away.

"Tommy, let go of the-" but it was too late.

Tommy had not only pulled the sturdy, metal truck from the younger boy's hand but he had bashed him over the head with it. Tom was stunned by the violence. Curt's eyes filled with tears and his mouth hung open, but no sound came out. The boy wasn't seriously hurt but he could have been. A Tonka truck was a formidable weapon.

Curt idolized Tommy and unlike all the other little brothers in the world he loathed seeing his older brother punished. Curt would take his lumps rather than get his brother in trouble, Tom knew it and so did Lydia. Curt would cry along with Tommy when Tom spanked Tommy and would beg his father to stop. Curt was too young to understand that Tom hated spanking Tommy, but the boy needed to be punished. Tommy needed to learn that he wasn't allowed to hurt his brother or kick his mother as he did that day in the supermarket, leaving Lydia with a good size welt on her shin. Tom made him regret it. Or did he?

Lydia spoiled him; that was the problem. Tommy wouldn't eat foods he didn't like, carrots or squash or spinach and she didn't force him.

"It's all right, Tom, he doesn't have to."

Growing up, Tom and Billy had to eat everything on their plate. Or else. Wasting food was a sin and yet, she permitted it.

That wasn't all. When Tommy was little, he'd climb into bed with his parents in the middle of the night and Tom allowed it, but when the boy turned five or six, Tom began shooing him back to his own bed. Soon after that, Tom began to wake up in the morning and discover Lydia had spent the night in Tommy's bunk bed.

"Tommy's sensitive" was her defense when Tom complained. He knew she kept half the bad things Tommy did from him. He could tell by the look on her face when he came most nights that the boy had misbehaved either at school or at home and she'd pretend everything was fine when he knew it wasn't. She was covering for him. Tommy would come to a bad end if something wasn't done and done soon.

How could two boys be so different? Curt never said a peep, half the time you didn't even know he was in the house. Tom would go look for him sometimes, wondering where he was, and find him playing with his trains or his army men quietly in his room. His report cards described him as a "delight" and "a pleasure to have in the classroom." His kindergarten teacher called him "delicious."

Tom got down on all fours and pulled the boys apart. While Curt cried and pretended not to cry, Tom picked up Tommy and pried the truck from his hand and dropped it to the floor. He carried his thrashing son up the stairs with the bannister draped in tinsel in preparation for Christmas.

As the boy's arms flailed Tom started to lose his grip but held on just long enough to deposit him on his bed. The boy rolled off the bed and onto the floor and he looked up at his father with tears and rage. Tom glared back at him, refusing to be intimated. In that moment while they stared each other down, he couldn't help but notice how handsome his son was. Such a handsome young boy, and smart, yet, he was like a wild colt who needed to be tamed.

"Stay here 'til I say you can come out" said Tom and he closed the door behind him. He decided not to spank the boy this time, nor whip him with his belt, it didn't seem to do any good. This called for more drastic action. No son of his was going to be wild or spoiled and an idea came to Tom as he descended the stairs.

It was a wicked idea and it coursed through his brain as he sat holding a paper towel filled with ice to his younger boy's head. Curt didn't cry and didn't speak. Tom sat silently as well, weighing his scheme for meting out justice. *Do I dare?*

Lydia was off doing some last-minute shopping, with Christmas less than a week away. It was his day off and Tommy's school was closed for the holiday. He knew that Lydia wouldn't have gone along with his scheme, but she wasn't home. She hadn't witnessed Tommy hit Curt with the truck, but he had. It was violent and cruel and willful, and the boy needed to be punished. Tom set Curt down and dropped the ice from the paper towel into the sink.

He got up and walked to the living room and peered out the tiny window at the top of the front door. One or two patches of snow were all that were left from a storm earlier that week. He looked past the unpainted backside of the wooden Santa on the lawn and at the gray, dented trash barrels, still full, near the street.

He remembered the fights he used to have as a boy with his brother Billy. *We were only a year apart. Besides, I never seriously hurt him, and I never hit him in the head with a metal truck.*

Tom looked at the Christmas tree. The living room always looked so tiny this time of year with the furniture bunched together to make room for the tree. It was the twentieth and Tom pictured the room filled with presents, presents that were hidden until the night before. They'd return home after midnight mass and the boys would sleep, he and Lydia would lay the gifts out. They'd be up to nearly three, the longest but happiest night of the year.

Tom and Lydia had finished shopping for the boys and hid their presents in the basement locking the door.

"The basement's flooded, you can't go down there" she had told them, hiding the key.

The boys didn't catch on that the basement "flooded" every year at this time, "flooded with presents" in Lydia's words. Tom looked out the tiny front door window, biding his time and convincing himself that his idea was the right thing to do. She wouldn't like it, but it would be done before she got home.

He stood there, just stood there for over an hour. Curt played on the floor nearby with any toy he liked in his brother's absence and barely made a sound. Tom weighed the pros and cons of the wicked idea that he couldn't get out of his head. There was a financial aspect, there always was, and both he and Lydia, hated to waste money. Yet, money wasn't everything, and Tom knew what the Good Book said about it. He was going to be brave and stamp out the evil even if it meant facing Lydia.

He heard the sound of the truck in the distance. He walked purposefully up the stairs, his legs pumping military style. "Tommy," he said outside of the closed bedroom door, "I want you to go to the window and look out into the front yard."

Tom walked back down the stairs and phase one was complete. He entered the kitchen and retrieved the basement key from above the door frame. He opened the basement door and closed it behind him, a minute later, he emerged carrying a shiny new bike. He set it down on the kitchen floor and relocked the basement. Curt, on his knees playing, looked at his father from the living room and wondered why he was holding a new bike.

Tom picked the bike up and slipped out the backdoor. He held it high as he walked down the driveway with it and stood on his lawn. He set the bike down and looked up toward Tommy's room and waved. He stood waiting for the truck. *I should have put my coat on.*

After a few minutes, the garbage truck pulled up in front of the house and man hopped off the side. The driver stopped and came around the front to help his partner. Tom picked up the bike and walked to the back of the truck and its bone crushing opening.

"Hey," the garbage man yelled over the din of the truck, but it was too late. Tom had heaved the bike into the truck and the truck had bit down on it and swallowed it up.

"That was a brand, new bike" the garbage man yelped. "Jesus, Mister, I would have taken it home for my kid."

Tom turned and began walking back to the house.

"You shouldn't have done that," the man yelled again.

He ignored him. He didn't take orders from garbage men. He looked up at the bedroom window and saw his handsome eight-year-old son's face pressed against the glass.

Chapter Thirty-Six

My Dad hated his Dad. I'm not sure if "hate" is the right word, it might not be strong enough. It was one of those Irish grudges that once begun never wavered. If anything, it blossomed and hardened.

You would think since my Dad hated his Dad that we would never see him, and I would grow up without knowing my grandfather, but it wasn't that way at all. My Dad was Irish and Catholic and very "old world," and there were things expected of you and my Dad did them. My Dad always honored his obligations as he perceived them, so we had my grandfather over every Thanksgiving, Christmas and Easter. He drove himself over while he could and when he couldn't any longer, we went and got him. He'd come for dinner and my Dad and he would barely speak. My Dad honored his obligations but he didn't have to like it.

On these occasions, my mother would be cheerful and pleasant but the two of them didn't have much to chat about. Mostly, my grandfather focused on me. He always brought me little gifts or candy even on Thanksgiving. He'd sit next to me and cut my meat and I'd tell him about my friends and teachers and activities. I wasn't sure he could hear me half the time, but he always pretended to be interested. We'd go to church and I'd hold his hand in the parking lot.

Although my Dad only saw his Dad thrice a year my mother would bring me over on the sly. She'd have me sing a song for him from the school play or dance my ballet steps or play my trumpet. (I played for ten weeks) He'd sit in his living room grinning from ear to ear. Sometimes he'd cry a little bit.

Later on, when I'd mention to my Dad that I saw Grandpa, he'd heave a heavy sigh and glare over at my mother.

"He's nice to her," she'd say. "He's an old man with nothing. Let him see his granddaughter from time to time."

And my Dad would say nothing back and the fight would be over.

On the way home from Grandpa's one day, my Mom said, "You don't need to tell your Dad that we visited Grandpa." "Are we lying to Daddy?"

"No, Sweetie, I never want you to lie. Remember how we talked about always telling the truth?"

"What if Daddy asks me?"

"If your Daddy asks, 'Did you visit your Grandpa today?' say 'yes.' Otherwise, don't bring it up. We don't need to tell Daddy everything. Not telling isn't lying, do you see?"

"No," I said.

She puffed out her cheeks, let some air out and strummed her fingers on the steering wheel.

"Earlier today, I took a poop. Now do you think Dad wants to hear about that?"

"He might."

"He doesn't. So, I'm not going to mention it to Daddy. Not everyone wants to hear about every facet of your life. Do you understand?"

I didn't understand but I didn't want to hear my Dad's heavy sigh and I didn't want my Dad mad at my Mom, so I learned to keep my mouth shut and I learned that some secrets were okay. My grandfather and I were about to keep a big one from my Mom and Dad.

Chapter Thirty-Seven

The two of them thanked Uncle Billy for the waffles and such and got into Curt's car. The rain had stopped but a gray gloom still hung about. For once, he wasn't the only quiet one as she stared out the passenger side window through three stop signs and five stop lights.

"Are you mad at me?" he asked.

"No."

The silence continued for three more lights.

"Are you mad that I told him I didn't want his house?"

She turned and looked at his face. This was a trap and she wasn't about to fall into it. They'd only been together for four months and if she said, "yes" it would appear she was after his money and was presuming commitment and marriage and all the things that would chase him and any other guy away. *Oh no, you don't.*

"I'm upset because I don't want your Uncle Billy to die."

"I don't want him to die either," he said, staring back at her.

A car behind them beeped and he drove on.

"He's a very sweet man," she said. She was on the verge of tears.

"He is," said Curt. He seemed amused that she was upset.

"How did he get so rich?" she said sharply.

They hadn't really fought before, and he was baffled by her tone. They were like two boxers feeling each other out in the early rounds.

"Um, well, my grandfather owned a lumberyard and he turned it over to Uncle Billy and he started making tables and cabinets and things and eventually, it became a successful furniture business. And now he owns four furniture stores, three in Massachusetts and one in New Hampshire."

She had heard of Morrissey Furniture and seen their trucks but hadn't associated them with Curt before. Morrissey is a fairly common Irish name in a city filled with Irish names. There was even a Morrissey Boulevard that snaked its way through Dorchester and there was a girl behind her in Catholic School named Jane Morrissey. How was she supposed to know he was related to the Furniture Morrissey?

"I'm mad because you're always keeping things from me."

"I thought you said you weren't mad?"

"Well, I am," she said. "You're always keeping things from me."

"Like what?"

She could see the muscles in his jaws tense.

"You didn't tell me how your Mom died or about your brother."

"Okay, but we talked about that."

"And I told you I insisted on total honesty and you didn't tell me about your uncle and about his furniture business."

He glanced over at her and let out an exasperated sigh.

"I didn't tell you about my uncle because it has nothing to do with me. His money and his furniture store are his. That's completely separate from me."

Why didn't he think about the future? Why didn't he look down the road and think about the two of them being married and where they'd live? Why didn't he think about Kevin and think about all the things he'd need? He was so selfish. She lapsed into another prolonged silence.

"I told Uncle Billy that I just want him to get better and I don't want to think about anything else."

"I want him to get better, too."

She wanted him to get better. She wanted him to be completely cured and live a long life. She didn't want to live in a house that made her feel like an awful person. Suppose he did get better, all better? Maybe after she and Curt got married, they could move in with him. He said he was lonely. He didn't exactly say that but he did say the house was too big for one person. What if she and Curt and Kevin and Uncle Billy all lived there together?

"How come I've never seen your apartment?" she said.

"My apartment?" he said.

His eyebrows were raised, and he seemed astonished.

"Why do you want to see my apartment?"

"Because we've been together for four months and I haven't seen it. What are you hiding?"

"What am I hiding?"

The rain started again, and he flicked on his wipers.

"I'm not hiding anything. I just thought it was easier for you if I picked you up at your place. If you want, you can come over tomorrow night?"

"Why not show me your place now?"

"Because we're almost at your place for one thing and for another thing, I'll have to clean it first."

"Clean it?"

"Yes, I clean houses and offices all day. Sometimes when I get home, I don't feel like cleaning. I'll clean it up and then you can come over tomorrow night.

He turned onto her street.

"Of course, if you do come over tomorrow night you can't stay over."

"Why not?"

"Because how are you going to get to work? You'd have to bring a change of clothes and your hair dryer and your make-up and it would take you forty-five minutes at least to get to work from my place."

He parked in front of her place.

"How 'bout Friday?"

"Okay," he said, "Friday night, we'll rent a movie and get some take-out and you can see my place."

"Good."

Chapter Thirty-Eight

Tom crept into the kitchen and turned on the light above the stove, giving himself just enough light to move around. He pulled the step stool out from behind the garbage can and set it down gently. He hopped up on it then reached for the bottle of scotch in the top shelf behind the pancake mix. He moved carefully and deliberately not wanting to wake anyone, especially Lydia. The slightest sound at night was enough to make her eyes pop open and her head jolt up.

He took a glass from the cabinet and poured himself a tall one. He never had more than one but that one was becoming taller and taller. A few years ago, it was a single shot, lately, they were triples maybe even quadruples. After he poured, he always put the bottle back behind the pancake mix and moved the step stool to its home behind the garbage can.

When he finished off a bottle, he'd slip outside and put it in one of the barrels. The next day, he'd sneak the new one in the house when Lydia was at the grocery store or giving Curt a bath. She knew he had a bottle but assumed the same one lasted most of the year. It had become a bottle a week.

When Tom didn't drift off to sleep right away, he was in trouble. Sometimes he worried about his finances and the stress of supporting a wife and kids. His brother Billy had opened a furniture store in Natick that seemed to be thriving. Tom even saw an ad for it in the Boston Globe one day and he canceled his subscription the next.

Most nights that he lay awake; more often than not, he worried about Tommy. The boy was acting up more and more both at school and at home. One weekend, Lydia went away to take care of her sister who was ill and now living in Philadelphia. Tommy had snuck into their bedroom and was playing with Tom's medals and his German Luger. Tom caught him and gave him what for. The gun wasn't loaded, but what if it had been? *What's going to become of that boy?*

When he lay awake thinking of Tommy, thoughts of the war would start to seep in, and he couldn't push them away with Hail Marys. On these nights, he'd tiptoe downstairs and drink his tall scotch. That would take care of things and he'd return to bed and fall asleep almost immediately. It wasn't a restful sleep, though, and he'd wake feeling lousy and a little groggy.

He had always prided himself on his self-control. He was pretty sure that his uncle Brendan had died of cirrhosis of the liver, "the Irish disease" his mother called it and Tom always wondered if it was the Great War that drove him to drink. Tom rarely drank in front of Lydia. He didn't come home and mix one. He didn't have a beer or wine with dinner, only the occasional high ball at a party and even then, just one.

"I've never seen you drunk," Lydia would tell him from time to time.

He once had a boss who drank. A cocky little worm who'd go out at lunch and get soused and come back chewing breath mints thinking no one was wise to him. Tom could have ratted him out but didn't and the old lush got canned anyway after getting belligerent with a customer. *Good riddance you old fool.*

Some nights Tom woke after a nightmare. He'd see Moretti's bloody corpse or Leckie without his head. Some nights he couldn't shake the image of the German boy he strangled to death. *He murdered Moretti. He had it coming. It was him or me.* Tom knew he was in the right but the boy's face appeared nonetheless.

He'd lie awake and think about Moretti and Leckie and Sims and wonder what would have become of them. Moretti would have gone back to New York and married his girl and taken over his father's mechanic shop. Tom would probably never see him except at an army reunion.

Leckie had plans for law school. He probably would have become some kind of big shot, maybe even entered politics. Voters like a witty guy on the stump. Sims was a loser who never would have amounted to much.

Tom took a sip from his glass and sat at the table. Tonight, for some reason, he thought about Plesac. Plesac was the corporal from Ohio who blew his own big toe off with his M1 before an upcoming battle and got himself out of the rest of the war.

Tom heard the shot, coming from the dark, not fifty feet away. He saw Plesac moments later, drunk and crying, his foot a bloody mess. He claimed it was an accident and Tom was naïve enough to believe him until Moretti set him straight.

"That was no fuckin' accident."

"Why would he do that?" asked Tom.

"Better to lose your big toe than your fuckin' head," said Moretti, "The yellow cocksucker."

After Plesac shot himself, Tom and another man helped him to the medic, each putting one of Plesac's arms around their shoulders. He blubbered and hobbled and babbled drunken nonsense and Tom had felt sorry for him. It wasn't until the next day after Moretti told him the real score that Tom became angry both at Plesac and at himself for not catching on.

Plesac sickened Tom for he was a coward who was a disgrace to his family and his country. He hadn't thought about Plesac in years and didn't know why he was thinking about him now but Plesac still sickened him. Tom grew angry, sitting alone in his kitchen at 2 a.m. when it occurred to him that Plesac is probably still alive while Moretti and Leckie and Sims are dead. *That no good bastard.*

Tom got up suddenly from the table and dumped his scotch down the sink. He moved the step stool back over from behind the garbage can and got on and took down the bottle. It poured the rest down the drain. He made a promise to himself that he would never drink again, and he kept that promise for more than twenty years until Tommy killed Lydia.

Chapter Thirty-Nine

"You're such a big girl, going off to sleep away camp."

I was terrified. I sat in the backseat while my mother drove. My Dad had to work, he always had to work. "That's the price you pay when you own your own business," he said, millions of times.

"I didn't go away until college unless you count a Girl Scout sleepover or two but those were only for one night. A whole week without your Mom and Dad, boy, are you going to miss us."

I had been tricked into going to sleepaway camp. It started because my friend Emily was going away to camp, and she wanted a friend to go with her and because Emily's Mom and my Mom got to talking, I ended up being drafted.

"You'll swim every day. You love to swim. And they have water-skiing and archery and arts and crafts. You and Emily will have a great time. I wish I could go. I've never been water-skiing my whole life and I'm in my mid-twenties."

That was one of her jokes. My Mom joked a lot about being in her mid-twenties now that she was closing in on fifty.

The reality was she had a conference to go to in Dallas so she couldn't drop me off at day camp and pick me up every day like she usually does. So, when Emily broke her leg on her stupid skateboard, and I said I didn't want to go to camp alone it was too late. It was all arranged. They'd paid their money and my Mom was going to be away that week anyway and my Dad was, of course, working, so I was going.

"Jello, you're going to have the time of your life."

She called me "Jello" whenever I was nervous and then she would imitate my trembling. She usually could make me laugh, but not today, not when I had been tricked into going to summer camp all alone.

We crossed the New Hampshire border.

"New Hampshire," said my mother reading the sign, "'Live Free or Die.' I guess those are our only options."

Was that supposed to make me feel better?

After another half an hour or so when we were officially in the middle of nowhere, we saw signs for Camp Abenaki. We followed a line of cars heading to where we were heading, and we turned down a long dirt road. Some college students were at the end, smiling and waving and directing us where to park. We pulled up to a painted log and parked. Each car had a kid or two, my age or older, inside.

I took my Mom's hand as I had always done in parking lots until I noticed none of the other kids were holding their Mom or Dad's hands and I let go. Too late. I'd already been seen and judged. I noticed a heavy blonde-haired girl, a year or two older, scowling at me. I had shown weakness which is something you never want to do in front of a wild animal or other children.

We went to sign in and a friendly college student asked me my name and my mother told her.

"Oh, she's in Cabin Hiawatha right down here," she said, pointing to a map. All the cabins had Native American names like Samoset and Sacagawea.

"Oh," she added, "And I love her name."

The college student actually seemed nice and I would have felt better if I hadn't noticed the heavy girl in line behind me, glaring at me and chewing gum out of the side of her mouth the way grown-ups smoke cigarettes.

We found Cabin Hiawatha and a teenager named Rose introduced herself as our cabin leader. She had a tattoo of a hawk on her shoulder and one of a shark, just above her ankle. My Mom flinched a little meeting Rose hoping I wouldn't notice. Rose didn't smile and didn't seem as nice as the college student who signed me in.

My Mom put my duffel bag on my bunk.

"Well, this is it."

She smiled cheerfully but I could see she was crying a little as she kissed me good-bye.

"You're going to have so much fun."

"Is that why you're crying?" I should have asked but didn't.

As my Mom left, the fat, scowling girl entered and picked out a bunk for herself. I thought she was around twelve but our cabin only housed girls nine or ten. She looked at me disapprovingly again and I avoided eye contact. *What did I do to her?*

Rose had all of us sit outside on the ground "Indian-style" and tell the group our names. Rose asked each girl if she had a nickname. A girl named Heidi liked to be called "Pat" because her last name was Patterson. The fat scowler's name was Michelle and she had a thick Boston accent but no nickname. When Rose got to me, I told her my name was "Kay" and Michelle said, "I've got the perfect nickname for her…chink." A couple of the girls laughed, and Rose said, "Settle down." I'd been at sleepaway camp for ten minutes and already been subjected to a racial epithet for which my assailant received the mildest of rebukes. A week seemed like a ten-year sentence.

Rose asked us to raise our hands if we knew how to swim. I raised my hand and so did everybody else.

"That's good," said Rose, "We're going to go to the lake and take the swim test to see if you're a guppy or a minnow. Minnows can swim past the dock, guppies have to stay inside the dock."

I was a good swimmer and I liked to swim but when we got to the lake something occurred to me. I liked to swim in pools. Pools were clear and you could see to the bottom. The lake was dark and you couldn't see for more than a few feet below the surface. I saw a couple of fish wriggle by. What else was in there? What if there were snapping turtles or crabs? What if a snapping turtle dragged me to the bottom and held me down there and nobody could see me and I drown?

We had to line up on the dock and we were instructed to swim one by one to the other side. Michelle went first and sputtered and flailed and made it to the other side.

"You're a minnow," the lifeguard said, and she beamed. A few other girls went and then it was my turn. I didn't want to jump into the dark, scary lake.

"I don't want to," I said softly.

"We just want to see if you're a guppy or a minnow," said Rose.

"What if I sink to the bottom?"

"You won't sink."

"Sink Chink," yelled Michelle and she and the other girls began chanting, "Sink Chink, Sink Chink, Sink Chink."

"Stop it," said Rose and the chant died out a minute or so later.

"Jump in," she said to me as harshly as she had told the other girls to stop with the racial slurs.

"I don't want to," I said. As I started to say something else, a male lifeguard grabbed me around the middle and tossed me in. For a second, I was under the dark water and I was terrified. I raced to the light at the top and popped my head above the surface. I had swallowed some water and began to choke and swim at the same time.

"Sink Chink" yelled Michelle and the chanting began again. I swam as fast as I could to the other side and upon reaching the dock, another male lifeguard plucked me out.

"You are definitely a minnow," he said with a smile. I looked back at him without one.

"I want to go home," I said.

I started to cry.

"I want to go home."

"But you're a minnow" said Rose, bending down to be at eye level.

"I want to go home" I said again, wiping away tears as the disgusting lake water dripping off of me. Michelle stood nearby watching us with a sly smile on her face.

"You'll feel better in a little while," said Rose.

I stayed out of the water while the other kids swam then we went back to our cabin and changed. No one spoke to me on the way back to the cabin or on the way to the cafeteria. I got a tray and got in line and a lady plunked some of their version of mac and cheese on my plate.

"Do you want some bug juice?" a teenager asked.

"No, thank you."

"It's really fruit punch."

"No, thanks."

I sat as far away from Michelle as possible, hiding near some bickering teenage boys who didn't seem to notice me. I'd never been homesick before, but I was now. I thought about what I'd be doing if I were home. I'd probably be playing alone in my room but for some reason, I pictured myself playing mini-golf with my Mom and Dad. We'd only done in once before, but for some reason I'd thought if I were home, we'd be doing it again right now. I imagined us finishing the game and getting an ice cream, the soft serve kind, and I'd get a mix of vanilla and chocolate like I always do. *Why can't I be doing that right now?*

After dinner, there was an assembly and Chief Ron, replete with a headdress, spoke to the entire camp. He called us "braves and squaws" and tried to teach us the camp song. I didn't feel like singing. Then, Rose gave us each a smooth wooden stick about the size of a pencil and one marshmallow. Each cabin took turns standing near the fire and toasting our marshmallows. Michelle held hers too long near the flame and it dropped off the stick onto the sand. She cursed and demanded another one, but Rose said she didn't have any more.

After that the counselors put on a skit where each one had an Indian name like "Fighting Head-Cold" and "Running Gag." The kids laughed and cheered, especially for their own counselors. Rose played the part of "Sitting

Pretty" and two of the "warriors" vied for her affections. Nothing she said was particularly funny, and as the skit was coming to an end I leaned back and felt something in my pants. I reached back to find Michelle's black, squishy marshmallow between my underwear and my shorts. I looked back at her, but she stared straight ahead as though nothing had happened.

After we sang the camp song one more time we walked back to our cabins and got ready for lights out. I tried washing the marshmallow off my underwear and my shorts, but it was sticky and some of it wouldn't come off. I changed my underwear in a bathroom stall and when I got back to my bunk, I found a folded over note on my pillow. I opened it up. It said, "Sink Chink."

Chapter Forty

"Do you want a comedy?" Julie asked.

"I don't care," said Curt.

It was early August, three weeks before the bank robbery or as Julie called it, "The Day We Were All Almost Killed." It was less than a month after she accidentally said, "I love you" or as she told it to Marjorie and only Marjorie, "That Time I Almost Ruined Everything."

With rain predicted the next day, the video store was packed on a Friday night. It was a small, independent shop with not a great selection and if they didn't grab something soon all the good stuff will be picked over.

"Do you feel like laughing?" she asked.

"Not necessarily."

"Do you feel like crying? Cringing? Smirking? Help me out here."

"Whatever you want," he said.

It looked like Julie would once again have to pick the movie. Michael never let her choose. Of course, those were the days where you actually had to go to the movie theater. Michael didn't want to be seen at a theater showing something unmanly. No musicals, no Woody Allen or Monty Python. Nothing intellectual or foreign. No romantic comedies or even dramas because God forbid, he might be seeing crying in public. Only stupid comedies or movies with explosions. The explosion didn't even have to make sense or fit into the plot; if something blew up, it was a good movie.

Dutch hated movies, all movies. It was strange. He didn't have the attention span. He'd start to fidget after a half hour and get up and go to lobby. They went twice and both times he left the theater.

"How can you sit and watch two football games back to back and not sit through a movie?"

"Because it's not real," he said, "Football is real."

Curt always let her get any movie she wanted, even a girly one. He probably figured they were going to fuck anyway so what difference did it make. She didn't care that much either. Not tonight. She just wanted to see his apartment. All week she wondered what kind of a place he had that he preferred to Uncle Billy's mansion. He said he lived "downtown" but that could mean anything. Did he have some kind of a penthouse bachelor pad with a heart shaped waterbed and silk sheets? Her imagination was getting the best of her. The guy owned a small cleaning business and needed a loan to expand.

While she was anxious, he seemed preoccupied. When he picked her up, he mumbled something about a "rough day" but didn't elaborate. At the video store, he didn't say much and let her chatter away. He'd been normal all week, staying over three times, but now that she was finally going to see his place he was withdrawn. *Is he hiding something, again?*

"Do you want action?" she asked.

"Pardon?"

"An action movie," she said, "Why? What did you think I meant?"

He shrugged instead of laughing.

"What's wrong?" she asked.

"Nothing," he said in a way that meant something.

She glared and he sighed.

"I had to fire one of my guys today."

"How come?"

A forty-year-old guy with a ponytail wedged between them and lurked nearby.

"Can we just go?" he asked.

She skirted past the "Drama" section. This guy has had more than enough drama the past few months. She decided what he needed was an escape.

"How 'bout a horror movie?" she asked.

"You like horror movies?"

"I do," she said, "I love being scared."

"Well, in that case, I could just drop you off in the Combat Zone and save two-fifty."

"I'm good," she said.

She picked something awful. If they were just going to fuck anyway, she'd rather not miss something good. Besides, the suspense was killing her. She wanted to get to his swinging bachelor pad as soon as possible.

He turned left on Comm Ave away from the Back Bay and Beacon Hill. *Where are you going? Don't you live in a penthouse apartment overlooking Boston Common? What are we doing in this shitty part of town?*

"It may take a little bit to find a parking space."

It did. *He doesn't have his own space? He took the stereo out of the front and placed it in his trunk. Uncle Billy doesn't need to remove the stereo from his car when he gets home.*

"It's in here" he said, pointing to a three-story building. So much for the panoramic view. They dodged a homeless guy and got on a cramped rickety elevator. He unlocked the door to his studio apartment.

Curt knew she was coming over, so he'd converted the futon bed into a futon couch. It faced the TV and the VCR inside a modest shelving unit. There was a homemade bookshelf at the opposite wall with an assortment of books mostly about World War II. The "kitchen" was a sink and a refrigerator and a counter. Kevin shuddered inside her.

"This is nice," she said

Curt gave her a look.

"Yeah?"

She should have been relieved. It wasn't a swinging bachelor pad. It was a dump. It would take some fancy talking, the kind he was incapable of, to lure a lot of women to this place.

"How long have you lived here?"

"Eight years."

That explains it. He got the place when he was just starting out and his business was brand new. He probably has been so busy he doesn't realize he can move. He just needs someone to explain to him that he's a grown man and no longer right out of college.

He plucked two take-out menus off the refrigerator.

"Do you want Chinese or pizza?" he asked.

Michael had always said, "chink food." He never said the N-word and would privately rail against anyone who did, yet he said "chink" was a regular part of his vernacular. When she called him on it, he'd say, "Chink isn't racist, it's cute." Curt handed her the menus then he played his answering machine right in front of her. *This guy has balls.*

"Curt, it's Brick. C'mon man, you got to give me another chance. Please, call me back." Beep.

"Curt, please, I know I fucked up. It won't happen again. Please, I'll work for free next week. I'll do anything. I promise. Call me back." Beep.

"What did he do?"

"He showed up for work high. One of my customers called and complained. I wasn't on that job with him so he thought he could get away with it, but the customer was home and smelled it on him."

"Oh."

What would I have done? Would I fire one of my tellers if they showed up high or drunk or coked up? Maybe I'd have to. How can I get Bob to show up high?

Julie never had to fire anyone. Her tellers were her friends or at least her "friends." The worst thing they did was show up hungover, and Julie had probably been with them the night before.

She ordered Chinese and he popped the movie in and the making out had begun when the doorbell rang.

"That was quick," she said.

They untangled and he hit the buzzer and scooped a twenty out of his wallet. He opened the door and out of the elevator emerged not a small Chinese delivery boy but a large white man with a baby face and a Frankensteinian gait.

"Curt, please."

"Brick, don't do this. You know I have to let you go."

"I've been with you six and a half years."

"I know Brick, that's why you should have known better. How many times have you done this to me? I just thought you worked slow."

"This was the first time. I swear."

"C'mon."

Julie lay on the couch, peering up at the two of them, just a few feet away. She wasn't sure if Brick had even noticed her.

"I swear on my mother I'll never do it again," he pleaded. *Is this big guy gonna cry?*

"You hate your mother," said Curt.

Brick shifted his feet while he tried to think of something else to say.

"You brought this on yourself. This isn't just about you. It's about the reputation for the business. If I lose my business everybody is out of work. Judy has a kid, Rojo has two. You didn't just let me down, you let everybody down."

Curt spoke calmly, almost paternally to the much bigger man even though they were roughly the same age. He looked over Curt and made eye contact with Julie hoping she would intervene on his behalf. Julie looked away. *I'd give him another chance. If it were me, I'd give him another chance.*

The buzzer buzzed again and without looking at it, Curt swatted it with his left hand like a bug.

"I'm sorry," Brick mumbled again.

"So am I," said Curt.

"Six and a half years."

"Not my problem."

They stared at each other for a moment. *Was the big man going to hit Curt? What would I do if he did?* The elevator door opened, and a small older Chinese delivery man stepped out. Curt reached around Brick and handed him the twenty.

"Keep it."

The man stretched two bags past Brick. "Thank you" he called over the big man getting back on the elevator.

Curt stood holding the bag looking at Brick and not moving.

"Please?" he asked.

Curt shook his head, "No."

Curt didn't budge with his Uncle Billy and he wouldn't budge now. The big man turned and left and Curt shut the door. He set the food on the counter.

"Let me get some plates," he said matter-of-factly but his hand trembled as he reached for them.

He was right, of course. His business ran by word of mouth. If word got out that his workers were high, his reputation would suffer. His little business could fold. Yet, she couldn't help but wonder if and when the time came, if Curt would dispatch her just as casually and with just as little fanfare.

Chapter Forty-One

The yelling began in the night waking Tom and Lydia up.

"Get away, get away," Tommy yelled.

Someone is in the house.

Tom bounded out of bed past Lydia, down the dark hallway. He burst into the boys' room and snapped on the light. Curt sat up in the corner of bunk bed, clutching his blankets and crying. His face was contorted with fear.

Tom looked at Tommy's empty bunk.

"Get away, get away, get away," Tommy screamed from inside the closet.

Someone has grabbed Tommy.

Tom opened the closet door and found Tommy sitting atop a pile of toys and games with his fists balled up near his face and his knees to his chest. There was a game of Chinese checkers, a basketball and pairs of sneakers around his feet. His eyes were wild with fear.

"Get away, get away, get away."

He kicked at Tom with both feet and then, cocked his feet for another kick.

"Get away," he yelled.

"Get out of there," said Tom.

He reached for Tommy's feet but Tommy kicked his hand away. *Ow.* He shook his thumb in pain.

"Tommy," yelled Lydia, "What is it, Sweetie? What's wrong?"

"They're trying to kill me, Mom. They're trying to kill me."

"Who is?"

"They're trying to rape and plunder and kill me."

Rape you? Plunder you?

Lydia nudged Tom out of the way and bent down in front of the open closet.

"No one is going to hurt you, Sweetie."

She reached out her hand, but Tommy kicked her in the knee, nearly knocking her over.

"Tommy," barked Tom, "Don't hurt your mother."

"They're trying to kill me," he said, kicking his feet out again causing a basketball to tumble out of the closet.

"Tommy, knock it off," said Tom angrily.

"Who is trying to kick you, Tommy," Lydia asked, her voice was frightened, but soothing.

"The Vikings. The Vikings are trying to kill me and rape me and plunder me."

The Vikings? The boy is afraid of Vikings?

"Get out of there," said Tom with disgust.

He reached for Tommy's legs again and when Tommy kicked, Tom pulled his hands back avoiding the blows.

"Tom," said Lydia.

"What?"

He looked at his wife. She held up an open hand. He could hear Curt crying nearby.

"Don't yell at him," she said softly, "He's frightened."

"Well, what do you want me to do?"

Her eyes were bloodshot.

"I think we should get Curt out of here."

He nodded.

"That's a good idea."

He scooped up Curt from his bed. The younger boy was crying silent tears and his body trembled. Tom put him in his mother's arms.

"Here."

Curt had almost grown too big for her to carry.

"Come, Sweetie," she said, kissing him on the head, "You'll sleep in our bed tonight."

The two of them disappeared down the hall. Tom stared into the closet and Tommy stared back at him, his fists and feet ready to spring.

"Tommy," he said quietly, "Nobody's trying to kill you."

"They're trying to kill me, Dad. They're trying to kill me and rape me and plunder me."

I am so tired.

"Tommy that's stupid. The Vikings haven't been around for hundreds of years. No one is trying to kill you or do anything else."

"They are," he said after a moment, "They are."

Tom pulled the chair from Tommy's desk and sat facing his son. He glanced at the clock shaped like a baseball on the wall. 1:50. *I need to go to sleep.*

"Tommy, I promise you," he said gently, "There are no Vikings."

Tommy looked back at him without arguing but without agreeing. *What do I do now? He has so much going for him. He's handsome and he's bright. His teachers tell us how bright he is all the time. The boy could go places if he would just stop acting up. When is he going to outgrow this stuff?*

Neither spoke for several minutes. Tommy yawned. *I'm tired, too. What should I do? Lydia will know.*

"I'll be right back," he said.

He walked back down the hall to the bedroom and found Lydia snuggled with Curt in the bed. Curt was just about asleep. She made a "shhh" gesture with her finger. Silently, she unhinged herself from Curt and tiptoed back down the hallway with Tom trailing behind.

They found Tommy sound asleep in the closet and exchanged relieved looks.

"Can you put him to bed?"

Tom nodded. He waded into the closet and pried the boy loose. *He's heavy.* He placed him in Curt's lower bunk, and they shut off the light and tiptoed back to bed.

In the morning, Tom awoke at his usual time. Though exhausted, his body woke every day at ten past six no matter what. Lydia and Curt were still asleep.

By the time he showered and shaved and dressed, Lydia was downstairs. Tom entered the kitchen to find her standing over Tommy, who was fully dressed and sat the table eating a bowl of cereal. His hair needed to be combed and he rocked back and forth a little, but he seemed perfectly normal.

"Hi, Dad," he said, slurping some milk from his spoon.

"Hi, Tommy," said Tom, feigning nonchalance.

Lydia looked at Tom and gestured towards the other room with her head. The two met in the living room and spoke in whispers.

"I'm going to take him to the doctor," she said.

"Why?"

She scowled at Tom.

"Why? You saw what happened last night."

Tom shrugged.

"He just had a bad dream, that's all. He should go to school."

"That was no dream. He was wide awake, and he was worried about…Vikings."

She spat out the word "Vikings."

"He seems fine now," said Tom, walking away from his wife and back into the kitchen.

"Come on, Tommy, I'll drive you to school."

Chapter Forty-Two

That night, I felt like I didn't sleep at all although I must have dozed a little here and there. I wondered what I had done to make Michelle hate me and I wondered what I had done to make my parents send me away to summer camp. When you're adopted you're a little more insecure. *Maybe my parents don't really love me.*

At first light, I was wide awake while everyone else slept. As far as I could tell, I had two options, I could murder Michelle in her sleep or I could get the hell out of there. Reluctantly, I picked "B." I slipped out of my bunk, changed into my clothes and put my toothbrush and towel into my duffel bag. While the others began to stir, I sat on my bed and figured out a plan.

"Good morning, girls," said Rose, trying to be cheerful though it wasn't in her. "Let's go the bathroom and wash up and then get some breakfast in the cafeteria. We have a lot of fun things planned today." *Sorry, but that's what you said yesterday.* I glanced over at Michelle who shot me a dirty look and I shot one back. Now that I was leaving I knew there was nothing more she could do to me.

Rose herded us out the cabin door and toward the bathrooms.

"I forgot my toothbrush," I said and I darted back into the cabin. I grabbed my duffel bag off my bunk and tiptoed out the backdoor. I ran as fast as I could, swapping shoulders with my duffel bag.

The office was also wooden and cabin-like and I burst in to find Chief Ron's wife, Chieftess Jean sitting behind a desk. She was talking to a troubled, older girl, trying to figure out if those bumps on her leg were mosquito bites or Poison Ivy.

"I have to call my Mom," I said, trying to catch my breath.

"What is it, dear?"

"It's emergency."

"What emergency?"

"I have to go home."

Her shoulders slumped and she looked at the girl with the bumps and frowned and looked back at me.

"Sweetie, a lot of girls feel homesick the first night but we have so many fun things in store. Tomorrow's "Backwards Day" where we have dinner first thing and sing the camp song with a fire in the morning while everyone wears pajamas. Doesn't that sound like fun?" *You're kidding, right?*

"Can I call my Mom?"

"All right, call your Mom," she said, handing me the phone. "I'm sure she'll want you to stay. I have to bring this girl to the infirmary. I'll be right back."

I dialed slowly, waiting for her and the itchy girl to leave.

"Mom."

"What's wrong? Are you hurt?"

"No, not exactly. I hate it here. The other girls are mean to me and I want to come home."

"Sweetie, you can't come home. I'm going to Dallas remember? You haven't even been there 24 hours. Give it a chance."

"The other girls hate me."

"How could anybody hate you? Now, I've got to go to the airport. Just give it one more day. I want you to call me tonight. Hang in there. Love you."

She hung up and I thought about calling my Dad but I knew he always went along with whatever my Mom said. I only had a minute before Chieftess Jean came back. I called information and asked for my grandfather's number and she connected me.

"Grandpa."

"Sweetheart, you're up early."

As quickly as I could I told him about Michelle and the racial slurs and the marshmallow and there was a brief silence.

"I'll come and get you. What's the name of the camp?"

I told him.

"I'll be there in two hours."

While I waited for my grandfather, Chieftess Jean came back and was eventually joined by Chief Ron. The two of them took turns, trying to convince me to stay. They seemed to take it personally that I wanted to leave their camp. True to his word, my grandfather walked in two hours later. He wore a suit and tie like he always did even though it must have been eighty degrees. "Force of habit" he used to say when I asked why he dressed that way.

He asked me to step outside and I did. I heard him yelling at Chief Ron and Chieftess Jean. He used the word "Goddamn" a lot. He came outside a minute later and his face was red and his eyebrows stood at attention. "Let's go home," he said.

Chapter Forty-Three

At this point, even the Committee had to concede that Julie and Curt were now girlfriend and boyfriend. They spoke on the phone every day; they went out a couple of times a week, if something funny or interesting or unusual happened at work, she would jot it down to remind herself to tell him about it later. She was into him, he was into her and there was only one missing piece of the puzzle, they hadn't yet had sex.

Withholding sex had never been Julie's strong suit. After her break-up with Michael, she went through a promiscuous phase when she was ten pounds heavier, drinking too much and more unsure of herself than before or since. In those days, she gave it up on the second or third dates and once on the first. None of them ever called.

"My vagina is the Bermuda Triangle," she told Marjorie, "Guys disappear in there and are never seen again."

With Curt, Julie was determined to hold off, knowing more than her pride would be hurt if he got away. While she took all the credit, he was partly to blame. His mother had just died, his brother was in custody and his whole family had disintegrated. He could hardly be faulted for not being quite as randy as he might normally have been.

The further they got from his mother's death, the more their romantic encounters escalated. His hands had been under her shirt and in her pants, but when they got to the edge, she would shut things down. She had promised herself to hold off for three months and she made it nearly five weeks.

It was the middle of May, a few days after Mother's Day. The older she got Mother's Day became less and less about her own mother and more and more about herself and her lack of achieving motherhood. She thought about Kevin all the time and didn't need any reminders. Mother's Day was like a persistent, nagging yeast infection.

On top of that, her boyfriend was a guy whose mother had just died tragically. They couldn't go out to brunch or the mall or a park and hang with the public that was celebrating the very topic they both wanted to avoid. So she called her Mom early before he picked her up and the two of them spent the day hiking in New Hampshire as far away from the general populace as they could get. Five days later, as she lay in bed contemplating their upcoming date, Julie made a decision, "tonight is the night."

She decided to proceed without the Committee's approval. Normally, on something as momentous as this, each member would weigh in and like the UN Security Council one dissenting vote could veto the whole thing. Like any deliberative body, the Committee wouldn't let you do anything impulsive.

Before "The Committee" signed off, it wanted to know when a guy called you and how long you talked and what about. It wanted to know what a guy did for a job and where he went to college and where he was from. It wanted to know how much a guy drank and what kind of drugs he did. The Committee let you know when to fuck a guy and when not to.

Not listening to the Committee was a mistake. Cara blew that software guy on the first date after the Committee told her not to and he never called her again. He was a cute guy with nice shoulders who'd been to a good school and Cara blew it. If she had listened to the Committee, she might still be with him instead of that loser Jimbo who even Cara knows is a loser.

You could defy the Committee, but where would that get you? After the software guy never called and the Committee said, "I told you so," Cara told them to go fuck themselves. Her actual words were "I don't need to listen to you. I can do what I want." And she was right, but where did that get her? It meant eating her lunch alone every day and only talking to customers unless it was about work. It meant not going for drinks on Thursdays or Fridays and only getting together with high school friends, most of whom have moved onto a husband and kids. Cara had no choice but to come crawling back to the Committee and beg for forgiveness.

Julie resented the Committee even though she was part of it and the Committee was always right. It was the Committee that told Sasha to stay away from the skeevy guy who wore the jewelry. She didn't listen and he tried to date-rape her and she was lucky to fight him off. She called them that night and they had to call a special meeting on a Sunday morning to make sure she was all right. The Committee looked out for you and didn't want you to get hurt either physically or emotionally.

Although its charter stated each member had an equal vote, the only vote that really mattered was Debbie's. The other Committee members waited to hear what she had to say and always abided by her decision. She was the most vocal and she didn't mince words. She had a look that bore through you like a district attorney. "You fucked him, didn't you?" she would say and with one look she'd know you had.

Yet, Debbie was pro-fucking when the time was right. Sasha had a guy she liked and was friends with him and they would make out here and there, but she didn't give it up when Debbie told her to, and he got some somewhere else and Sasha never heard from him again.

"You had him on the hook, and you let him go," Debbie told her.

While the possibility of her becoming a lesbian remained open for the time being, Debbie claimed that she liked men even though no one could recall ever seeing her with one. Yet, miraculously, no one understood men better than her. She was like a brilliant campaign strategist who knew just how to get a candidate elected but was not a good candidate herself. Truth be told the other women on the Committee didn't really like Debbie either, but they feared her, and they respected her and her advice was sacrosanct.

After some consideration, Debbie had given Curt her okay. Curt had come in hoping to be approved for a loan and had never discovered that wasn't the approval he needed. The loan was a formality. He had a good business and good references and good credit. Winning Debbie over was much more difficult. Debbie couldn't let a guy just walk into the bank and pick up Julie even if Julie was technically her boss. Julie wasn't the Chairwoman. Curt would have to prove he didn't already have a girlfriend, that he was a stand-up guy and wouldn't screw Julie over. Debbie nodded with approval when Julie told her there wasn't another woman at the funeral. If he had a girlfriend or two, she or they certainly would have been there for that. Although Debbie lamented Curt wasn't quite as tall as she would have preferred, she liked that he and Julie had long talks on the phone. It showed he had "sincerity." While Curt was winning Julie over unbeknownst to him, he was also winning over Debbie.

On this Friday night in May, Julie and Curt were making out on her couch, when she suddenly stopped him, slid out of his grasp and stood up.

"Let's go in here," she said, gesturing to her bedroom with her head.

"Are you sure?" he said.

"No, not really," she said quietly with a sly smile.

He chuckled and she took his hand and pulled him off the couch and towards the bedroom.

They kissed fully clothed on top of her bed for a while and then she removed her pants and he removed his. He took a condom from his wallet.

"How long have you had that condom?" she asked.

He gave her a look of surprise. She loved playing the wise ass.

"This old thing," he said, holding it up. "It's been in my family for years. My grandfather meant to use it before my father was born and my father meant to use it before I was born."

She laughed. *See, he can be funny.*

"Every girl dreams of a guy with an antique condom," she said, and she helped him put it on.

"*This is it*," she thought.

There was a lot at stake. Julie tried to pretend she only cared about the deeper values: about how she wanted a guy with character, a guy who wouldn't lie or cheat, a guy who was intelligent, a guy who was kind to old ladies and dogs and small children. Those things did matter to her, but they weren't the only things that counted. She also wanted a guy who was good in bed.

She took off his shirt and he took off hers. After a few moments, it was clear that he knew what he was doing and so did she. Though, she was often ashamed of her younger promiscuous phase, and sometimes wondered if she was the butt of former lovers' crude jokes, the phase was not without its benefits. She had learned how to have sex. It was a skill that Curt had picked up somewhere along the way as well. The two of them were like veteran stage actors with impeccable timing and perfect repartee. They followed up this performance with an early morning matinee.

When Julie left for work in the morning, running late, she was more in love than ever. As she rode the train, she found herself suppressing a smile so those around her wouldn't find her insane. She hurried along the two blocks from the T stop to the bank trying to recall a time when she'd been happier. She couldn't think of a moment that topped this. She entered the bank only twenty minutes before it was to open, and the tellers looked up from their trays. She could feel her face become hot and she knew she was blushing.

"You fucked him, didn't you?" said Debbie.

Chapter Forty-Four

It was ten after three and Tom lay awake alone. Two months after the Viking nightmare there had been another incident with Tommy and Tom had come home to find Lydia in tears at the kitchen table. The boy was fourteen now and too big for her to cuddle with in his bunk bed. So, instead, she slept in a sleeping bag on the floor in the boys' room.

Ever since he had quit drinking, Tom had stopped getting out of bed in the middle of the night. Instead, he would just lie there in the same position, sometimes for hours, willing himself back to sleep. He prayed so much for Tommy, yet his problems persisted.

It had become a pattern; there would be an episode followed by a few weeks of calm, then out of nowhere another episode. Sometimes Tommy would have a run-in, real or imagined, with another classmate. Sometimes he saw or heard something that wasn't there. Once, he bit another boy. The other kids were afraid of him and he had no friends.

After each outburst, Tom and Lydia would be called in to meet with his teacher and the principal. They wanted him to go to a special school, but Tom said "no." They couldn't dispute the fact that Tommy was very bright, and Tom was insistent that he go to the regular high school and onto college.

On this night, after Tom calmed her down, Lydia told him what had happened that day. She had picked Tommy up at the bus stop when he suddenly began rocking back and forth and screaming and cursing.

"The words that came out of his mouth," she said.

She was able to coax him out of the car and into the house where he eventually calmed down.

Tom tried to convince Lydia as he had many times before that Tommy was bright enough to overcome his problems. He'd mature and figure out what was real and what was imaginary but so far he hadn't and she was unconvinced that he ever would. She thought Tommy should go to the special school but Tom knew that would kill his chance for college and a better life.

Tom had been to war and seen and done unspeakable things. One of his buddies had his head blown off. His best friend was killed in front of him and he had choked a German boy to death with his bare hands. Yet, he hadn't lost his noodle.

What had Tommy been through? They lived in the suburbs in a quiet neighborhood. Tom had quit smoking and quit drinking. He had never masturbated and had never run around on his wife. He had resisted evil his whole life. Why couldn't Tommy? Why was he strong and his son weak? God was testing him and he didn't know why.

As he lay there, the way he always slept, with his arm tucked under his head and his knees bent, he hatched a plan to save Tommy. It was so simple. Why hadn't he thought of it before? Tommy was tormented by demons. It was time to cast the demons out.

What he needed was an exorcism. The doctors had done nothing for Tommy. It was time for Tom to turn to the church. In the morning, he'd take the boy down to St. Zepherin's. They'd be happy to help. He was sure of it. *What if Lydia objected? She didn't have to know. Besides, he was doing it for her, too.* He knew how troubling Tommy's behavior was to her. She was a nervous wreck. She'd thank him when saw that the boy was cured. He'd put his plan into effect first thing in the morning. Tom closed his eyes, said a Hail Mary and went to sleep.

Chapter Forty-Five

When I told Grandpa I hadn't had breakfast, he took me to the nearest IHOP, and I had the silver dollar pancakes. I poured strawberry, blueberry and something called "boysenberry" syrup on top.

"What's boysenberry?" I asked.

"Search me." he said. He often used expressions I never heard from anyone else like "search me."

"My Mom is going to be mad that I left camp."

Whenever my Mom got mad, my Dad got mad right after, but I left that part out.

"She's in Dallas," I said, "It's in Texas."

"That so?" he said.

"She's going to make me go back to camp."

He sipped his coffee. He drank his coffee black without any cream or sugar, and he didn't like coffee ice cream which I never understood.

"What if you go to camp with me?"

"Grandpa, you can't go to camp."

"What if there's a camp for just you and me."

"There's no such camp."

"There could be."

The waitress came by and he asked for the check. Whenever we went to lunch and he asked for the check he always asked for the waitress to bring me the check. It was one of his little jokes, but he didn't do that today, he just asked for the check.

"What were you going to do today at camp?"

"I don't know, swimming, arts and crafts…"

"Well, why don't we do that?"

"The lake was scary," I said. "It was dark and had things in it and you couldn't see the bottom."

"What kind of things?"

"Fish."

He chuckled.

"Why don't we swim in the town pool? You can see the bottom and it doesn't have any things."

We drove all the way from New Hampshire to his town in Massachusetts. He let me sit in the front seat which my Mom and Dad never do even when there's only two of us. He even let me play whatever I wanted on the radio and all he said was, "Are you sure that's music?"

When we got to his house, we changed into our bathing suits and he made a joke about changing from one suit to another and he chuckled to himself. He drove me to the town pool which had a high chain link fence all around it. He flashed his permit to the lady at the gate and picked up a guest pass for me.

"This is my granddaughter" he said, "Can't you see the resemblance?" That was one of his favorite jokes.

He had his bathing suit on but didn't go in the water.

"I'll watch you," he said.

I found some kids about my age, a brother, two sisters and a cousin, playing Marco Polo and they let me play with them. We played for almost two hours and they didn't call me a racial slur the whole time, and then, they had to go and my grandfather said we should too.

"See you tomorrow," they said.

"Yeah," I said.

When we got to the car, I told my grandfather, "They never asked me my name."

"That's okay," he said, "You can still be friends with someone and not know their name."

"Really?"

"Sure. I had lots of friends in the army whose names I didn't know."

We went back to his house and changed out of our bathing suits and he let me watch TV even though the sun was still out which wasn't allowed in my house. He let me pick the show and fell asleep next to me on the couch.

"Grandpa, you were sleeping."

"No, I wouldn't do that," he said, "I like to close my eyes and pretend it's a radio show."

Grandpa always called "dinner" "supper" and he had it at five o'clock. In my house, we didn't eat dinner until seven o'clock when my Dad came home from work. For supper, he made fat hamburgers and baked beans. I don't like baked beans but there was a rule in Grandpa's house that you have to eat everything on your plate, so I had to eat my baked beans.

I started to get nervous during supper because I remembered I had to call my Dad.

"I have to call my Dad," I said. "He's going to be mad I'm not at camp. He's going to make me go back."

I started to cry.

"But you are at camp," he said, "You're at Camp Grandpa."

He gave me a bowl of ice cream, (he only had vanilla) and while I ate it he got a piece of paper and wrote some things down.

"Here," he said, handing me the paper, "I want you to read this."

I read it out loud to him at the kitchen table.

"Hi Dad, I'm having a nice time at camp. I swam for two hours. I made some new friends. I have to go now."

He smiled when I finished.

"I didn't have a nice time at camp."

"You had a nice time at Camp Grandpa, didn't you?"

I nodded.

"Read it again," he said.

He had me practice it five more times.

"Let's call him," he said.

"Grandpa, it's only 5:30, my Dad doesn't get home until seven."

"I know," he said.

I knew our number by heart and my grandpa stood next to me holding the piece of paper with what to say. I got the machine and listened to my own voice on the outgoing message.

"Hi, we're not home right now, we're out doing important stuff, leave a message at the beep."

The part about the important stuff was my Mom's idea and she had me rerecord the message over and over until I got it right. The machine beeped and I read the message my grandfather wrote for me.

"Hi Dad, I'm having a nice time at camp. I swam for two hours. I made some new friends. I have to go now."

I hung up and he smiled.

"Let's go play miniature golf" he said. He always called mini-golf "miniature golf" and when I asked him why he said, "I'm funny that way."

The rest of the week when I woke up, my grandfather was already up and wearing a tie. He'd teach me how to make my bed "military-style" and we would have pancakes for breakfast with just regular syrup. He'd take me to the playground near him that had the sign that read, “This equipment is made entirely of recycled materials.”

“Oh, brother,” he said.

At the playground, he’d push me on the swing then we’d go home and change into our suits and go to the pool. My friends were never there again, and I had to swim alone.

He let me watch TV during the day and he’d sit next to me and close his eyes and snore a little bit. I got a little bit bored here and there but being bored is better than fearing for your personal safety.

Each afternoon at five-thirty, he would have me call home and read a new message that he wrote for me. Then, we would play miniature golf except for the time it rained, and then, we played checkers.

As the week was drawing to a close, the thought I was trying to avoid kept seeping back into my head. How am I going to get home without my Mom and Dad finding out that I hadn’t been at camp all week? I asked my Grandpa on Saturday and he said, “Don’t worry, I’ve got it under control.”

Chapter Forty-Six

The morning after Julie and Curt had consummated their relationship, before the bank opened, Julie took some good-natured ball busting.

"So, Julie, you gonna have that smile on all day?"

"You know Julie, next to you, the megabucks winner looks kinda bummed out."

Usually, it was Julie who did the poking and the prodding with wisecracks but today, she had no return volleys and silently basked in her post-coital glow.

She was friendly and warm as each customer entered. It was suddenly a party and Julie was the hostess, thrilled that each guest could make it. When an old cow came in to bitch about a certain bank policy, Julie listened with genuine concern and co-conspiratorial outrage. She was very cheerful and sweet and very un-Julie.

This lasted from nine o'clock until nearly nine-twenty when a sudden thought hit her. *What if he doesn't call? He will*, she said to herself, dismissing it out of hand but a minute later, the thought was back. *But what if he doesn't? What if he's like all the others?*

Curt wasn't like that, she decided. This wasn't a fling or a one-night stand. She'd gone to his mother's funeral and his brother's hearing. They'd gone to multiple movies and had multiple dinners. They'd had long talks on the phone and shared personal matters. They'd played miniature golf together. This was a real relationship.

Sex was the next logical step. She had enjoyed it and was sure he had too. Of course, he'll call. He usually called around 10:30. She was certain he would call around 10:30 today. *But what if he didn't? He hasn't said he loved me yet. What if he doesn't call?*

Would she call him? Would she call him this morning? Would she call him in the afternoon? No, she wouldn't call him from work. If he didn't call, she would wait until she was home at night, alone, in case he was breaking up with her and she could cry it out and not make a public scene. She wouldn't give the Committee the satisfaction.

Her phone rang; some inarticulate boob with an attitude who hadn't heard back from his loan application, blah, blah, blah. *What kind of an asshole would call at 10:20 when Curt was going to call any second?* Julie dispatched him quickly.

A minute later, Debbie called her over to help with a customer. *Is she fucking with me? Does she know he should be calling soon? Is she trying to undermine our relationship?*

Julie, reluctant to leave her desk, came any way. She could hear her phone from where she stood but she looked back any way, two or three times, to see if her button was lighting up. It wasn't. Julie got the woman out the door mollified but the solicitude she displayed at nine a.m. was long gone.

Her phone rang again. Julie scurried to answer it drawing raised eyebrows between Debbie and Cara. It was another customer and Julie slumped in seat imagining herself as an old maid. As they spoke, Julie's other line rang and Julie put the man on hold.

"Hey," said Curt as if nothing were wrong.

"Hold on a sec," said Julie as she punched line one, "Sir, our fire alarm just went off, you're going to have to call back this afternoon."

"I'm back," she said.

"Last night was fun."

"Oh, so this morning wasn't?"

He laughed. It felt good to make him laugh.

"This morning was fun, too," he said.

Her other line rang, and she ignored it.

"I have class tonight" he said.

He was taking a marketing class in hopes of improving of business.

"I thought you showed some class last night."

"Oh, boy," he said. She could hear his eyes rolling over the phone.

"What? It's not enough, I have sex with you? I have to make you laugh, too."

That got him and she was back on track. A customer, a blue-collar guy in grimy, possibly smelly overalls approached and stood near her desk.

"Maybe we could go to the movies tomorrow night" he said. She wanted to say something about the new Tom Hanks movie, but she knew she couldn't say "Tom Hanks" and look as though she was conducting bank business. Instead, she said, "Yes, I think that's an excellent proposal."

"Do you have to go?" he asked.

"Yes, Mr. Morrissey, I'll have my supervisor call you."

The two of them tended to linger when their phone conversations were over, neither saying anything but neither hanging up, just listening to each other breathe not wanting to let go.

"Okay, you're with a customer. We can talk later," he said.

"Yes and I'll look over your assets."

He laughed and hung up.

"Can I help you, sir?" she asked the blue-collar guy, smiling broadly and looking at the clock over his shoulder. It was 10:29.

Chapter Forty-Seven

In the morning, he woke up, urinated, showered, shaved and decided to forgo breakfast. Lydia was out but would be back soon, so he had to act quickly. He burst into Tommy and Curt's bedroom reached down and shook Tommy awake.

"C'mon, c'mon, get up, you're coming with me." Tommy stirred and looked at his Dad through half-opened eyes.

"What?"

"C'mon, we got an appointment. Up" he said sharply this time.

Curt knelt nearby with a toy car in his hands and supervised the proceedings. A few minutes later, Tom stood over Tommy in the kitchen while Tommy ate his cereal. Tom peered out the window at the driveway. "Let's go, hurry up."

"Where we going?"

"You'll see."

He peered out the window again and this time saw Lydia's station wagon pull in. "Shit" he said, not quite audibly.

"Finish eating, brush your teeth and let's go."

He disappeared out the backdoor and watched her get out of the car.

"Don't tell me you're going to help me" said Lydia when she saw him coming. "It's not my birthday."

Tom ignored her and scooped up three bags of groceries, one under each elbow while squeezing one in between.

"I'm taking him to get his haircut."

"Who?"

"Tommy."

"Tommy? Tommy doesn't need his haircut."

"I think he does."

"How is he?"

"Fine, I'm just taking him for a haircut."

"Why don't you take both of them?"

"No, just Tommy."

Lydia, with a bundle in each arm, eyed him suspiciously. "You're selling him on the black market, aren't you?"

He wasn't in the mood for a wise ass. He simply wanted to take his son down to the rectory so the priest could perform an exorcism on him, and he wanted to do it without being hassled by his wife.

"What are you up to, Tom Morrissey?"

"Can't a father take his son out once in a while?"

"All right," she said, "These bags are too heavy for me to stand here and fight with you. I don't know what you've got up your sleeve."

Tom corralled Tommy and got him into the car.

"Where are we going?" Tommy asked as they pulled out of the driveway.

"You'll see" said Tom.

"Am I in trouble?"

"No."

They drove on in silence. *What did we used to talk about? Little league, I guess and Cub Scouts.* He remembered how both boys would constantly ask him about animals. "Dad, who would win in a fight a polar bear or a crocodile? A tiger or a grizzly bear? A lion or a boa constrictor?" They were obsessed. He smiled to himself remembering those days.

He peeked over at Tommy. The boy's eyes stared straight ahead betraying nothing. *What goes on inside that brain? What does he think about? What are his day dreams? Does he like girls yet? Is he thinking crazy things right this minute? Is there a demon inside him right now?*

"Why are we going here?" Tommy asked as they parked in front of St. Zepherin's.

"We're going to have a little talk with Father Henry," Tom said, leading the boy to the front door of the rectory. Tom pressed the bell and looked around afraid to make eye contact with his son.

Mary opened the door. He had forgotten about her. She was a pitiful and wretched soul. A sixty-year-old amalgamation of hideous birth defects with a deformed and misshapen head and enlarged eyes. Her arms were flaccid, and she was missing fingers and walked with a limp. The boys were frightened of her when they were younger, as were all children. They would see her at mass from time to time and once in a while about town but mostly she hid in the rectory where she worked, a modern-day Quasimodo banished from view by a cruel and superficial world.

Tom didn't recoil as others did when face to face with Mary. He'd seen his share of soldiers more damaged than her. He'd seen half-blown off faces and missing limbs and bodies sheathed in burnt skin. When Lydia first saw Mary and remarked, "The poor dear," he could only nod. He'd seen too many "poor dears" and now could only muster resignation instead of pity. Life is cruel.

"Can I help you?"

"We're here to see Father Henry."

"Father Henry is administering to the sick, but Father William is here."

Shit. Father Henry is the fire and brimstone type. He'd cast out the demon and give it a boot in the ass. Father William was younger and more modern, the kind of priest Tom didn't care for. *What choice do I have?*

"Okay, we'll see Father William."

"Come in. I'll see if he's free," she said, limping away.

Tom gripped the back of Tommy's neck gently between his thumb and index finger and led him inside. They stood wordlessly in the hall waiting for the deformed lady to return. "You can come in" she said, finally.

Father William was adjusting his Roman collar when they entered, the equivalent of a normal guy straightening his tie. He was a few years out of the seminary and far too young to have served in Tom's war or the one in Korea. His hair was a blondish-brown and touched his ears.

The rectory study was dark with heavy burgundy drapes and deep brown mahogany furniture. The priest shook their hands and had a smile for each of them. He had them sit in front of his desk while he sat behind it.

"What can I do for you?"

"I'm here for an exorcism" Tom said, getting right to the crux. Father William's mouth sprung open and his eyebrows rose to their full height. Tommy flinched and turned sharply and looked at his Dad. Tommy had been emotionless but now his eyes were suddenly alert.

"An exorcism?"

"For my son."

Tom and the priest looked at over Tommy. He seemed perfectly normal at that moment the way a car stops making that funny noise as soon as the driver pulls into his mechanic's garage. The priest bit his lip and furled his brow. He pressed a button on his phone and asked Mary to come in.

"Could you take Tommy into the kitchen for a moment? I think we have a few Tollhouse cookies left."

"He's too old for cookies," said Tom. "He's fourteen."

"You're never too old for cookies," said the priest escorting Tommy to the door. Tommy seemed even more terrified as Mary led him away.

The priest returned to his seat. "What is all this about?" Tom gave him a brief history of Tommy's escapades giving specific details. The priest nodded gravely after each one. When he finished the priest asked, "What do the experts say?"

"They don't know anything. They want to put him in the special school. It's for bad kids, troublemakers and kids from bad homes. Tommy's a good kid with good grades. I want him to go to the regular high school and have a normal life. That's why I thought an exorcism could help."

The priest smiled, "Half the parents I know would want to bring their teenagers in here for an exorcism."

His attempt to lighten the mood failed as Tom glowered back at him. The priest rubbed the back of his head and looked away from Tom's glare.

"Mr. Morrissey, it sounds like Tommy has problems but, the boy's not possessed."

"How do you know?"

The priest let out a long and deliberate breath.

"Exorcisms are extremely rare and only for cases of demonic possession."

"Well, how else can you explain his behavior? The boy hears voices, aren't those demons?"

I got him there. He's so used to dealing with little old ladies who can't get their husbands to go to church he's not used to doing real priestly work. Tom wasn't about to let him wriggle out of it.

"Let me talk to Tommy alone for a minute."

Father William got up and opened the door and called to Mary.

"Do you mind waiting in the kitchen?"

Tom exhaled but acquiesced. *Can we just do the exorcism and be done with it? I still have to take the boy for a haircut.*

Tom sat in the kitchen with an empty plate in front of him. Mary dropped a couple of cookies onto the plate with her two-fingered hand.

"Thank you" he said, remembering his manners. He wanted to tell her, "I know a lot of guys worse off than you. Young fellows who can't see at all or lost their legs. I knew one eighteen-year-old private with burns over ninety-five percent of his body. You ain't got it so bad." He said none of those things of course, he just ate his cookies quietly like a good boy.

After a few minutes, Father William called him back in. "You have a fine young man here, Tom" he said.

"What about the exorcism?"

The priest sighed loudly, and his shoulders slumped. "Tom" he said, "I wouldn't even know how to do one. Let's do this." The priest scurried behind his desk and lifted up his chair. He hoisted it over the desk between the two chairs that Tom and Tommy had been sitting in and set it down. He gestured for the three of them to sit.

"Let's pray together" he said.

Father William sat and they followed suit. He reached out his hands and grasped Tom and Tommy's and then gestured for Tom to hold Tommy's other hand. The three of them sat linked together. Tommy's eyes darted nervously from his father to the priest and back again. "It's going to be all right," thought Tom.

Father William closed his eyes and began, "Our Father, who art in heaven…" Together they recited three Our Fathers and three Hail Marys. Tom opened his eyes from time to time make sure Tommy was saying the prayers along with them.

"Louder Tommy" and the boy did as he was told.

After they finished, Father William said, "Dear Lord, please take care of our son Tommy. Fill his heart with the Holy Spirit and guide him to the light and away from the darkness. Shield him from the forces of wickedness and despair and lead him to the light and eternal happiness, amen."

Tom opened his eyes and smiled at the priest. *That should do the trick.*

Chapter Forty-Eight

It was six in the morning when he woke me.

"It's 0600," he said.

I didn't know what O600 meant and I was still sleepy.

"We have to get there before your Mom and Dad do."

That got me up. I peed and put my clothes on and made my bed the way he taught me before I came down stairs. He had poured me a bowl of cereal with a banana, forgetting that I don't care for bananas. As I ate, he pulled out a map he had drawn of my camp.

"Here's a map of your camp" he said. It had a rectangle where the office/cabin was some smaller rectangles for the other cabin. There was a big circle that said "Lake" in the middle. It looked nothing like my camp. He left out the ball fields and the basketball court and the fire pits and the wooden stage and the cafeteria tent.

He looked at me very seriously.

"This has to be like a military operation," he said, "It will require precision and execution. Your Dad hates me enough as it is. You don't want your parents to know you weren't at camp all week."

That was true, I didn't. He informed me that he had called the camp and that parents were picking up their kids between nine and eleven.

"I need to drop you off early so your parents don't see me driving away and wondering what the heck I'm doing there."

He was making some good points. It was as if he kept kids away from their summer camps all the time.

"So, I'm going to drop you here at 0830 hours."

He pointed to the map in front of the cabin office where he had picked me up. I had no idea what he meant by 0830 hours.

"You need to kill about twenty minutes to a half hour. Here's what you do. You take your duffel bag and you walk all the way around here."

He drew a line all the way around the lake.

"That should take a kid your size a good twenty minutes."

I nodded.

"Then, when you come back there should be lots of kids milling about. Do you know what "milling" means?"

I shook my head. He smiled, "It just means walking around. It'll be chaos with kids walking helter-skelter with their duffel bags and what have you."

I didn't know what helter-skelter meant either but it's impolite to interrupt.

"Just stand with the other kids while they wait for their parents. When you see yours, just go and get in the car with them. It's very simple really."

"What if someone sees me?"

"Like who?"

"Rose, my counselor."

"Just stay away from her. What's she going to do, kick you out?"

That's true. What could she do?

"We got to go," he said.

He gave me an English muffin to eat in the car. It just had butter on it and no jelly the way I like it. On the way, he tried to explain to me about military time. I was able to understand that 0800 was eight o'clock and 1100 was eleven o'clock but I didn't see why 1400 was 2 o'clock and 2100 was nine. That made no sense at all, but I didn't tell my Grandpa that.

It was a two-hour drive and I took a little nap on the way. When I woke up, we were pretty close, and I got quieter the closer we got. He pulled into the giant camp parking lot with the painted logs.

"I'm scared," I said.

"In a half hour or so, you'll be in a car with your Mom and Dad driving home and you'll never have to see this place again."

That sounded good. He parked the car and walked me to the entrance carrying my duffel bag. He handed me the bag and kissed my head.

"I have faith in you," he said.

He walked away quickly and I picked up the duffel bag. It was heavier than I remembered and I walked as quickly as I could past the office/cabin. What if Chief Ron or Chieftess Jean saw me? I scurried along towards the lake. *What if Michelle sees me?*

The camp was eerily quiet. "They must still be having breakfast" I thought.

The lake looked more blue than black this time and the sun shimmered off it making it look pretty but still not worth going in. A sign said, "Closed" and I walked along the outside by the trees. I stopped every few minutes to put my bag down and catch my breath. I even threw a rock in the lake just to show I wasn't afraid of it.

By the time I returned from the lake, there was a mass migration of children, some with parents and some without, moving towards the parking lot like animals on the savannah lumbering toward the watering hole. I was able to blend into the herd without difficulty, and as we got closer, I picked out Michelle. She was with a plump, hard-faced woman who was undoubtedly her mother. When Michelle saw me, she looked puzzled momentarily than cursed at me. The hard-faced woman shook her by the scruff of the neck and had she been anyone else, I would have felt sorry for her.

We filed past the office/cabin and I didn't look to see if Chief Ron or Chieftess Jean were inside. The children with parents, Michelle among them, dispersed into the parking lot while the others crowded together as a line of new cars arrived.

There was a counselor with a bullhorn. As each car pulled up, he would announce the name of the camper who would then emerge from the pack and disappear into the car. From a distance, I saw Rose towards the front talking to some of the girls in my cabin. They were kids who might have been my friends had Michelle not turned them against me. I moved to the back behind some of the older kids so she wouldn't see me.

The whole process seemed to take hours. One by one, a child's name would be called and then a suitcase thrown in a car and then the next one would step up. I stood waiting by myself whispering, "Please, Mom, please, please."

She was always late. It makes my Dad angry and he always mumbles about it but never says anything directly to her. Finally, I spotted her maroon Jeep Cherokee in the distance entering the parking lot and joining the back of the line.

The line of cars got shorter one kid at a time. I left my safe hiding spot behind the bigger kids and moved to the front of the dwindling crowd.

"Hey," said Rose from the back of the pack.

I ignored her and lugged my duffel bag to the curb. My mother was now third in line. The college kid with the bullhorn called my name.

"I'm right here," I said.

"Hi, Honey," My Mom said.

She hopped out the car and kissed my cheek and hoisted my bag into the trunk. I jumped into the backseat and as I clipped in, I saw Rose staring at me and walking with purpose towards my car.

"Mom, you should go, people are waiting."

"Okay, okay, let me get my seatbelt on."

She looked back at for a moment, taking me in and she smiled broadly. Rose got closer.

“Mom.”

Rose yelled something at my mother but was drowned out by the sound of the bullhorn. My mother put the car in drive and pulled away down the dusty road back towards the highway and home.

“So how was camp?”

“Good.”

“See, you were worried for nothing.”

Chapter Forty-Nine

Before Julie and Curt had sex, they had fun. She made sure of it. With all the heaviness that surrounded them with the funeral and the hearing and the impending trial and the general air of sadness, they both needed a break. Now that it was mid- May and spring in Boston had finally arrived, they could do something outside and they landed on miniature golf. The plan was for him to swing by and pick her up and they'd play mini-golf and maybe get an ice cream and smooch a little bit and have the kind of fun every other young couple in the world was having. It may have even happened that way, if she hadn't played her answering machine.

Curt and his employees worked long hours on weekends cleaning office buildings that were closed Saturdays and Sundays. During the week, most of their business was in private homes which were nowhere near as large or as taxing, so Curt preferred to go out mid-week when he wasn't likely to doze off.

On this particular Tuesday, their designated "night of fun" she got home late from work. There was a transfer that should have gone through and didn't and it was a lot of money and there was a threat of a work stoppage, and who gives a fuck, she was late. Curt was there waiting for her. They had plans to play miniature golf.

She apologized and kissed him and scooped up her mail and came in her apartment with him. She'd quickly change out of her suit, put on a sweater, her new jeans and some sneakers and they'd be out the door, but she saw the light blinking.

Why shouldn't she play it? She had nothing to hide. She had no other boyfriends, didn't owe money to gamblers, wasn't part of a criminal enterprise. What harm could come from playing the message?

She pushed the button and when she heard Marjorie's voice, she felt her throat constrict.

"Hey, it's me. Just called to say 'hi.' How's Kevin? Bye," beep.

Had Curt heard? He was near the door. She was in the kitchen. *Maybe he didn't hear. How could he not hear?* Her apartment consisted of a living room, a tiny kitchen and a bedroom. The answering machine was on the kitchen counter and there was no wall dividing the kitchen and the living room. *He must have heard her say, "How's Kevin?" This could ruin everything.*

The crazy thing is there was no Kevin. Not yet anyway. Like most things in Julie's life, it started as a joke. Marjorie was Julie's best friend in college, her roommate junior and senior year. Theirs was a friendship Julie had never been able to replicate. Fifteen years later, they were still best friends.

Graduation weekend they were loath to leave each other. Julie was going to stick around Boston and Marjorie was going to medical school in Minnesota. There were alumni strewn about campus in five year waves. While nursing hangovers and sipping coffee they spotted two women, old friends, celebrating their 25th reunion.

"That's going to be us" Julie said, "You'll be a famous doctor, I'll be a wealthy venture capitalist…"

"I'll be here with my 23-year-old daughter Jennifer and I'll introduce her to your 23-year-old son…"

"Kevin" Julie said, taking it from there. "They'll fall instantly in love and be married, and your family and my family will get beach houses next door and spend all the holidays, Christmas, Easter, Flag Day together." It was a gag, but one that hung on.

Marjorie really did become a doctor, though not a famous one. She had two kids, the eldest, a girl named "Jenna"—close enough. "How's Kevin?" became code for "How are things?" or "Seeing anyone?" or "How close are you to realizing your dreams?"

When work was going well and Julie's love life looked promising, Kevin was a healthy, robust 10 lb. new born. When things weren't so good, which was more often than not, Kevin was a sickly preemie clinging to life in an incubator. It was in bad taste, of course, but it was just between the two of them and it allowed for shorthand with busy schedules. A quick update on Kevin's prognosis said it all.

As Julie got older, she began to dream of Kevin. She never even told Marjorie that part. Day dreams, mostly, of nursing Kevin, strapping him in a stroller, pushing him on the swing. Kevin never grew past the toddler stage. She'd given up all the whole venture capital nonsense, but Kevin was a dream that she refused to let go of. That was the irony, now that she was with Curt and in love with him Kevin was healthier than ever. If she had gotten home on time and called Marjorie back she would have told her or her machine that "Kevin was five pounds and four ounces and breathing on his own."

"Ready to go?" she asked, now clad in sneakers and jeans as was he. She's never seen him in either. She'd only seen him dressed up in suits or at least button-down shirts and never in his "play clothes." He looked cute and noticeably more boyish.

His mood, for once, was upbeat. He must not have heard. If he had, it hadn't bothered him. He had promised her a night of fun and seemed determined to keep his promise.

They breezed through eighteen mini-holes, not really keeping score and letting a group of teens play through. Their conversation was light and carefree for the very first time and she kept him distracted with her fusillade of anecdotes. He laughed in all the right places.

It wasn't until after the game, while they licked their soft serve cones from the snack bar, sitting on picnic benches, that he asked, "So who's Kevin?"

He's a cool customer. He heard the message, filed it away not showing a trace of annoyance or concern.

She couldn't let him think she was seeing someone else. He had introduced her as "his girlfriend." She didn't want him to think it was okay to see someone else, not at this point. He was "the one" and she couldn't let him think otherwise.

Julie stopped licking and looked him dead in the eye.

"He's a little boy from my neighborhood. He was in a car accident."

Curt's face expressed alarm. She went back to her cone.

"Is he okay?"

"It was quite serious, but he'll be all right, a few broken bones but no permanent damage."

"That's good."

"It is," said Julie, cramming the last of her cone into her mouth.

Chapter Fifty

Tom drove home carefully, hunched over the steering wheel, through a half-snow, half-rain combination, trying his best not to be dizzy. He had left work abruptly after throwing up, having caught the flu that was going around that December. He said a little prayer that he'd recover by Christmas. He'd never missed a mass on Christmas Eve his whole life, not even during the war.

As he turned the corner on his cul-de-sac, he saw an unfamiliar car in his driveway. It was a sports car, red and foreign, and he knew it didn't belong to one of the neighborhood's Moms. The sick feeling, he had a minute earlier was nothing compared to the one he had now. He pounded his fist against the steering wheel.

The car in the driveway wasn't a complete shock. He had had his suspicions, but Lydia was evasive when he questioned her. The two of them had been fighting so much about what to do about Tommy that he didn't press her. Now he wished he had.

He parked in front of his house and sloshed his way angrily up the driveway towards the backdoor. His head was spinning as an icy rain pelted his face. It was barely three o'clock and no one was expecting him.

He popped open the backdoor, jarring the bell which announced his arrival. He spotted a pair of men's shoes on the floor that weren't his and an expensive overcoat with an Italian label hung on his coatrack. He slammed the door behind him.

Lydia burst from the kitchen with an astonished and guilty look on her face.

"You scared me half to death. What are you doing home?"

"Sick," he snarled, brushing past her with his hat and coat and shoes still on.

"Your brother stopped by," she said to Tom's back with a slight quiver in her voice.

He entered the kitchen to find his brother Billy seated at his table holding a tea cup with a half-eaten Danish on a dish in front of him.

"Hey, Tom," Billy said jumping up.

He started to extend his hand but quickly retracted it.

"Isn't this cozy?" hissed Tom.

"Tom," Lydia said.

"C'mon, Tom, don't be like that," said Billy trying to maintain a smile.

"Get out."

"Tom Morrissey, stop that," said Lydia, sharply.

"Tom, how long are you going to hate me?"

"As long as it takes," hissed Tom, "Get out of my house."

Billy stood up with his hands out in front of him trying to placate his brother.

"Okay, okay. You didn't used to hate me, Tom. It's only since my business took off."

Tom went to grab Billy but wavered and almost fell and turned and grabbed the sink instead. Lydia stepped in between them.

"Tom, Billy just stopped by before Christmas. He brought the boys presents."

"We don't want your goddam presents."

Tom staggered under a wave of nausea and leaned over the sink fighting back the urge to vomit.

"You don't look so good, Tom. Let me help you upstairs."

He put his arm on Tom's elbow.

"Get your goddam hands off me and get out of my house."

Lydia put a hand on Tom's other elbow.

"Tom, you're sick. Let him help you upstairs."

"I want him out of my goddam house," said Tom, still bent over the sink, his face purple.

"Okay, Tom, if that's how you want it. Thanks for the tea, Lyd."

No one spoke as Billy slipped on his shoes and bent down and tied them. He stood back up and took his time putting on his fancy Italian coat and buttoning each button. Tom gripped the sink tightly with both hands enjoying the tension. Lydia stood nearby glaring at his profile.

"Merry Christmas," said Billy, finally.

"Merry Christmas" said Lydia over her shoulder.

Billy shut the door behind him.

"How often does he come?"

"Once in a while. The boys like him."

Her arms were crossed defiantly.

"So the three of you are conspiring against me."

"No one's conspiring against you, Tom Morrissey. He's your brother. You should be ashamed of yourself."

"He should be ashamed of himself."

Tom took his coat off and shooed her away when she tried to help him. He sat down in the chair Billy had just occupied and bent down to take off his shoes.

"You didn't tell him, did you?"

Lydia hesitated and he knew she had told him about Tommy. She had told him the family secret; Tommy had been diagnosed as schizophrenic.

The exorcism had done nothing. If anything, the hallucinations, the voices and the violent episodes had gotten worse, and the boy was now sent to a special school despite Tom's objections. Tom gave in only when they assured him this would offer Tommy his best chance of going to college. He would be medicated and monitored the rest of his life. Tom never told anyone, not a soul, and now she had told Billy. *Billy. Of all people.*

"How could you?"

He glared at her, his face a deep red, his eyes blazing. She trembled as she looked back at him. She had never been afraid of him before.

"Tom, he's your brother. He's very concerned. He offered to help. He knows some very good doctors."

"I don't want his help. I've never wanted his help. I don't want him here. Do you understand? Ever."

"He's family."

"He is not family," said Tom, shaking his finger at his wife.

"It's Christmas time. He's trying to be Christian, Tom. It wouldn't hurt you to be Christian and forgive someone once in a while."

"I'm plenty Christian" said Tom emphasizing the "I'm."

He untied each shoe and pried them off with just his feet. There were wet, messy footprints now on the kitchen floor.

He stood up gingerly and Lydia handed him a large plastic bowl in case he needed to throw up. Tom shuffled to the living room stairs.

"You're really mad at your father, you know" she yelled to his back. "He's the one who gave him the family business."

"He's the one who took it. My mother would never have forgiven him for leaving the church and my father would have disowned him if he knew he'd turn out to be a fag."

Chapter Fifty-One

My parents never found out about Camp Grandpa although there was a close call a few days after I was back home when my Dad noticed me making my bed, military-style.

"Where'd you learn to make a bed like that?"

"Camp."

Prior to the Michelle incident, the most traumatic thing that ever happened to me was in the second grade when my teacher handed out parts for the Thanksgiving show and I got one. I don't like speaking in public. In fact, I'm terrified of speaking in public. My fiancé David likes to tease me about my chosen profession.

"Lawyers have to speak in public, you know."

"Courtroom lawyers," I'd tell him, "Not environmental lawyers, and besides, I might have flunked the bar exam."

Of the twenty-four kids in my class only five were chosen to speak. The odds were in my favor. Had Mrs. Werner held auditions, I wouldn't have auditioned. I would have been happy to build the scenery and then blend into it. I'd always liked Mrs. Werner and thought she liked me, and I couldn't understand why she was punishing me this way.

"Each of you has a slip of paper telling you what part you have. If you have a line, it will be written on your slip of paper."

The boy next to me was Dylan Huelsman. His slip of paper read, "Native American." My friend Alexa's said, "Puritan woman." Mine said, "Pocahontas," and underneath it read, "Welcome Pilgrims, you have braved the mighty Atlantic and we will teach you our Native American ways of medicine and agriculture."

"What's Pocahontas doing there?" My mother asked that night when I showed her the slip of paper. A good question, considering that Pocahontas lived near Jamestown, Virginia and the Pilgrims had the first Thanksgiving way up at Massachusetts Bay. The whole show made no sense. Sir Walter

Raleigh was there, and he died in 1618, two whole years before the Pilgrims landed in Plymouth. Walter's line made no mention of tobacco although my mother liked to tell people he was smoking an e-cigarette.

Shortly after receiving the bad news, I sidled up to Mrs. Werner at her desk. She was putting a frowny face on Dylan's math homework.

"I can't do this," I said softly.

She was writing and stopped and looked at me in surprise.

"Why, of course you can. I chose you because there are some big words there and you have the best vocabulary of anyone in the class."

I told my babysitter Annika about it when she picked me up from school that day. Annika had black fingernails and wore only black and dyed her hair a purplish black color. "I like her," My Mom said to my Dad when she hired her, "She's funky." I didn't know what funky meant and I'm not sure my Mom did either. I liked Annika, too because she never made me do stuff I didn't want to.

"Just tell her you don't want to do it," Annika said. "She can't make you say those things if you don't want to, and neither can your parents."

I looked into it. It turns out, they could make me say those things even if I didn't want to.

"What's the big deal about speaking in public?" My Dad asked.

This from a guy who barely speaks in private.

"I'm scared," I said.

"Sweetheart," My mother said, "Conquering your fears is part of life. I'm afraid of clowns and I still took you to the circus last year."

"No, you didn't, Dad did."

My Dad chuckled.

"I meant to," said my Mom, "and it's the thought that counts."

Two days later, my mother fired Annika after Annika was arrested for shoplifting from the boutique store in our town. (Something black, I bet) Her name was on the police blotter in our town paper and my mother called her up and told her she wasn't a good role model for her daughter, and even accused her of taking her watch which she found in her desk at work a week later.

Suddenly, I had two working parents and no babysitter and in desperation, my mother turned to my grandfather who was always "happy to help." My dad didn't approve but desperate times and all that and for a week straight, my grandpa picked me up from school. I confided in him my dilemma.

"Just picture everyone in their underwear."

"Why would I do that?"

That stymied him and he became embarrassed and mumbled, "Never mind."

Instead, he had me practice my line every afternoon for a week, telling me to pretend he was the only person there. Since he was the only person there, I had no trouble telling him my line and I said it to him over and over.

"Welcome Pilgrims, you have braved the mighty Atlantic…"

We started out with me saying it at the kitchen table while I ate some Fig Newtons, which were his favorite cookies, but not mine. Gradually, he moved further away until he was all the way in the living room, and I would have to yell my line from the kitchen.

"Welcome Pilgrims, you have braved…"

The day of the performance, he wrangled an invite from my mother. Our little classroom was packed with parents and one grandparent and most of the dads held video cameras. If I stumbled or forgot my line or peed myself, it was to be recorded for all time. I'd never been so scared, even more than the time that big spider was on my bed. I stared at my grandfather and only him as he sat in the front row smiling back at me.

When my turn finally came, I said my line directly to him and next thing I knew, it was Walter Raleigh's turn then Massasoit's and the show was over. The whole production lasted five minutes leaving parents puzzled wondering, "I skipped work for this?" I spotted one dad who was crying, and his daughter didn't even have a line.

When it was over, the parents and one grandparent stayed and mingled and we gave them apple juice and cookies (Fig Newtons again, what gives?). My grandfather hugged me and told me I was "best one." The phrase "you were the best one" reverberated around and around my tiny brain. Maybe I could speak in public. Maybe I could become an actress and star in movies. I'd be the famous actress with the boy's name.

I daydreamed about my new career the whole day until my mother drove me home from school.

"Sweetheart, you looked so beautiful up there, but I couldn't hear a word you said."

My grandfather was just being kind, I wasn't the best one. I was the worst one. I'd never be an actress and I'd never become the famous movie star with the boy's name. I knew I was a disaster, and I vowed never to speak in public again. Seven years later, I learned what an actual disaster is.

Chapter Fifty-Two

For their first date, Julie decided they should see a movie like every other normal couple in America had been doing since the turn of the century. Later on, she would joke that for their first date he took her to a funeral, but it really began with a movie. She wanted to lighten the mood, so she picked what she thought was a comedy.

They had dinner beforehand and Curt passed the table manners test. She'd been out with guys who chewed with their mouths open or ate with their fingers like a Neanderthal and if she was going to stare across the table at somebody for the rest of her life, he couldn't gross her out. He didn't.

During dinner, she told her Sister Beatrice and the condom story. It was her best bit and she liked to pull it out on first dates for two reasons. One, she liked to start strong, make a good impression, and let the guy know what kind of delightful conversation would be headed his way if he stuck around. Two, the story was a good gauge of his sense of humor. If he barely laughed or didn't at all, he was a dud and she wasn't going to spend the rest of her life performing for a guy who was a bad crowd.

She told the condom story flawlessly and Curt laughed long and hard. She was relieved for although he smiled pleasantly throughout dinner, he wore his air of sadness like a Hazmat suit, bulky and impossible not to notice. The tragedy was still too fresh so despite his efforts to be a good sport and her attempts at humor, his mood kept slipping back to somber. "The movie should help," she reasoned.

In truth, it was Debbie who picked the movie.

"You've got to see it," she said, "It's hilarious."

And it was. Julie laughed frequently always with a sideways glance at Curt making sure he too was enjoying himself. He seemed to be although, he didn't laugh as often or as loudly as she did, it was enough to make her feel that he was enjoying her company and her movie, and everything was going well, until Julia Roberts suddenly died.

Why did she die? It was a turn Julie wasn't expecting. Why in a "hilarious" movie would Julia Roberts suddenly die? Curt's mother had just died unexpectedly and now Julie had brought him to see a movie about a young mother with a small child who had a seizure and died. *Good lord.*

Julie was stunned and upon realizing what she had done, turned and grabbed Curt by the arm.

"We should go," she said.

"Why?" he said, his face confused.

"Because," she said while being shhh'd from someone nearby.

She stood up and bolted for the exit, nearly crashing into a gaggle of old ladies in the lobby before Curt caught up to her.

"What's the matter?" he asked.

"I am so sorry," she said, "I had no idea that anybody died."

"Oh," said Curt with a chuckle.

Julie didn't handle death very well. After her break-up with Dutch and the subsequent "drinks with the girls" on Thursday night, she lamented how she was destined to die alone.

"We all die alone," said Debbie.

"What do you mean?" asked Sasha.

"Men die first," said Debbie. "Men die first around seventy-two while women rattle around an empty house until they're eighty-seven so even if we get married eventually, we'll die alone."

That conversation stuck with Julie like a tattoo. Men die first at seventy-two and women hang on 'til eighty-seven and here were Julia Roberts and Curt's Mom breaking the rules. They weren't eight-seven, and this wasn't what nature intended, and she started to cry.

"Let's go back in," he said.

"No."

She sniffled.

"C'mon, you're enjoying the movie. Let's see the end."

He took her hand. *He took my hand.* He led her back to their seats where they sat still holding hands. *He still has my hand.*

Since he wouldn't cry, she cried for the both of them, partly out of empathy for Sally Field for losing her daughter and partly out of guilt for making him watch. She apologized from the credits all the way to the car.

"It's fine," he said, "Seriously."

On the way home, she decided to make it up to him. She didn't invite him in because she didn't feel that guilty. He'd have to settle for a long and passionate make-out session that could have ended two or three times had she not kept it going. She kissed him as sexily as she could, doing her best to make things right. They made plans for another date and she gave him one last kiss good night and long meaningful leer as she backed out of the car. Although Curt never let on, it wasn't until Julie was in her apartment alone staring at her bathroom mirror that she discovered her face was lined and streaked and smeared with mascara and she looked more ridiculous than sexy.

Fifty-Three

Tom was putting his handkerchief back when he felt the little slip of paper in his pocket. He'd just been arguing with a customer, a middle-aged woman who was trying to return a scarf she had already worn and put through the wash. *Sorry, lady, rules are rules.*

He didn't like to blow his nose on the floor, but sometimes it couldn't be helped. He fished the paper out of his pocket and opened it up. Every once in a while, Lydia would a leave little note for him to find later in his trousers or suit jacket. The notes would say something like, "I love you" or "You're handsome" or some little private joke just between the two of them.

This one read, "We're having spam tonight."

Tom laughed, then, looked around to make sure no one was watching lest he appear a lunatic laughing all by himself. *What had made her think of that?* It had been years since he told her of his revulsion of spam and anything else found in his k-rations.

He decided to check on the boys on the loading dock when he heard his name being paged.

"Tom Morrissey to the office, please, Tom Morrissey to the office."

He was paged a few times every day but never as "Tom Morrissey" always as "store manager." That was protocol. He headed to the office. Being paged by his name meant something was up and he had a sick feeling. *Not again.*

Five times in the past year, he had gone home early because of a Tommy-related emergency. The boy had spontaneous, unprovoked fits of rage. A month earlier, he had badly cut his hand after punching a window and needed stitches.

Tom was becoming numb to all of it and he was aware of his numbness. He and Lydia were on high alert all the time. He left the house each morning praying that nothing bad would happen while he was at work. He learned how to get through each day just by going through the motions the way he had during the war.

On the other side of the door, marked "Employees Only," Helen was waiting for him. She was a plump, phony blonde busybody who always had an ache or a pain she liked to tell you about.

"It's an emergency" she said, "You have to go to St. Luke's."

"St. Luke's? Is it Tommy?"

"He didn't say" she said, "He only said it was an emergency and the name of the hospital."

"He?"

"The man from the hospital."

"Why didn't Lydia call?" he thought as he hurried to his car. *What did he do this time?* He knew there were whispers about his son at work. They knew he didn't go to the normal school. *What else did they know?* He had kept his son's schizophrenia from them, but someone was bound to find out and once, one person found out, everyone would know.

Tom drove with his mind elsewhere only vaguely aware of red lights and pedestrians. He wondered if Tommy liked embarrassing him, if making him and Lydia look like bad parents was a game for him. *Was it something he enjoyed? Was it just part of being a teenager? Was it a rebellious phase that would come to an end some day?* He still clung to the hope that the boy would straighten himself out and go to college someday.

Tom parked in the hospital parking lot as he had before. He walked, knowing that he should run, but his dread and his dignity wouldn't allow it. The automatic door opened, he skirted past a colored man mopping the floor and approached the woman sitting at the white desk. She was heavy, gray-haired and bespectacled and she flinched when he gave her his name. She disappeared for a minute down the hall and came back with an older blonde woman, older and taller with an air of authority who took Tom aside.

"Your son tried to kill himself, but he was unsuccessful."

Kill himself? The boy tried to kill himself?

"They brought him in with your wife, who had some type of episode."

The woman's eyes never wavered from Tom's as she delivered the news. They were brown and blood-shot.

Lydia? Something has happened to Lydia?

"What does that mean? Some type of episode?"

She hesitated.

"It appears she had a slight heart attack, but she's going to be fine."

On hearing the word "heart attack" Tom closed his eyes and for an instant thought he was going to topple over. *No. A heart attack? A suicide attempt?* He had steeled himself for news about Tommy but not about Lydia.

"Can I see her?"

"If you like."

"What about my son?"

"The doctor is busy with Thomas right now, but you can see him afterwards."

"Can I see my wife now?"

"Certainly, but she's been sedated."

Tom followed the nurse. He was vaguely aware that she must have been attractive in her day and that's where her confidence came from. She wasn't afraid to look a man in the eye and be authoritative. The room Lydia was in was on the second floor. They rode the elevator in silence up one floor.

"Here she is" the nurse said.

Lydia was sound asleep with her mouth opened an inch or so. She could have been at home sleeping, yet she never slept on her back, always curled up on her right side with her arm tucked under her head. She wore a hospital johnny and a plastic bracelet with her name on it around her wrist. She was pale and looked skinnier than usual. Tom felt like he was at the morgue identifying her body.

"She'll sleep like this until morning," the formerly pretty nurse said, "She was just so frightened, poor thing."

She led him back to the waiting room to see the doctor. The sight of his wife lying there that way made him queasy. *What if she had died?* Tommy was sixteen and going off to college in a couple of years but what about Curt? He was only eleven. A boy that young needs a mother.

Tom stood in front of a chair in the waiting room, but couldn't bring himself to sit down. His thoughts shifted from Lydia to Tommy. The boy had tried to kill himself. *Suicide is a sin, a sin worse than murder because there is no chance of repentance afterwards. Didn't the boy realize his soul could be damned for eternity?*

Tom felt tears coming on and cleared his throat. He wouldn't allow that and he forbade himself from crying. As he quelled his tears, his anger rose. His son had tried to kill himself and had nearly killed his mother in the process. He balled his hands into fists.

"Mr. Morrissey."

The doctor was Oriental. Whether Chinese or Japanese, he didn't know. Tom was a good eight inches taller and couldn't tell if he was older or younger than the man. *It's difficult to tell with Orientals.*

"Thomas is sedated now. The boy had tried to kill himself."

"How?"

"The boy slashed his left wrist and bled quite profusely. Fortunately, your wife was home and the ambulance got him here quickly."

The Doctor spoke in facts without emotion. Being Oriental, he was probably unaware that Tommy had committed a mortal sin.

"Can I look at him?"

"Certainly."

The doctor led Tom to the elevator and once inside being alone, he continued the conversation.

"We're going to need to keep him here for a few days for observation, but we may need to transfer him to another hospital."

Tom knew he meant a mental hospital. *The looney bin. My son is going to the looney bin. He's lucky he's not going to hell.*

They got off on the sixth floor. *Six is the devil's number, 666.* The irony was not lost on Tom. He wondered what religion the doctor adhered to. He'd seen some Orientals at mass and didn't know if they saw the light when they came to this country or if missionaries had shown them the way in their own homeland.

"He's in here" the doctor said. Tommy lay on his side with his left wrist heavily bandaged. There were constraints on his other wrist and around his ankles keeping him in the bed. He wore a white johnny too and looked even paler than Lydia.

Looking at the bandage, Tom felt the lump in his throat return and again he began to cry. This time he couldn't stop. "I'll leave you alone for a minute," the doctor said and exited quickly.

He looked down at his pathetic son and realized for the first time that he had been deluding himself all along and that the dreams he had for the boy would never come to be. *He's not going to college. He'll never marry and have children. He'll be lucky to ever hold any kind of a job.* Tom stood bent over with his left hand tucked under his elbow and he began sobbing into his right wrist. *Damn you, Tommy. Damn you for making me cry.*

Chapter Fifty-Four

Jenny was my best friend, and she died. We were fourteen and she had gone skiing with her family in Vermont, but their car skidded on some black ice and Jenny was killed, her Dad had a traumatic brain injury and her brother broke both legs while her mother emerged with cuts and bruises, and no family to speak of.

Jenny and I had been friends since her family moved here from Bethesda, Maryland. Like me, she played field hockey and she danced, and our friendship began one day in Honors English in the 8th grade. Ryan Hesketh was pontificating about Shakespeare, pretending that he, unlike the rest of us, understood Julius Caesar. As he blathered on, Jenny got my attention by tapping her pen on her notebook and as I glanced over, I saw one word written down in large, bold letters. It was the word "lame." That one word written for my benefit alone began our friendship. It was the signal to me that here was someone who thought the way I thought, someone, who behind that mask of innocence and benevolence was actually scathing and perspicacious and vicious.

I marveled at her ability to skewer every single boy in the school. Tyler Drummond was the best-looking boy in our grade, and he knew it. As he strutted by one day she whispered, "His bathroom mirror must have to tell him, 'okay, that's enough,' and send him on his way." She told me which boys would end up in prison and which ones were gay. She was a teenage sphinx who said nothing but saw everything and shared her insights and her wit only with me.

The day she died, it was really the next day that I got the news, was the worst day of my life. I'd always been afraid of death; I remember crying at bedtime as a five-year-old having caught on to the fact that we're all going to die. My Mom and Dad would try and console me that it wouldn't happen for years and years, but they couldn't deny that it would happen, and I was not consoled. Now here it was, arriving much too early to take my best friend away. I cried more that day that I ever had or ever would.

Here's the thing, I didn't go to the wake. My parents had a commitment that they couldn't get out of, so I was to go alone, and I lied and didn't go. I didn't lie exactly, I just didn't tell them the truth, their rules. I went to a Starbucks and had a mocha something and sat by myself. Jenny was Catholic like me and I feared her dead body would be on display. I never wanted to see a dead body and I especially didn't want to see my best friend's dead body, so I sat in the corner of Starbucks and cried my silent tears.

I barely slept the night before the funeral and my mother woke me up that morning. My Dad had already gone to work.

"I can't go to the funeral," she said.

She had some sort of meeting that she was running, and she tried to get out of it, but her boss wouldn't let her.

"Don't worry," she said on her way out the door, "I spoke to your grandfather and I've arranged for him to take you."

This was a stroke of luck. I didn't want to go to funeral. I couldn't bear the thought of seeing the coffin and knowing my best friend's dead body was inside. I just couldn't. I knew my grandfather wouldn't make me go. Unlike my parents, he never made me do anything I didn't want to. An hour later, he arrived, all dressed up in his dark suit. I explained to him about Jenny and the black ice and that while I appreciated him coming, I didn't want to go.

"Get dressed," he said, "We're going."

"But Grandpa, I don't want to."

"Hurry up," he said.

His tone was gruff and although I'd heard his gruffness many times, I'd never heard it directed at me. I had a sudden glimmer into my Dad's life and why he both feared and loathed this man. I wanted to defy him, but I didn't have the courage and moments later I was dressed and in his car.

"We'll just sit in the back," he said after a few minutes of silence.

We arrived right at nine, but it was starting late. There were hordes of teenagers, most of whom I knew, all dressed up and many of them were crying. I saw girls that Jenny barely knew or barely liked that were inconsolable. How dare they?

My grief was now more rage than anything else and I snubbed my classmates and slipped in a side door with my grandfather trailing behind. I was furious that he had brought me here. I sat in the last row and he sat next to me and I didn't acknowledge him or anyone else.

I knew that any minute the funeral would begin, and the coffin would Jenny's dead body would be brought in. I should just run. I should just run out right now and run home. My grandfather could never catch me.

He knelt down to say his prayers and he bade me to do the same. This guy was pushing his luck, but I humored him while I planned my escape. I had to get out of there.

I finished pretending to pray and I sat back down. The organ music began, and Jenny's Mom walked past. She was blonde and petite and cute and about ten years too young for her and my Mom to be friends. My Mom's friends all seemed to be about her age and body type. I always felt I could watch a group of women walk by and pick out which ones were my Mom's friends. My Mom's friends all looked like her.

Jenny's Mom did yoga and was slim and made Jenny and me egg white omelets after sleepovers. Her normal erect posture was gone now, and she was hunched and helped down the aisle by an older man. Was that her father? Jenny's grandfather? The church became eerily silent now as even the teenagers stopped talking and everyone stared at Jenny's mom as she slumped down the aisle with the help of the old man.

My grandfather nudged me.

"Why don't you go sit with her?" he whispered.

"I don't want to," I whispered back, shaking my head.

"Go on," he said.

I rose from my pew automatically and thought about turning left and running out of the church, but I turned right and followed them down the aisle. Jenny's Mom sat in the front row with her Dad to her right and I slide in to her left and sat down. She smiled a tightlipped, non-tooth-showing smile and took my hand. I could see the cuts and the stitches in what until recently had been a very pretty face. They wheeled in the coffin and I burst into tears.

I don't remember much about the funeral. I know that sounds odd, but my mind kept wandering away from the prayers and the rituals to thoughts of sleepovers and English class and lunch in the cafeteria. I have no idea what the readings or the Gospel were about, but I remember the eulogy making me mad. The priest, a doddering old man, not much younger than my grandfather, spoke of Jenny's "kindness" and "her gentle nature" and he completely missed the point. She wasn't like that at all.

Throughout the mass, Jenny's mother would give my hand a squeeze from time to time. I wasn't listening but I gleaned it was triggered by something the priest said. Every time she squeezed my hand I would cry. I was like a dish rag. She squeezed and I dripped.

When the mass was over, Jenny's Mom didn't release her grip and she held onto my hand all the way down the aisle and out the door. My grandfather looked on as I stood with her on the bottom of the steps as people approached and offered condolences. The priest had invited everyone to the cemetery, but these folks didn't want to go to a cemetery any more than I did.

Suddenly, she turned and looked right at me. I could see her face would be scarred under her left eye, on her forehead and along the side of her right cheek. These were deep grooves that would never fade away.

"Would you ride with me in the hearse?"

The hearse? With my friend's dead body? No fuckin' way.

"Sure, she will" said my Grandpa. *Where did he come from?*

I was helped into the hearse and once seated, Jenny's Mom took my hand again. Jenny's body was right behind us. I was in a car with a corpse and not just any corpse, the corpse of my best friend. I felt a wave of nausea and began to sweat. "Please don't throw up" I said to myself.

We drove slowly through red lights while non-grieving cars stopped and waited. Halfway there, her mother squeezed my hand again.

"She loved you so much," she said, "You were her best friend."

I tried to speak but something blocked my throat, and nothing came out. My eyes were so laden with tears I could barely see her. It was like looking through a car windshield with the wipers broken.

At the cemetery, a fraction of the packed church was there. It was for VIPs only of the world's worst after-party. The priest had changed from his white robes and wore only his black walking around clothes with the little white collar. He read from a small prayer book and I paid attention this time. It was the old "ashes to ashes, dust to dust" routine they show in movies.

It was over soon enough and Jenny's Mom hugged me and thanked me for coming. "Anytime" I said. Anytime? Meaning what? That I'd come to her daughter's funeral anytime? Am I a fucking idiot? This was all my grandfather's fault. I didn't want to come to the funeral. I didn't want to sit with her mother. I didn't want to ride in a car with her dead body and I didn't want to go to the cemetery and now I said, "Any time." I got into his car and stared out the window and ignored him the whole ride home. Fuck him.

Chapter Fifty-Five

Their second date was another movie, this one something foreign and metaphorical and dull, and Julie and Curt ended up making out in the back row like two newly pubescent teenagers in the 1950's. Things were progressing nicely. With dinner plans scheduled for their third date, Julie decided it was time for "The Talk."

When you're in your early or mid-twenties you don't need "The Talk" but once you're both past thirty there needs to be some discussion. "The Talk" was a two-step process. First, each party had to explain why they weren't already married. After all, at that point in your life, most people have found somebody so you had to explain what was wrong with you, at least that's how Julie looked at it. Sometimes someone was simply focused on his/her career. Often, someone had been in a long-term relationship that had ended badly just before marriage. Occasionally, there was a more exotic excuse like a stint in the Peace Corps, or having to overcome a spinal injury. In any event, each side had to explain why they were where they were.

The other part of "The Talk" was that each side had to establish the ground rules, like "Are we still seeing other people or not?" Julie, given her family's history, had very specific rules about alcohol. So far in two dates, Curt had a total of one beer which was a good sign. Julie didn't mind a guy who smoked pot occasionally, but she drew the line at coke or anything more exotic.

Sometimes religion came up during "The Talk." Once, while on a last date, a guy told Julie he'd never get serious with her because she wasn't Jewish.

"I'm only dating Muslims from now on," she told the Committee the next day.

Julie was funny about religion. She didn't want a Born Again Christian or a Mormon or a Jehovah's Witness or anyone super religious. Yet, she didn't care for atheists either. She wasn't much of a Catholic, but she still believed in God and wasn't ready to turn her back on the whole thing.

"The Talk" can be complicated and messy but it needed to take place. If a guy says he never, ever wants to get married, she'd rather know that upfront. So just after they had ordered and handed the menus back, Julie leaned forward and asked, "So, how come you're not married?"

He stopped chewing on his breadstick and gave her a funny look.

"Oh, you want to talk about that?"

She shrugged with her palms to the ceiling in a gesture of "Why not?"

"Okay," he said, "I had a girlfriend for two and a half years but we broke up. How 'bout you?"

"My last boyfriend and I broke up when I caught him cheating on me."

She left out the part about finding the other woman's panties.

"My college boyfriend cheated on me, too. The only rule I have is I want total honesty."

"The only rule?"

"Yep," she said, "I'll date a serial killer as long as he doesn't lie about it."

The waitress came by.

"Can I get you another drink?" she asked Curt.

It was obvious the waitress thought he was cute. She would glance Julie's way, but her gaze stayed mostly on him. Such are the hazards of dating a good-looking man.

"No, thanks," he said, and Julie shook her head "no."

She smiled at him and moved on.

"How old are you?" she asked.

"Thirty-three."

"Me, too," she said.

She was thirty-five, but guys didn't like it when the woman was older. Besides, the two years she had spent battling Bob to be the alpha dog at work shouldn't count. She had to put her love life on hold while she concentrated on her career and that shouldn't be held against her.

"What is it that you're looking for?" she asked.

He lifted his eyebrows and sucked in his cheeks and then exhaled.

"Well, I'd like to be with a woman who is smart and kind and fun to be with."

"Uh oh," said Julie, "That rules me out. I wished you'd said something sooner."

He laughed. She was glad she could make him laugh. He wasn't an easy laugh as Sasha was, but Sasha laughed at everything. He was more discerning.

"Why did you and your girlfriend break up?"

"There were a few things," he said. "She accused me of being a workaholic."

"Are you a workaholic?"

"Absolutely," he said, wiping his mouth with his napkin. "I own my own business. I can't just punch in and punch out, I'm responsible for everybody on my staff and everything that goes on in my company."

"Do you believe in God?" she asked.

"Sure," he said.

"Do you do drugs?"

He laughed even though for once she wasn't going for a laugh.

"I own my own business. I can't be out partying and getting shitfaced and what not. I have to set a good example."

So far, so good.

"Are you or have you ever been a member of the Communist party?"

He laughed hard at that one. *I am fun to be with.* The waitress was back and she brought their salads with her.

"Here you go," she said. *Is it my imagination or does she only smile at him?* Julie waited for the waitress to walk away before she asked the big question.

"Do you see yourself as getting married and having kids?"

"I see myself getting married," he said, "But I don't see myself as having kids."

Julie kept a poker face. He'd been doing so well. He was a hard-working, non-atheist, non-drug addict, a straight shooter who was super cute.

"You're not dying to have kids, are you?"

"No," she said softly.

What was she supposed to say? She couldn't bring up Kevin at a time like this. Curt met 90% of her requirements and that was pretty good. Guys always say they don't want kids. Michael used to say that and now he's got three. She had had enough of "The Talk" for one night. *He'll change his mind.*

Chapter Fifty-Six

Tom came home from the hospital and took off his coat. He remembered nothing of the drive home. *How do people do that?* His mind so preoccupied with thoughts of his wife's heart attack and his son's near suicide that the car drove itself home.

He looked at the clock in the kitchen. It read 1:25. He could have gone back to work. *How would that go?*

"So, where were you, Tom?"

"Oh, my son tried to kill himself and my wife was so traumatized she had a slight heart attack. How's business today? How's that sale on women's blouses going?"

He knew he'd make up something tomorrow. *Maybe I'll tell them about the heart attack. No shame in that. How many years before I can quit?*

He decided to eat something. He didn't feel hungry, but he knew he should eat. He ate every day between 11:15 and 11:30 before they got busy during the customers' lunch hour. He took some cold cuts and mayonnaise from the refrigerator and white bread from the counter. He remembered the bread his mother baked every Sunday morning. *Freshly baked bread, right out of the oven.* His life, like his bread, had gotten so much worse.

He took a butter knife from the drawer and began to put mayonnaise on two slices of bread when he stopped abruptly and put the knife down. *There must be blood. Tommy had slashed his wrist, there must be blood.* He moved quickly from the kitchen through the hall and started up the stairs.

On the third step, he saw a large red drop of blood. He hovered over it for a moment then proceeded upwards. There were larger drops on the fifth and sixth steps. The higher he went the more drops of blood he saw. He moved slowly, taking his time on each step. There were puddles of blood in the hall when he reached the second floor.

Oh God. Look at all the blood. This is my son's blood.

He hugged the wall, stepping over the puddles, and entered the bathroom. There was blood on the floor and blood on the walls, the mirror, in the bathtub and the toilet. The toilet paper poodle had blotches of red on its green knitting.

He was nauseous now and dizzy. He reached out for the towel rack which snapped under his weight, and he fell to one knee. He saw that he had dipped his knee in his son's blood and the blood began to slowly spread on his pants. He quickly lifted his knee out of the puddle.

He closed the lid of the toilet and pulled himself up and sat. All the blood made him think about Moretti and he realized he was out of breath. *I'm all right, I'm all right, I'm all right.*

He sat on the closed lid of the toilet for a few minutes. Then, he bent over and picked up the towel rack which was now in two pieces. He held both pieces in his right hand and sat back on the closed toilet lid. It was then, he noticed the razor blade.

It was half submerged in blood. Holding the broken towel rack in his right hand, he leaned forward and carefully, plucked the razor blade from the blood. It was one of his. Tommy had only shaved once or twice and didn't yet own his own razor or any blades. He stared at it. It was just an ordinary razor and he knew it was very nearly a murder weapon. He started to cry again and then, pushed the tears back down.

He held the razor between his thumb and finger. He thought about Moretti's parents, his little Italian father and his big Hungarian mother. They must be long dead now, like his parents. He had wished he had contacted them after the war to tell them what a wonderful son they had. He had always wanted to find them and tell them, but he never had. *How would I have found them? There are ways. Why am I thinking about them now?*

He noticed the blood stain on his knee, and he lifted himself up, holding the broken towel rack in one hand and the razor blade in the other. He retraced his steps avoiding the puddles again and stepped delicately down the staircase.

In the kitchen, he opened the cabinet door below the sink and placed the razor blade and the broken towel rack in the trash and closed the cabinet door. He opened the other cabinet door and took out a plastic bucket and began filling it with water. He took off his suit jacket and tie and draped them over a chair while water filled the bucket. He rolled up his sleeves. He felt the water. Cold. *What is wrong with me?*

He dumped it out and began filling it again this time with hot water. It was already 2:30. *How is it 2:30 already?* He began to feel hungry. *Why was this taking so long?* He shut the water off, took a sponge and a spray bottle from under the sink. He put the sponge in the bucket and lifted it with his left hand. In his right, he carried the spray bottle and made his way up the stairs, again tiptoed around his son's blood.

He'd do the bathroom first and work his way down. He sprayed the mirror. *God, I look old.* His eyes were blood shot and his hair receding. After the mirror, he cleaned the blood from the tub, squatting with one leg inside the tub and one leg out. He then washed the blood from the sponge, avoiding looking in the mirror this time. Somehow, he knew if he made eye contact with himself, he would cry again.

He sprayed the toilet lid and flushed it twice to get rid of red stains inside the bowl. He sprayed around the bowl and the wall behind. *How did it get all the way back here?* It must have ricocheted. He washed the sponge again and opened the medicine cabinet to avoid looking in the mirror.

He sat on the toilet lid and leaning over, began washing the floor. It occurred to him that he should be using a mop, but he continued with the sponge anyway. He was rinsing the sponge when he heard the backdoor open. *Curt's home.* Tom had forgotten about Curt and now he was home.

He threw down the sponge and with a surge of adrenaline, scurried down the stairs swiftly but mindful of Tommy's blood. It was just a few seconds before he reached the kitchen. Curt, still in his coat and hat, looked at his father. He saw the blood on his father's pants and hands and became frightened.

"Dad, what are-"

"Curt, I need you to play in the cellar."

Tom placed a bloody hand on each of Curt's shoulders and moved him backwards towards the cellar door.

"Dad, I…"

"Curt, just listen to me. I need you to play in the cellar."

Tom opened the cellar door and with his right hand, he grabbed Curt roughly by his shirtsleeve and swung him down the first two steps. Curt stood on the second step looking up at his father in the doorway. Some of Tommy's blood was now on his shoulders and his sleeve.

"What happened Dad?"

"Curt, I need you to play in the cellar, right now."

"Dad, what happened?"

The boy was screaming now.

"Dad!"

Tom closed the door and locked it.

"Play in the cellar, Curt."

Curt tried the door handle. It was locked.

"Dad" he yelled, "Let me out. Dad, let me out."

But Tom had gone, gone to destroy what was left of the evidence.

Chapter Fifty-Seven

For my family, the three big holidays, Thanksgiving, Christmas and Easter, had always been virtually interchangeable. Granted, we didn't go to mass on Thanksgiving or hunt for eggs on Christmas or watch football on Easter, but the basic template was always the same. I'd go with my father to pick up my grandfather and since the two of them didn't speak I did all the talking. I'll tell him about the Girl Scouts and piano lessons and soccer games. Once home, we'd either watch the game, open presents or collect the eggs and then, we'd eat a huge meal and drive my grandpa back to his house. This happened three times a year my whole childhood.

Things changed slightly the Thanksgiving after I turned sixteen, and the changes were too subtle for me to grasp at the time. Life is kind of like the game "Chutes and Ladders" but in reverse. You start at the top and move gradually a few spaces at a time until occasionally, you land on a chute and plummet a great distance all at once. Sometime between the previous Easter and that Thanksgiving, my grandfather plummeted. He went from a proud and dignified gentleman to a puzzled, bumbling fool. I found it hilarious.

When we picked him up on this particular Thanksgiving, he was his typical well-dressed self, and although his brown tie didn't really go with his blue suit, he seemed perfectly normal. Like always, he greeted me with a smile and my dad with a scowl and it wasn't until we reached my house that things began to go south.

My grandpa and I sat in the living room watching the Detroit Lions get pummeled when my Mom suggested I tell him about the school play. I had a small part in our school's production of "Our Town." I was still terrified to speak in public, but I loved the theater so with each school production I would sign up, feign illness and miss the auditions and then happily take my part as one of "townspeople" or "crowd" or as one of the "villagers." In "Our Town" I had landed the role of "woman." As I began to tell him about it, he dozed off and even made snoring sounds.

"Mom, he's asleep," I yelled towards the kitchen.

"Sweetheart, not everybody likes Thornton Wilder," she yelled back.

My Dad woke him up for dinner and he murmured something about his new medication.

The holiday meal began like it always did with the saying of grace. My mother, for some reason, liked to pretend that we were religious whenever my grandfather was around. In years past, she would go on and on about my first communion or confirmation or the girl's Catholic high school she went to. She always initiated the saying of grace as though we did it even when he wasn't there.

A few minutes into the meal, there was a lull in the conversation and my grandfather became confused and began to say grace again. To be polite, we stopped eating and joined in, but this time I noticed my grandfather's brown tie protruding out of his blue suit jacket onto his plate into a pool of gravy. I began to giggle and after my mother scolded me, my giggling became uncontrollable.

I pulled myself together and the meal continued and while my mother was mid-story, my grandfather interrupted her and began saying grace for the third time. Once again, we joined in and I began laughing again and couldn't stop. I even excused myself and went to the bathroom to try and laugh it out. It didn't work for just when I would stop and begin to exit the bathroom, I would get the giggles again and would have to retreat and try to regain my composure.

When I finally returned to the table, both of my parents shot me dirty looks. When I sat down, he began saying grace again and I tried biting my tongue and pinching myself in the leg to keep from laughing. We must have said grace ten more times and after the last time, my mother reached over and plucked his tie from him plate. She tried stuffing it back into his jacket when I noticed a tiny cranberry clinging to it. That cranberry stayed on his brown tie defying gravity, velcroed in place by a combination of fabric and gravy. It was the funniest thing I'd ever seen, and no amount of scolding or tongue biting could make my laughter stop.

A few minutes later, when my mother attempted to serve pie, my grandfather fell asleep again, sitting up with his head leaning over the table, and we had to cut dessert short. My father drove him home without me while my mother lectured me on being insensitive and immature.

"I couldn't help it," I said, "I mean…that cranberry."

My friends never found the story as funny as I did, but in my mind, I finally had an anecdote that could rival one of my Mom's. Two years later, when he was diagnosed with Alzheimer's, it stopped being so funny. Now when I think of that day, none of the mirth returns. I think only of how stupid I was and how callous, and I'm filled with shame.

Chapter Fifty-Eight

The morning after "The Talk" Debbie stood holding the Boston Herald waiting for Julie as she entered the bank. Julie was late, having lain in bed that morning reliving the night before. After "The Talk" she and Curt had engaged in some ferocious heavy petting and though she was tempted she was proud of herself for not letting things go too far. She was horny and reflective and didn't feel like getting out of bed. Even Sasha had beat her to work.

Debbie pointed to a story in the paper and handed it to Julie.

"Is this your boyfriend?" Debbie asked.

Julie took the paper from her. She knew all the Committee members plus Melvin the Security Guard and Bob the Idiot were watching her. She took the paper without looking at it, tucked it under her arm and strode towards the ladies' room. Whatever it was, she would look at in private.

She locked the door behind her and opened the paper.

"Son Accused of Murdering Mother" read the headline.

The gist of the article was that the Suffolk County DA was going to pursue murder and assault with a deadly weapon charges against Thomas P. Morrissey for killing his mother and attempting to kill his father.

Someone knocked on the door.

"Miss Rossi," said Melvin, "It's nine o'clock, you mind if I open up?"

She wasn't surprised that Bob couldn't make the decision to open the bank at nine even though the bank always opened at nine. *Can't he do a fucking thing?*

"Yes, Melvin, you can open" she said through the locked door.

She threw the paper in the trash and exited the ladies' room. She walked to her desk without looking over at The Committee.

"Isn't that his family?" said Debbie from behind the Teller's glass.

"Yeah," said Julie nodding.

She took a file from her desk and pretended to examine it. There was only one customer in the bank now and she knew all the tellers were staring. She could feel her face reddening, but she wouldn't look up.

Curt acted like everything was rosy. He took her to the movies and to dinner and engaged in near sex without the slightest hint that his brother was soon to be tried for the murder of his mother. He didn't think to mention any of this? Even after she had told him that she insisted on "total honesty."

She placed her elbows on her desk and her head in her hands. *There had to be "a catch." There was no way a handsome, sensitive, principled, unattached guy was going to walk into her bank and fall for her without there being a catch. Check the fine print.*

"If it sounds too good to be true, it probably is," one of her professors was fond of saying. He taught advertising and was one of those teachers who only had two or three things to say and said them over and over and over.

"If it sounds too good to be true, it probably is."

Curt was too good to be true. She should have suspected something. She joked about it during lunch with Sasha.

"You know anyone you want to set me up with? Someone from the Manson family perhaps?"

Sasha laughed. It was so Julie.

"I attract this sort of thing, don't I?" she said, "My life is like a bad sitcom."

Despite the jokes and the self-deprecating remarks, she was genuinely hurt and the more she ruminated the angrier she got. He was just another deceptive guy. *They're all the same. Full of shit.*

She was with a customer when he called.

"Hey," he said, his voice warm.

"I'm sorry," she said to her customer.

"Bob, could you help Mrs. Crimmins with her transfer?"

He probably couldn't, but she foisted the nice old lady onto him anyway.

"Hey," she said, without warmth when she returned to the call.

"I had fun last night," he said.

There was a moment before she replied. Part of her just wanted to say, "Me, too" and pretend nothing was wrong, but she couldn't.

"I saw the story in the Herald today," she said.

Now it was his turn to be silent.

"Yeah," he said, "I've been meaning to talk to you about that."

"I wish you had," she said.

She spoke just above a whisper. She was at work and the doors were open and customers and Committee members lurked nearby. She had to maintain at least the guise of professionalism.

"We had a long talk about total honesty" she said, "That's the one thing I insist on, remember?"

"You're right, you're right," he said, "It's just…"

He stopped talking for a moment. *Was he getting emotional?*

"It's a hard thing to bring up, you know. My brother didn't kill my mother. It's total bullshit. He loved my mother."

He was getting emotional. Suddenly, she was the bad guy, prodding her grieving boyfriend into discussing matters he didn't care to discuss.

"I just want you to be honest with me, that's all," she said.

Now she was on the verge of becoming emotional. She glanced towards the tellers. Debbie, sans customers, was staring straight at her from behind the glass. *She's too far away to hear me.*

"Well, listen, there's a pretrial hearing on Friday morning. It shouldn't take too long. His lawyer is just going to enter a plea of not guilty. It should take five minutes. You can come with me to that if you want."

"Okay" she said, holding the phone in one hand and squeezing the cord with the other.

"It's at the Suffolk County courthouse at nine a.m."

"All right," she said, "I better go. I'll see you there."

Fuck, what did I just agree to?

Chapter Fifty-Nine

"Tom, pull over," said Lydia.

"I hear him, I hear him."

He pulled over and let the ambulance pass. They were on their way home from the movies on a Sunday afternoon. It was something they never do any more. Who has the time, and the movies had gotten so smutty. If they weren't smutty, they were preachy, always foisting the Negro and their problems on us. He didn't have anything against Negros. There were Negros who worked on the loading dock and a Negro woman who worked behind the perfume counter. Tom didn't have a problem with them as long as they did their job. He just didn't need to see movies where Negros and white people got married, that was all. Negros should marry Negros and white people should marry white people.

This movie was safe, not smutty or preachy. You can't go wrong with Walter Matthau and Jack Lemmon and Lydia needed a laugh. It was nice to hear her laugh again.

After trying to kill himself, Tommy had spent 48 hours under suicide watch and then another 17 days in a mental hospital. When he came out, he was medicated and googly-eyed and spoke slowly and carefully like a drunk trying to pass as sober. Lydia wouldn't leave his side until Tom and Tommy's teachers finally persuaded her that it would be best if he went back to school, where he could continue his education under constant supervision with kids with similar problems.

Lydia had changed the most. Her liveliness was gone and her humor, once constant, now rarely made an appearance. She was placed on a blood thinner and ordered to quit smoking. She had trouble sleeping now and Tom would catch her sneaking cigarettes at the kitchen table in the middle of the night and make her put them out and come back to bed. She'd be a mess the next morning and get the boys off for school and take a nap.

She was tense all the time now, always on edge.

"How could he try and kill himself? He knows how much we love him."

"I don't know," Tom said, each time she asked. He didn't know. *Why would he do that?*

She'd always been so witty and carefree. She used to make him laugh all the time but that was before the suicide attempt. He couldn't remember the last time she'd said something funny. She'd changed. They'd all changed.

The movie was Tom's idea. Tommy was doing better, and he seemed genuinely contrite about what he had done. It had been eight months since he tried to kill himself and there hadn't been any new incidents or violent outbursts.

A movie would do them good. The two of them barely did anything together these days. They rarely had sex. A few times at Tom's urging she gave up and he did his business as quickly as possible. This was their first "date" in nearly a year.

The ambulance took a left up ahead on Burton Road. A left on Burton was part of their way home, too.

"Tom," said Lydia.

He saw the ambulance and he sped up and took the same left. Tom was going to take a right up ahead onto Pine and as long as the ambulance didn't take a right on Pine there was nothing to worry about. The ambulance took a right on Pine.

"He's going to our house," shrieked Lydia.

"He's not going to our house," said Tom, but he knew that he might be.

He never drove over the speed limit, but now he now he pressed on the gas hard, desperate to get home.

"We shouldn't have gone to the movies. We shouldn't have gone to the movies and left Tommy all alone."

"He's not alone. Curt is with him. Curt wouldn't let him do anything."

"But what if he did?"

"He wouldn't do anything with Curt there."

Tom turned right on Pine just in time to see the ambulance take a left on Wheeler Circle, the cul-de-sac where they lived. There were only eight or nine other houses on their street.

Lydia began to cry while simultaneously reciting the Hail Mary. He didn't cry, but he said the Hail Mary along with her. She didn't finish it.

"I'll never forgive myself. Please God."

He took a left on Wheeler Circle. The ambulance was parked in front of the Kostopoulus' house. *Thank God.* Mr. Kostopoulus was an eighty-seven-year-old widower whose wife had died the previous winter. Tom pulled into the driveway of his own house and looked at Lydia. She was still crying and breathing heavy. He reached for her hand, but she shooed him away and opened the car door.

She got out of the car and headed towards the house. He got out too but walked down driveway on his way to the Kostopoulus house. Three or four neighbors had gathered outside to feign interest. Tom and Lydia had been friendly with them until recently. Everyone knew that Tommy had tried to kill himself and Tom sensed they were keeping their distance. The Morrisseys were now the "weirdo" family.

"You're imagining things," Lydia told him, but he didn't think so.

The families with kids didn't want his crazy kid infecting their kids.

Mr. Kostopoulus was wheeled out of the house on a stretcher and placed in the back of the ambulance. It left with its siren blaring a minute later. Tom kept his distance. Frank Krause from across the street strolled past.

"What happened?" asked Tom.

"Not sure if he had a stroke or a heart attack," said Krause.

Tom nodded and turned back towards home. His heart rate was back to normal and he felt tired now that the excitement was over. He entered the back door and could hear the television on in the den.

He heard the bedroom door upstairs close and found the two boys sitting on the couch in the den watching something called, “Creature Double Feature.”

“What’s wrong with Mom?” asked Curt.

“Nothing.”

Chapter Sixty

I knew something was wrong right away. It was the day before Thanksgiving, and it was my first day back home after having left for college three months before. I was going to see him tomorrow anyway, but I thought I'd stop by and say hello and spend some time alone with him before he and my Dad began baring their teeth at one another over turkey and pumpkin pie.

He answered the door in his pajamas. It was one in the afternoon and he answered the door in his pajamas. I'd never seen him in his pajamas before even when I had stayed with him during Camp Grandpa. He knew my name but seemed more perplexed than happy to see me. It wasn't the reaction I was hoping for.

"Grandpa, are you sick?"

"No, I'm fine. Fine."

He let me in, and I followed him into the kitchen.

"Grandpa, why are you wearing pajamas?"

The question caught him off-guard.

"Pajamas?"

He looked down and seemed quite surprised to discover I was right. He was, in fact, in his pajamas. He turned at stared at me with an angry face as though I was the one responsible. He then limped away from me through the living room and up the stairs to his bedroom.

I looked around at the state of his kitchen. There were dirty dishes and cups and pots and glasses in the sink and on the counter and on the table. There was an open jar of jelly on the table next to a packet of hot dogs with three remaining. The kitchen stank of rotten food.

"Grandpa, you're going to get mice," I called to the upstairs knowing he wouldn't hear me.

On top of the refrigerator, I spotted an uncooked hot dog with a bite taken out of it. Fuck, mice were the least of his problems. I threw the raw hot dog away.

Slowly, I walked in the living room with my head scanning slowly from one side to the other. There were newspapers strewn about and plates with food on the coffee table and on the floor. One of the couch cushions was missing.

In my freshman psych class, when the teacher described the anal-retentive personality I had thought of my grandpa. Everything in his house had always been just so. He made his bed when he first woke up. He showered and shaved and dressed in a suit. His home was immaculate.

I had seen him just before I left for college but not at his home. My mother had invited him and a few of my friends over for a barbecue before I left for central New York. He only stayed an hour or two and he seemed old but himself. How did he slide from his normal self to this in just a few months? How long has he been living in squalor?

I spent the rest of the afternoon cleaning his house. I put away the jelly and the hot dogs and did the dishes in the sink. I threw away food in the refrigerator that seemed roughly my age. Halfway through, he came downstairs. He had shaved and put on a shirt and a tie and a jacket. He seemed pleased with himself. I didn't mention he still wore pajamas bottoms and had slippers on his otherwise bare feet.

He seemed happy to see me again when he came down. He knew my name and I had him sit and talk to me while I cleaned. He told me stories I'd heard many times, the story of meeting his wife and the time he proposed and the day his first son was born. He left out the part about his son being confined to a mental institution.

I found no mice, only ants and sprayed them with a can I found under the sink. Does bug spray go bad?

After I finished cleaning the kitchen, we moved to the living room and he sat and told me the same stories he had just told me. I picked up the newspapers and found the missing cushion behind the couch. How did it get there? While I vacuumed, he kept talking and I smiled at him, not hearing a word.

I went upstairs cautiously, not knowing what to expect and to my surprise found it immaculate, even the bed was made. Coming back down, I examined the dining room and found it dusty but otherwise perfectly preserved. He had somehow confined his shenanigans to the kitchen and living room. How did he eat? How did he get groceries?

That night, my parents sat silently as I told them the horrors I'd seen.

"He needs full time care," I said, "I don't know how he hasn't starved himself to death."

"Sweetheart, full-time care is expensive," my mother said.

Everything with her was always about money. My father mumbled something that sounded like, "He's not living here."

The next morning, on Thanksgiving, the three of us drove there to get him. He greeted us in his usual suit and tie with pants and socks and shoes this time. He was happy to see me and called me by name and was civil but reserved with my parents. He was his old self.

When we entered his house, there was a plate with some crumbs on it on the table. but otherwise, his home was in the same condition I left it in. My parents saw nothing wrong and I realized I had ruined everything. I had contaminated the crime scene. By cleaning his home, I had destroyed the evidence that this was a man who could no longer live alone. I had completely ruined my own case. *Holy fuck, I'm going to make a terrible lawyer.*

My parents looked at one another and looked at me and shrugged.

"He seems fine," my mother said.

"No, no, he's not fine," I whispered, "He needs help."

"Sweetheart," my Dad said, "People get old."

"He isn't just old," I said, "Something is seriously wrong."

I couldn't convince them, and I blame myself for what happened next.

Chapter Sixty-One

On Friday morning, Julie went with the black dress once again. She'd never been to a pre-trial hearing before, and didn't really know the protocol, but she knew better than to go with something too revealing or too clingy or too colorful. Black was always safe.

On Thursday afternoon, as she was leaving work, she once again told Bob that she'd be late the next day, and when he looked at her funny, she leaned close and whispered, "Boob job." *Fuck him, it was none of his business.*

She then had to feign illness to get out of going for drinks with The Committee. She knew she'd face a barrage of questions about Curt and his family and wouldn't be able to put them off with jokes about boob jobs. The Committee believed nothing was "none of their business."

It was late March and an inch of snow had fallen during the night as winter decided to be a dick one last time. While she warmed up her car and brushed the snow off, she wondered, "*What is it with this guy?*" *First, a funeral and now a hearing and sometime down the road a murder trial, this guy's a lot of laughs.*

With the roads slick, the traffic was worse than usual and Boston drivers were as ornery as ever. She was grateful she no longer had to commute downtown to work. She found a garage to park in knowing she might not be able to run out every hour and feed a meter. Ten bucks for the day, who can afford that every day?

She slipped on the way up the courthouse steps and nearly fell. *Whoa, that's just what I need a broken neck. I hope this fuckin' guy appreciates this.*

She was nervous entering the courthouse. *What am I afraid of? I'm not on trial.* A cop directed her where to go while simultaneously looking her up and down. She entered a room that looked more like a college classroom than a courtroom. There were only a handful of people there, and the solemnity reminded her of church. She was tempted to kneel instead of sit. *Why the fuck am I here?*

A minute later, Curt entered and slid onto the bench next to her clasping his hand with hers. He didn't kiss because they were in court, but he pressed his shoulder against hers in a gesture of unmistakable intimacy. *Holy shit, he's cute.*

"Thanks for coming," he said.

"Sure, sure."

"It shouldn't take long. They'll enter a plea of not guilty and we can leave. You'll be back at work by eleven. Promise."

"I'm not worried," she said.

She wasn't worried, in fact, she was suddenly glad she had come. The stylish thin man from the funeral burst through the doors and Curt stood and waved and he waved back and made his way towards them. He was well-dressed again, this time in an electric blue suit. Julie stood as he got close.

"Uncle Billy, this is my girlfriend Julie. Julie, this is my Uncle Billy."

Everybody shook hands and Billy spoke of the snow and his drive in.

"It's practically April, I thought winter was over."

Julie had stopped listening. Curt had called her "his girlfriend" and she had to quell the urge to leap in the air. They'd only been on three actual dates but "girlfriend" implied exclusivity and commitment and the possibility of a life together for her and him and Kevin. She smiled and nodded and kept her joy to herself.

An older man entered using a cane. That must be his Dad. She recognized him from the funeral when he'd been in a wheelchair. He was taller than she expected and not as frail. Uncle Billy waved and Curt's Dad ignored him and limped toward the front.

"He hates me," Billy said to Julie with a shrug and a wink, "And yet, I'm so loveable."

Julie laughed hoping that was appropriate. A short, big bellied man burst through the doors and sauntered quickly down the aisle into a seat next to Curt's father.

"That's the lawyer," murmured Curt, "We should probably sit."

"I'll just stay here," said Julie.

"You sure?"

She nodded. She'd rather sit in the back and not get too close. Curt and his uncle sat in the front with the lawyer between them and his father. *What is up with that?*

A side door opened, and court officers led a handcuffed man in the room. His hair was thinning and unkempt and his eyes looked glassy and his expression frightened. She could see bits of Curt in his face and the more she looked at him the more she wanted to cry.

The bailiff spoke and they rose for the judge's entrance. *This is like church.* The judge was cherubic and non-threatening. The lawyer entered a plea of "not guilty" which the judge accepted, and just like that, the crazy brother was whisked away. The remaining Morrissey men stood up and Uncle Billy reached a hand towards Curt's father. He slapped it away violently, and Curt interceded and calmed him down and the bailiff came over to tell them to knock it off. Julie witnessed the whole scene and recoiled at the violence.

All week, she had joked about his family and her love life and how bad her luck was when it came to men, but what she saw now wasn't funny. She saw a family that had been shattered into a million pieces and would never be whole again. She saw hatred and despair and psychosis.

I could leave. I could run from here and duck his calls and never see him again. I'm still young. I'm pretty enough. I'd find someone else, someone whose family was free of criminals and violence and schizophrenia. She could leave right now and everyone, even Kevin, would understand why.

Chapter Sixty-Two

"Have you seen my necklace?"

"Oh, yeah, sure" said Tom, "I wore it to work yesterday. I must have left it there."

"I'm serious. I saw it this morning."

Tom straightened his tie in the mirror. Twenty-four years today. Next year would be the big one. They'd have to go somewhere but where? She'd want to go to Rome or Paris, but he'd been to Europe and hadn't cared for it.

"But, Tom, the Nazis aren't there anymore" she'd tease, but he still didn't want to go.

He wanted someplace exotic like Hawaii or Tahiti. Tommy was twenty-two now and Curt nearly sixteen. *Maybe her sister could come and look after Curt for a week. A quarter of a century couldn't go uncelebrated.*

He studied himself in the mirror for a moment to see what kind of damage twenty-four years of marriage had wrought. His face was lined, and he was completely bald now. *Maybe I should wear a rug? Too late, now, I'd look foolish showing up for work pretending I have a full head of hair.*

The weight was the biggest difference. He must have put on two pounds each year. *I'll be enormous on my 50th anniversary.* He'd seen joggers on the road and laughed at them. No one from his generation jogged. Y*ou only ran if someone was chasing you.* Tom felt his middle. *Maybe they'll have the last laugh.*

Lydia seemed the same to him, maybe not quite as skinny but she'd been too skinny before. Her hair when they met had been what she called "mud brown." It had since gone through several transformations, there was even a blonde phase which was temporary and didn't fit the Lydia he knew.

"It turns out, I don't want to have more fun," she said after dyeing it back to her natural brown.

Tom slapped aftershave on his face. Twenty-four years is a long time. Longer than the lives of both Leckie and Moretti. Most guys he knew weren't in love with their wives anymore. One or two had a woman on the side. Divorce was no longer uncommon even among Catholics. *Catholics who were divorced. Shameful.*

"Twenty-four years and still going strong," he told her that morning.

He meant it, too. Though they weren't nearly as randy as they once were and it had been years since she slipped little love notes into his pockets, she was still "his girl" and she still excited him and he hoped he still excited her, even with his bald head and paunchy belly.

He had plans for a romantic evening. Curt was sleeping at a friend's and Tommy was off doing God knows what. He and Lydia would have a romantic dinner downtown, and the romance would continue when they got home. It had been several weeks since they last made love and he began to feel aroused at the thought of her naked body against his.

Tom exited the bathroom to find his wife seated on the bed crying. *Women, everything was a crisis.* He sat down next to her, trying to suppress a wry smile. Lydia with her hands to her face and tears sneaking out the sides couldn't see him anyway.

"What is it?"

"The necklace," she said, her voice sounding like a child's. She always sounded like a child to him when she cried.

"Oh" said Tom, after a moment. "I thought you suddenly realized you'd been married to me for twenty-four years."

Lydia sniffed and put her hands down. She stood up retrieved a handkerchief from a drawer and blew her nose. This was supposed to be a romantic evening.

"I'm going to have to do my make-up again."

He couldn't argue. Mascara ran down her face and her cheeks glistened. Their reservations were for seven, but they'd never make that now.

A late start meant getting home later and suddenly their anniversary love-making was in jeopardy.

"You've got other necklaces. Why don't you fix yourself up and we'll go?"

"I don't care about the damn necklace," she said, looking at him through red, glassy eyes. She almost never swore and when she did, it got his attention.

"All right, then, what are you upset about? You saw it this morning. It's around here somewhere. Let's not let it spoil our night."

It's just a goddam necklace.

Lydia sighed and looked away.

"It's not the first thing that's gone missing."

"What do you mean?"

"Two of my bracelets are missing and my diamond earrings."

The diamond earrings he had bought for their twentieth. He didn't like to buy expensive things. At that time, Tom thought both Tommy and Curt were headed for college, but twenty was a big number and big numbers were important in a marriage.

"Did someone break in?"

Lydia's jewelry and the color television set were the only expensive items in the house and the TV was still there.

"No, no one broke in."

His stomach clenched when it dawned on him what she was getting at.

"Tommy?"

"Who else?" she said bursting into tears and fumbling for him like a blind man. He stood and hugged her and could feel her tears on his shirt.

"Why would he take them?"

She sniffled and reached for a Kleenex on the dresser.

"He must be selling them," she said, before blowing her nose. Her voice sounding like a child's once again.

"He even took the promise ring."

"The promise ring?"

Goddam him. What could he have gotten for that? Diamond earrings were one thing but their promise ring meant nothing to the outside world. He couldn't have gotten more than a few bucks.

"He must have taken them when I was out this afternoon."

They had discussed the possibility that Tommy was doing drugs but dismissed it. His behavior had always been erratic. When he was on medication, he was lethargic but harmless. Sometimes he didn't take it and his mood swings were intense. He threw things and broke things, once smashing a guitar Curt have saved for six months to buy. He screamed threats at his mother and father. Tom had suspected that Tommy was on drugs but Lydia insisted the boy was sick. He'd always been sick and that it was the sickness not drugs that made him this way.

It was clear now that Tommy was doing drugs and he was stealing his mother's jewels to pay for them. His own son was as bad as the punks who stole from his store; juvenile delinquents on God knows what and his son was one of them. He's not even a juvenile any more.

She cried but he wouldn't. *I can't believe he would stoop so low. That goddam son-of-a-bitch.* Tom knew they wouldn't be going out to dinner. The mood was spoiled. There would be no romantic evening and no love-making that night. Tommy had stolen one more thing.

Chapter Sixty-Three

I was on my way to my Poly Sci final when my mother called me. It was December in Syracuse and my roommate Brooke and I had gotten into the habit of greeting each other with, "I'm freezing my balls off." We had overheard a maintenance man say to his buddy a couple of weeks earlier and it tickled us and became our catchphrase.

I was freezing my balls off, metaphorically speaking, when my mother called, and it took me a minute to remove my gloves and fish my cell phone out of my pocket from between my layers. I almost let it go to voicemail but Poly Sci was my easy class and for once, I wasn't nervous.

"Sweetheart, I have something to tell you…"

My mother is a jokester and when she adopts a serious tone it's always a trick to lure you in, so you don't see the funny part coming. This time, there was no funny part.

My grandfather had either fallen and broken his hip, or his hip had snapped causing him to fall. Either way the result was the same and the broken hip wasn't the worst part; there was no one there to call 9-1-1. He lay on his bathroom floor coming in and out of consciousness for roughly thirty-six hours. Thirty-six hours with no food, no water, just agony.

It was a minor miracle he was discovered at all. His letter carrier thought he heard something while slipping the mail through the slot. According to my mother, he had told police he almost walked away thinking it was his imagination. What if he had? My grandfather might have died on his bathroom floor.

I tanked my Poly Sci test. This was all my fault. If I hadn't contaminated the crime scene three weeks earlier and had convinced my parents he could no longer be left alone, none of this would have happened. He would have had a nurse or someone keeping an eye on him, but because I fucked up, he was left alone. I probably wrote three sentences on my exam. I just sat there, self-flagellating, feeling too guilty to give a shit.

I did okay on my history final after talking to my mother the night before. She assured me he was in stable condition and though dehydrated, they had pumped fluids back into his system. He had a broken hip and a nasty gash from a shattered bathroom mirror but for the time being was no longer in pain.

"How does he look?" I asked.

"Like an 85-year-old man who spent two days on a bathroom floor."

The following day, I got up early and drove six hours straight to the hospital, only stopping once for a quick pee. When I got to his room, he was wide awake and alert and happy to see me. His right leg hung in the air and yellow skin stretched across his skull and stick arms hung from his shoulders. He spoke slowly, but with surprising lucidity.

"I'm getting a new hip."

"That's nice," I said.

"I've been shot in this one once before you know."

It didn't but then again, he never talked much about the war.

"It's about time I got rid of it."

I should have laughed but instead I cried.

"Grandpa, I am so sorry."

"Why, did you push me?"

I didn't know what to say. I couldn't say what I was thinking. How do you tell someone that you love and admire, someone who has looked after you that they can't look after themselves anymore and that brain no longer works right? Especially, when his brain works just fine some of the time.

I spent the afternoon there. We'd talk for twenty-minute intervals and then his eyes would begin to blink slowly and he'd doze. I'd text and play a game on my phone and then he'd wake up a half-hour or so later and we'd resume our conversation.

"Do you remember when I called you from camp?"

"Camp Grandpa?" he said with a smile.

"My parents never found out."

"Not everybody is meant to know everything."

He napped again and then he told me the story of meeting his wife. He told it to me three times in a row the exact same way and then, he dozed some more.

Each time, he awoke, he slipped a little more and late in the day he woke up angry. He called out for his wife who had died before I was born. He yelled each of his son's names.

"They're not here now, Grandpa."

He scowled. It seemed like a good time to leave and I was saying my good-byes when my parents entered. They seemed surprised to see me and a little hurt that I came here first instead of going home. My Dad nearly said something.

"When did you get here?" My mother asked.

She was dressed in a business suit and my dad was in his yellow work uniform. They always looked like a mismatched couple. My grandfather looked at the two of them with his mouth slightly open, seemingly unable to place where he knew them from.

"I wished you had come home first we could have driven together," said my Dad.

"If only they would invent some way of allowing for people to communicate over some sort of device," said my mother.

Her sarcasm could be exhausting.

"I came early because I was worried about him," I gestured towards my grandfather who up until this point they hadn't even acknowledged.

"I'm glad I did, he was much more lucid earlier."

"That's too bad," said my mother, "The doctor asked us to be here at five for the Alzheimer's' test."

Sixty-Four

The night before she met Curt, she had a date and not just any date, a computer date. The ads for them were everywhere, on TV, on the radio, there were leaflets in her mail. She mocked them at first but bit by bit, her own junk mail wore her down. How did they even know she was single? Did her mailman tip them off that it had been months since a man was seen leaving her premises?

It was during one of her fallow periods, a time of intense loneliness that she signed up. She told no one, no one on The Committee, not even Marjorie. Even after the man chosen as her perfect mate by state-of-the-art technology called and set up a date, she told no one. If he had abducted her and dismembered her body, he might have gotten away with it. After all, she said was staying in that night. No one at the bank knew anything about a date, computerized or not.

They met at the comedy club. That was her one smart move, she realized after. She didn't let pick her up at her place. They were strangers and she didn't want him knowing where she lived. He seemed normal enough on the phone, but you can't always tell from that. The phone had tricked her many times before when friends had set her up on blind dates. Guys with deep resonant voices turned out to be nebbishes and guys with soft voices turned out to be built, well, one guy but the point is the phone never revealed anything as far as she was concerned.

That first glance told so much. Not that she believed in love at first sight or anything like that. She was too old for such chimera, but that initial spark had to be there. That first handshake and that blink-of-the-eye "would I fuck this guy or not?" test had to be passed if things were going to progress. There were guys who passed the initial test but were rejected minutes later or sometimes weeks later but a guy who flunked the first test never ever changed her mind. She sometimes wondered if she were superficial, but a guy who she didn't find attractive right away never became attractive down the road. You either had it or you didn't.

The comedy club guy didn't have it. He was older, for one thing. There was no way he was thirty-two. He had to be pushing forty, but he lied to the computer's face about his date of birth and not by a year or two the way

Julie had. He colored his hair and combed it over. He wore a tight shirt over a baggy torso. Naturally, he had a moustache. He had also lied about his personality. He wasn't "the life of the party" as much as he was a loud mouth, pure and simple.

He insisted they sit in the front row. Julie knew better but there they were in the front row when the show started. The host, a pudgy twenty-something named Steve, had barely gotten on stage when Gary began to banter with him. Almost immediately, the focus of the show became Gary and "Janie" (Steve had misheard her Julie's name).

"Are you fucking her?" Steve demanded.

"Sure am," Gary responded with a hoot and raised clenched fist. "No," Julie wanted to stand up and announce. "We are not fucking. We're not even kissing. This is our first and last date." Instead, she sat silent and mortified as Steve segued into own made-up sexual escapades by first referencing the similar antics of Gary and Janie. Gary laughed and pounded the table as she maintained a frozen, "try and be a good sport" smile.

The next comic, an alcohol and drug laden veteran of the comedy scene capped his long, horrifying and probably mostly true tale of receiving oral sex from a "tranny" with a similar joke about Gary and Janie. Gary hooted with delight and his clenched fist returned to the air triumphantly. Julie seethed but feared getting up and leaving would only draw more abuse and she hated a scene more than anything.

The final comic was a guitar act who sang parody songs, and Julie might have found him amusing had her evening not been ruined. During a parody of "Love me Do" entitled "Love me Pooh" about gay sex between Winnie the Pooh and Tigger, Gary tried to slip his arm around Julie. It was quickly dispatched with a flick of her hand and a withering glance. The show ended with Steve eliciting applause for all the comics and the wait staff and finally, "Gary and Janie." They had been the stars of the show and this night had entered her "bad date pantheon." Her one consolation of a night of pure hell was she could always weave it into a funny tale and this one needed little embellishment.

With the lights up and canned music playing, Gary grunted, "I've got take a piss."

Julie nodded. *Well put.*

"I'll be right out" he said.

Julie had to pee, too but a long line by the ladies' room was already forming and she needed to make her escape. She ducked behind a curtain into a narrow passageway. Tucked in a little backroom sat Steve and the guitar guy.

"Janie" said Steve, "You're not supposed to be back here."

"Shut up" she snapped, "You ruined my night."

The guitar guy chuckled.

Julie was peering out the curtain when Gary emerged from the bathroom. He stood near the bar stupidly, looking around for her. When the line for the ladies' room disappeared, he grew anxious. Julie chuckled to herself.

"Are you going to wait til he leaves?" Steve asked.

"That's the plan," Julie said.

A few minutes later the bouncer informed Gary they were closing up. "My girlfriend's in the bathroom."

Girlfriend? No chance, Fuckface.

Minutes later, a waitress exited the ladies' room, "Sorry, but there's nobody in there." Gary snorted and stormed out.

Julie turned to the two comics. "I need to wait a couple of more minutes til the coast is clear." She turned to Steve, "Then you're going to give me a ride home. You owe me that much." The guitar guy seemed tickled and Steve didn't object. She didn't have enough money for a cab. Sometimes even people who work at a bank forget to go to the bank.

It was a mostly silent, awkward and uneventful drive home until Steve pulled up out front of her place and tried to make a pass. "You're shitting me, right?" said Julie with a slam of the door.

Chapter Sixty-Five

Lydia was at work the day Tommy came back. Tom wasn't big on women's lib but her doctor thought it would be a good idea for her to get out and do something instead of sitting in the house all day smoking cigarettes and worrying about Tommy. So now, four afternoons a week, she was a hostess at a local family restaurant.

"They don't think I'm smart enough to be a waitress," she'd crack.

The day Tommy came back, Tom was in the kitchen making himself some soup and watching college football. BC was trailing Florida State by two touchdowns. Curt was in his room, studying for the SATs. Tom was startled by the bell announcing the backdoor had opened and closed.

Tommy had been gone for nearly a month and his hair was shaggy and his beard unkempt as he took a handful of steps into the kitchen. He wore a sweatshirt unzipped with a torn tee-shirt underneath. He looked thin and glassy-eyed and there were scratch marks on his neck that begged for an explanation.

"Hi, Dad," he said.

Tom grabbed him and pinned him to the wall and pressed his forearm into Tommy's windpipe. Tommy struggled to breathe, and his glassy eyes were big as he stared at his father with a bewildered expression. Tom put his face close to Tommy's.

"You are not welcome here. This is no longer your home. Get your shit and get out."

Tommy tried to speak but his complete shock and his father's forearm prevented him.

"We can't take it anymore. Your suicide attempts, your stealing, your drugs, your being away weeks at a time, coming home whenever you feel like it, no explanation of where you've been. Your mother can't take it anymore. You're breaking her heart."

Tommy began to cry. This was the longest he'd been away but over the summer, there'd been two stretches of four days and one stretch of nine when he hadn't come home and hadn't bothered to call. The police would no longer look for him. He was over eighteen now, no longer a child. The Windham police had had enough of chasing Tommy Morrissey around.

The first night Tommy didn't come home, Tom and Lydia waited up all night. They were still sitting at the kitchen table when Curt got up for school in the morning. Lydia, nearly catatonic, barely spoke to Curt when he saw her. By mid-morning, Tom had to call her doctor who prescribed valium for her nerves.

Tommy came home a few days later with a wild story of where he'd been. It involved a friend they'd never heard of and a trip to Philadelphia where they were robbed. His story made no sense, but Tom and Lydia were happy he was home and alive didn't press him on it. He'd behave for a few weeks, take his medication, look for a job and by all accounts behave like most kids his age and no different from the ones in college.

A week or two later, he'd disappear again then eventually return, always bringing with him a half-baked story and tears and contriteness. Lydia and the doctor would then beg him to take his medication and he'd swear up and down that he would.

Tom would have banished the boy the last time he had come me home, but Lydia wouldn't have allowed it. She'd spoiled him his whole life and would have gone on spoiling him forever, but Tom had decided enough was enough. He would be strong if his wife couldn't be.

Tommy tried to push Tom's arm away from his throat and the two men tussled, knocking a framed copy of the Irish Blessing onto the floor and shattering the glass that protected it. *May the Road Rise Up to Meet You.*

"Don't hurt him, Dad."

Tom turned to see Curt standing in the doorway, his eyebrows high and his face alarmed.

"Your brother can't stay, Curt. He's got to get his things and go."

Tom dragged Tommy by his collar past Curt and pulled him quickly up the stairs. Tommy gagged and cried and called, "Dad" over and over. When they got to the doorway of Tommy and Curt's room, Tom pinned him against the door once again.

"I found your drugs" he said. "I found your drugs and I flushed them down the toilet."

A few days earlier, Tom had searched their room hoping to find some clue as to where his son was. He found a clear plastic bag with some marijuana and three blue pills he couldn't identify. Tom only knew they weren't the white pills Tommy's doctor had prescribed. Tom had indeed flushed the contraband down the toilet.

"Do you see what kind of an example you're setting for your brother? Are you trying to make him a drug addict like you? Ruin his life the way you're ruining yours?"

"No, I wouldn't," Tommy said and the crying became genuine blubbering.

Tom shoved Tommy into the room.

"Dad," said Curt.

"Keep out of it, Curt."

Tom reached into the closet and pulled out a duffel bag. While Tommy lay on the floor crying helplessly, Tom opened his dresser drawers. He grabbed clumps of underwear and socks and tee-shirts and shoved them violently into the bag. He plucked shirts and pants from the closet and shoved them on top.

"There" he said, "That should hold you for a while. Get up! Get up!"

Tommy staggered to his feet and Tom thrust the duffel bag into his belly. Just then, the smoke detector on the kitchen ceiling began to squawk. The soup had overflowed onto the flame.

"Curt, shut the stove off."

Tom dragged Tommy once more but by the collar this time down the stairs.

"Let him stay, Dad, let him stay."

"Please, Dad," Tommy yelled, "I'll be good."

"No, you won't," Tom yelled, as all three moved together in a cluster.

"Out you go," said Tom at the bottom of the stairs and once again when they reached the front door, "Out you go and never come back."

Tom pushed Tommy out the door with the duffel bag opening up. Pants and socks and shirts fell onto the steps and onto the ground.

"Now go to hell," Tom yelled, slamming then locking the door.

Tom, red-faced, brushed past Curt into the kitchen. The smoke detector squawked again and again. He turned the knob on the stove off and grabbed a potholder and then the pot. He swung the contents into the sink and down the drain.

"I told you to shut this off."

"You can't kick him out Dad. You can't kick Tommy out." Tom turned the faucet on, and steam rose from the burnt pot. He shut the faucet off.

Curt stood crying and pleading with his father. Curt wasn't a crier and Tom was stunned by the boy's reaction. *Didn't he see he was doing it for him? Jesus said if your right hand causes you to sin, cut it off and cast it from you.* He couldn't allow a drug addict to share a bedroom with his young son.

Tom grabbed Curt by his lapels and shook him to stop him from crying. Curt pulled away and lost his balance and the two of them fell over onto the floor. Tom cut his elbow on a small piece of glass. *Shit.* They grappled briefly then Tom got his younger son in a headlock and Curt cried and his body shook.

Tom held Curt that way until both of them stopped moving.

"Settle down, settle down, it's all over. I had to do it. He gave me no choice."

Tom spoke softly to his son without loosening the grip of his headlock.

"Your brother is killing your mother. Do you understand? Stop crying, stop crying, stop crying."

Curt began thrashing again but Tom held on.

"Listen to me. She can never know he came back, understand? She can never know he came back. Promise me you won't tell her he came back."

Curt cried and couldn't stop. Tom squeezed the headlock tighter.

"Promise me, promise me, Curt."

"Okay, okay, Dad, I promise."

Chapter Sixty-Six

"Alzheimer's?" I asked, "He has Alzheimer's?"

My Mom looked at my Dad and my Dad looked at my Mom.

"That's what we're here to find out," said my Mom.

I must have looked shocked. I wasn't prepared to hear Alzheimer's.

"You were the one who said there was something wrong," said my Dad.

He had me there. I did think there was something wrong after all, I was the one who saw his home in complete disarray.

"I don't know," I stammered. "I thought maybe he had a vitamin deficiency or cancer."

Even I knew how dumb that sounded. I mean, "Who roots for cancer?"

"A vitamin deficiency?" said my Dad.

"I don't know."

I didn't know much about Alzheimer's, but I knew it was incurable and I knew it would take parts of his brain away bit by bit until there was nothing left. Some people bounce back from cancer, but no one bounces back from Alzheimer's.

"I was hoping he had something treatable, that's all," I said quietly.

The doctor entered and said "hello" to my parents. He was in his late thirties and prematurely gray which is probably a plus when treating geriatrics.

"And who is this?" he asked looking at me.

I introduced myself.

"Oh, he talks a lot about you," he said with a smile.

He seemed pretty happy for a guy about to deliver terrible news. "And, how are you?" he asked my grandfather, who looked back at him blankly.

"Fine," my grandfather said.

The Doctor looked at the three of us who were standing. It was a little after five and I still had my coat on.

"Why don't I administer the test?"

"Will it be multiple choice," asked my Mom, "or a series of essays?"

The Doctor chuckled but I didn't. I wasn't in the mood for her bullshit.

"Listen," I said to the Doctor, "my grandfather was much sharper earlier today. Is there any way we could do this in the morning instead?"

The Doctor jerked his head back as though I'd struck him.

"I'm afraid not," he said, "we need to know the extent of his condition."

"It's just that later in the day he gets tired…"

"Sweetheart," my Dad said, "He has to do it now."

"Why?"

"Because we're all here now," said my mother.

I couldn't believe that no one was on my side. The three of them were determined to go ahead with this test whether I liked it or not. I could feel my face getting hot, but I stepped aside and said nothing more.

The Alzheimer's test turned out to be a lot less formal than I had imagined. The doctor just sat down in a chair next to my grandfather and asked him some questions. He knew his own name and my name but couldn't quite come up with my mother's.

"I've never been very memorable," my mother said with a chuckle.

"I know the feeling," said the Doctor with a laugh.

The two of them seemed to be having a marvelous time.

The questions continued and my grandfather knew his wife's name and his sons' names, but he didn't seem to realize one of his sons was a few feet away wearing a yellow jumpsuit.

"Where are you from?"

"Boston," my grandfather said.

He technically lived in Windham about 15 miles away but close enough. Maybe he doesn't have Alzheimer's.

"What day is today?"

"Tuesday?"

It was Friday but that didn't prove anything. Anyone could lose track of what day it is during a hospital stay. Every day is the same.

"What month is it?"

"September?"

"It's December."

"They rhyme," said my mother, "Sort of."

Even the doctor didn't laugh at that one.

"Who is the president?"

My Grandpa looked up at the ceiling tiles, bit his lower lip and thought for a long moment.

"It's not Kennedy," he said finally.

He was right. It wasn't Kennedy. It hadn't been Kennedy for fifty years.

"Ask him his prayers," my mother said.

She said she'd heard him recite his prayers with the hospital nun the day before. He did them now for the doctor, reciting both the Our Father and the Hail Mary perfectly. When he finished, he saw me smiling and he smiled back. Way to go.

"Could you recite the alphabet?"

This is silly if he knows his prayers, he knows the alphabet. He got as far as "I." He couldn't come up with the letter "J." He tried and we let him try but he could not come up with the letter "J."

"That one always stumps me, too," my mother said.

Shut the fuck up.

I looked at the doctor in stunned silence. To be polite, he pulled the three of us into the hallway.

"I'm afraid he has Alzheimer's," he said.

No shit.

"So, what happens now?" I asked.

"Well, it'll be another week or so before his gash heals and two months before he can walk again but even after that, he's going to need permanent twenty-four-hour care."

He made prolonged eye contact with each of us to make sure we heard what he was saying.

"Either a full-time nurse or to be put in a nursing home. He'll need someone to cook his meals and keep an eye on him at all times."

I waited for a wise crack from my mother, but for once she restrained herself. She looked at my father waiting to hear what he had to say. "He can live with us," he said.

Oh, boy, this isn't going to go well.

Chapter Sixty-Seven

Julie spotted Curt as soon as he walked in. How could she not? He noticed her at the same time and headed straight for her. Did he find her pretty or merely authoritative? She was behind a desk after all and he was looking for a loan so naturally, he would ignore the tellers and approach her.

"Can I help you?" asked Bob, trying to intercept him. *The one time he actually tries to do something. Oh, no, you don't.*

"I'll take care of this Bob. Please have a seat."

He wore a one-piece yellow jumpsuit with a white shirt and tie underneath. Who wears a tie with a jumpsuit? His jumpsuit looked smudged but not filthy like a mechanics and she wondered what he did for a living.

She liked his eyes and kept hers focused on them while they talked.

"What can I do for you?"

"I'm looking for a loan."

"I can help you with that, have a seat."

They sat.

"There are some forms to fill out," she said, taking her eyes off for the first time since he walked in.

She found the forms she needed after a moment and pulled them from her drawer. Normally, she let the customer fill them out on their own but it was a slow day and he was cute so…*fuck it, I'll do it with him.*

She asked him his name and he told her and while she was transcribing it into the boxes, he asked her name. She asked his address and he asked where she was from. He told her about his cleaning business and how he needed three more vans and more cleaning supplies to keep up with the demand. Every time she asked a question, he'd answer and ask her one. She forgot about the form while they each revealed where they'd grown up and had gone to college and how many siblings they'd had. It was suddenly a lunch date without the lunch.

He had a straight forward demeanor and none of the arrogance that good-looking guys always seem to have. She kept it professional but could feel color coming into her cheeks. She liked the way he cocked his head and lifted his eye brows and nodded along while she spoke.

She was halfway through a funny story about her train ride in that morning; the man sitting next to her was so busy doing a word puzzle in the paper, the one where they scramble the letters, that he missed his stop.

"It took him twenty-five minutes to figure out a five-letter word. I wanted to yell, "It's apron, A-P-R-O-N."

She became aware of a customer waiting and the tellers eyeballing her. *Fuck you, Debbie, mind your own business.* She finished her story, acting out the man angrily muttering under his breath, got her laugh and went back to the form.

He told her his date of birth. 8-6-54. He was a couple of years younger than her, but it was still within reason.

Now, the big question.

"Are you married?"

"No," he said maintaining eye contact, "I'm not."

She checked the box marked single. *Are my ears red? They feel warm.*

"Do you have any children?"

"No," he said softly, "I'm not doing that."

Chapter Sixty-Eight

The marriage retreat was just about over when Tom enraged Lydia. It was an innocuous comment really. They were mingling, drinking fruit punch from Styrofoam cups, nibbling a stale cookie or two. The workshops were done. The retreat was basically over. He was like a quarterback throwing a last second interception when all he had to do was take a knee and the game would be won.

How did she even hear him? He was chatting with Arlene, a simple but earnest woman who loved her six cats and wished her grandchildren didn't live all the way in Michigan. Lydia was all the way over by the cookie table talking with Gil, Arlene's husband. How did she hear him? But she did, and she glared at him from across the room to let him know he was in deep shit. *Uh oh.*

Tom immediately began to take great interest in Arlene and her cats.

"What are their names?" he asked.

He asked one probing question after another, never taking his eyes away from her and nodding along while she spoke. He was stalling as best he could; hoping to avoid the inevitable car ride home.

Some couples had left when Tom caught a break. Father Ronald, a roly-poly priest who liked his desserts in lieu of sex, called the stragglers back together for one last prayer. Lydia wouldn't look at Tom. The group put their Styrofoam cups down and came and sat in folding chairs arranged in a circle. Father Ronald had them hold hands and close their eyes. Lydia placed herself so there'd someone in between her and Tom. He was forced to hold hands with a hen-pecked slob named Ned on one side and Arlene on the other.

"Dear Lord," began Father Ronald, "We gathered this weekend to strengthen our faith and our commitment to you. We ask for forgiveness from you and the ones we love, and we ask for a new beginning."

Yes, exactly. I ask for forgiveness for what I said five minutes ago. And a new beginning.

Father Ronald continued, “We think of the friendships we’ve made this weekend and how each one of us here has touched us. We leave here much like iron that has been forged to become steel; our faith has been forged by your love, and grown even stronger, and so has our love for one another.”

Tom wasn’t so sure about that. He was leaving with a very unforgiving, angry wife. *I want my money back.*

Father Ronald moved into the home stretch, “We leave here better neighbors, better husbands and better wives, we leave here better fathers and mothers, better brothers and sisters, better sons and better daughters, but most importantly, we leave here better Christians, Amen.”

“Amen,” the group said, and they could open their eyes now.

Tom hoped that maybe the prayer and the feeling of good will had cooled his wife down but no such luck. When he glanced over at her, she scowled back at him.

This was the third “Renewal of Faith” retreat that they had attended. It was available for couples of various parishes to come together for what Father Ronald called “a tune-up.” They met Friday night for a short mass followed a group discussion. Saturday began with Morning Prayer then breakfast then a series of talks and discussion. Special “guest couples” were invited in to explain to other married couples what married life is like. At first, Tom found the whole thing absurd, but eventually, somewhat begrudgingly he grew to like it.

The retreat was, of course, her idea. She wanted to go because she thought they should “work” on their marriage. That’s what modern couples do, they “work” on their marriage. *Our parents didn’t do that. They got married and that was that. If they had problems, well, too bad.*

Tom grew to like it for a different reason. Each year, the guest couple told basically the same story. They got married, were happy, grew apart, had some sort of crisis and got past it through their faith and were happy again. This was the template much like a weekly TV drama where each episode fit a certain formula.

The first-year guest couple’s marriage nearly crumbled because the husband drank and became abusive. With the help of Father Ronald, the man quit drinking and their marriage was saved. The second year, the man gambled away their life savings. He spoke of "Vegas" never once calling it "Las Vegas" telling chilling stories of days on end spent at the craps tables, convincing himself his bad luck was about to change.

The marital troubles for each guest couple were always the fault of the husband, and this year's couple, Rick and Nancy, were no different. Rick confessed to the group that he "strayed." A woman gasped. Rick didn't elaborate, he simply admitted that five years ago, he had strayed, and Nancy was ready to divorce him. Once more, Father Ronald had intervened and worked his magic and kept the couple together.

She should have divorced him, thought Tom. *What exactly did he mean by "strayed?" Did he have an affair? Did he have multiple affairs? Did he frequent prostitutes?* One year, at his office Christmas party, Tom's boss Frank had a few too many drinks and ended up kissing a salesgirl under the mistletoe. Frank was married and avoided the girl the next day and every day after that. Tom was certain that there were no meetings in hotel rooms or motel rooms, no sex other than a few drunken kisses, but as far as he was concerned Frank had strayed and Tom held him in contempt for all eternity.

Tom always left the marriage workshop feeling pretty good about himself. He had quit drinking years ago and he had never gambled and had certainly never "strayed." He may not be the world's best communicator but did his wife really want to hear his every waking thought? It was obvious he was better than these men. Surely, Lydia could see that. His marriage would be strengthened thanks to some comparison shopping. Tom and Lydia always returned home in a good mood. Nothing like seeing what a mess other marriages were in to feel good about your own.

They should have left this year's retreat happy, too, but Tom had misspoken.

When Arlene asked, "Do you have any children?"

Tom said, "We have a son who's not married, and he owns his own house cleaning business."

That's all he'd said. It was simpler this way. He didn't want to say, "I have two sons," and face the inevitable follow-up questions.

"They're in their thirties."

"No, they're not married."

"The younger one owns his own house cleaning business, the older one is a drug addict who unbeknownst to his mother, I kicked out of the house several years ago and could be dead or living on the streets for all we know."

So, for the sake of simplicity, he said, "We have a son who's not married, and he owns his own house cleaning business."

Just a little white lie to avoid embarrassment or worse, pity. *It was no goddam business of Arlene's how many children we have. Besides, she's moving to Michigan, we'll probably never see her again anyway.*

Tom and Lydia said their good-byes and walked to the car in silence. The only sound was the click-clack of Lydia's heels on the pavement. "It's gotten a little chilly," he said to no response and he realized the unintended double meaning. *It had gotten chilly.*

He reached to open the car door for her when she pushed his hand away.

"I can do it myself."

She opened the door and got in. He shook his head, walked around and got in the driver's side.

"That guest couple was something," he said, buckling his seatbelt. "I can't believe she didn't divorce him." *You could do a lot worse than me, you know, you could be with a cheating bastard.* No response.

Tom started the car then reached over and turned the radio on, and just as quickly Lydia reached over and turned it off. Nothing like a marital spat on the way home from a marriage retreat.

"You have two sons, Tom Morrissey," Lydia suddenly barked. Her eyes were narrow, and she clutched her purse tightly with both hands. He glanced at her quickly before putting the car in reverse and backing slowly out of the space.

"I know," he said calmly.

He'd be the reasonable one.

"I am well aware we have two sons."

"You may wish you only had one, but God gave you two."

Tom's anger started to rise, and he tried to check it.

"I just didn't want to explain the situation to a total stranger. It's none of her goddam business how many children I have. What is she, writing a book?"

Another car started to back up and Tom leaned on the horn for a full two seconds.

"Don't beep at these people, we just did a retreat with them. That's Rick and Nancy."

"Serves him right for cheating on his wife."

She shook her head and then waved at Rick and Nancy to smooth things over. He pulled out of the parking lot and she turned back towards him with both of her eyes staring at the side of his head.

"You can't just crumple him up like a piece of paper and throw him away. You can't pretend Tommy doesn't exist."

"I'm not pretending any such thing."

Yet, Tom was done with Tommy. He was done with Tommy the way he was done with Moretti after the whores, the way he was done with his boss after the mistletoe kisses, the way he was done with Kennedys after Chappaquiddick. Couldn't she see he was done with Tommy because of what he had done to her?

"He's coming back, you know. People recover from addictions all the time and lead long, productive lives. Betty Ford cleaned up her life and so did Kitty Dukakis. Tommy can get straightened out. I know he's coming back. He'll come back clean and sober with a new lease on life." *No, he won't.*

He had never regretted kicking Tommy out, although he wished he hadn't told him to go to hell. Only God gets to decide who goes to hell and who doesn't. Yet, he knew he had done the right thing for Lydia and for Curt. While she longed for his return, he knew Tommy wasn't coming back.

Yet, he was wrong, but Lydia was wrong, too. Tommy did come back. It took two more years, but Tommy did come home. But he wasn't clean and sober, and he wasn't straightened out.

Chapter Sixty-Nine

I was asleep when the yelling started. It was Christmas morning and my Grandpa had been brought into our home two days earlier. The bandage on his upper thigh from the fall in the bathroom had to be cleaned and changed twice a day and my mother had assigned that task to my Dad.

"The two of us," she said, gesturing to herself and me, "Aren't about to go flitting about the old man's crotch."

Amen.

With my grandfather occupying my room, I was relegated to sleeping on a mattress in our unfinished basement not far from the washer and dryer.

"What's it like down there?" asked my Dad.

"Quaint," said my Mom, answering for me.

My Dad had changed my Grandpa's bandage three times without incident, though I had been in the kitchen for two of those changings and I hadn't heard them exchange a single word. My father must have walked in without a greeting, ripped the bandage off, cleaned the wound, applied ointment to the new bandage and placed it on my grandfather's nether region all in a stony silence. The threat of death often puts an end to grudges, but not in my house, not even at Christmas.

My grandfather's voice woke me out of a sound sleep from two floors above.

"You think you're perfect."

"I never said that."

"You give me that look. You don't know what I went through. You have no idea."

"I have a pretty good idea."

"You have no idea," my grandfather shrieked.

I entered the room, just after my mother, the two of us still in our pajamas, my Dad being the only one in the room who was dressed. He sat in a chair, holding a bloody bandage in one hand and a fresh one in the other while my grandfather lay on my old bed with his legs splayed open. I accidentally got a glimpse of his open wound and I cringed.

"What's going on?" my mother asked.

"I'm changing his bandage and he starts yelling at me."

"He was giving me that look," my grandfather said.

"I wasn't giving him a look," my dad mumbled.

They were like two small boys each pleading his case to their mother. Everyone was quiet for a bit while my mom looked around deciding what to do.

"Let me just finish," said my dad and he reached for my grandfather with the unused bandage.

"Get the hell away from me," my grandfather yelled, "I had to do what I did. He was killing your mother."

"He was sick," my dad roared back at him, catching everyone by surprise, "He was mentally ill."

"Get the hell away from me," my grandfather said again just as loudly.

"Fine," replied my father. He threw the bandage down and stormed out, followed by my mother and me. The three of us met up in the hall.

"Dad," I said sharply.

He pointed a finger at me, and his eyes were intense, "You don't know our history. You have no idea what he did."

I looked down, too afraid to challenge him. Nobody moved.

"Should we open presents now or…" said my mother, "or should we go to church?"

Normally, I would have laughed but I felt sick.

"What are we going to do now?" My Mother asked.

"I'm not going back in there," My father said. "He can change his own fuckin' bandage as far as I'm concerned."

My Dad didn't swear a lot. My Mom did but my Dad didn't. I waited for my Mother to say something and when she didn't, I said, "I'll do it."

The two of them looked at me and then at each other.

"He has an open wound. It has to be done," I said, "So, I'll do it."

Neither of them fought me over it so I walked back into my childhood bedroom, where my stuffed animals once roamed, where my sleepovers were once held, and I sat down where my Dad had been sitting. I had been with my Dad when the doctor gave him the instructions, so I knew what to do. I cut little piece of tape and then I took a fresh bandage and dabbed it with ointment.

"What are you doing?" My grandfather asked, catching on to what was happening.

"Grandpa, you need a bandage. Your cut can't be open."

"You're going to do it?"

I nodded and he winced but said nothing. He looked the other way as I gingerly placed the bandage close to his privates. I brushed his pajama shirt out of the way and could see white pubic hair poking out from his underwear. I had lost my virginity earlier that year, but I had only had sex twice in my life and I wasn't that comfortable around any man's genitals, especially my grandfather's. Yet, there I was Christmas morning, taping a bandage to my Grandpa's thigh as best I could. The two of us endured the same horror twice a day for the next three weeks.

Chapter Seventy

"Who was that cute guy today?" Cara asked during Thursday night drinks, the day Curt came in.

It was so rare that a good-looking man was seen on the premises. When one did show up, the tellers were like zebras or impalas on the Serengeti. They sniffed the air and cocked their ears alertly. They craned their necks and turned their heads in all directions. In concert, they all simultaneously sensed raw, carnivorous, predatory danger and their pulses quickened.

There were false alarms to be sure, men with a right look, but the wrong marital status or sexual preference. It seemed two or three weeks might go by before someone "fuckable," as Debbie liked to put it, came through those doors. When a young lion did approach their watering hole, what were they expecting? He'd wait in line, perhaps, exchange some small talk while conducting his business, and then leave. It could take months to develop any kind of a rapport. If he tried to strike too soon and ask one of them out too early, he was branded a "creep" and dismissed by the herd.

This was where Julie had caught her break, for Curt came in, not to cash a check or deposit coins, but for a loan. A loan required filling out forms and sitting across from each other and fifteen or twenty minutes of conversation that could stray into non-work-related areas if she so chose.

"He was applying for a loan."

"You spent a lot of time with him."

"There was a lot to go over," said Julie.

"It's funny how the cuter the guy the more there is to go over," said Cara and Julie blushed.

Sasha sat down at the table.

"I just checked my answering machine. He hasn't called."

"Sorry," said Debbie.

"What did I miss?"

"I was just asking Julie about that cute guy today" said Cara.

"I didn't think he was that cute," said Debbie.

Julie's eyes narrowed.

"I thought he was really cute," said Cara.

"You think every guy is really cute," said Debbie.

Now Cara's eyes narrowed.

"Personally, I thought he was too short," said Debbie.

"I'd say he's five-nine," said Julie.

"Five-nine is short" said Debbie.

"Five-nine isn't short," said Cara, "it's average."

"That guy was more like five-seven," said Debbie, not letting the point go. *Okay, so he's a little short.*

"You're five-seven and he's five-seven," said Debbie, looking directly at Julie. "You wouldn't catch me with a guy who was five-four." *I wouldn't catch you with a guy.*

"I thought you were five-three," said Sasha.

"I grew an inch recently," said Debbie.

The three of them laughed, not quite sure if she was kidding.

"Besides," said Debbie, sipping her "Mai Tai" while staring straight at Julie, "You don't want a guy who wears yellow overalls."

Debbie had her there. Curt's cleaning crews each drove a bright yellow van and wore bright yellow overalls. He had explained to her the bright yellow served two purposes, it advertised his business and it put people at ease. Customers were letting workers into their homes after all and the more harmless they appeared the better.

Cara laughed at Debbie's crack about the overalls and then Sasha said, "I didn't realize he was so short."

"Yeah," said Debbie, shaking her head, "Too bad."

Debbie had turned them all against him in a matter of minutes. Unaware that he had been undermined and then dismissed, Curt called the next day while Julie was with a customer.

"Hi, Julie, this is Curt Morrissey. I came in for a loan yesterday."

"Oh, yes, Mr. Morrissey," said Julie playfully, "I think I remember you."

"That's good," said Curt.

He seemed amused and she smiled involuntarily.

"I'm afraid we won't know if your loan is approved for another week or so."

"Oh, I was actually calling to see if you wanted to go out for dinner some time."

Julie paused and held up a finger to the woman across from her indicating she'd just be a second.

"Yes, Mr. Morrissey, I think that can be arranged. Let me give you the proper number for such an undertaking."

"Are you with a customer right now?"

"No," said Julie, "This is just how I talk."

Curt laughed and Julie was proud of herself. She gave him her home number and let it slip to the Committee after the bank closed that he called and asked her out.

"Congratulations" said Cara while Debbie said nothing.

Tough shit, Debbie. I don't care if he does wear yellow overalls.

He called her at home the next day and they chatted pleasantly about nothing and he listened and laughed in all the right places. They made dinner plans for the following Wednesday and Julie got off the phone feeling exhilarated. *Maybe Kevin will like this guy.*

She flaunted her defiance at the Committee for the next few days, mentioning his name here and there and gloating unabashedly. Her joy lasted until Monday night when she came home and played her answering machine.

"Hi, Julie, this is Curt Morrissey, I'm afraid I won't be able to make it on Wednesday."

Chapter Seventy-One

Tom and Lydia were watching TV when they heard the sound of the motorcycle. They were watching a cop show where none of the actors looked remotely like cops. He sat passively on the couch, his mind wandering. She sat next him with knitting on her lap and her head bobbing, nearly asleep. The motorcycle sound grew closer.

Their street was quiet at night. Their street was even quiet during the day. The neighborhood contained older empty nesters like Tom and Lydia or young couples with babies and toddlers and not much else in between. Not a lot of noise after nine and with the clock inching towards ten-thirty, the sound of a motorcycle caused heads to look up and faces to peer out windows.

When the motorcycle turned down their driveway, Tom jumped from his chair.

"What the hell is that?"

Startled, Lydia's head stopped bobbing and her eyes were fully open.

"What is it?"

"There's a motorcycle in our driveway."

He moved quickly, quickly for him, quickly for a man his age, towards the backdoor and the sound of the motorcycle, with Lydia close behind.

He marched through the kitchen and flicked on the outside light. He went out the backdoor. The bell jingled. The motorcycle was parked in the shadows and a figure in black leather removed his helmet and placed it on the seat. The figure stood away from the light and Tom couldn't see who it was.

"Hey, what the hell do you think you're doing?"

After a moment or two, Lydia emerged from the house and leaned against him trying to get a look. With both hands she latched onto Tom's arm and squeezed fearfully, digging her nails into him. "Ow," thought Tom.

The man walked from the shadows. He was tall and balding with a slight paunch.

"Who the hell are you?"

The figure moved towards the house. Towards Tom and Lydia.

"It's me, Dad."

"Tommy?" said Lydia, giving Tom's arm another squeeze.

"Hi, Mom," said Tommy.

He got closer and Tom saw the gun.

"He's got a gun," yelled Tom, and with careful, deliberate movements he detached his wife's hand and gently pushed her behind him.

"Tommy," Lydia shrieked.

She started to move towards her son when Tom stuck out his arm and barred her path. Tommy continued towards them with his gun pointed at Tom. He stared directly at Tom and the pupils in his eyes were huge. *He's on something.*

"Get in the house," he said sharply to his wife.

She didn't budge.

"Tommy," she said.

Tommy stared at his father with a menacing grin.

"I've got a gun this time so you can't hurt me, Dad. You can't tell me to go to hell and you can't hurt my neck."

"Tommy, Sweetie, we're happy you're back," said Lydia.

Tom said nothing.

"You are maybe," said Tommy.

He kept the gun on his father and didn't look at his mother. He was so much older. It had been seventeen years. He was balding and what hair he did have was long and unruly. His face was fuller, and his cheeks and belly were pudgy. Otherwise, it was still Tommy. The same eyes. The same grin. Now that Tom could see his face, he would have known him anywhere.

Lydia began crying. She tried moving around Tom and towards Tommy.

"Lydia, go in the house," said Tom and he stretched his arm out and pushed her back towards the house.

"I'm so happy to see you. Put the gun away, Sweetie."

"I can't, Mom. He'll hurt me."

"No one will hurt you, Tommy. I want to hug you."

She spoke to him as though he were still a little boy and not a grown man pointing a gun at his father.

"No, he'll hurt me."

Lydia took a step towards Tommy and so did Tom to keep her from getting too close. Tommy cocked the gun. Everybody froze. Tom could see sweat on Tommy's upper lip. It was the same spot he used to sweat as a child, and here it was all these years later.

"This is my gun," said Tommy.

"Yes, it is your gun, Sweetie. Can you put the gun away?"

Tom wished she would stop talking and go in the house. He could handle Tommy alone. Just as he handled the German boy.

"You can't take the gun from me," said Tommy, his wild eyes focused on Tom.

"Tommy, Sweetie, put the gun away and come inside."

Tom didn't look at Lydia, but he knew from her voice she was crying. The wind blew and he had a vague, faraway sensation of being cold.

No one spoke for three or four seconds.

"This is my bike, Dad," said Tommy, gesturing behind him to the motorcycle. "You can't take this bike from me, Dad. You can't throw this bike in the garbage truck."

"Tom, what's he talking about?"

Tom shook his head at her. *That was thirty years ago.*

"Tell her, Dad. Tell her."

"Tommy," said Tom, "we don't want you here. Get on your motorcycle and be on your way."

"Tom," snapped Lydia. "We do want you here, Sweetie. Put the gun away, Sweetie. Come in the house. I'll make you some pancakes."

"No, there will be no pancakes," said Tom.

He was ready to pounce. If Tommy took one step closer.

"Tommy, I'll make you some pancakes. You always loved pancakes."

Why are we talking about pancakes?

"I don't want pancakes, Mom," and the gun pointed at her for an instant and then back at Tom. Tom lurched towards him and then stopped. All three were like an equilateral triangle, each about three feet from the other.

The German boy's face flashed in Tom's mind.

"You made me leave, Dad. I didn't want to."

Tommy began to cry. *He has never grown up. He will never be a grown man.*

"I'm your son and you told me to 'Go to hell.''

Tommy's voice sounded different now that he was crying, and Tom stared at him with more contempt than fear.

"No one threw you out, Tommy. We want you here. We've been waiting for you," said Lydia, her voice slow and soothing.

"He did, Mom," squealed Tommy, jabbing the air with the gun. "he told me to 'go to hell.'"

Tom grabbed at the gun. It went off. With a loud crack.

Chapter Seventy-Two

When his gash healed, my parents put him in a nursing home to die but he wouldn't. He hung on and hung on for years just to spite my Dad.

"Pretty soon the only thing he'll remember is that he hates your father," my Mom would say but she was wrong because even when he stopped having good days and bad days and only had bad days, he always remembered me. He knew my name and he knew my face though he couldn't always put the two together. Neither of my parents believed me but I know he knew me. When he'd mumble to himself the way my Dad still does, I'd be able to decipher two names, his wife's and mine, his two great loves.

When I'd visit him in the nursing home, almost always unaccompanied, he'd more often than not be sitting in the chair next to his bed with his back to the window facing the open door where occasionally someone would walk past and not look his way. The first year someone would dress him and even put on his shoes. By the second year he was down to a hospital johnny and a diaper and his shoes were now slippers.

They put the TV on for him until they realized he wasn't watching, and they shut it off and he never noticed. He'd just sit in that chair, staring and mumbling, day after day, year after year.

Once or twice a day, one of the Jamaican orderlies would get him up on his feet and tether him to his walker and drag him up and down the hallways so his body would stay strong. They were so cruel. If ever there was an argument against staying in shape, it was Thomas Morrissey, Sr. Better to let yourself go then have a fit machine that outlasts your brain. Who wants to be a rudderless boat adrift at sea?

When I first came to visit, I'd go into great detail about my classes and my roommate and the job I had in the campus cafeteria. Every so often he would interrupt to ask, "When do I go to mass?" and I realized he absorbed nothing of what I said. My attempts at reminiscing also failed. He no longer remembered my school plays or our holiday meals or even Camp Grandpa. His mind was now mush.

I'd come and visit him anyway, all the way through college and into law school. After my frustration with him wore off, I discovered it felt good to talk to someone. I'd have long, one-sided, candid conversations with him that I wished I could have with my parents. I've never been the tell-your-problems-to-a-stranger-on-the-bus kind of person, but I started to see the advantages. There are things you don't want your boyfriend to know and there are things you don't want to tell your friends because they might judge you and hold it against you. I was slowly starting to learn about men, and it took Alzheimer's for me to find one who was a good listener. It was the summer of my first year of law school when I decided to tell him about my alcoholism.

The irony was I didn't drink in college. Not really. Not by college standards. I got drunk once freshman year and got sick and slept on the bathroom floor and spent the whole next day in bed recovering and vowed never to do that again and I didn't. I'd nurse a beer or a glass of wine to be polite or at least not to be the only one not drinking.

My drinking began in law school and it culminated during something called "mock trial." I never drank at parties or on New Year's Eve or at the end of final exams. Alcohol wasn't for celebrations, it was medicine. It was an anti-anxiety pill in liquid form.

I had gotten through college without having to speak in public. In group projects, I was happy to do the behind-the-scenes work and let someone else be the spokesperson. They could use my words since I couldn't. When a professor would call on me in class I would blush and answer quickly and then spend the next few minutes trying to calm myself. In law school, there's no place to hide.

As first years, we had to present something called "oral argument." I spent weeks preparing and my research and my notecards were meticulous. I rehearsed over and over in my room and my roommate even let me practice on her the way my grandfather had all those years earlier. I couldn't have been more prepared but the night before I barely slept. My stomach was in knots and I fantasized about meeting with my professor beforehand and getting excused for being shy. Shyness is a trait you're born with like high cheekbones or male pattern baldness. There is even a gene for shyness and since I have it, it's simply not fair to make me do this.

I knew none of this would fly and then the next morning, after my roommates left, I stayed behind, paralyzed with fear. When time was running out, I remembered my roommates' boyfriend had a bottle of tequila in our cabinet. I took it out and did a quick shot and then one more. I stopped at two knowing that's all I could handle, and I grabbed my notecards and headed off to class.

The tequila did the trick. I wasn't great by any means, but it gave me just the confidence I needed to stand up there and stare at my well-prepared notes and read them one by one. My professor's only criticism was that I should "look up more," but he found my argument "persuasive." Tequila had saved the day.

I had other oral arguments and tequila rescued me each time. Two quick shots and then I was out the door. I convinced myself that all successful people have certain rituals. Professional athletes were famous for their superstitions. This was mine.

In third year, after class one day, my boyfriend David commented on my breath. It's hard to keep something like that from someone you're kissing. Police departments across the country could save a fortune on expensive Breathalyzers by having their cops simply make out with suspected drunk drivers. I switched to peppermint schnapps, so I'd be minty fresh.

Eventually, I learned that peppermint schnapps has another advantage. It's usually sold in a much smaller bottle than tequila, one that fit comfortably in my purse. It was tucked safely inside the day of my mock trial.

Three of us, James, a handsome, but arrogant black man and Patty, a gangly and bossy white woman were foisted on each other as teammates. We were pitted against my friend Krisha and two cohorts. The case was nearly twenty years old and involved a fifty-eight-year-old man who had hit and killed a pedestrian in broad daylight. He was neither drunk nor speeding and was being tried for negligence. In the real world, the case ended in a hung jury, which theoretically made for a fair fight.

Our team was assigned the task of proving negligence and James and Patty were soon battling to be the alpha dog which left me in the role as peacemaker. I was frightened enough without the added tension.

The mock trial took place inside a real courtroom in front of a real judge. When I arrived that morning, I was shocked to see how many people were to be in attendance. Aside from my professor who I expected to see, there were dozens of high school students bussed in to learn how our judicial system works. I was prepared for the case, but I wasn't prepared for this. I got in line for the metal detector and x-ray machine behind them and slipped my schnapps bottle from my purse into my coat pocket.

The clerk of the court admonished the students before they could enter the courtroom.

"No soda cans, no food, no coffee cups, no gum in my courtroom."

He made no mention of peppermint schnapps. I ducked inside the ladies' room, sat in a stall and took my two good luck swigs.

The trial began with James, who'd won a coin flip with Patty to go first. He stumbled out of the gate, was uncharacteristically nervous and was easily outshone by the defense. Patty didn't fare much better and then the defense unleashed Krisha.

Every law school class has a star, someone who's "going places" and for our class it was Krisha. She was half-black and half-white and strikingly beautiful. The jury, made up of high school students, was instantly charmed. She was cool and they liked her. Everyone liked her and she turned the felonious driver into a kindly grandfather victimized by bad luck.

I couldn't follow her. I was cold and robotic, and the teens stared at me wanting Krisha back and not wanting to be my friend. I stated my case and sat back down without so much as a nod or a wink from James and Patty.

The judge ordered a short break and I ventured back to my same toilet seat and took two more healthy gulps. I sashayed back into the courtroom suddenly aware that the judge was staring at me. I felt dizzy and sweaty and I waited my turn to present the rebuttal.

I didn't watch Krisha this time. I stared at my feet and practiced my opening line over and over in my head. Krisha finally sat and the judge said something I didn't quite make out.

"Get up," said James through gritted teeth so I got up.

I began to say what I'd prepared, but the judge cut me off. He ordered me to approach the bench and I did so slowly and fearfully. When I arrived, he leaned towards me and spoke in a whisper.

"Are you drunk?"

The jig was up. I tried to stammer out a denial, but he'd been a judge a long time and knew a drunk when he saw one. He called my professor out of the crowd so the three of us could "sidebar," a term now painfully apt.

The two of them spoke in hushed tones so the high school students couldn't hear. This wasn't the lesson they were here to learn. After a moment, my professor turned red-faced in my direction.

"Have you been drinking, Ms. Morrissey?"

I got even more dizzy and I leaned over and threw up into the empty witness stand. Court adjourned.

I met with my professor the next day and the two of us worked out a deal. If I wrote the judge an apology letter, quit the law review and joined AA, he would give me a D and not have me kicked out of school. I agreed and joined AA that day. I've been going to meetings once or twice a week since, although I still have yet to stand up and speak. How can I? How could I possibly stand in front of people and talk without the help of peppermint schnapps?

I explained away my D to my shocked parents claiming I had the flu during the final. I've never told them about my drinking or AA, but I poured it all out to my grandfather that day. He sat staring at me silently not sure what to make of me. No matter, I knew he'd never remember a fucking thing.

Chapter Seventy-Three

Julie played the message Monday night, getting home late after shopping for jeans.

"Hi, Julie, this is Curt Morrissey, I'm afraid I won't be able to make it on Wednesday. My mother died yesterday and there are some things I have to take care of. I'll call you." Beep.

Her first thought was that he was full of shit. Guys will say anything to get out of an uncomfortable situation. She'd been lied to before with some pretty flimsy excuses, but that was usually after the guy had had sex with her.

Dutch had cheated on her for a while before she finally caught on and she wondered if everyone knew but her. She had vowed she'd never play the sap ever again. If she had learned anything in thirty-five years it was that men weren't to be trusted.

Would a guy really lie about his mother dying? Maybe he was married or engaged or had a girlfriend that he thought about cheating on and then reconsidered. Maybe he decided he wasn't interested and wanted to spare her feelings. She played the message three more times. *He seemed sincere.*

In the morning, before she showered or ate or even peed, she retrieved the paper from her front porch and scanned the death notices. There it was: "Lydia Morrissey, devoted wife of Thomas J, beloved mother of Thomas P. and Curtis J..." *Okay, so he wasn't lying.*

Julie arrived at work brandishing the newspaper at the Committee members.

"Some guys will do anything to get out of going out with me," she cracked.

Julie had amassed quite a few hilarious, horror stories from her dating life and here was one more for her collection. Cara laughed. She always laughed at Julie.

"I don't think he could help it," said Bob.

Shut the fuck up, you eavesdropping imbecile.

Sasha scurried in late and Julie thought about reprimanding her but decided against it. It would look as though she was angry about something else and taking it out on her. While Sasha set-up her till, Debbie filled her in on the news.

“Are you going to the funeral?” asked Sasha.

“Of course not,” said Julie.

The idea hadn’t occurred to her.

“Why would she?” said Debbie.

“I would,” said Cara.

“*Of course, you would,*” thought Julie, “*You make out with guys you met five minutes ago.*”

“She barely knows him,” said Debbie.

“I just think he’d appreciate the gesture,” said Cara.

“I’ve got a gesture you’ll appreciate,” said Julie with a smile and everyone but Bob laughed.

It was nine on the dot.

“Melvin, would you mind unlocking the doors?” said Julie.

It was a particularly slow day. A young couple came in and talked to Julie about a loan they were never going to get. They were both twenty and looked younger, high school sweethearts who got married without a job and without a clue. Julie listened politely to their unrealistic dreams and even let them fill out a loan application knowing that unless one of them had a very rich Daddy willing to co-sign, there was no bank in the world that would say yes.

Her mind wandered while the 80-pound husband made his pitch. *Maybe I should go to the funeral?* It had dawned on her that if Curt did have a wife or a fiancée or a girlfriend, she would certainly be at his mother's funeral. This way, Julie would know exactly what she was up against.

"*And*," she reasoned while the adolescent groom blathered on, "*if he wasn't seeing anyone, he'd appreciate her thoughtfulness and sensitivity. She'd show him she was the type of woman who'd stand by him during the hard times. Who wouldn't want that?*

He finished making his insipid pitch.

"I've got big plans," he assured her, "Big plans."

She nodded politely and shook hands with both of them. She knew she'd be calling them in a day or two to let them know they'd been turned down.

She daydreamed some more during her lunch break at the sandwich shop across the street. *Let's just say he is "the one." We get married and the two of us raise Kevin together. Wouldn't I be mad at myself for missing out on one of his major life events? Maybe he'd tell Kevin that what won him over was how kind and considerate his mother was when they first met.* By the time she'd finished her tuna melt she had convinced herself to go.

Chapter Seventy-Four

The bullet grazed Tom's side. He lunged for Tommy, knocking the gun to the pavement. The gun bounced on the driveway twice making a metallic sound. Tom grunted in pain, but his adrenaline propelled him forward and his hands reached for Tommy's throat. He squeezed Tommy's throat the way he squeezed the life from the young German more than forty years earlier. Lydia screamed and Tommy's voice made gurgling sounds as Tom applied pressure to his throat. Tommy was heavier than the German boy had been. Tom's hands couldn't reach all the way around this time.

Lydia shrieked, "No! No! No!"

She reached for Tom's arm. He elbowed her away. The two men fell to the ground now with the older man on top, his hands tight on his son's throat.

Lydia stood over them and screamed, "Tom, stop, you're killing him. Sto-"

Before she could finish the word "stop," she hissed out a strange, gasping sound and collapsed to the ground. Tom choked Tommy. Both men's eyes were wide, wide open now, Tom's with fury and Tommy's with fear. The two of them turned at the same time and looked at Lydia.

She was lying lifeless on the driveway with her eyes and her mouth open. Tom let go of Tommy and moved to her. He felt a sharp pain in his side and blood seeped down his leg. His hands trembled as he knelt next to Lydia.

He yelled, "Hey, hey, hey" and he shook her body. Tommy stood over them, crying, with his hands around his own neck.

"Call 9-1-1!" yelled Tom, and he looked up at Tommy. Tommy looked at his father and blinked, not knowing what to do. Tom grunted at him before he stood up and limped towards the house. *Oh, God, oh God, please.*

He was aware of the pain in his side now. He saw blood drip down his leg. He opened the backdoor, swinging his bloody leg into the kitchen. He grabbed the phone and punched 9-1-1.

"Operator, what's your emergency?"

"We need an ambulance. My wife is lying in the driveway. We live at 58 Wheeler Circle."

"Sir, there is a cruiser on its way."

"Never mind the cruisers, send an ambulance. She collapsed."

"Sir, remain calm. Is she breathing? Does she need CPR?"

"I don't know," yelled Tom, slamming down the phone.

He limped back down the steps, wincing in pain. Before he reached the backdoor, he heard the sound of a police siren. *Someone must have heard the gunshot.*

He bolted from the house. Tommy was on all fours on top Lydia hugging her body.

"Get away from her," he yelled.

He hobbled towards the two of them. He fell on top of Tommy and began to pry him off of his wife. Tommy wouldn't let go of his mother.

He struggled to pull Tommy from Lydia. A police cruiser careened into the driveway. Its siren blared. Its blue light swirled. The cruiser doors sprung open. A bright white light suddenly flooded the area.

"Freeze! Don't move!"

Tom and Tommy stopped struggling but each held onto Lydia. Tommy's gun lay on the ground just a few feet away.

The police officers, one young and black, the other old and white, pulled the two men from Lydia's body. More sirens blared as another cruiser swooped in behind the first.

The young black officer placed two fingers on Lydia's jugular.

"There's no pulse," he said without emotion.

Tom stared at him.

What do you mean 'No pulse'? Please God.

"Do something," screamed Tom.

"There's a gun," yelled the older cop, noticing it for the first time.

"Do CPR," Tom yelled at the black officer.

The two new cops, both white, grabbed Tom and Tommy and pinned them to the pavement.

"What the hell are you doing?" said Tom, more bewildered than angry.

Tommy kept saying, "No, no, no," over and over like a yogi chanting his mantra.

The ambulance pulled into the driveway now.

"She has no pulse," the black officer yelled to the EMTs.

"She needs CPR," yelled Tom.

The older officer on top of Tom frisked him and suddenly pulled his hand away as though he'd been burnt. "This one is bleeding," he said in surprise.

"Just give her CPR," Tom yelled.

The red ambulance light and the blue cruiser lights swirled together. The EMTs rushed to Lydia's body. Tom's face was pressed to the pavement so he couldn't see them administer CPR but he could hear the rhythmic counting. Tommy kept saying, "No, no, no."

"Shut up," said Tom.

God, please save her. She never hurt anyone, please, she doesn't deserve this. Please, I'm begging you.

"She's not responding," said an EMT.

"No, no, no," continued Tommy.

The EMTs lifted Lydia onto a stretcher and hurried her to the back of the ambulance. Tom closed his eyes, his face resting on the cold pavement. *Our Father, who art in heaven…*

Chapter Seventy-Five

My mother was stunned and more than a little annoyed when I postponed my wedding. She had to get on the phone with her sisters and my cousins and tell them to rearrange their hotel reservations and their flights and whatever else they had planned.

My Dad, on the other hand, was like a death row inmate receiving a call from the governor and getting a stay of execution. Ever since I got engaged the mere mention of my wedding was enough to make his eyes well up and for him to bolt from the room. I don't know what weird things go in on men's heads regarding their daughters and I don't want to know.

In any event, the next day, the three of us went to visit my grandfather. Anyone watching would have thought we were a normal happy family but maybe there is no such thing. Maybe all families are just as full of shit as ours.

On the way there, my Dad was quieter than usual if that's possible. I wondered what was going on with him. Did he feel guilty now that his father was dying and the two of them had barely spoken my entire life? I never saw them have what anyone would call a "real conversation," unless you count the shouting match of a few years earlier.

When we got to his room, my grandfather's eyes were open and he was conscious or at least reasonably so for him. He looked blankly at my father and mother but when he saw me his eyes flickered with delight. Did he really know who I was or was he merely responding to the love I was propelling his way? Was there a vestige of the bond between us or was he like the moon reflecting light from the sun but emitting none of his own?

He was hooked up to an IV which gave my mom a chance to start in on some jokes.

"What you have there, Tom, vodka or is that gin?"

"That's not really the 'Breakfast of Champions' now is it?"

He no longer knew what vodka was or gin was or even what breakfast was, and my father and I weren't in the mood to laugh. After a few minutes, my grandfather was asleep, and my father began taking lunch orders.

I wasn't particularly hungry, but I know my dad is always happier when he has a task. As much as he hated my grandfather, if my grandfather had asked him to come over and build a brick wall, brick by brick, my father would have done it without complaint.

I sat staring at my grandfather while my mother pulled a book from her purse.

"What do you think he's dreaming about?"

"He's like a little baby at this point," she said, "so he's dreaming about whatever babies dream about. Boobs, I guess."

I made a face.

"Men probably dream about boobs their whole lives."

She was probably right.

After a few minutes, my dad was back with the sandwiches. He and my mother proceeded to discuss their mundane bullshit with my grandfather's unconscious body in between them. It was as if they were in their living room and my grandfather was the coffee table. I wanted to say, "Hey, there's a person here," but I didn't.

After lunch, my dad ducked outside to make some calls and check on his crew. My mother sat reading her book. I called David a couple of times, but I spent most of the day sitting and holding my grandfather's hand while he slept. He woke up once or twice and murmured a few words though the only one I could make out was "Lydia."

He was asleep again when my father came back and it wasn't long before my father said, "We should go." I could tell he was antsy. The guy can't sit still. I ignored him.

"We should go," he said again.

"Not just yet," I said, and he and my mother exchanged looks. A few minutes later, she finished her chapter and said, "Sweetheart, we really should go."

I gave in this time and bent down and kissed my grandfather's forehead. He opened his eyes and squeezed my hand and pulled me close and whispered something just to me.

Chapter Seventy-Six

Julie didn't tell the Committee she'd decided to go to the funeral. She casually mentioned to Bob on her way out the door the day before that she'd "be a bit late tomorrow morning." The Committee might have supported her decision, but they might not have, and she couldn't afford to risk it. *They can't tell me what to do. I'm their boss, they're not mine.* But she knew better. She was as susceptible to peer pressure and social convention as anyone else.

She only had one black dress in a closet full of business suits, which made her choice of what to wear easy. It reminded her of her Catholic school days with only one option every morning. She left the house early knowing she was going to an unfamiliar part of town and couldn't risk getting lost and arriving late. It did her no good to sit in the back of a crowded church and go unnoticed. He had to see her otherwise the whole mission would be a failure.

When she arrived at 8:45 for the 9 o'clock mass she felt something was amiss right away. The church parking lot wasn't full or close to being full like she had anticipated. There were at most a dozen cars. When her uncle died the year before his funeral was packed and her uncle was an asshole. Granted, he was an Elk, and his whole herd, or lodge or whatever it's called, was there with their secret handshakes and other nonsense, but still, *"Where was everybody?"*

Julie picked up the newspaper section off the passenger seat to make sure she had the right time.

"The funeral mass will be held at St. Zepherin's at 9 a.m. on Thursday."

She had the right place and the right time. *Should I be doing this? Will he appreciate the gesture or think I'm some kind of crazy stalker? Is this dumb? He's hasn't seen me yet. I could just leave and go to work, and no one would ever know.* Her stomach felt the way it used to before her tennis matches in high school. Once before a big match she had even thrown up. She checked her make-up in the rear-view mirror and got out of the car.

An older, but not quite elderly couple climbed the church steps just ahead of her. She could feel herself perspiring despite a bracing March wind. *I can still leave. I can turn and run. He'd never know.* The old man held the door for his wife and Julie.

"Thank you," she said, entering the church. *Too late now.*

There were no more than twenty-five people sitting or kneeling. She had anticipated the church being crowded and had schemed to sit on the aisle where he'd be sure to see her. Now it didn't matter. He'd spot her no matter where she sat. She found an empty pew about eight rows from the altar.

"I'm the youngest person here," she thought looking from one white head to another. *I don't see anyone who could be his girlfriend. Unless he had a thing for sixty-somethings.* Her stomach loosened up a little.

A thin gentleman in his sixties made his way to one of the front pews. He had a shock a gray hair and was impeccably dressed in a tailored suit and the yellow handkerchief in his top pocket matched his tie. He seemed a little too stylish and out of place among the crowd of working-class Catholics. *Who is that? That's not Curt's father—is it?*

Julie was startled when the organ sounded and played a dirge she'd heard before but couldn't name. She rose with the others and looked back as the pallbearers glided the coffin down the center aisle. Curt trailed behind pushing a man in a wheel chair who had to be his father. He was older and balding with a paunch, but with the same dark eye brows and eyes.

Curt looked stricken, his face laden with grief. His eyes, reddened by tears, looked at Julie for a full second as they passed. Her body stiffened when she saw him. *What was I expecting? Was he supposed to wave and smile and say, "Thanks for coming?"* She had come to be supportive and scope out the competition yet, this was real grief and real pain and she felt like an imposter. *I don't belong here. I shouldn't have come.*

Curt sat in the front row with his Dad next to him in the aisle. The priest entered from the front. He was a million years old and Julie remembered the ancient priest from her high school who'd say mass for the girls on the first Friday of every month.

"That priest is so old he played Little League with Jesus," Julie was fond of saying in those days. This guy looked even older than him. *We might have a double funeral on our hands.*

The priest called Curt's mother "a saint" and spoke of her "wonderful sense of humor" and "cheerful disposition." He praised her as "one of the pillars of the church." The woman in front of her sniffled.

The gospel was the story of Lazarus, which to Julie seemed cruel. Lazarus was brought back to life. That wasn't going to be the case here. The embalming probably ruled that out entirely she thought. She had a habit of thinking of a rebuttal whenever a priest or a professor or pretty much any authority figure was speaking.

Julie looked around without moving her head. Her eyes scanned one way than another. She saw varying degrees of grief from stoic concern to devastating sorrow. *She felt nothing. Why would she? Why am I even here? This is stupid.*

The priest invited Curt up for the eulogy. From the front row, Curt rose and moved toward the pulpit, bowing to the seated priest on his nearby throne. Curt stood behind the microphone surveying the crowd making eye contact with as many as possible, catching her eyes for just a second. His handsome face remained neutral, betraying no strong feelings either way. He took out some papers from his inside pocket and unfolded them and placed them in front of him. He gripped the sides of the lectern with both hands and looked down at his notes and then back up.

"I'm a Mama's boy," he said in a clear voice, "Always have been. Those of you who knew my mother can understand why." "*He's looking at me,*" Julie thought, "*Isn't he? I think he's looking right at me.*"

"My mother," he continued, "was the kindest person I know and the wittiest. No one was ever ugly or mean or stupid in my mother's world. An overweight girl was 'uniquely proportioned.' A confrontational person was 'spirited' and stupid person was described by my mother as 'not a knower of things.'"

The congregation laughed a tentative laugh. Julie began to think about Kevin. *Would he give her eulogy some day? Would he call himself a*

"Mama's Boy"? Would he describe her as "witty"? Maybe. "The kindest person he knew"? Probably not.

Curt placed one piece of paper behind another and then began again.

"I know people are wondering how my family could have fallen apart like this. How could that happen? The real question is how was it able to stay together so long? The answer is that she held us together for years longer than anyone else could have."

Someone coughed and Curt paused.

"When I was little," he continued, "like most little kids, I was afraid of what was under the bed and the monster in the closet and my mother assured me there was nothing to be afraid of."

There was a catch in his voice now for the first time.

"Yet, in my house, the monster was real, it was schizophrenia, an insidious form of mental illness that was always lurking under the bed or in the closet and in the shadows."

The woman next to Julie started to cry and she grabbed for her husband's hand.

"We never knew when the monster would show up and what form it would take. Sometimes it took the form of violent outbursts and other times it curled up in a ball and cried for hours on end. My father wanted to fight with the monster and cast it from sight when he saw the destruction that it was causing. But my mother knew how to tame the monster and with her soothing voice she would calm it with love and understanding."

Julie became aware of herself now and she realized she was crying along with the others. She could hear sniffles and see the tissues and handkerchiefs being raised and lowered.

"As my brother's life spiraled downhill and he began to be shunned by friends and neighbors and lost the support of teachers and everyone else close to him, my mother clung to his side. She would lie next to him, all night sometimes, while he cried. She would whisper to him for hours on end that she still loved him no matter what. This tiny, frail woman fought the monster to a stalemate for years until the monster finally won and my brother lost his battle with schizophrenia. There are always casualties in war and a few nights ago my mother became a casualty in the war against mental illness."

Curt stopped for a second now, and as the silence lengthened Julie leaned forward willing him to go on. He gripped the lectern tightly again, looking at his feet as he composed himself. Julie wanted to rush over to him and hold him, but she knew that she shouldn't.

"The autopsy revealed," Curt said with his voice quavering, "That her heart was too big for her body."

Tears began to spill down his cheeks.

"I didn't need a doctor to tell me that."

He stopped now and put his papers inside his jacket. By the time he returned to his pew Julie had fallen madly in love with him.

Chapter Seventy-Seven

Tom went to mass on Lydia's birthday. It was the first time he'd been since her funeral. Tom Morrissey had stopped going to church after God took his wife from him. *Why would God do that? Why not take me instead of her? She never did an evil deed her whole life.*

He never went back to work after Lydia died. His hip had pretty much healed and he could have gone back, but what for at his age? He had their savings, the money he never spent on Tommy and Curt's college, and the insurance money. All his old co-workers were long gone. His boss seemed relieved when Tom called to say he'd had enough.

He got drunk a couple of times after she died. He stopped at a liquor store and bought himself a bottle of scotch. He discovered he no longer had a taste for it and didn't care for the effects. He knew she wouldn't approve if she were looking down on him if there were such a thing as heaven. He dumped it out, the way he had the previous bottle twenty years earlier.

Her birthday, November 17th, fell on a Thursday in 1988. The weekday masses were always at 12:05 and lacked the pomp and circumstance of a regular mass. The priest never even gave a sermon, the idea being that people with jobs could attend a quick mass on their lunch hour, grab a quick bite and go back to work. Yet, no one with a job ever came. It was always just a handful of old people, old ladies mostly, a small but dedicated gaggle that went each day taking up only two or three pews.

Tom was on the young end of this crowd. "The average age has to be 85" thought Tom looking around. *I feel like a kid.*

Father Henry said the mass in Lydia's honor. They had made arrangements on the phone.

"I'd be more than happy to," Father Henry had said, "She was one of the Lord's favorites, you know."

Father Henry wouldn't perform an exorcism for Tommy, but he'd say a mass in Lydia's name. Tom put a fifty in the collection plate, not wanting to be beholden to anyone.

He knew what Lydia wanted from him for her birthday. He'd been putting it off for months. Ever since the pre-trial hearing, he'd been ashamed of himself for pushing his brother. *I shouldn't have pushed him.* He tried to dismiss it from his mind. *He shouldn't have tried to shake my hand. He knows the rules. We have a deal.*

It was obvious his brother was dying. Tom had seen enough death in his life to know when it was lurking nearby. He knew she'd want him to call Billy for her birthday. If he waited another year it would be too late. Billy would be dead. *I shouldn't have pushed him.*

The day after the pre-trial hearing and a half a dozen times after that, Tom picked up the phone to call his brother. He even called information and got Billy's number. Most rich guys had unlisted numbers, but not Billy. He didn't care who called him.

Each time, he would think about the millions of dollars Billy made off the family business while he was nothing more than a glorified clerk. He'd get angry and hang up the phone and stew for hours afterwards. *The hell with him.* It didn't take much to put Tom right back in that meeting with Billy and his father the day his birthright was stolen from him.

There other moments, usually in the middle of the night, lying awake, that Tom was honest with himself. His father was right, Billy had a better head for business. If he had been running things, it wouldn't have turned into a furniture chain, it would have remained a lumberyard and may have even gone under. Billy was the one who spun it into gold. During those nights, he'd resolve to call Billy but always changed his mind the next day.

Lydia used to prod him.

"So what if he got the business?" she'd say, "You've got two wonderful children and a wife with movie star looks."

When her attempts at humor failed to persuade him, she'd try a different tact.

"Even Esau forgave Jacob," she'd say, and Tom knew she was right but still he couldn't let go of his hate. It was like an old friend whose company he'd gotten used to.

Kneeling after communion, during the mass on her birthday, Tom thought about shoving his brother in the courtroom. He remembered the pretty woman in the red dress gaping at him like he was a monster. *I shouldn't have pushed him.*

Sometimes, he'd think his wife was right, he had won. *I'm the one with the family.* Other times, he'd think Billy had won. Billy was successful, the one with the mansion and the millions. He used to drive by his house just to gape at it. *Billy won.* Now Billy was sick, and Tom's family was gone. *No one won. No one ever wins.*

When he got home from her mass he decided to call. He always liked to get her something nice for her birthday. He'd start thinking about what to get her three or four months beforehand. Now she was gone. *I still have to do something for her birthday. This is what she wants.*

The number had been on the notepad on the little table in the living room since the day of the pretrial hearing. He picked up the phone and dialed. Billy answered.

"Billy, it's your brother."

There was a moment of silence.

"I've been expecting your call," said Billy.

Chapter Seventy-Eight

"Sweetheart, wake up. The hospital called, they think your grandfather is going to die today."

My mother never had a light touch, never could ease into anything.

"Your grandfather is going to die today"—that's how you wake me up? How 'bout you wait 'til I've had a bowl of cereal? How 'bout "I've got some bad news"? Anything. She didn't have to wake me up with a punch to the gut but she did anyway. Always has to be blunt and we know what that rhymes with.

I stared at her in disbelief.

"What are you shocked about? We all knew this was coming. We all knew last Saturday he wasn't walking out of that hospital room. Today is the day, that's all."

She was right, of course. It was three days ago that he whispered to me and since then he had slipped into coma. I had gone to visit him all three days without my parents, once with David, but he just lay there more dead than alive.

I don't know what I was thinking. Was I expecting some sort of miracle? That overnight they'd come up with a cure for old age and his Alzheimer's that would have worn off like the flu? I knew he was dying. I postponed my wedding because he was dying, and yet, hearing my mother say, "he's going to die today," in that casual "who gives a shit" tone was what wounded me. I lay there for a few minutes, quietly sobbing to myself until my Dad pounded on my door and said, "Get up, we have to go."

A half an hour later, showered and fed, I was in the backseat of my father's car. Staring at the back of his head, I was struck by how gray my Dad was getting. One old guy down and now he's next in the pipeline. Someday, it'll be my turn.

My mother was chatty and carefree and unaffected by the day's agenda, but it was my Dad who angered me. After all, it was his Dad who was soon to be gone for good and I never detected a hint of sadness.

I admit I hadn't seen my grandfather from the middle of August 'til the beginning of November and I felt guilty about it, but I had a pretty good excuse. The bar exam and my wedding were two major life events. My parents knew he'd been transferred from the nursing home to the hospital for five days before they told me. Why hadn't they visited? My grandfather was dying, and my father didn't give a shit. How would he like it if I behaved that way on his death day? I began lashing out.

"So Dad, do you have any fond memories of your father?"

"What?"

"When you were growing up, did you and your Dad ever have fun?"

My Mom glanced back over her shoulder at me.

"What do you mean by 'fun'''?

"Sweetheart, why are you asking this?" My mother butted in.

"I was just wondering if he had any fond memories of his father. Any summer vacations, camping trips, Disneyworld…"

"Disneyworld? Do you think Tom Morrissey ever set foot in Disneyworld?"

"Why are you badgering your father?"

She was angry now and I considered backing down but decided against it.

"I'm not badgering anyone. I was just wondering if Dad had any fond memories of childhood."

"Yes, yes," he said. He was angry now. Finally, some emotion from the inscrutable one.

"I have some fond memories."

"Like what?"

My father looked over at my mother who looked over at me.

"What is your problem?"

"I don't have a problem. I'm just asking Dad if he had any fond memories of his childhood, that's all."

"Well, let's see," he said, "My Mom would take us swimming in the summer and sledding in the winter."

"You sure it wasn't the other way around," My mother said, never missing an opportunity.

"She'd take us sledding and then make us hot chocolate and she was a good story teller."

He was a slippery one. His Dad was dying and here he was telling me things about his Mom I already knew.

"What about your Dad?"

"What about him?"

"Did you have any fun with him?"

"Your father is not on the witness stand. You're not a lawyer yet, you know."

"I'm not interrogating him."

"It sure seems like it."

The two of them were exasperated.

"Look, my grandfather is dying and I'd like to hear some fond memories my father has of him, that's all."

My father got quiet for a moment. With him, you never knew if the moment was going to last the rest of the day but this one didn't.

"If I think of one or two, will that put an end to the discussion, Sweet Pea?"

I almost laughed when he called me "Sweet Pea" through gritted teeth, almost.

“That sounds good.”

He sighed heavily and released one of his patented harumphs.

“When I was little, we’d throw the football around the backyard and that was fun. Sometimes he’d take your uncle Tommy and me to the park and hit us flyballs and that was fun.”

“How ‘bout when you got older?”

He became quiet then responded carefully.

“When we got older, my brother got sick and the fun stopped. There was no more football or fly balls and certainly no Disneyworld.”

I could hear a quiver in his voice for the first time in a long while and I decided to back off having gotten what I wanted.

“Let’s just say he was better at being a grandfather than he was at being a father.”

Chapter Seventy-Nine

Tom sat in the chair against the wall near the window. Billy lay a few feet away, unresponsive. He'd been in a coma for the past four days. Tom had come to visit each day sitting for hours in Billy's private hospital room staring at his brother and the mint-colored walls.

After their Thanksgiving dinner together, Tom and Billy spoke on the phone every day for nearly two months. They had long talks about their parents, Uncle Brendan and the old days. They reminisced about Eddie Curran and the other kids from the neighborhood and their old teachers.

Sometimes after they spoke, Tom would remember a funny story that he'd forgotten since childhood but was now rediscovered like an old fossil. He'd jot it down on the notepad he kept by the phone and bring it up to his brother the next day. Sometimes, it was Billy who would reach back into the archives to retrieve some nugget that Tom had long since discarded. The two lingered on the phone for roughly an hour each day with long silences but plenty of laughs in between. They were finally friends again after their own decades-long cold war.

Tom stood up and looked out the window. The sun shone brightly in a blue sky uncluttered by clouds. It looked to be a beautiful day, but he knew better. It was February first and the temperatures had dropped to the single digits. From the 9th floor, he could see little figures scurrying to and from their cars fighting against the coldest day of the year.

"Hi, Dad."

He turned to see Curt standing in the doorway, his bulky coat open with his bright yellow jumpsuit underneath clashing with the mint-green walls. Tom had worn a dignified suit, dark blue or gray, each day to the department store. His son wore a ridiculous, garish get-up.

The two shook hands.

"How's it going?"

"No change. He hasn't opened his eyes in three days. The doctor should be here soon."

Curt nodded and took off his big coat and draped it over a chair. They both sat now on opposite sides of the room with the motionless body of Billy Morrissey in between.

"It's cold."

"Yeah."

"How's work?"

"Fine."

Two weeks earlier, Tom had been at Billy's when Curt arrived for a visit. Billy asked Curt about a girlfriend that Tom knew nothing about.

"We broke up," said Curt.

"I'm quite sorry to hear that," said Billy.

How does he know about her and I don't?

Curt was always correct with Tom. He shook his hand, looked him in the eye and gave him quick and clear responses but he never revealed anything to his father. Tom didn't know if his son liked his job or he was doing well. Curt never brought a girl home for Tom to meet even when Lydia was alive. He never discussed his employees or what he did on his down time. Tom couldn't name a single one of his friends.

The two had never been close but since Lydia died, Tom could feel the boy's contempt. The two never exchanged a harsh word but he could tell from the way his son looked at him that he blamed him for what happened.

It wasn't my fault.

Tommy was crazy. He always had been. Anyone could see that. It wasn't Tom's doing. He had to choose between Tommy and Lydia, and he had chosen Lydia. He'd make the same choice a million times over if he had to.

The doctor came in a little after two. He was an Irishman of about fifty who could have passed for one of Tom's cousins. Tom had always wished Curt had become a doctor. Now he'd settle for just about any profession that didn't require a yellow jumpsuit.

They'd met the doctor before, and he greeted each of them with a breezy familiarity.

"Cold out there."

Tom and Curt smiled. The doctor checked Billy's vitals, looked over his chart for a moment or two then, put it back. He shook his head and his breezy air disappeared.

"His body is shutting down. He probably only has another day or two."

Tom remained impassive but while the doctor spoke Curt began to cry. Not a sound came from him, but tears dribbled down his cheeks, and he made no effort to wipe them away.

Will he cry like this when I die? Tom knew he wouldn't, and he resented the affection the boy had for his uncle. *I'm his father. What had Billy ever done for him? A few presents at Christmas? Crumbs from a rich man's table.*

He had raised Curt, not Billy. It was from the sweat of his brow that his son was clothed and fed and sheltered. He was the one who had taught him how to throw a football and pitch a tent. He had taken him to his Boy Scout camping trips and brought him to mass every Sunday.

When the doctor left and they returned to their seats, Tom's resentment shifted from Curt to Billy. This was all Billy's doing. He has stolen his son from him the same way he had stolen the family business fifty years earlier. Tom sat with his fists clenched, glowering at his brother. Billy, even unconscious with his body disintegrating, had outfoxed Tom once again.

Chapter Eighty

Julie saw Billy's name in the paper and decided to go to the funeral. Thanks to Curt, going to funerals was her new hobby. *Why shouldn't I go? I was friends with him. I had had brunch at his house and we played tennis together once.*

She told them at work she'd be a little late and when the committee probed further she fended them off with a lie about "the dentist." She was so tired of them and their outpouring of sympathy since her break-up with Curt. Debbie, in particular, was consoling and sympathetic and unabashedly triumphant.

"I never liked him," she confided to Julie during Thursday night drinks. *Fuck you.*

After she and Curt broke up, she began to look for Billy's name in the obituaries every day, feeling ghoulish, like a vulture circling in the air. One February morning there it was, featured prominently with a whole four paragraphs and a photo. The photo had to be thirty years old and she could see some of Curt's face in his. A handsome, unmarried, younger Morrissey brother, sound familiar?

The paper said he died of pneumonia and, technically, he may have but Julie knew better. He suffered alone and died alone, the poor man. Would that be her fate as well?

Tom threw his paper down on the kitchen table in disgust. The Boston Globe had heaped praise on his brother calling him "a furniture mogul" and giving his life four full paragraphs and a picture. The brain surgeon who died at fifty-seven while hiking only got three paragraphs and a smaller picture.

He looked at his reflection in the door of the microwave and straightened his tie. He knew his obituary wouldn't garner four paragraphs and a picture. He'd be with the also-rans, the inconsequential, the shitheads. *Who decides whose life is important and whose isn't?*

What did they say about Lydia? It wasn't that long ago but his memories from that time remained hazy. He seemed to recall the phrase "devoted wife and loving mother." Bland and generic praise that didn't come close to telling the story of what a woman she was.

What would they say about me? *Devoted husband and loving father? Was I a loving father?* They'd have to mention the war. He had fought in the Battle of the Bulge and had a medal to prove it. That was one thing he had over Billy. He had served his country honorably in its time of need. A thousand years from now his descendants would recall that one of their ancestors had fought Hitler. *What descendants?*

She put on the same black dress that she'd worn to Curt's mother's funeral but this time she wore a push-up bra. The dress wasn't low cut enough to show cleavage, but it offered a hint of what lay underneath, just a little reminder to Curt of what he'd been missing.

She took longer than intended getting ready and her car took longer to defrost than she expected and by the time she got to the church the funeral had nearly started. This wasn't the plan. She had wanted him to see her on the way in and think about her all through the mass, but she was too late. She could only see the back of his head and his shoulders as he sat with his father in the front row. She took a seat near the back in a church filled with furniture, employees and gay men. She'd never seen so many sixty-something gay men in her life. She lived in Boston after all, *where had these gay guys been hiding?*

The priest, young and progressive, seemed to know Billy remarkably well, and if he objected to his lifestyle he didn't let on. He spoke of Billy's "charitable donations" and his "charitable spirit" and his "unflagging sense of humor." He was "a kind boss" and "a loving uncle" and a "good friend." Julie didn't cry but she did well up from time to time, and although she had an ulterior motive for coming, she did have a great deal of affection for this sweet and gentle man.

Curt sat next to Tom in the front pew and to Tom's relief didn't cry. The two of them sat stoically, staring straight ahead, their impassive faces revealing nothing. The priest, smiling and ebullient, called it "a happy occasion" and a "celebration of a life."

He's probably gay, thought Tom.

The church was packed, and he wondered if it was mostly his employees or had Billy really touched that many lives. He grew angry when he thought of the low turn-out for Lydia. She was a saint and deserved better, but as Tommy's outbursts grew more frequent, their number of friends dwindled until they were left with a hearty few.

Tom's mind wandered during the eulogy and he wondered what kind of reception Billy will receive in the afterlife. What's valued on Earth is not valued in heaven. So, what if the church was full? Billy had lived a life of depravity and sin. He may have been a big shot here, but it was easier for a camel to pass through the eye of a needle than it was for a rich man to enter the Kingdom of God. Maybe Tom would have the last laugh after all?

At communion time, Julie passed by the front row and snuck a peek in Curt's direction desperate for eye contact, but he knelt with his head bowed seemingly unaware of her presence. When the mass ended and it was "time to go in peace and love and serve the world," she stood at the end of the pew. Curt and his father escorted the coffin down the aisle. He glanced her way and held her gaze for a second or two. *Was he glad to see me? Surprised? Angry? He's so fucking inscrutable.*

As she descended the church steps with everyone else, he stood at the sidewalk staring up at her. His hair was freshly shorn and his cheeks rosy in the February cold but he was still his cute self.

"Thanks for coming," he said, "You didn't have to."

"Why wouldn't I? I liked him."

Curt nodded and breath escaped from his not quite closed mouth.

"Did you want to ride in the hearse with us to the cemetery?"

"I don't want to ride in the hearse."

"You can. You can ride in the hearse with me and my Dad."

"I don't want to ride in the hearse. I have to go to work."

"All right," he said.

People got in their cars and began to line up behind the hearse. Curt and Julie stood for a moment looking at each other. She shivered and pulled up her collar.

"I miss you," he said.

"I miss you too," she said.

"I rang your doorbell when I brought your purse over, but you weren't home."

"I didn't know that," she said.

"Well, I did," he said softly.

She nodded. Damn, he's cute. Short but cute.

"I love you" he said, "And I want to marry you."

"Too bad," she said with a shrug, trying to appear casual, "If you won't have kids, you can't have me."

She'd been rehearsing that line ever since they broke up.

"Julie, you know I can't" he said.

"Sure, you can."

Both of them spoke just above a whisper.

"Don't you see? Mental illness runs in my family. It's not just my brother, it goes back generations. How'd you like to be the mother of a serial killer? Do you want to bounce Ted Bundy on your knee? Or little Charlie Manson?"

"Sure, why not?"

"You say that now, but you wouldn't."

She looked a way for a second and then looked back.

"Do you think your mother regretted having your brother? Did she regret being a mother?"

Another line she had rehearsed since their break-up.

Tom was helped into the back of the hearse; his hip had stiffened up with the cold weather. Most of the people his age had moved to Florida or were making plans to. Not Tom. He had lived in Boston his whole life, save for a year or so in the European Theater. Boston was where he would die.

They loaded Billy's casket into the back. Tom had seen so much death. He had watched his wife die, he had seen Moretti murdered and had sat with Billy when he passed. He was there for each of their deaths, his three best friends.

He remembered how hot it was for his mother's funeral. She had died July 3rd , and he remembered standing at the cemetery in his dark suit, dripping sweat while the priest read the final prayers over her body. His mother, his father, Uncle Brendan, Lydia, Moretti, Leckie, Sims, Billy, all gone. He would be next. There was no one left.

"We're ready to go onto the cemetery," said the driver, "Whenever your son is ready."

Where is Curt?

"Heart disease," Curt said.

"What?" said Julie.

"We have mental illness on my Dad's side and heart disease on my Mom's. I could go at any moment."

"You look healthy to me."

He looked down and shook his head as a man from the funeral home approached. She glared at Curt waiting for him to respond.

"Sir, we're ready to go to the cemetery now."

"Just a sec," he said, and he turned back to Julie.

"We don't need children to be happy."

"I do."

"Why can't we be happy just the two of us?"

"Because," she said. *Because? Is that the best I can do?*

"What if we adopt?" she said.

She was going off book now. She didn't want to adopt. She had always dreamed of being pregnant. She'd fantasized many times about rubbing her pregnant belly and looking at herself in the mirror. She'd even dreamed of nursing baby Kevin, but she was desperate now and willing to compromise.

"No," he said.

Tom hadn't eaten breakfast. His entire life he had never eaten before mass even though the Church had loosened it rules decades earlier. He still had fish every Friday. He'd remain steadfast even as the Church wavered.

"Sir, everybody is ready," said the driver.

It was time to go. They couldn't keep the priest or the other celebrants waiting. It was time for the procession to drive to the cemetery for the final prayers over the body. Where the hell was Curt?

Tom opened the door to the hearse and peered out. Curt was on the steps on the church talking to a pretty woman with light brown hair. Something about her seemed familiar. Had he seen her before?

"Curt," he called, "We have to go."

Curt ignored him.

"She can come in the hearse with us."

No response.

"Tell her she can come in the hearse with us."

"She doesn't want to get in the fuckin' hearse," yelled Curt.

The pallbearers backed away after Curt said "fuck." He cringed.

"Look what you made me do," he said softly.

“Sorry,” she whispered.

“I have to go,” he said.

“Why can’t we adopt?” she asked.

“No.”

“Why not?”

“Because with adopted kids you don’t know what you’re getting. Their genes could be worse than mine.”

“What about a little Chinese girl? When was the last time a little Chinese girl became a serial killer?”

“I’m sorry,” he said, “I just can’t.”

Goddam it, thought Tom, swearing on the church steps. *What is wrong with him?*

The head pallbearer approached Tom.

“Sir, the priest is ready, everyone in the cars are ready, we really have to go.”

“Curt,” Tom yelled, “We have to go.”

“I’m sorry,” Curt said. “I have to go.”

She nodded.

It’s really over.

Curt turned to look at Tom. Tom could see the look of contempt that Curt flashed him from time to time. He hates me. My own son hates me.

“Wait,” said Curt sharply.

Julie stopped.

Curt stopped abruptly and walked back at her.

"Okay, you win," he said.

"What?"

"We can adopt a little Chinese girl."

His tone was angry, and she wondered if he was being sarcastic.

"Seriously?"

He nodded.

"You seem pissed."

"I am."

This isn't how I want it. I don't want him agreeing to marrying me and raising a child with me if he's going to be angry and begrudging and resentful. On the other hand, he said "yes" so fuck it, I'll take it.

"Okay" she said, "We can get married."

"Fine," he said with disgust.

She rushed towards him and kissed him while pallbearers looked on. She kissed him as hard as she could and then pulled back.

"All right," she said with a smile, "I'll get in the hearse."

She slipped from his grasp and ran and jumped into the open door of the waiting hearse and slid into the seat next to Tom. Tom moved over and looked at her, too surprised to speak.

"I'm Julie," she said, and the two shook hands for the very first time. Curt climbed in and closed the hearse door behind him. She reached for his hand and entwined it with hers.

So, what do you know? After all that, Kevin is alive and well and he's a little Chinese girl.

Chapter Eighty-One

I ducked into the sacristy before the funeral. The priest, ancient and stooped, was donning his white robes and was too old to hear me come in. This guy is lucky to be attending someone else's funeral, I thought.

I'd never been in a church sacristy before and there wasn't much to it, a closet or two and some drawers. As a child, I pictured the priests' changing room to be like a football player's with lockers that they could bang their heads against to psyche themselves up before the "big mass."

Of course, "changing" in this case just meant throwing a robe on top of the black pants and black button-down shirt that priests wear. I have no idea what they did in the summer in this old church with no AC. This church and this priest were both barely hanging on.

"Knock, knock, knock," I said pretending to rap my knuckles on the wall.

He looked up, surprised to see me, and pulled down the robe from about his neck, messing up his few remaining wisps of white hair.

"Hi, I said, "I'm Tom Morrissey's granddaughter, Kevin Morrissey."

He chuckled and opened his mouth wide enough to reveal a less than complete set of yellow teeth.

"You don't look like a 'Kevin'."

I'd been hearing that my whole life which is why I sometimes go by "Kay" but I smiled and played along as though the idea were new.

"I'm Father O'Laughlin."

Sounds about right, I thought.

"My father asked me to do the eulogy."

"Oh," he said, "Fair enough. How 'bout when I say your name you come up to the pulpit?"

I detected just a hint of a brogue. His hair, his teeth and even his accent were all leaving him bit by bit.

"Sounds like a plan," I said, and we shook hands for some reason and then I entered the church. I'm fine one on one but when I saw the crowd I'd be addressing, sitting there in their pews, getting ready to judge me, a sudden fear, old and familiar, came over me. I slipped into a pew with my Mom and my Dad and my fiancé David. I knelt like a good Catholic girl and said my introductory prayers while David remained seated next to me like the good Jewish boy that he is.

When I agreed to do the eulogy (who else could do it, really?) I expected the turnout to be not much more than us. My grandfather was over ninety, an irascible old fellow who'd been out of it for years and had been an irascible middle-aged fellow before that, with his wife gone and his best friends not surviving the Battle of the Bulge.

Yet, despite this, the church was filling in. There were some of my Dad's employees and my Mom's co-workers and one or two my friends and some of my parents' friends and a few, as far as I could tell, church regulars. The throng swelled to thirty-five or forty. *I'd have to speak to that many?*

I got a sick feeling in my stomach reminiscent of my hearse ride with Jenny's Mom. My palms began to sweat, and David let go of my hand and gave me a mock dirty look, pretending to wipe his hands on his pants. I would have laughed if I weren't so frightened. I longed for my bottle of schnapps.

Organ music played and then abruptly stopped right before the mass was to begin. I once read of the old days, the 1800's or so, when a parish would hire a woman or two to come and mourn for the newly departed; women who would wail from time to time and sob and provide the appropriate atmosphere. What a gig! I could have used one of those women now as the eerie silence terrified me.

The organ music resumed with a flourish and we all stood and greeted the priest's entrance. We followed the church regulars lead on when to stand when to sit and when to kneel, the Morrisseys being a bit rusty. While Father O'Laughlin spoke and said his prayers I wasn't listening, too preoccupied with what I was going to say.

Pretty soon, I heard my name and grabbed my notecards from my bag and ascended the pulpit on the altar. I peeked at my notecards then looked out at the crowd. I glanced at the casket and I remembered how my grandfather sat in the front row of my class play, and realized he was front and center once again, cheering me on.

My voice sounded different at first as I was cotton mouthed but gradually it sounded like its old self and I looked less and less at my notes as I spoke.

I told them of the school play and then saw the faces of my parents drop as they learned for the first time of "Camp Grandpa." I spoke of Jenny's funeral and of long afternoons sitting with him by the television. I spoke of his service in World War II and told the story I had heard many times of the day he met his wife.

I finished by telling of his final days and what, as far as I could tell, were his last words. It was just before he slipped into his final near-week long coma when he no longer knew what was what and who was who. He saw my friendly face and held my hand and pulled me close and whispered, "Be brave."

About the Author

Brian Kiley has been a staff writer for Conan O'Brien for 23 years. He's been nominated for 16 Emmy Awards (He won in 2007)

He's appeared 7 times on the David Letterman show, 12 times on Late Night with Conan and 4 times on the Tonight Show.

He has his own Comedy Central half-hour special.

His jokes have been featured in Reader's Digest, Prevention Magazine, GQ and the New York Times Sunday Crossword Puzzle.

Made in the USA
Las Vegas, NV
07 July 2021

26090577R00197